MIDNIGHT
IN
ST PETERSBURG

MIDNIGHT
IN
ST PETERSBURG

VANORA BENNETT

CENTURY

Published by Century 2013

2 4 6 8 10 9 7 5 3 1

First published in Great Britain in 2013 by
Century
Random House, 20 Vauxhall Bridge Road,
London SW1V 2SA

www.randomhouse.co.uk

Addresses for companies within The Random House Group Limited can be found at:
www.randomhouse.co.uk

The Random House Group Limited Reg. No. 954009

A CIP catalogue record for this book
is available from the British Library

ISBN 9781780890036

The Random House Group Limited supports the Forest Stewardship Council® (FSC®),
the leading international forest-certification organisation. Our books carrying the FSC
label are printed on FSC®-certified paper. FSC is the only forest-certification scheme
supported by the leading environmental organisations, including Greenpeace.
Our paper procurement policy can be found at:
www.randomhouse.co.uk/environment

Printed and bound by CPI Group (UK) Ltd, Croydon, CR0 4YY

For the Karpovs in St Petersburg

ACKNOWLEDGEMENTS

I would like to offer heartfelt thanks both to Selina Walker, my wonderful publisher, and her team at Century/Arrow, and to Natasha Fairweather, my equally wonderful agent, who between them have spent longer than I like to remember patiently coaxing this manuscript into existence in published form.

My family has been no less forbearing, especially Chris, who has had the grace to read many drafts, over many months, and make many wise suggestions.

So many other people have contributed to the writing of this book. Of course my first debt of gratitude is to every larger-than-life character I ever met at any alternative art show, *khappening*, war zone, nightclub, crime scene, party or concert while living in Russia in the 1990s. At the very, very beginning of thinking about writing on this subject, the jeweller Kenneth Snowman, chairman of Wartski antique dealers and a leading expert on Fabergé, whose 1953 book mentioned Horace Wallick, filled in many gaps in my knowledge over lunch at the Connaught. More recently, the family of the late Felix Youssoupoff kindly answered my Facebook questions relating to an early draft, and several experts have shared views on Rasputin. From Moscow, Olya Shevtsova found me information about the real-life Anatoly Leman and his splendidly eccentric family. Toby Faber lent me violin books and shared his encyclopaedic knowledge of the violin world. I hope my violin-making teachers in Cambridge – Quentin, José, Bob, Kit, and of course Juliet – will find an oblique reference or two in the text that will make them smile, and that Olina the Cleaner will be pleased that her insult of choice, 'you filthy haemorrhoid', made its way into the text. Nina Wilsdon, née Brodianskaya, my first Russian teacher, set me on the road to enjoying Russian poetry, St Petersburg and the kind of wistful émigré stories I still love hearing from other friends with Russian backgrounds, including Shura Shihwarg and Peter Obolensky. The Russian-accented grannies of London friends of Jewish descent – who didn't want to speak Russian – prompted me, many years ago, to start finding out why those families might have wanted to come west. John and Penny Morrison were expert guides on all things Russian throughout my research. And my dear St Petersburg friends the Karpovs may recognize their address, their kitchen, and their apple *sharlottka*.

PART ONE

SEPTEMBER–DECEMBER 1911

CHAPTER ONE

The train was still hurtling through the darkness, with hours to go before St Petersburg and dawn, when Inna had her fortune told.

Not that she'd ever meant to show her palm to a gypsy. She'd slunk on to that train in terror of being noticed at all.

Of course, she couldn't help hearing what was being said by all the raucous men crowded together on the bottom bunks of the communal compartment, drinking, eating sausage and chicken legs and eggs, and singing along to a squeezebox playing sad songs far too loud and fast. She couldn't help being aware, either, that there was a gypsy woman on the bunk below hers, reading the drunks' hands.

But she'd spent the first part of the journey pressed up against the wall of her top bunk, keeping very quiet, like all the other shadows in all the other corners she didn't dare look at, shying away from the noisy talk. In an attempt not to be overwhelmed by the racing of her heart, she'd been repeating, hypnotically, in time with the rhythm of the wheels, 'Nearly safe, nearly safe, nearly safe . . .'

She'd never have imagined, alone with her fear, that anything or anyone could have persuaded her out of the prickly darkness. Until it happened. The talk had been enough to keep her hidden – the talk that kept coming back to the assassination.

The Prime Minister, shot dead in the theatre in Kiev by a terrorist. The Tsar, down south on a visit, standing in the brilliantly lit royal box, frozen-faced as a photograph, watching Stolypin hold his chest and stagger to his knees.

What I don't understand is, how did he get past the security police in the first place?

He had a pass, can you believe? I was told he was a police informer himself.

An anarchist, I heard.

Or some sort of Red. An SD, an SR . . .

But a Jew, of course.

There, of course. Her heart thudded. It was only ever a question of time before the conversation turned to the Jews.

Reds, Yids, what's the difference? Always the Yids, isn't it? A viper in the much-suffering Russian breast.

The door kept banging. Word must have gone around in the restaurant carriage that there was a gypsy telling fortunes down in the third class. New drunks came, wanting to cross the woman's palm with silver.

Miserably, she heard: *Yeah, give them a good kicking.* And, after a rustle of newsprint, another voice, less obviously belligerent, but nasal and full of hate: *Yes, like it says here . . . 'The Government must recognize that the Jews are as dangerous to the life of mankind as are wolves, scorpions, reptiles, poisonous spiders and other such-like creatures. These are destroyed because of the risk they present to humanity. Yids must likewise be placed under conditions that will make them gradually die out. This is the task of the Government and the best men in the country.'*

There was a roar of approval. Inna cringed back. Here, too, she thought; they're the same even up here.

And then it died away.

She risked a peep over, down from her bunk.

A thin man of medium height was stepping into the carriage. He had the longish hair and beard of an Orthodox religious man, and a big gleaming cross at his breast. He was dressed like a peasant.

She waited for him to join in too. But then she saw he was shaking his head. 'Did the Lord Jesus preach hate, brothers?' he said. His voice was quiet.

In the embarrassed throat-clearings and shufflings of buttocks on seats that followed, she heard the rustle of *Zemshchina*, the right-wing hate newspaper, being stuffed back into a pocket. No one liked being caught with a red angry face, baying for blood. Not up here in the safety of the north, anyway. Good, she thought, savagely. Good for the little father.

The peasant didn't press his point. He just moved on to the fortune-telling gypsy, right below Inna, and held out a coin, then his hand.

Inna hoped the gypsy would have a happy-ever-after fortune for him.

But instead she dropped his hand and said, 'I'm not telling *your* future. Take your money back.'

'What's wrong, my dear?' the peasant said in his burr. Now he was so close, Inna saw he had the soft expression of a countryman approaching a skittish horse, apple in hand.

Then he looked up at Inna, caught her looking down

at him from her top bunk, and shocked her again with the directness of his gaze. He had extraordinarily pale eyes. 'Ah, well, all our hands are full of troubles,' he said to the gypsy woman. 'No escape from troubles, in these wicked times . . .'

'Don't you go hunting for that coin any more,' he went on cheerfully, patting the gypsy's bedding for the coin she'd let fall. 'Tell the little lady's fortune instead . . . the one up there.'

The gypsy squinted up at Inna in surprise; then, abruptly, she pulled Inna's hand down, as if to get the whole business over with as fast as possible.

Inna was too surprised to resist.

The peasant wasn't put off by the gypsy's hostility. As Inna felt the woman's bony fingers on her palm, he murmured, 'A happy future, mind: flowers in the field, a chicken in the pot, a handsome husband . . .'

But the gypsy didn't look at Inna's hand for more than a moment, either. Then, with a scowl, she pushed it away too. 'Another one,' she muttered. 'One thing's for sure. We live in evil times.'

Inna kept her hand out. Her fear had receded a bit now and she wasn't going to let this woman make her cringe away as if she'd done something wrong. 'What did you see?'

But the gypsy shook her head, tied her scarf over her head and picked up her purse, as if she was off out shopping.

'Come on, tell me,' Inna said. She didn't know why her voice was trembling.

Perhaps the gypsy heard that. At any rate she looked reluctantly up and took back Inna's hand. 'Lifeline, here, see?' she said, jabbing at the palm, all round the base of the thumb.

Inna nodded.

'Well, it stops, doesn't it?' the gypsy said irritably, as if Inna was being stupid. 'Look. Just peters out. Nothing.'

There was a silence.

'You asked, Abramovna,' she said, loudly enough for Inna to think others might hear the contemptuous Jew slur.

Hating herself, Inna shifted hastily backwards into the darkest corner of her bunk as the gypsy flounced off towards the compartment door. She let her breath out. No one except the peasant had heard, and he was safe.

He was spreading his hands in resigned acceptance. 'Five kopeks wasted, that's for sure,' he said peaceably. 'Both of us doomed. Ah well, God be with her, poor thing, with her nasty thoughts – and at least we'll have each other for company on the road to Hell, if she's right . . .'

He nodded and turned to make his own way out of the carriage. Once again Inna was left on her own, with her arms wrapped tight about her knees, and the rowdiness below gaining in volume, and, for comfort, only the rhythm of her phrase, 'Nearly safe, nearly safe, nearly safe,' in time to the wheels.

But now even that lullaby had stopped working so well. Different words to the rhythm were coming unbidden into her head. The gypsy's words: 'Peters out, peters out, peters out . . .'

The poorer passengers were out of the third-class carriage almost before the train had stopped in St Petersburg.

They rushed guiltily in the grey light along the platform of Emperor Nicholas Station towards the station building, ignoring the weight of their parcels and packages. It was only

September, but already their quick breath came out white in the chilly air.

Anyone watching the fast-emptying green carriages would have seen the long-legged spider of a girl who emerged last, with only a smallish bag in each hand. She stood on the step for a moment, blinking, seeming bewildered by the pace of the retreat into town.

Then she jumped down, too, set her worn woollen coat with its respectable bit of beaver at the throat straight, adjusted her plain hat over her black hair, and strode off to catch up with the crowd.

In her head, she was reciting the address she was making for. Strictly speaking, she didn't need to. Next to the passport in her wallet she had folded the much-fingered piece of paper on which she'd written it down. She didn't know where it was, exactly. She didn't even know her way out of the station. But she knew she'd be safe once she'd found it.

She let her hand brush against the pocket in which she could feel the wallet. She was already walking fast. But she speeded up.

'You there, girl!' Inna heard a man's rough rasp just behind her, talking in the exclamatory way the lower classes of Russia talked to their women, labelling everyone either 'girl!' 'woman!' 'aunty!' or 'granny!'

She ignored him, raised her nose a fraction higher and speeded up. That kind of voice meant trouble.

'*Baryshnya,*' the voice said, sounding less certain as it moved up the social scale with its forms of address, but following her, all the same. Definitely her. Footsteps still right behind. '*Mademoiselle?*'

Inna had left her own Jewish documentation behind in

Kiev. No point in keeping it when all it allowed her to do was live in the south of the empire, in the Pale of Settlement, where Jews were supposed to stay under strict police control. It wouldn't get her anywhere here, up north, in the imperial capital.

She didn't need her papers any more anyway, since she'd been lucky or quick-witted enough to pick up Olya Morozova's evening bag in the panic at the theatre. She'd known what was in the bag because Olya had spent the whole of the first interval showing it off to her classmates: a travel passport to spend a month with her grandmother in St Petersburg, missing the start of term at their secondary school in Kiev. It was something Inna could only dream of, and, oh, didn't Olya, impeccably Russian, and the daughter of the city's deputy police chief to boot, know it, and didn't it sweeten the pleasure for her in showing Inna the pass.

But Olya hadn't had time to think about her bag in the second interval, once the man in the shabby coat had walked in and they'd heard the shots and the entire audience had erupted in panic. She'd been too busy screaming.

Somewhere up ahead, in the echoing heights of the station building, a melancholy brass-band version of the overture of 'A Life for the Tsar' could be heard. They'd been playing the same patriotic Glinka in the theatre, too, Inna remembered; the music brought it back.

The frightening crowds in Kiev after the assassination had also had the Tsar on their minds. The leaflets which had covered the town like a snowfall by dawn, with their ugly, hastily put-together type, full of grammar mistakes, telling the people the assassin was a Yid, as well as a Red: they all had the same message. It was time for patriotic citizens to

9

show their loyalty to the Tsar by ridding the Motherland of this noxious nation of Christ-killers.

Inna had picked one up late the next day, once she'd used Olya's passport to buy her ticket for the night train. Her fear had lessened once she was on the move and taking control of her own destiny: it was still a series of stifling rises in the gorge, but at least not that numbing helplessness. After a glance, she'd trodden the leaflet into a puddle, outside the station. She'd ground it underfoot, and watched it disintegrate into the wet black of the water.

There'd been more crowds of patriots out all that day: snub-nosed, tow-headed, thickset men, in and out of the pubs, in and out of their Black Hundreds meetings, with their double-headed eagle pins gleaming on their lapels, carrying their pictures of the Tsar and his family, handing out the leaflets, chatting to the burly policemen in their midst as if they were brothers (which all too often they were). No blood had been shed; there had been no screams, or shop windows broken, or bonfires in the street, which Inna knew from hearsay was how things went when a real pogrom got going. But still, these people were dangerous as they milled around staring at those others – the shadows flitting by lugging parcels to the station, or to carts or carriages or motorcars. Tonight's escapees were all hoping not to be tomorrow's victims, and Inna was glad to be away.

Well, now she was away. But was she safe?

She turned and stared down her nose at the greasy jowl of a man in a dark uniform with silver and red facings. She felt something rising in her throat, but her voice sounded steady as she said, 'Yes?'

He looked suddenly uncomfortable as he wriggled in

his too-tight tunic. She could see him thinking that he'd mistaken the shiny thinness of the cloth at her elbows for the submissiveness of the poor, and got his tone wrong. Dropping his eyes, he said, 'Begging your pardon, *mademoiselle*,' with an extra note of respect.

Not that there was any need for a man in uniform to apologize. If you were a subject of the Russian Emperor, and wished to go more than fifteen miles from your home, you needed permission from the police and the Ministry of the Interior that ran them. It was the ministry's task to stop terrorists throwing their bombs or sticking their knives into ministers' throats in the secret civil war everyone preferred to pretend wasn't convulsing the land. You could be watched, searched, fingerprinted, arrested, interrogated, exiled, fined or handed over to military justice on nothing more than a policeman's hunch that you might be doing something political or were a Jew – since Jews, it was believed, were especially prone to dangerous politics.

Yet even so a lowly individual policeman, like this one, could always fear that the next person he dealt with might just be privileged enough to harass him back, ensuring he lost the certificate of trustworthiness without which he would be banned from public employment.

'Your documents, please,' he said, definitely less sure of himself now.

She put down her bag and got the wallet out, looking straight at him.

He unfolded the wallet, tsking at the thin sheets of paper in the little internal passport booklet that wouldn't separate, and making a big performance of blowing on them while giving Inna vaguely menacing looks. But there was nothing wrong with the red stamps and dates, Inna knew, or the permission from the Kiev Ministry of the Interior that the passport gave for Morozova, O. A. (occupation: student of Fundukleyevskaya Academy; age: 18; faith: Orthodox; residing at: Kreshchatik 86, Kiev; social class: hereditary noblewoman; facial features: dark hair and no distinguishing marks; daughter of: Morozov, A. P., hereditary nobleman, 6th-grade colonel of the Corps of Gendarmerie, Kiev department) to visit Morozova, A. A., hereditary noblewoman, her grandmother, residing at Italian Street, St Petersburg, for family reasons, from last week, for the month of September.

After a lengthy examination of the booklet, the policeman gave it back. Somewhere in his reading, perhaps at the mention of Morozova, O. A.'s father's exalted status in the services of state repression, his expression had become timid. He bowed, now, too low for comfort given his girth and the tightness of his tunic. 'Checking for passengers from Kiev . . . have to, after . . .' he muttered. He didn't want to say the word assassination, Inna saw, and she felt a momentary pang of pity for him, with his cruel, stupid job.

'Looking out for Yids on the run,' he added in a stronger voice, straightening up. Inna noticed that he had a double-headed eagle pin on his stand-up coat collar. 'Murderous Red swine. Scared they'll get their come-uppance. Don't want to stay and take the punishment they've got coming. Running everywhere, thousands of them – like cockroaches. But we don't want that filth here, do we?' If he was expecting an answering leer from her, he was disappointed. 'Well . . . well . . . I wish you a pleasant stay in our city, your excellency.' He handed back the booklet and, avoiding her eyes, turned to seek out a new victim among the hurrying third-class passengers.

Inna watched as he moved to intercept one of the other shadows she'd been aware of, a man in his early thirties, with the sadness in his soul clearly visible. He had a deathly white face behind his dark Jewish-looking beard and shadows under his eyes, and, every time Inna had glimpsed him, on both trains, he'd been holding tight to the hand of an unnaturally quiet little girl of about ten. No mother; Inna had tried not to wonder what had happened to her. Now, as he saw the approaching gendarme, the last flicker of hope left him. The little girl's face crumpled into panic.

Inna hurried on. So they had no passports. But since hers was stolen, and Olya Morozova's father might at any moment think to telegraph his colleagues to watch out for imposters, there was no time for pity.

But, when she looked more closely at the station building ahead, she realized it offered no safety. Instead there were more gendarmes guarding the doorway and pouncing on people in the crowd. Some were converging on youths in scruffy overcoats, filleting leaflets from their pockets; others were grabbing urchins, and flicking wallets from their hands. But most were looking for incomers.

Inna stopped dead. Someone bumped into her from behind. Scurrying feet shifted course. Then she felt a hand on her arm.

Inna closed her eyes and bowed her head. So this was it, she thought: how your lifeline petered out.

'I thought so . . . you're the little lady from the train who had your fortune told, aren't you?'

It was the peasant from the train.

'I saw you, and I thought, Well, you must be new to the city if you're trying to leave through the station building. Police everywhere, snooping through your papers – waste half your day if you give them a chance. So why don't I walk you out the way Petersburg people go, the ones who've got any sense. You don't want to look like an outsider, do you?'

She nodded gratefully, noticing his extraordinarily calm pale-blue eyes again.

'Come on, then.' He set off briskly to the left into a narrow lane that went straight from the train platforms all the way round the side of the station hall to the street.

It only took a minute.

Inna looked round and realized that the great modern square they'd come out into, with its grey cliff-faces of hotels, and tramlines, and squealing motorcars and carriages and pedestrian crowds all rushing here and there under a lowering sky, was actually outside the station. There wasn't a gendarme in sight.

'So . . . that's it? Are we out, in the city?' she asked. 'Really?' She took a deep breath, dizzy with relief. She was in St Petersburg. She was safe.

CHAPTER TWO

She began walking, one bag in each hand, impatient to be off and free of the peasant.

Yet the fact remained: she didn't know where to go. She knew she had to walk into the centre, along Nevsky Prospekt, the great avenue which ran through the city in a dead straight line. But she had no idea which of the roads leading off this square would get her to Nevsky.

From behind her came a chuckle. 'That's the road out of town,' she heard the peasant say, sounding amused. 'I'm heading into town, along Nevsky. Shall I put you on your way?'

She turned, with dignity, to reject his offer, but when she met his eyes she could see there was no malice in them. He'd helped her till now. Of course he wasn't about to start pestering her.

Chastened, she nodded. 'I'm going to Hay Market,' she said, realizing – to her surprise – that she'd be glad of the company.

'I've known that lane since I had troubles of my own with

the police,' the peasant said, shouldering one of Inna's bags (she kept the smaller bag, which contained her violin, in her own hand) and setting off beside her along a big straight ugly boulevard lined with tall grey buildings. What troubles? she wondered, but he went on: 'That's the thing about policemen: they get everywhere, like cockroaches. No way to actually stamp them out – but it never does any harm to keep out of their way.'

Inna couldn't help but smile. It was a delicate gesture, she thought, to invite her to remember the terrifying gendarmes, who liked to call Jews cockroaches, as no more threatening than kitchen creepy-crawlies themselves.

'Especially if you're a Jew.' The peasant gave her a sideways glance.

It was an invitation to frankness. She hesitated, and then took it. 'Like me, you mean,' she said.

Noncommittally, he nodded.

His casual mention, out loud, of Inna's national identity, the fifth point on the passport, that inescapable evidence of her membership of a shameful race (if she hadn't temporarily escaped it by borrowing Olya's papers, at least), didn't make her flinch in the way she usually did. She just felt distant from the proposition. Aunty Lyuba, who was Russian by blood, had raised Inna, with *her* Russian first name, to be just like any of the young Russian girls in their city apartment block. Inna's last name, Feldman, could be Yiddish or just innocently Volga German; there were only ever difficulties if people raised their eyebrows on hearing Inna's unchangeable middle name: the patronymic she was called by on formal occasions, 'Inna Venyaminovna', which was made from her father's un-Russian-sounding, un-German-sounding name,

Benjamin. Yet there'd never been religion in Aunty Lyuba's life, or in Inna's. They were progressive and scientific: no ancient Talmuds and Judaic chaos in Aunty Lyuba's genteel apartment, thank you, just dead Uncle Borya's books on medicine, Dahl's dictionary, the Russian classics, freshly laundered white lace everywhere, and lessons, lessons, lessons all day long. Inna didn't remember much about her own parents, but they'd been close to Aunty Lyuba, so she thought they must have been like her in this. Still, even if Inna, like Aunty Lyuba, had no Jewish ways, they were never unaware of what people might say, or think, or do. Inna remembered starting at the Academy, and pirouetting excitedly in her new white lace pinafore, ready to walk the three streets to the school by herself for the first time, and how her carefree happiness had curdled when Aunty Lyuba, shaking her head over Inna's lustrous black hair tied in a big white bow, and the exotic curves of her cheekbone and nose, had murmured, 'They'll always *know* . . . but they'll always expect a Jew to show fear. So walk tall . . . stare them down, like a princess.'

And Inna had done her best. She'd given every man on the way to school the fiercest look she could; yet even now she could never banish the fear.

The fear is all that's really Jewish about me, Inna thought now. She couldn't see anything else she had in common with the Jews they were always writing about in the papers (people she'd never actually seen for herself): those banned both from countryside and big cities, who filled the little towns of the south, the *shtetl*s, with their wailing music and strange clothes, the ones behind the revolutionary movements, or the monstrous ones drawn, hunchbacked and grinning,

17

who were said to bake matzos with the blood of murdered Russian children. (Not that this was likely. Everyone knew that; everyone with an education and some common sense, anyway. But still, there was the Kiev man they'd arrested a few months back – Mendel Beilis, his name was – on precisely that charge: the arrest that had started all the pogrom talk that was resurfacing now. So you couldn't help but wonder, a bit.)

'*I* don't drink children's blood or steal chalices from churches, if that's what you mean,' she said tartly.

'No . . .' the peasant replied. His voice was calm, absorbing her flash of defensive anger without seeming to notice. 'Of course not. You're just a person, getting on with your life.'

Inna bit her lip.

He went on, sidestepping the oncoming Number One tram without a second glance: 'I know a man, Simanovich. He's a jeweller in Kiev. They're always on to him, the police: making out he's a loan shark and a gambler. Evil-minded nonsense. He's a dignified man. Loves his people. Tries to help them: he's got several of his Jews papers to stay up here, for instance; and why not, if they like the city, why not? They're people like anyone else. Simanovich should be rewarded, not tormented.'

She'd underestimated him, Inna thought, touched. He might be an unlettered peasant, but his goodness shone through. She liked his gentle garrulousness, too: that unhurried way of following a thought right through.

'. . . But there's so much hatred now. Maybe it's just because of that man who's been killed. Stolypin: the Prime Minister, the Chief Policeman.' The peasant paused, then continued in a stronger voice. 'Yes, the Chief Policeman . . .

Because the police are people like everyone else. They take their style from the top. And him, Stolypin, they called him a reformer, but he was a cruel man too. No good for any of us. His days were numbered . . .'

He muttered something inaudible. Then, shaking his head, as if regretting his harshness, he made the sign of the cross, and said, rather reluctantly, 'Well, God be with him.'

Inna nodded, keeping her face still. She didn't want to tell him that she'd actually been in the theatre when Stolypin was shot, because in truth she didn't have much to tell. She almost wished she *had* seen more than a stir in the crowd when the two shots rang out, and then the hysterics on all sides, women fainting in chairs and people pushing for the doors as word passed through the hall like fire of who it was who'd been attacked.

'So you know Kiev? Were you there for the Tsar's visit?' It surprised her, now she came to think of it. What would take a Siberian peasant so far from home? Come to that, what was he doing here, in the capital?

He turned his gaze on her, slowing down as he felt towards his answer. His eyes were vague. Then the deep lines around them crinkled, and he laughed.

'Why, I've been to Kiev many a time,' he said. 'This time in a train, like a gentleman, but oh, in the pilgrim days of my past, many's the time I've walked all the way from Siberia on my own two legs . . . rejoicing in God's sunlight, or shivering under His snows. I'm not a young man, and sometimes I feel I've walked every inch of the empire on these two legs.'

He was shaking his head at the memory of his travels. Then he stopped walking, as if a more important thought had just struck him. He pointed at a side street – another gulch of cobbles between grey cliffs of apartment blocks. 'That's where I live now. Nikolayevskaya Street, House Seventy. I won't ask you in now as we've got business in the centre. But mind you come and see me there when you've settled in. You'll be welcome.'

Inna nodded, politely but guardedly. She knew she wouldn't be back.

So, she thought, still piecing together the puzzle, he'd be one of those peasant pilgrims she'd read about, the *stranniki* who found God in a thunderclap, and left their villages to wander the land for years, in religious ecstasy. That would explain his cross, and his godly air, though not why he'd left the land to come here to the city.

Not that it really mattered. What she wanted to know most, as they started walking again, was when would they get past this dull bourgeois avenue and reach Nevsky Prospekt, and the beginning of the gorgeous but frightening imperial Petersburg that every Russian novel described so vividly?

Inna had always imagined Nevsky as a place of wonders: classical columns, arches, caryatids, French bonnets, Guards officers, gleaming carriages, palaces pulsing with electric light and chandelier-lit shops full of lobsters, jewels and candied cherries.

Not like this street. The only salesman here was a scruffy man with a brazier on the pavement, selling pumpkin seeds roasted in salt in twists of newspaper, and giving her a lecherous wink as he called, 'Seeds, seeds, I'll give you seeds, darling.' She swept past, nose up.

'It's that house just there, do you see, on the corner with Nevsky,' the peasant was saying. 'My house. Don't forget that.'

Nevsky?

'Nevsky?'

This couldn't be it, surely? This – a street distinctly less glamorous than many in Kiev? This dull jumble of stolid ugliness – Nevsky Prospekt?

He roared with laughter again. 'This is Nevsky. The most famous street in the land.'

'But where are the palaces? The theatres, the concert halls, the shops?' she asked.

'Ah,' he said, nodding. 'Just up ahead. But don't be impatient. There's all the time in the world for palaces and shops and vanities.' He paused. 'Yes, I know Kiev well, and I was sad to see it the way it was this week, with everyone so frightened, and disaster in the air, and all your people leaving . . .'

Inna shrugged, and said, as coolly as she could: 'Yes, the people I've been living with this year – kind of relatives – *they* were scared. They're leaving for Palestine.'

She couldn't suppress a sigh. The Kagans were the closest thing to family she'd had left. She'd been so grateful when they'd come out of nowhere and taken her in after Aunty Lyuba's death. Not that they'd ever been close, once she was there; the Kagans were always too taken up with their fearful plans to be off. But now they'd gone, and it was so far away, Palestine. And she had no one else to keep her in Kiev.

'I've been to Palestine,' the peasant was saying. 'Last spring, I went.'

Inna turned and stared at him. 'Did you go *there* on your own two legs, too?' she asked, letting scepticism into her voice.

'No, no,' he replied, almost absent-mindedly. 'Kiev to Odessa, and from there over the Black Sea to Haifa on the

21

Lazarus. You sleep on deck, and how beautiful the sea is, with the sun glittering on the waves. You only have to gaze on it for your soul to become one with the sea. And after that: Jerusalem.' He sighed, but his breath was full of joy and love. 'An earthly realm of tranquillity . . .

'Not expensive, either,' he added, perhaps understanding how trapped Inna was feeling. 'Twelve roubles each way on the boat, third class. That's how pilgrims go. No comforts, but why would you give up your share of suffering? It's suffering and persecution that purify the soul. You could go, too, if you wanted. See your folks.'

'Well, one day maybe I will,' she said. She didn't really think she would, but the idea it might be possible lightened her heart anyway.

Or perhaps it was the gleam of pale sun on water ahead . . .

Her eyes widened. She could see the road transforming itself into the Nevsky she'd hoped for.

On her left, looming up, was a great dark-red palace. And, beyond that, over the dark glitter of what she knew must be the Fontanka, was a bridge frilled with delicate iron tracery, and topped with four enormous statues of horses with rippling muscles . . .

She stopped, exhilaration chasing away her tiredness and worry. She was here, at the very centre of things. She'd made it.

'I was glad to be away from the centre of vain and worldly things when I got on that boat,' came the companionable voice at her side, sweeping her forward. 'But sometimes, when you see the sun on the water, you can't help but marvel at the beauty of Creation, even here.'

He squinted at her. 'You like it, eh?' He seemed amused. And as they walked on, he told her stories about the buildings they were passing, and about the grand duchesses or starving ballerinas or savvy Armenians or merchants behind each stucco façade. He knew so much. He breathed the gritty air with its smell of salt and industrial fog as naturally as if it were the country air of home.

Inna was impressed by his composure. On the corner of the Merchants' Yard Market, two young dandies with gold frogging over their fronts forced her off the pavement, and she had to scramble back to safety out of the path of an oncoming carriage. Yet he glided through the crowds of tight-waisted gentlemen in braid – so many uniforms: army, navy, Guards, civil service; Inna couldn't tell them apart – and of ladies in sweeping robes and feathers, as if he hardly felt their imperious jostling.

'So this is why Dostoyevsky found Nevsky so tricky,' she said breathlessly. 'I feel like the Man from Underground now, too. Invisible, and black and blue from all these aristocratic elbows, and full of secret bile, you know?'

He put a hand out to steady her, but his only reply was a vague, uncomprehending, 'What's that you say?'

Then, without warning, he turned off the boulevard down another broad avenue.

'Oh!' Inna cried, forgetting Dostoyevsky because her head was still spinning with excitement. 'But we haven't seen half of it. Where is the Yeliseyevsky store, with the pineapples and fresh lobsters? And the Defence Ministry, and the Kazan Cathedral, and—'

'Further on,' he answered matter-of-factly. 'But you wanted Hay Market, didn't you? And that's down here.'

Understanding that if he really did live way back on that street he'd shown her near the station, he must already have put himself out considerably to bring her so far, she said, quickly, 'Of course, I understand,' and hurried on behind him.

'Where are you going, anyway?' he asked, over his shoulder. 'Who to?'

Inna paused, unease creeping back into her heart. 'To a cousin. A kind of cousin.'

'You have a lot of "kind of" relatives,' he said.

'Well,' she replied, trying not to feel defensive, 'he's the son of the other "kind ofs". I'm going to stay with him.' She took a deep breath to steady herself. 'He works for Leman, the violin-maker.' She wanted to give the impression that she knew exactly what she was talking about. She didn't want her companion to realize that she'd never actually met Yasha Kagan.

But she felt tears painfully close as she strode on, round the corner into the new street.

She was remembering her flight back from the theatre through the restive crowds that suddenly seemed to have filled the Kiev streets, her feet hardly touching the ground, and finding the Kagans packing their trunk. They'd held off emigrating for the entire year, even though they had papers, because they'd kept thinking that their Yasha might come too, if things didn't work out for him up in St Petersburg. Yet there they were, not mentioning the frightening news of the night, just saying, with shame in their eyes, that they could get a passage from Odessa on Tuesday.

'Of course,' Inna had told them stoutly, wondering where she'd go, but not wanting to add to their burden by making them feel guiltier about her than they probably already did. 'I'll find somewhere new to stay tomorrow.'

She remembered retreating to her room – their son's old room, where she'd been lodging for the year since Aunty Lyuba died.

It was full of memorabilia. There was the first violin he'd made, during his apprenticeship, which his mother had kept and which Inna had taken to playing since she moved in. There was a photo, too, from Yasha's last year at school. The youth in it was tall and slightly out of focus, with his head held high, a long neck, and curls of black hair at nape and temples.

Inna had lain down on the bed, looking at that stranger's photograph. It was late, but there was a lot of movement on the street outside: men's feet running and urgent talk, and the uncertain light of lanterns.

It was only then that she'd realized exactly what she was going to do, instead of finding a room and clinging on here, alone, for another year of school.

'I'm coming to you,' she'd told Yasha's portrait. 'And I'll bring your violin,' she'd added as she heard a crash of wood splintering on something hard outside. 'No point in leaving it to get smashed by *them*.'

The next morning, she'd gone to the bank and withdrawn all that remained of Aunt Lyuba's small inheritance.

By now, Inna and her peasant were in Garden Street (though, as the peasant said scathingly, 'Who knows when there was last an honest garden in it?') and going down the side of the glittering Merchants' Yard Market. The market arches sparkled with foreign goods, but once you'd got a bit further, past the Empire Bank, the traders under the next row of colonnades looked poorer, and the wind felt more brutal. By the time they reached the square at the end, the magical grandeur had gone out of the air altogether and they were surrounded by the grime of an ordinary city again: traders, trams, rubbish underfoot, and a brass band of old men hunched up against the wind by a small white church.

'Hay Market,' the peasant said, stopping. 'And now?'

'Well . . . I mustn't keep you any longer,' Inna said, looking hesitantly around. The address she wanted was just off here somewhere. It shouldn't be hard to find. Yet the streets leading back from the square looked suddenly threatening. The men lurking all around were not wearing the bright military or civil service uniforms she'd admired on Nevsky, but threadbare working-men's padded coats or smelly sheepskins. Women stared assessingly out from under battered hats, and the eyes of the ragged street children were frankly frightening.

'Nonsense,' the peasant replied. 'Leave a young lady like you alone at the Hay Market? Why, you'd be stripped down to the bone within seconds. Look at all these scallywags. No, no, I won't think of it.'

All at once, it was too much, and Inna felt the tears hot and wet behind her eyes.

Looking down, she said, in as near to a level voice as she could: 'I'm not exactly sure where he lives. It's Moscow Prospekt, just round the corner somewhere . . . but . . .' Here, to her horror, she heard herself gulp. 'I don't exactly know him, you see.'

After a moment, she felt a heavy arm move slowly across her shoulders. 'Does he know you're coming, this cousin?'

She didn't answer. She could feel her face, turned down behind her hand, scrunching up as she tried to stop the tears. But they coursed down her cheeks anyway, out from under her tight-pressed eyes. Her shoulders were shaking under his arm.

'Don't you fret, now.' The peasant's voice was low and soothing. 'We'll find him and everything will turn out all right. You'll see.'

Looking up, Inna said, still shakily, 'I'm all right now. '

'I'll ask someone then,' he said matter-of-factly, stepping away. 'Moscow Prospekt, you say?'

He stopped one of the hard-faced traders, and Inna, still worried about crying again, saw the man answer him with a jerk of the thumb, to the left.

'House Number Two,' she said, and they set off into the biting wind with a new sense of companionship.

The address she had written down turned out to be in a dark, fetid courtyard off one of the big ugly avenues nearby.

Even the peasant looked doubtful as they pushed open the door to a prison-like staircase, which seemed never to have been cleaned, and began to make their echoing way up the wide stone steps to the first-floor flat.

Inna stood tall, took a deep breath and rang.

Part of her felt journey's end just ahead, and safety, and wanted the peasant gone. But another part of her was full of gratitude for his help and panic that he'd just slip away before Yasha came to the door.

So she did nothing – didn't meet his eye, didn't speak – as they both strained to hear voices or footsteps from inside the leather-padded door.

It was only when footsteps did become audible that she

looked at him. He looked back, thoughtfully nodding his head.

She feared he might make the sign of the cross, or say something pitying in farewell.

'You forget about that gypsy woman, and her foolishness. What does she know? The future is a matter for God,' he said simply.

She was about to shake her head and say, No, it was a matter for her. But the door was opening and a stripe of warm yellow light came from within. The peasant, as if unwilling either to intrude or to leave before Inna had found her relative, stepped back into the shadows.

A tall, muscular, close-shaven man in his twenties was looking out. 'Can I help you, *mademoiselle*?' he asked Inna politely.

She stared at him.

Could this man possibly be . . .?

There were none of the luxuriant dark curls she remembered from the photograph. This man's hair was cropped close to his skull. Following the bluish line of stubble from the long throat and lean jaw upwards, she saw how it receded at the temples and appreciated the small vanity that must have prompted the Spartan style he'd chosen. Still, he was handsome, in a sportsmanlike way: long-legged, with a torso whose muscles she could guess at under his white shirt, and that elegant throat, with his head set on top with almost military precision, chin down, crown high, in a way she'd never have guessed at from the picture.

But she recognized the straight nose with its flaring nostrils, and the wide, straight mouth, and the cheekbones, and the brown, almond-shaped eyes, with the possibility of softness suggested by their thick lashes. There was no softness in them now. Yet she'd never seen a face so arresting.

'Yasha?' she asked.

It was only as he nodded, and confirmed, still in that neutral voice, though with just a hint of impatience or surprise, 'Yes, I'm Kagan . . . how can I help you?' that Inna was aware of the peasant slipping away down the stairs. She was too preoccupied with the man in front of her to turn or call goodbye. It was only later that she realized she'd never even asked the peasant his name.

CHAPTER THREE

Yasha had been about to go out when he heard the doorbell. He'd have been long gone already if, earlier on, Madame Leman hadn't taken it into her head to bring out all the coats and hats and boots from storage, ready for winter. She'd dumped them in armfuls in the lobby, but then got distracted, as usual, and gone off leaving the job half done. So it was pandemonium in the windowless little room, and he'd been pushing through piles of furs, looking for his jacket in a cloud of mothball smell, and feeling exasperated for what felt like hours.

Before opening the door, though, he'd taken the precaution of shoving a couple of children's moulting rabbit hats on top of the box of leaflets he'd been planning to take round to Kremer's. You never knew. Better safe than sorry.

But when he looked out into the gloom of the landing – as stern as he could in case it was the police who'd come calling – what he saw, in the yellow stripe of light from inside the flat, wasn't a fat man in a uniform at all, but a girl.

An unnervingly attractive girl, too: very tall, slim, with

lovely ankles visible below her threadbare coat and shining black hair escaping from under her hat. A girl half stepping forward to look at him (his face must be in shadow, he realized), with a face too pale for classical beauty and huge green eyes.

He stood up straighter. He'd never seen her before. He'd remember if he had. She wasn't the kind of girl you'd forget.

Yet, uncertain though her expression was, she seemed to know his name.

'Yasha, I'm Inna,' she was saying.

Her name meant nothing to him. And he could hear Kremer's uncle's voice in his head, saying, 'A good revolutionary keeps his trap shut,' and, 'Never trust a stranger.' So he looked watchfully back at her, waiting.

She hesitated before plunging on in her attractively low voice, 'I've been living at your parents' flat.' He was shocked to hear her use the informal, family way of saying 'you' and 'your'. 'Since my Aunt Lyuba died . . . I'm a kind of cousin of your father's . . .'

He noticed a beseeching look in her green eyes.

Of course. Mama had mentioned the cousin's turning up, in one of her very long and inconsequential letters, which were all full of gossip about people he'd left behind, and general aimless fretting about the bourgeois kinds of things his parents did fret about. It had been one of the few pieces of news he'd taken in, because he'd remembered hearing stories about the Feldmans as a boy. 'So you're Inna Feldman?' he said.

She nodded, still looking expectant.

Yasha remembered old Kremer's warnings about women. 'Always be on your guard,' he'd been fond of saying, in that wise, smoke-choked voice of his, 'especially with women. You never know what they want – but you always know they'll want something. Anyway, there's only ever room in a man's heart for one love, lads. Let it be the revolution, and not some rouged-up hussy.'

'You're their lodger in Kiev,' he said brutally, noticing the way she flinched as he said this. 'But what are you doing *here*? In St Petersburg?'

He'd made a point of replying using the formal 'you' – *vy* – as if she were a stranger. Respected, but not his family, not his nearest and dearest. For the first time since he'd seen her and been thrown into this state of near-paralysis, he was taking control. He could think again.

He watched her register that, then decide not to take offence, just answer.

'Well, because they've left,' she replied quickly, too eagerly, with the beginning of an anxious smile that both twisted his heart and angered him at the same time, 'and I've brought . . .'

'Left?'

If there was one thing Yasha knew about his parents it was that they never went anywhere. The concert hall, the shops, the theatre, neighbours' apartments, and a week at the coast in the summer, taking the Crimean air: those were the predictable parameters of their universe.

'Are they here?' he asked, in what felt like a gasp. Turning; half expecting to see them coming up the grimy stairs any minute. 'With you?'

'No,' she said. 'They went to Odessa. Where the boat goes from, to the Holy Land. For the Tuesday passage.'

'But they can't have,' Yasha heard himself objecting.

'They didn't tell me. They didn't write. They *always* write.'

He had piles of letters, most of them barely read, in a drawer in his room.

'They did,' she said. How calm she sounded. 'I've brought you the letter.'

He went on staring at her as his world turned upside down: as he stopped being the bold young man venturing far from his claustrophobic home to have adventures and change the world and sneer with his mates at his parents, who were pottering around safely back home, doing their best to forget they had a drop of Jewish blood in their veins; as he became . . . well, whatever you did become when your family suddenly just vanished into thin air.

After a long silence, he said, almost to himself, 'But why?'

'They were scared there would be a pogrom. We all were.'

Her voice was controlled, but he could hear the wobble in it.

'But there's not going to be a pogrom,' Yasha said. He felt confident of this. All his comrades in the Bund had discussed this question, at length, and had decided that the appointment of Kokovtsev as the new Prime Minister – not a bloodthirsty man – meant the authorities had no interest, this time, in egging on the more uncouth elements of society to shed Jewish blood.

'Nothing's happened so far, and nothing is going to happen in future, either,' Yasha added, aware that he was sounding too angry. 'Everyone knows that. They should just have stayed put.'

Her eyes flashed with indignation. How green they were.

'Well, it was completely natural to be frightened!' she burst out. 'Anyone would have been, with the way things got . . . the streets full of those thugs, the things those leaflets were saying. You would have been scared, too, if you'd been there. And what does it matter if it hasn't happened yet? It still might. Any day. Why do you think so many people have been trying to leave?' He noticed that she'd gone on calling him the familiar 'you', *ty*, as if insisting on their closeness.

'Palestine is for cowards,' he said flatly. 'Better to fight than run away.' It was what his comrades told each other at their political meetings. Yet here, before this girl who actually knew his parents, it didn't sound so convincing. He tried not to think of his father's shortness of stature; of his bent back and timorous, scholarly ways; of his thin cracked voice; of his multiple minor medical problems and silver-topped cane. Because if he did, he'd know how absurd it was to imagine the old man going out and facing street gangs of hoodlums.

He didn't want to see mockery in her green eyes. He looked down.

'Did you say you'd brought a letter?' he asked after another pause, still saying '*vy*'. He'd take it, she'd go away, and he'd have a chance to find out where Mama and Papa were heading, at least. Think it through on his own.

He could feel, hear, that she was nodding. 'Well, where is it?' he said. He met her eye at last, but only to look expectant as he put out his hand. 'Their letter?'

'At the bottom of my bag,' she said shortly, looking away in her turn. He could see, now, that she was less mocking than he'd expected, and also angrier. Her lips were tight. There were white dents at her nostrils. 'I'll find it once I've unpacked.'

And then, to his astonishment, she picked up her bags

and pushed determinedly past him and through the door. 'Because I'll need to stay.'

At a loss, Yasha followed her into the lamp glow of the vestibule in time to see her stop just inside the door and stare at the chaotic mounds of boots and coats and hats facing her as she put down her bags. With disquiet, he saw that one of the bags was now resting against his covered-up box of leaflets.

He watched her glance around, taking in the mortifying mess. Just for a moment, her nose – a straight, elegant nose, Yasha noticed – wrinkled. She must be smelling the mothballs. He saw her take in the full-length mirror, and the armchair for sitting on to pull on boots, and the little table beside it, with its lamp, the little dish for Madame Leman's hairpins and eau de Cologne and brush. Her eyes moved next to the shelves crammed with candles, lamps (some broken), Lucifer matches, and jars of jam, pickles and preserves, all hand-labelled in Madame Leman's flamboyant scrawl. He saw them widen at the fat magazines and periodicals, mostly very scuffed, piled up in front of the shelves lining the third, coat-free, wall.

For what seemed an eternity, Yasha couldn't think beyond his own agonizing awareness of the terrible impression all this clutter must be making. From behind the door onwards into the apartment, he could hear all the usual family din: banging and clattering from the kitchen, children squawking, and someone picking out a waltz on the piano.

And then he saw the look of painful longing on her face, and realized she wasn't despising it at all. He let out the breath he hadn't known he was holding.

Suddenly everything felt simpler. Now she was inside, he

could also see how young she was: tall, but hardly more than a kid really, with shadows under her eyes.

Well, of course. Naturally she'd be tired. She must have been in trains, alone, for a good three or four days.

He wasn't going to let in any foolish thoughts about it possibly being right to have left Kiev in the past week for fear of a pogrom. But, thinking of the rowdy types who'd packed the communal compartments he and his friend Kremer had met in, travelling here together a year ago – those hard-drinking men and all the policemen who'd wanted to check the Jewish pair's papers – he could see how frightening the journey north must have been for a young girl on her own.

'You must be tired,' he said, trying to restore a politer note to the conversation. 'Were you all right on the train by yourself?'

'Yes.' She looked at him challengingly – another flash of green. 'Yes, I was all right, because I stole a passport,' she went on baldly. 'A Russian one. And just as well I did. They weren't letting Jews out. And they had police at the station here too, looking for people coming in.'

His eyes widened a little at that. He wasn't going to admit to being impressed, though, or to there having perhaps been any real danger in Kiev. He just shrugged, uneasily, and let it pass.

He'd better ask Madame Leman if she could stay the night, at least, and just hope to God there wouldn't be a big to-do about it, like there had been when he'd sneaked Kremer in to sleep on his floor for those few days. She could have a bath. Get some rest. Get back on her feet. And then she could go off and do whatever it was she'd come here to do. Kremer and his leaflets would have to wait a day.

There was nothing else for it. He squared his shoulders. 'Come on,' he said, and picked up one of her bags.

Yasha stopped at the open door on the left and led her into the spacious living room, sunny yellow, with big divans and armchairs with books left open on them, and a pack of cards on the table, decorated with Tarot images, not the hearts and spades anyone who didn't know Madame Leman might have been expecting. Seeing her eyes open wider still, he remembered the effect this room had had on him, too, when he'd first got here. It was quite unlike the small, tidy, careful rooms of his parents' apartment, where you had to remember to do the right thing at all times. This was the warm kind of place where you could feel free to say anything you liked. There were pictures everywhere: big expansive things, peasants in sunlight, woodland scenes, portraits of sleeping children or men in suits; and one odd one that was just a red rectangle on black. But the most eye-catching image was the charcoal portrait of Monsieur Leman: a giant of a black-haired man with laughing, intelligent eyes, looking straight out into the room and a cloud of dark beard half-visible against the grey shadow of the loose top he was wearing; a flash of white cuff, a clean wrist.

Yasha was pleased when she took a step towards it. 'Everyone stops at that one: it's a Repin,' he said, and he couldn't keep the pride out of his voice. He could see her catch her breath. He could imagine what she was thinking: What, the famous Repin! She'd have seen reproductions of his paintings: the wild Cossacks in fits of laughter at a letter from the Sultan; the Tsar's dejected prisoners pulling a barge under a happy blue sky. Yasha couldn't resist basking in the glory of it: 'He's a friend of the family, so he drew the master.'

She nodded, entranced.

'Wait here,' he said gruffly and put down her bag. 'Take a good look while I go and tell Madame Leman you're here.'

Madame Leman was in the kitchen. Pink-faced, with fading blond hair escaping from a bun, she was supervising a child with plump cheeks folding mincemeat into little cabbage parcels. 'Neatly now, Agrippina,' she was saying with a smile. There was steam rising from a boiling soup pot on the stove, next to a frying pan with the first batch of finished darling doves in it. The little girl looked excited. She was licking her lips. The smell made Yasha hungry too.

When Madame Leman heard Yasha wanted to have someone else to stay, her smile faded. 'Oh, Yash,' she said. 'Not again?' Her eyes went to the big book open on the table. It was full of tight little sums; notes, red-circled calculations, lists of expenditure. At the sight of it she sighed; then she caught herself. 'Well,' she said, probably regretting that glance. 'After all, we've just got the payment in from the orchestra; that'll tide us over for a bit. But one night only, mind.'

That suited Yasha fine. Honour satisfied. He nodded.

'Who is it?' she added. Some of her usual warmth returned to her manner as soon as she saw he wasn't going to argue about how long. 'One of your Jewish group friends?'

'A girl,' Yasha said, then, realizing that this might be giving quite the wrong impression, added, hastily: 'A cousin, I mean. She's been living with my parents. Up from Kiev.'

'Why?' Madame Leman asked, looking wary again. 'What is she here for?'

He shrugged. 'She's brought a letter from my parents. Who've gone to Palestine. Apparently. They were scared there'd be a pogrom.'

At that, Madame Leman's eyes went soft. Stepping away from Agrippina, she embraced him, the smeary spoon waving behind him. 'Oh, Yasha, I'm sorry,' she murmured. He hugged her mutely back, very hard, and this time felt obscurely comforted to hear her add, 'You'll miss them, darling, won't you? But if they had to go, they had to go. They'll have been afraid.'

The little girl, who, living in this household, was used to flamboyant hugging, chided matter-of-factly: 'Now, Mam, you're getting mincemeat in his hair with that spoon.' And the embrace broke up, with 'tsssk' noises and laughs and fingers smoothing away any traces of onion.

When Yasha looked round, still smiling bashfully – she might be irritatingly all over the place at times, and she'd gone far too hard on him about Kremer, but Madame Leman was a good sort really – he realized Inna was standing in the doorway, watching.

She was quite still. She looked pinched and left out and tight about the shoulders, but even this couldn't hide the willowy sway of her movements. Yasha held his breath. He saw Madame Leman's eyebrows rise slightly.

Then, with a determined smile, Madame Leman said very quickly, 'Welcome!' and, 'Yasha's family is like family to us!' Turning briskly to Yasha, she added, 'Now, we'll put your cousin in the little room at the top tonight, Yasha, the one next to yours. I'll send Agrippina up with sheets in a minute. But I know you've got it full of your junk. So run along and clear it all out, will you? Put your boxes on the landing, all of them, so she can move, and don't grumble, please. After all, it's only for one night.'

There was something very final about those last words.

Yasha cleared his throat. 'Can I have that letter now?' he asked Inna.

Inna nodded, seeming dazed. She'd probably never heard anyone talk as fast as Madame Leman, Yasha thought. He knew how bewildering it could be. He watched her go out and come back with the letter in her hand.

Inna gave Yasha the letter.

'Now, dear, tell me your name, do,' Madame Leman went on, advancing on Inna with a chopping-board, a knife and some potatoes.

Yasha went out, grinning despite himself. There'd be no resisting the mistress of the house today, he could see. He could hear Madame Leman's determination, even from the corridor: 'And while they're getting things ready upstairs, perhaps I can get *you* to give me a hand with the lunch?'

Yasha raced up the stairs, three at a time, past the doors of several other flats, all the way to the attic floor where he slept, before ripping open his parents' letter in the privacy of the top landing. There was no need to go into his room to read it. This was his space, all of it, the corridor and stairwell as much as his box room and the neighbouring room: one dusty, crowded, private domain.

But it took only a moment to see that the letter wasn't going to offer him any comfort. There was nothing much at all in the brief note beginning, in his father's tiny, neat hand, 'Dearest boy, after much soul-searching, we have decided . . .' It contained only a poste-restante address in Haifa where letters might reach his parents through the society they'd entrusted with preparations for their emigration, and the pious hope that they would soon write again from Jerusalem. There was nothing about recent events in Kiev, nothing to suggest things had come to seem unbearable. There was nothing in it about Inna, either: no mention that she was on her way north, no recommendation that he take care of her . . . not a word. But then, their letters were always like that. Missing out all the important stuff. Hiding behind trivialities. Cowardly. Cowardly. Why hadn't they said anything before about planning to leave? Why hadn't he guessed?

He groaned out loud with the sheer frustration of it. Barely thinking, he screwed up the unsatisfactory letter in one of the fists he was cramming into his eyes, then threw the scrunched-up ball, hard, into a corner, and banged the flat of his hand, hard, against the nearest chest of drawers. That furious thump, that sting of wood on skin, was as close as he could get to relieving his feelings. But he was still raging against his parents as he started throwing boxes and bags out of the room where *she* was to stay.

It was his father he was angriest with. Yasha had been raging for years against his father's spinelessness. 'When I was, oh, twelve or thirteen or so, still a skinny boy with a treble voice,' he remembered telling Kremer's uncle, the first time they'd talked, 'I was on a train coming back from the dacha with my father. It was just after some terrorist bombing: I suppose the one when Grand Duke Sergei was blown to pieces in his carriage, entering the Kremlin gates. Do you remember? His wife ran across Red Square, weeping and picking up the pieces of his body? And their foster children ran after her? It was the only story in the papers that week, and so the train my dad and I were in was full of people all shouting about the Jews, you know, how something should be done about them.'

And Kremer's uncle had nodded in understanding. 'Because everyone knew that it must have been the Jews, because Grand Duke Sergei had expelled all twenty thousand of them from Moscow. And by the time it turned out it *wasn't* the Jews who'd thrown that bomb, but just some Russian Social Revolutionary, they'd all stopped caring.'

Old Kremer was a good person to talk to, Yasha thought. With his great square close-shaven head propped on one reassuringly brawny hand, with his broad back and his knack of getting right to the heart of things, old Kremer really listened.

Yes that was how it was, Yasha remembered confirming. 'So there we were in this packed train with these big men swearing and egging each other on – nail their whores of wives, burn their shops, you know the kind of thing. All round me, because I'd got kind of caught up in the middle of the crowd when they all poured in, drunk from their picnic. And there was my dad, sitting down in his corner, burying his nose in his newspaper, trying to pretend he wasn't there . . .'

Old Kremer, still nodding.

'. . . and then they noticed me.'

Yasha could see from old Kremer's wise eyes that he didn't need to describe the things the men had started yelling at *him* in that train. The taunts.

'Your father did nothing,' old Kremer prompted.

All Yasha needed to do was shrug. But he wouldn't forget the short, stout old peasant woman who *had* left her basket of apples on her seat and got up to defend him. The indignant, if absurd, way she'd started swatting at the jeering brute threatening to pull down Yasha's trousers to demonstrate to the carriage at large that he was a Jew. Her cracked country voice, screeching, 'You should be ashamed of yourselves, all of you! Bullying a harmless little lad with no one to protect him!' Or the way the men's focus on him had transformed, in an instant, into mockery of their friend, being battered by a crone in a flowery headscarf. The proof: it only took a bit of courage, from someone.

And then the train stopped, and he'd jumped off, leaving behind the gales of laughter. A second later, Papa slipped furtively out, too, hunched under his hat.

'We never mentioned it again,' Yasha told old Kremer. 'He never said a word.'

'That's the danger with fear,' old Kremer said. 'It silences people.'

You should become a doctor like Papa, his mother always used to tell him. But after the incident in the train, Yasha had stopped paying attention at school. He'd failed his exams, and refused to retake them or think of university. To his parents' barely suppressed distress, he signed himself up instead as an apprentice at a violin-repair workshop, like a poor boy from the *shtetl*.

So here he was. And it was because of the Kremers that Yasha now had all these boxes of leaflets he was piling up on the landing – especially old Kremer, who wasn't afraid of anything. In fact Yasha had met the younger Kremer first, on the train north, but when *he'd* whispered eagerly about a Jewish political organization Yasha hadn't really taken much notice. It was only when he met Kremer's uncle, recently out of jail in Warsaw, that he started to listen, because old

Kremer was impressive. He was looking for recruits, he said, replacements for all the thousands of young men arrested by Prime Minister Stolypin after the failed revolution a few years back. Mostly he was looking in the Jewlands, down south; but there were gaps even up in this relatively Jewless city, too, now that Kremer's uncle's tiny branch of the General Jewish Labour Federation – the Bund, they called it; a secular socialist party fighting for political rights for Jews in Russia – had fallen foul of the authorities.

Yasha remembered how old Kremer's eyebrows had risen at his fumbling, hesitant confession that he didn't even know Yiddish, let alone Hebrew, and that he wasn't religious, and what was the point. He remembered the indignation in the old man's voice when he'd snapped back, 'Religion? Why, I'm not talking about *religion*. I'm talking about the rights of man; the right to be proud of what you come from, and to live where you choose, and work where you're qualified; to have the same rights as the Russians you live among, rather than skulking around in the shadows, waiting to be picked on.'

Yasha was ready to listen. When he came to think about it, he had no more idea than old Kremer why his parents would have been so shortsighted as to have thought they were protecting him by cutting him off from his past. He'd started Yiddish lessons the next day. He'd gone to every meeting since, even when old Kremer had gone off south again, proselytizing. When that had left the younger Kremer without a room, Yasha had taken young Kremer in. And even after Madame Leman had kicked him out, the spare room next door had been a Godsend for the leaflets.

He heaved another two boxes out and dumped them, in

a cloud of dust, on the messy pyramid rising on the landing.

There were so many of them (the brothers were enthusiastic writers) but the leaflets were harder to distribute than they were to produce. There was nowhere safe for them; not over on the islands where he met the other Bundists, in pub rooms that stank of rotting plaster and cabbage. And now there was no room for them here, either – because this green-eyed girl from Kiev, Inna, had arrived.

Yasha couldn't bear to look inside the boxes. Not now.

They were so brave, the arguments in the wobbly type in there, about the need to fight back, right here, inside the Russian Empire, against official anti-Semitism. Not just take fright and emigrate, as so many thousands had in the past decade or two. Zionism is escapism, Yasha had half shouted, half whispered, aware of the possibility of police informers, to last weekend's nervous little gathering. Palestine is not the answer. Don't run from your troubles. Face them down. *Doykayt* – their made-up Yiddish word, 'hereness' – is where it all begins.

And now his parents had gone.

It was only once Yasha had emptied the room that he went into his own room and pulled out his parents' other letters. He was sweating. They'd never once said, he was muttering accusingly. Never . . . once . . . mentioned . . .

But they had.

He'd just never read any of them properly. He'd always flicked through their letters, chuckled over the first few careful phrases: still fretting over the doorman's thieving; still giving money to the school (whatever for?); still anxious about the quality of herring at the market; still at war with the officious nuns who nursed at the hospital. And once he'd got that far he'd put the letters back in their envelopes, to read properly later. He'd not noticed the anxious questions squeezed along a fold or as a PS or in a margin somewhere, in almost every one. When he might come home? Would it be prudent to get travel permission for the three of them, just in case? The careful mentions of so-and-so's visit to Haifa, and someone else's trip to Jerusalem itself. Each one, now, a knife in his side. Why hadn't he seen? Why hadn't he written back?

Yasha sat down heavily on his bed and tried to imagine what they were going through: Mama, tossing up and down on a boat deck, pale with travel sickness, with her fluffy mohair shawl damp and bedraggled round her shoulders and her hair all blown everywhere, surrounded by goaty old Orthodox pilgrims in rags and beards; and Papa letting bureaucrats fleece him blind, knowing something was wrong but not *how* they were cheating him – poor, flustered, helpless Papa, who'd never have the amused calm of Monsieur Leman or the granite strength of old Kremer.

It wasn't that Yasha didn't love them. But he'd been so angry, so resentful, so full of his new life that he hadn't made enough effort to respond when they'd tried to tell him about what they wanted to do.

Yasha groaned. He'd been the strong one all along, he saw now. He should have been better able to protect them. But he hadn't been there.

'You're very quiet, Yasha,' Monsieur Leman said at lunch, lowering his newspaper and peering over the top at him.

He shrugged. Just as well if he was. No one else was being quiet.

Barbarian and Agrippina were giggling at the children's end of the table, with no one disciplining them. Marcus, who was supposed to be in charge, was too busy gawping furtively at the guest, or giggling too, more uproariously than anyone, in his up-and-down donkey-bray of a teenage voice.

Madame Leman had been giving Inna Feldman the story of the Lemans' lives since the food was dished up: her husband's career, from classics scholar (hence the children's names) to reluctant army cadet to billiards strategist to ingenious manufacturer of profitable false teeth; their brief, idealistic emigration to live among the People, in the countryside near Kiev; their disillusioned return to St Petersburg on the eve of the revolution in 1905 ('Country people – so *narrow-minded*!'); the liberal newspaper Monsieur Leman had set up that had nearly got him jailed in the police crackdown after the revolution failed; and his return, in the past decade, to his first love, violin-making.

Her face was pink. She was smiling. Hairpins tinkled unnoticed on to her plate. Well, at least talking about herself and her family was putting her back into her usual easy mood.

While Madame Leman talked, Monsieur Leman was reading, chuckling and every now and then saying, 'Unbelievable!' as he pored over an allegedly eyewitness account from the assassination scene in Kiev. It was a gasp-and-stretch-your-eyes article that Yasha had already turned away from in disgust, claiming that the Empress's current favourite crackpot mystic, that goaty holy man, what's-his-name, had been in the crowd watching the Prime Minister pass on his way to the theatre, and started howling and wailing, 'Doomed! He's being followed by death!' before collapsing to the ground.

Yasha, meanwhile, was watching Inna. Madame Leman was clearly determined not to let another Kremer situation develop, and had kept the new guest working in the kitchen, without let-up, till the meal was on the table. Inna was still grimy and travel-stained, but she was gamely trying to be polite. She nodded, from time to time. She used the pauses in Madame Leman's monologue to say yes or, occasionally, no! Mostly, though, she just ate, with the concentration of the very hungry. She had three helpings of the potato purée he knew she must have made herself before her face lost its sickly ashy colour and she finally put down her fork.

'Did you not have any food on the train?' he asked, gently.

Eyes down, she shook her head.

Briefly, Yasha was aware of Monsieur Leman's eyes, peeping over the top of the newspaper at him again, looking amused. Shaking his head.

Hastily, Yasha got up, leaving his plate with the darling doves untouched to one side (he'd known Madame L. would have used minced pork as well as beef – she didn't approve of his new faddishness about pork – so he was secretly pleased that she'd made Inna peel enough potatoes to make purée for an army).

'I'm off to the workshop,' he said, avoiding the master's eye, suddenly wanting to be alone again. 'I got behind this morning.'

He didn't expect the tumult of reply that came as he scraped his chair back and prepared to slink quietly away downstairs.

First Inna, saying, in a stronger voice than he'd heard from her all through the meal: 'Oh! Can I come too? I'd love to see your workshop.'

Then the rustle of a newspaper being put down, and Monsieur Leman's rumble and Marcus's eager multi-register cry, at the same time, 'Of course!' and 'I work there too, now! I'll show you round!'

And finally Madame Leman's forlorn squawk, as the men of the house all headed for the door: 'But who's going to do the washing up?'

Yasha stopped. This might need careful management. It was just the kind of thing that had so annoyed her about young Kremer ('Eating us out of house and home and never lifting a finger to help!'). But Inna had understood instantly. She'd already turned, and was saying in pleading tones, with an enchantingly furrowed brow, 'Please, Madame Leman, just leave everything. I won't be long. I'll be happy to do it. And, by the way, it was a delicious lunch.'

That was enough, it seemed. Apparently at least half mollified, Madame Leman nodded and smiled faintly before turning energetically to Agrippina and Barbarian to say, 'Well then, you two, isn't it time we sat down together to look at your homework?'

CHAPTER FOUR

You could get to the workshop by the building's back door, at the bottom of the communal staircase that connected the Leman's first-floor apartment with the other flats above, and also, several flights up, with the two box rooms of Yasha's domain, though the shop front opened onto the avenue outside.

Yasha sat straight down at his stool, put on his apron, turned on his lamp and picked up the violin he was making. He'd let the others fuss around her.

So he said nothing when Monsieur Leman started telling the girl, with his sly smile, 'Best thing we ever did, hiring Yasha. His work is so quick and neat and elegant . . . and he's strong, too, does a week's work in a day without even noticing . . .' (though he did, for a moment, feel a quiver of secret pride).

It was frightening all the time, of course, this work, but a small, manageable fear – a fear born of love. You lived with it as you scraped away, a shaving at a time, never quite sure you'd mastered the tools, hoping you didn't cut your wooden infant's throat before it took its first breath. 'I like my apprentices a bit scared,' Leman was saying to Inna, laughing with her over his gold-rimmed spectacles, until she relaxed and smiled her unexpected, enchanting smile back. 'It makes me feel more like a master when I can set 'em right. Marcus, now: he's just beginning. Scared all the time. But Yasha's beyond that. Shaping up as a master.'

Yasha grinned, not looking up. He was carving a bass bar, whittling away at the delicate curves, making the arc of it higher in the middle, and broader and flatter towards the scooped ends. As always in this warm, comfortable, happy space, lit by pools of golden light, he felt cradled by the knowledge of the big, strong, broad-shouldered man for whom he worked, who could be relied on to have all the answers and who wanted to pass down his skills to a new generation. It had been the luckiest moment in his life when Leman had walked into his tough former master's workshop in Kiev and noticed him; when he'd invited him up here, to work for him; when he'd helped Yasha obtain the papers he'd need to get away from the brutal difficulties of the Jewlands to this new, gentler, life in the centre. Yasha was good at the job, and he knew himself to be useful; but if he was, it was because here, feeling a success, he worked with all his heart, because he loved the gentle promise of redemption that Leman had shown him in the work. Mistakes you can mend. Splinters can be glued back; cuts filled with glue and sawdust; unintended holes cut and lined and carved and sanded back into three-dimensional existence. Wood forgives.

'Bit of a mess,' he heard Marcus apologize. 'Shavings everywhere.'

'Let me sweep up,' Inna said eagerly from outside his field

of vision. 'No, really.' He heard Leman rumble something appreciative in reply as he showed her where the apprentices' brooms were. Leman liked a tidy space.

Yasha found he was whistling under his breath as his hands flew over the wood as, somewhere behind him, she started kicking up clouds of shavings. He didn't even mind that he could feel her peeking over his shoulder at what he was doing.

Everyone was always whistling or humming under their breath as they worked down here. Sometimes they chatted: quiet, meditative talk, on the subjects closest to their hearts, easy streams of consciousness that flowed on and intermingled, quickly becoming familiar to their companions.

But not today.

Today, after twenty minutes of unusually loud talk by the two Lemans, and of poking about and rather boastfully demonstrating the work they were doing, between her ener- getic bursts of sweeping – he could see from the sweeping that Inna Feldman was as eager to please the Lemans as the male Lemans were to interest her – Leman and Marcus took her back upstairs again, at her request, so she could wash up.

'Back in a minute, Yasha,' Leman said cheerfully from the door.

He nodded without looking up.

'I play the violin a bit myself,' he heard Inna tell Leman before the door shut. Alone, he breathed a long, long sigh. She wasn't going to get into Madame L.'s good books, not after the Kremer episode. But she just might with the others. And she was certainly doing her best. You had to give her marks for trying.

As Yasha worked, he went on trying to remember the Feldman story, calling to mind the details his parents had told him, long ago. Hinted at, anyway. It had been coming back in wisps. It went something like this, he thought: young couple, distant cousins, living in a flat in a smallish town an hour from Kiev with their little girl; both of them teachers. The apartment set alight, in one of those nights of anti-Jewish violence that the little towns down there were so prone to. Both killed. The little girl would probably have been killed, too, only she ran away, and was brought up by a neighbour.

'So was it smoke from the fire that killed them?' he remembered asking, trying to imagine the smell of it in his nose, and wondering whether those people been scared or just asleep. What an innocent. Still, even an innocent couldn't help but notice the way Mama's eyes had shifted sideways, and the discomfort in Papa's as he muttered, 'We don't know the details.'

He didn't know how old she'd been then – four, five? But of course she'd never forget something like that. So when she'd seen hateful crowds in Kiev last week, what could have been more natural than for her to draw the fearful conclusions she had?

Gently he blew the shavings off his workbench. She had guts, but he could see that she couldn't have been anything but afraid. He might, just might, have been too angry with her at the door this morning. It was possible he'd over-reacted, he thought, holding up his fiddle front to the light, to caress the shape he'd been making with a loving eye and see whether the curve needed correcting.

It was good to be on his own again, down here in the

calm, thinking. Seeing the whole shape taking form under his hands.

He was thinking, too, about that letter from his parents.

He'd crumpled it up so fast he hadn't really examined the envelope.

But now, looking back, in this more reflective state of mind, he remembered that it hadn't had the words 'By hand' written on it, any more than the letter inside had mentioned that Inna was the courier.

In fact, now he came to think of it, there'd been a stamp in the top right-hand corner – as if they'd intended to post it.

He thought his parents' first letter mentioning her, nearly a year ago, had said she was in the final years of school. What *could* a schoolgirl be planning to do, up here, so far from home? With a pang, he realized that none of them, so far that day, had asked.

Then, suddenly, he knew.

He put the fiddle front gently down in its padded cradle, so he could think.

His parents *hadn't* asked Inna to bring him that letter at all, had they? She'd just picked it up in the flat – pinched it, the same way she'd pinched a passport. It had been her own initiative to bring it here herself, because . . . because . . . he scratched his head, feeling increasingly uneasy . . . well, obviously, because she didn't have anywhere else to go. She'd had no other plan in her mind beyond finding him, and digging in.

Remorse struck him like a blow. He should have been protecting her. Helping her find a way to stay a bit longer. Taking the fear out of her eyes.

He turned off his lamp with a gentle hand and went slowly back upstairs.

He was wondering, as he went, what his parents could possibly have thought would happen to her once they'd gone? If they'd thought at all, because the likeliest thing was that they'd got so absorbed by their own fear that they'd just left her to fend for herself . . .

He opened the apartment door, imagining himself standing up to Madame L., insisting – no, *demanding* – in the face of every counter-argument, that Inna be allowed to stay for a few days, or even weeks. He'd make it up to the mistress.

He paused in the still chaotic lobby to compose himself. And, as he did, the conversation inside the yellow room died away, and the sound of a violin rose into the air.

A shiver went down Yasha's spine at the first wild, sweet, zany notes. He'd never heard anything like *that* here. Anywhere.

Everyone in this family played a bit, of course. He wasn't much of an artiste himself, but recently he'd taken to pouring his heart out, in the privacy of his room, into the mournful songs of the *shtetl*. Monsieur Leman, meanwhile, liked the mathematical purity of Bach; Madame Leman, who was literary, enjoyed the German romantics; Marcus preferred sentimental café music and soupy folk tunes; and the children sawed cheerfully away at whatever beginner's music they were made to practise.

But this?

It was frisky and catchy and modern. Playful, though it sounded fiendishly difficult, too: in thirds, and in a dancey three-beat rhythm, with odd accents on the third beat. Syncopated, like American negro jazz. It was composed of pointed little runs of six staccato notes, moving up and down the instrument, getting faster and louder and wilder, before dying away, from time to time, into a beautifully phrased, wistful, legato sigh.

Yasha stopped right where he was, among the coats and boots: entranced, lost. But his feet were tapping. He couldn't help himself.

The piece was being played with tremendous sophistication, too: with as much knowledge of emotional light and shade as technical confidence. Yasha found himself thinking, more poetically than usual: the flight of the soul . . .

And then it was over, moments after he'd recovered the power of movement, just as he reached the drawing-room door.

There could only have been one person playing, yet he was astonished, standing in the doorway, to see Inna there in the crook of the piano, with flushed cheeks and huge green eyes, looking around in apparent surprise at the tumultuous clapping, and only gradually, when she fixed her eyes on Barbarian and Agrippina, jumping up and down and cheering in their corner, letting her lovely face lift into a smile.

She had a violin cradled under one arm. After one shy glance around the room, she put it and the bow she'd been holding down on the lid of the piano.

Yasha couldn't see Madame Leman, who must still be sitting down in a chair out of his line of vision, but Monsieur Leman was standing up, beaming, and Marcus, too, spluttering joyfully beside him.

They hadn't even noticed him standing in the doorway. They were too enchanted by the girl. A feeling Yasha didn't understand clutched at his heart.

'I'm wondering', Leman was saying appreciatively in his

big booming voice, 'who in Kiev can have taught you to play Scriabin?'

Yasha watched Inna shake her head. 'Oh, I had lessons when I was younger,' she said awkwardly, not seeming at all the mature player of a moment ago. 'From my Aunty Lyuba. I lived with her. But she's dead now. I just mess about on my own. And I heard that piece at a concert, and liked it . . .'

She looked over at Yasha, staring at her from the door.

'And I do have a lovely violin to play on,' she added, and smiled tentatively at him, as if inviting him to share in her triumph. But he couldn't. Her playing had been better than anything he, or the rest of them, could draw from the instruments they spent their lives working on – so much better that it had made him feel a primitive by comparison. He could tell now that she must also know precisely how pretty she looked, and how vulnerable; she was knowingly *using* her charms.

'Look,' she was saying. 'It's the first violin Yasha made.'

The children whooped and squawked and surged closer: 'Really . . .? Let's have a look!' They grabbed it. Smiling – smirking, as it now seemed to Yasha – Inna was holding it up, out of their reach. From the chair, inside, there was a pained female cry of 'Children!'

At the same time, but much more quietly, Yasha said, 'That's *my* old violin?' It was too much. He thought of her passport, his parents' letter. Was there no end to the things she'd taken?

But she didn't appear to notice his ominous tone. With apparent artlessness, she said, as if he'd be pleased she was waltzing around Russia with her bag stuffed full of his things: 'Your mother let me play it. I brought it . . . I thought—'

But Leman cut her off. Turning to Yasha, he boomed excitedly, 'Ah, come in, come in, my boy! So you heard, too? Good heavens, why ever didn't you tell us what a marvellous musician your little cousin is – the real thing! I was bowled over – especially since all I was expecting was more of that mournful Jewish caterwauling you go in for upstairs!'

He laughed so hard at his own joke that he didn't notice Yasha's scowl. Yasha looked at the children. At least they weren't laughing at him; though it wasn't much better that Agrippina was gazing so adoringly at Inna. Barbarian, meanwhile, was taking advantage of being unobserved. He was down on the ground, quietly tying Agrippina's shoelace to a chair.

'Inna reminds me of you, my dear,' Leman remarked to his wife, who was still sitting behind the door. 'One of those women who, without any real teaching, can master the great arts.' He turned back to Inna and gestured proudly towards his life-companion. 'You know Lidiya Alexeyevna here taught herself all the European languages? Before she'd travelled further than Moscow? Before she'd even turned twenty? Sheer dedication . . . I admire that. I really do.'

"'S not just women. Men do it too. You taught yourself billiards in the army, Pap,' Barbarian called from the floor, grinning broadly.

Leman pulled a wry face. 'I was locked up in a closed cadet school for years. Enough time for a boy like me to learn the oddest things,' he answered. 'And, Barbarian, undo that shoelace right now or there'll be trouble,' he added, with no change of tone.

Grinning over the scuffle that ensued, he turned back to Inna.

'So. You play beautifully, we're all agreed on that.' He paused. 'Would you like to *make* a violin?' His voice sounded genuinely hopeful, as if the answer were up to her.

Inna's mouth opened. Her flush deepened.

Yasha's heart was pounding. To just let her in like this – so easily – when *he'd* had to learn his trade beforehand, and wait for months for papers, and struggle . . . When he'd been thinking she was an innocent who needed protecting, and had been rushing up here ready to fight her corner for her, only to find that with one dewy look, and one showing-off tune, she'd already got them wanting her here for good. If he didn't look out . . . well, the injustice of it took his breath away. Maybe old Kremer had been right about women, after all.

'Women don't make violins,' Madame Leman's voice said, into the silence.

'Not *ordinarily*,' Leman said sweepingly. 'But that was no ordinary playing.'

'But . . . are you actually looking for someone?' Inna asked.

'Well, we're training Marcus. But we get a lot of work in these days. And I've been thinking of taking someone else on for some time. Though you know how it is. One's always too lazy to start the wearisome business of actually looking for someone, and wondering if they'll get on with everyone, because by the time they start it's already a bit late to say we don't like the cut of your jib, and we're all at very close quarters here, as you know, and who wants to see a quarrelsome face at breakfast? Now, if only it were you, well – you're already in the family, so to speak, and the question simply wouldn't arise.'

Inna's disbelieving smile widened, and so did her eyes.

59

There was a silence as Yasha waited, with diminishing hope, for Madame Leman, at least, to say no, quite impossible. But she didn't.

Eventually, Leman turned to him, nodding excitedly. 'Good idea?'

Yasha only knew what he was going to do as he did it.

'She can't,' he said, stepping forward into the room, composing his face into a half-smile. 'She has no documents. She got here on a stolen passport.'

The smile hovered on Inna's face, diminishing over several agonizingly slow seconds as she struggled to understand what he'd done. And what did, finally, replace the hope that had been written on her was unmistakably the crumpled misery of a child with no home to go to.

Yasha watched, feeling terrible. Even then, she didn't turn the accusing eyes he deserved on him. Instead, she looked first at Madame Leman, who kept her own eyes carefully fixed on her feet, and then at Monsieur Leman, whose own excitement had been replaced by the cautious, hurt expression of a man realizing he's being taken advantage of.

'But . . .' she said, pleadingly, a note of desperation in her voice, 'even if it's not mine . . . I showed it to a policeman, at the station, and he let me pass . . . wouldn't it do?'

She reached into the violin bag, pulled out a passport and held it out to Leman.

Yasha stood in the middle of the room, as Leman flicked sadly through the passport. 'Hereditary noblewoman,' he murmured, shaking his head, 'daughter of the deputy chief of the Kiev police . . .'

'It's my friend Olya's,' Inna said.

He handed it back. 'They'd find you out, sooner or later,'

he told her, regretfully. 'It would be naïve to think they wouldn't. I'm sorry, my dear.'

She nodded, as if she was used to defeat, picked up the bag – leaving the violin out, Yasha noticed; she wasn't going to claim it, then – and said, very quietly, 'Do you mind if I go and rest now? I'm a little tired. But I'll be fine to leave in the morning.' From the doorway, she added, in a small voice, 'It was a very kind offer.'

'Look,' Yasha said, defensively, as soon as she was out of the door. 'It's not *my* fault. You know the way things are.'

But he couldn't help also remembering that Leman had found a way to register him as a resident in St Petersburg. A Jew was allowed to live here only if he was serving in the army, or was rich, or a qualified craftsman. The craft couldn't be too glamorous, either. So when the ministry had rejected Yasha as a violin master, he'd been in despair. But Leman hadn't been discouraged. 'There's always a way,' he'd said, and Yasha now had a residence permit as a carpenter. There were twenty-five thousand Jews in Petersburg, so there were probably twenty-five thousand ways to get in.

But there weren't any if you didn't have a passport in your own name, or a sponsor.

'I wish the law was made by liberals, too. But it's not. The ministry would never let her in. There's no use raising her hopes,' Yasha said now, trying to ignore the accusing looks from Marcus and the younger children.

Nothing went right after that.

Yasha went angrily back to work, so angrily that he stupidly splintered an edge of his violin, and had to put it aside. Until he calmed down, he knew, he wouldn't be able to figure out how to make the wood forgive his mistake.

No one else came down to join him. They were avoiding him, clearly. He retidied the workshop. He hounded wood shavings, and dealt death to spiders' webs.

Eventually he flung back upstairs, hoping for supper. But when he got to the kitchen door he could hear a tense conversation inside the room between Monsieur and Madame Leman, which he didn't like to interrupt.

He skulked uncertainly in the corridor, wondering what to do. The blood rushed hot to his face when he heard Madame Leman's alternately weary and exasperated voice, saying, 'But we had that other idiot friend of Yasha's to stay, don't you remember, while he was supposed to be looking for a proper room? And all he did was sit in the attic writing leaflets, and eat our food with never so much as a thank you, and never lifted a finger – for *two months*, Tolya!'

Surely it hadn't been two months? Yasha thought. But it had; he knew it had, really.

'Well, maybe she could help you in the house, just for a while?' he heard Leman reply cautiously from behind the door. 'Because we could all see today that *she's* willing enough to help, and that travel passport she's got is valid till the end of the month, even if it's not hers, and really, dear heart, look at the state of her; we can't just send her straight back tomorrow, can we?'

Yasha couldn't bear the idea of her going off to the station in the morning, either, holding herself tall and trying not to look scared.

But Madame Leman wasn't having any of it. 'I don't need help,' sang out like a slap in the face.

Yasha had never been able to be cautious for long. Now he opened the door and walked in.

'Or perhaps she could help out in the workshop for a few days – just till the end of the week, say,' he suggested boldly, catching Leman's eye. 'Sweeping up. Running errands. There's plenty she can do to make herself useful.'

Leman looked back at him in relief, and raised his eyebrows hopefully at his wife.

But Madame Leman was looking hard at Yasha. 'You've changed your tune,' she said.

Yasha blushed. He had, and for reasons he couldn't quite understand. But Inna was family, and, as he was telling himself now, families must stand together.

It was Madame Leman who gave Yasha a bowl of soup and some bread to take up to Inna in her room.

He knocked on her door, but he was inside before she answered. He only stopped when he saw the red-rimmed eyes in the tight white face she turned towards him. The brittle pride she'd displayed downstairs hadn't lasted once she was alone. She'd been crying.

Appalled, he muttered, 'Oh . . .'

She was sitting on the bed, with her back to him. Only her neck and head moved. She had a flowery shawl wrapped around her shoulders, over a night robe. The tears were in the past, at least, though only the very recent past. When he'd come in, he realized, she'd had her dark head down, concentrating on something in her lap.

As soon as she'd understood who was standing there, having broken into her privacy, her face had gone cold, though her eyes were flashing.

'Oh . . . *you*,' she said, quickly looking away. She put all the scorn she could into the formal word *vy* – his choice, earlier, he recalled, ashamed. He heard something small drop as she got up, carefully, standing cautiously behind the bed, with her hands behind her back. With exaggerated unconcern, she bent and quickly picked up whatever the small item was that she'd dropped, putting it, and the hand holding it, quickly into the pocket of her gown.

She was hiding something.

'I didn't mean to startle you,' he said. Calling her *ty* now was the closest he could get to an apology.

His cheeks were hot again. She must think he'd come to gloat. It wasn't an unreasonable thing for her to think, either, given how he'd been. Shame at his outburst earlier made his heart thump so hard he couldn't bring himself to speak. All the flood of other things he'd so wanted to say, while he was hastening upstairs – to tell her he'd guessed about the letter, and about how his parents must have left her – just faded away.

'I've brought you some food,' he tried again in a penitent tone.

'Thanks,' she said, shortly, looking down.

'And I wanted to say that Madame L. says it's all right for you . . .' He corrected himself. '. . . that she'd be happy for you to stay till the end of the week. You can help us out in the workshop to earn your keep.'

For a moment, he thought he caught the green gleam of relief he'd hoped for in her eyes, but then her face tightened again. She wasn't grateful to *him*. She still didn't want him near her.

'That's kind of them,' she told her feet. 'I'd like that.' She paused. 'Just put the food on the floor. I'll come for it in a minute. I was just . . .' She didn't want to pick up the food, he now realized, because she didn't want him to see that hand.

He put down the bowl on the floor, as she'd told him to, but as he straightened up he looked more closely.

She'd put her other hand to the shawl at her throat.

It had a handkerchief wrapped around it, which hadn't been there when she was playing downstairs.

'You've hurt yourself,' he said, concerned. As he spoke, her hand shifted on the shawl. He could see spots of blood, from her palm, coming through the hanky. 'Are you all right?'

He couldn't stop himself stepping forward. He so wanted to take her hand; to see for himself. He only just managed to stop himself.

'I'm fine.' She bit off the word.

'But what's wrong with your hand?'

She didn't answer at once, though she did at least look at him. She took the other hand out of her pocket and held it out, as if daring him to be shocked. There was a knife lying in the palm, the kind you take on train journeys to cut up your bread and sausage with. There was blood on the blade, and a mess of blood, some fresh, some congealing, in the line of small cuts across the palm it lay on.

Yasha recoiled. Shutting his eyes, he fumbled in his pockets for the clean hanky he knew was there.

'I've got a hanky, thank you,' he heard, still in that bitten-off, brazening-it-out tone.

'But what . . .' he muttered, still not able to look at her or that accusing gash, '. . . what the Hell are you doing to yourself?'

She stepped forward, using the same trick as before, and he retreated. It was only when she was closing the door that she answered. But the door had clicked shut, leaving him in the dark outside with a fuzzy, glowing image of her on his retina – this time uplit by the little lamp, with her fragile dignity and her wounded, defiant green eyes – before the words sank in.

'I was cutting myself a better lifeline,' she'd said.

CHAPTER FIVE

The next morning, Inna went straight out, without breakfast. She was pale. She had her hands in a muff.

Why had she been such a fool? she now wondered, mortified by the spots of rusty blood staining the sheets that she'd woken up to this morning. It wasn't as if she actually believed that gypsy's prophecy. She wasn't superstitious.

It was clear now that, after last night, Yasha would have nothing more to do with her. She'd seen that from the bewildered, shocked distaste with which he'd shrunk back, the look that signified: But that's not how things are done here. She'd been acting like someone from down there, someone so desperate she'd stopped being able to think. Someone alone.

But she wasn't helpless. She wouldn't just give in. And she wasn't alone, either, or at least not quite alone. There might not be anything she could do, by herself, to get papers, but there was at least one person she knew whom she could ask to help her get what she wanted.

The idea she woke up with was to go and see her friend the peasant. She'd ask for an introduction to his friend

Simanovich, the one who could get residence papers for Jews. She'd ask *him* what it would cost to get her a permit. She still had some money. It would be well spent, on that.

If Monsieur Leman wanted to keep her, and would train her (which he'd sounded genuine enough about), but just didn't know how to get documents (which she could imagine he didn't), well, there was nothing for it but to organize it herself.

Half an hour later, she was in the dark stairwell of Nikolayevskaya 70, feet clattering on worn tiles.

A gaggle of rumpled youngish men were lounging on the doorstep outside, standing on discarded cigarette ends. They didn't frighten her. They weren't in uniform. They barely looked at her, either, as she slid among them.

Inside, the doorman looked wearily up at her from behind a dusty arrangement of dried flowers. 'I'm looking for . . .' she hesitated. She didn't like just to say, 'the peasant'.

'The peasant,' the man said, scratching his ear. 'First floor, door on the left.' Gratefully, she flew upstairs.

The door opened a crack. Eyes looked out: eyes half hidden in deeply lined flesh above a straggly beard; unfriendly eyes.

Suddenly the eyes opened wide, and Inna was relieved to see that pale-blue blaze of recognition, the kindness dawning again in his face.

'Why, it's my young friend from the train!' he exclaimed warmly. Then a slight frown crossed his face.

'I was passing . . .' she stammered. 'And there was something I wanted to ask you . . .'

Her voice died away as he glanced back into the dark

vestibule behind him. His eyelids lowered till his gaze was lost in deeply lined flesh.

'I'd ask you in. It's just that these fools have all turned up.' He sounded vexed.

Inna's heart sank. He hadn't really meant it when he'd invited her to visit him. He'd just been saying something polite. Her cheeks flamed. She was about to whisper, 'If it's a bad time,' and flee, when he shrugged.

'Well, let them share,' he said, almost to himself. Then, looking directly at Inna, he added, with a determination she couldn't doubt: 'Come in, come in.'

The room she followed him into was very basic: a big window curtained in cheap yellowing lace, a table and stools on one side and a screen hiding a bed on the other. But it was full of people. There must have been a dozen of them sitting at the table, murmuring together.

There were no other peasants: no apple-cheeked Dunyas or little ragamuffins giggling under the table. All these guests were in city clothes. Very good dark clothes, too, with none of the darns and patches she'd seen on the Leman children's elbows (though with none of the Lemans' arty dash either).

For an instant, Inna was appalled. She'd never be able to talk privately to the peasant with them here. She'd walked uninvited into a party.

But, almost at once, she began to wonder who they were. Almost all were women (although there was a stout, pompous young man in a dark morning coat hovering behind the stool of a young, pretty woman with a flower of a face and the most beautiful oyster-coloured silk blouse Inna had ever seen). And, grand though they clearly were, almost all had

69

a look in their eyes that suggested life hadn't treated them as kindly as they might have hoped.

They should have been intimidating to a provincial schoolgirl. But they looked so helpless that Inna couldn't find it in herself to be scared.

When they became aware of her, the buzz of talk stopped.

It wasn't quite a party after all, Inna realized. They were all staring at her, furtively, jealously, as if each one was privately assessing a potential rival.

The only exception was a middle-aged lady in a feathered hat above her modest robe, who was at the samovar, pouring out tea.

'Father Grigory, may I offer your guest some tea?' she asked.

Father Grigory? So he *was* some sort of religious man? The peasant didn't seem pleased by the honorific, and just nodded.

Handing Inna a glass, the lady said, 'I'm Lyubov Vassilievna Golovina, my dear . . . and that's my daughter, Munya.' She indicated a girl scarcely older than Inna, with timid blue eyes, a sweet, plain face and a shawl.

Inna felt tempted to bob a curtsey in gratitude for Madame Golovina's well-bred graciousness. 'My name is Inna.' She paused and then added, 'Feldman,' omitting her Jewish patronymic. The Golovinas were clearly nobility even if their clothes weren't grand; and if 'Munya' were enough of a name for the daughter to go by, then 'Inna' without 'Venyaminovna' would do for her.

'How do you know each other?' Inna asked Munya, indicating the peasant with a nod.

'Oh, I was introduced to him by my cousin's wife – Sana,

70

over there,' Munya replied, nodding at the pretty young lady in the expensive oyster-silk blouse. 'Sana thought he would help me come to terms with my tragedy . . .'

In the renewed silence, Inna noticed how oddly the table was set. Around the big samovar there was an incongruous feast: sumptuous tortes, laden with cream and cherries, and crystal bowls of fruit, exotic items which wouldn't have been out of place at Yeliseyevsky's (as Inna imagined it) but looked odd in this plain room; but also little piles of home-made peppermint gingersnaps and heaps of large crude rolls. There were two smeary jars of jam, with teaspoons propped against the saucers. A luxurious sturgeon in aspic lay on a platter next to a rough basket of plain black bread and a deep bowl of hard-boiled eggs.

The peasant, too, was a little different from how she'd remembered. Had he been wearing those luxurious clothes in the train yesterday: peasant trousers made of black velvet? His knee-high boots gleamed – patent leather? His shirt was definitely made of silk. Perhaps the clothes and the food were gifts from these anxious-looking gentlefolk who called him 'Father' and gazed at him silently with those hungry eyes?

Inna hoped they weren't about to pray. Yet there was nothing religious in his room – just a photo, propped up against the window, of St Isaac's Cathedral, with white ribbons tied to the frame.

She didn't understand, but it didn't matter. Excitement was replacing her embarrassment. She'd find a way to talk to him before she left, she was sure. And meanwhile this was an adventure.

She did wish they would eat, though. It was still only ten

71

in the morning, but Inna was hungry, and the food looked delicious.

The peasant caught her eyeing the food, and grinned. Loudly, to the room at large, he said: 'Drink your tea, dear guests. Eat.'

A few guests sipped. Still no one touched the food. He shook his head, seeming irritated; then he stood and took a handful of the eggs from the bowl himself. The women's eyes lit up. Inna heard a rapturous murmur of, 'Father, an egg!' from all sides. He rolled his eyes and almost snorted. But he walked around the table, presenting them to his guests, one by one, on an outstretched palm, with a solemnity so exaggerated it looked to Inna almost like mockery.

'There . . . *now* eat, for God's sake,' he growled. He sat down, crossed himself, and started eating a piece of bread with a pickle on it.

Inna caught herself staring again – not at him, because, after all, he was just sitting there chewing; but at his guests, who were still not touching the food but, instead, silently watching the dark bread disappear into his mouth.

Well, more fool them, Inna thought. She put some of the magnificent dill-perfumed sturgeon on a plate and took a modest mouthful. Finishing his sandwich, the peasant looked approvingly at Inna. 'You're hungry, so you eat,' he said. Then, 'They're all so rich and educated, but sometimes these fools don't understand the simplest things.' There was a sting in his voice. Yet the eyes all swivelled back to him again with that same rapt look as if he'd made a sacred pronouncement. On Inna's right, Munya even made a genteel little grab for the notebook Inna could see lying on the table, and scribbled an urgent note.

Contemptuously, the peasant told the ladies beside Inna, who were looking anxiously at their eggs: 'Look, you won't dirty your hands with simple honest food. Take those eggs and roll them on the table. They'll crack. Then you take the shells off. Then you can eat them. Even a fool should know that.'

Wincing as if they were being asked to humiliate themselves – which, Inna felt uncomfortably, they were – the pair cast their eyes down and set to rolling the eggs around on the table until the shells cracked. Fastidiously, they picked bits off. One even put her white egg to her mouth and nibbled.

Inna was relieved when the bell rang, breaking the tension.

The two newcomers were men, who came in murmuring together. One was young and languid, with a mocking half-smile on his startlingly handsome dark face. The other, who had a frosting of grey in his black hair, was also tall and well set-up, but a little older: his carriage was athletic but somehow more solid, and he had laughter lines at his eyes. He had a bottle in his hand.

It was this second man to whom the peasant turned, much more cheerfully, to exclaim: 'Mis-ter Wallick!' A foreign name. Father Grigory stood up. 'Late, as usual.'

Unapologetically, Mr Wallick waved the wine. 'I know you don't, Father, but I'm made of weaker stuff.'

The younger man only smirked, watching the greeting through heavy lidded eyes before wafting towards Munya to bend over her in a practised bow and murmur, 'Why, darling girl . . .' and kiss her hand. There was no particular feeling in the kiss, Inna thought, and Munya submitted limply to it, though her mother nodded in satisfaction when the beautiful

73

young man remained standing, looking casual and elegant, beside Munya's chair, ignoring Inna.

The foreigner, Mr Wallick, was bolder. He unstoppered the wine and helped himself to a glass, then a plate of sturgeon. That perked everyone up. As Mr Wallick poured a second glass and put it, with a nod, into his languid young friend's hand, the rest of the group moved eagerly towards the fish and started to eat, too.

The beautiful young man didn't touch the food, but he did sip at the wine before moving a few steps to murmur into Madame Golovina's ear. Something amusing, Inna thought, because that lady started to smile. The room quickly became so noisy with the clatter of talk and forks that it put even Munya a little more at her ease. Unexpectedly, she leaned forward and started confiding: 'Sana sent *me* to the Father a couple of years ago, after a beloved friend of mine was killed in a duel. I'd been going to séances to speak to him from the Beyond . . . doing experiments in the raising of spirits . . .'

Half flattered by the confidence, half appalled, Inna nodded.

'The Father was so straightforward.' Munya sighed. 'So blessedly straightforward. He saw right to the heart of things . . . He just said, "Why?"'

Inna remembered the peasant's common-sense tone of voice from her talk with him the previous day. The memory reassured her. She tried not to smile.

'And he said, "You know how long hermits pray to prepare themselves for visitations of the spirit, yet you want to commune with a spirit right in the middle of your social life . . ."' Munya opened her glistening eyes wider. 'He said I'd drive myself mad like that.' She put both hands on her notebook, as though it contained every golden word of the peasant's advice (which Inna thought it probably did), and subsided back into a dreamy silence.

Inna thought this conversation was over. But, after a long pause, Munya suddenly added, 'My friend who died was Felix's brother.' She nodded mournfully towards the beautiful young man, who must be Felix. 'So now, you see, I'm hoping the Father will help *him* too.'

Inna couldn't see what help Felix could possibly need. He didn't look as though he had any secret sorrows. In fact, she'd never seen anyone so sleek and pleased with himself. She'd taken an instant dislike to him.

'And his friend?' she asked. The foreign gentleman, up at the other end of the table, was being supplanted next to the peasant by other admirers. As they advanced, he shrugged and looked down the room at Felix, with what Inna thought was amusement. Felix grinned back.

'Oh, him . . .' Munya said vaguely. 'An Englishman, I think. He paints miniatures at Fabergé's: to go on the top of cigarette cases, you know . . . Felix is just back from Oxford, you see, and needs some gifts with English scenes. And they've made friends . . .' She sounded puzzled. 'A very good person, of course, the Englishman,' she added, as if trying to convince herself. 'If he's here with us, then he must be a believer . . .'

The peasant, meanwhile, was looking at his admirers without enthusiasm. 'How to lead the good life, is that your question?'

Inna had the impression he was breathing deeply.

Everyone fell silent, as they waited expectantly for him to go on.

'All anyone needs to do to find God is to walk right away

from this stinking city, as far as they can, and stand in a field, where the air is clean,' he eventually growled. 'No pips on the sleeve. No bickering or one-upmanship. No fancy ideas – and no fools. There'll be God in that field, all right.'

Inna wasn't sure she liked either the worshipful way the ladies looked at the peasant or the theatrical flavour of his grumpiness. Why did he let all these people into his home, she caught herself wondering, if he disliked them so? And why did he dress up for them in his odd silken finery? He'd seemed more genuine yesterday.

But a blissful look spread over almost every face (though Inna didn't dare look at Felix or the Englishman). Munya scribbled.

'Which is exactly what *I'm* planning . . .' the peasant was continuing, scowling around at his admirers, when there was a ring.

Everyone shifted. Munya stopped her feverish writing and stared around with scared rabbit eyes. The peasant stumped towards the door. So did the fat young man in the morning coat, as if he was trying to get there first. But languid Felix, who was mischievously eyeing them both, was closer.

What Inna was most aware of was the hands of the ladies coming out to the table to restock plates with those delectable-looking petits fours and fruits. They weren't so holy when no one was looking, Inna thought.

She was expecting the peasant to disappear and then return from the front door with a new guest. Instead, he went towards a box on the wall in the doorway. The ringing was coming from there, she realized.

With an oddly disrespectful swerve of the shoulder, the young man barged in front of the peasant. Looking amused,

Felix, who was taller, beat them both to it. He reached out a long arm, unhooked a device from the front of the box and put it to his ear. As he did, he grinned at the fat man, who stared balefully back.

Inna realized that, unimpressive though this room was, the peasant had a telephone installed in it, just like Olya Morozova's father.

Felix's triumphant grin quickly turned to comical bewilderment when he listened to the noises coming out of the receiver. Then his lips formed an 'o,' like a naughty child caught in a prank, and he hastily passed the instrument back to his fat rival. 'Pistolkors here; I'm listening,' the fatty said in a loud, self-important voice. 'Put her through.' Then, in an utterly different and repellently obsequious tone, he smarmed, 'Why, delighted, *utterly* delighted, dear lady . . . Of course, he's right beside me.' He held out the mouthpiece to the peasant, who grabbed it.

'Yes,' he grunted.

A shiver of – what? excitement? satisfaction? passed through the room. Munya looked proudly at Inna and muttered: 'Tsarskoye Selo . . .'

Inna knew what that was: the Emperor's out-of-town palace, just outside Petersburg, where she'd heard he and his Empress preferred to live than in town. Did the peasant have friends at the palace, too? The voice, now faintly audible crackling out from the other end of that instrument, was female. For all Inna knew, they might be eavesdropping on a call from the Empress herself. She gasped.

'What, all the way to Livadia?' the peasant was saying – crossly, Inna thought, and definitely with much less smarm than Pistolkors had mustered. She was already laughing at herself for having fancied that he might have been talking with the Empress. 'What for? I was planning to go home.'

After a moment: 'But they need me in my village of Pokrovskoye too. I haven't seen my own family for—'

Then he nodded, a few more times. Reluctantly.

When he put the mouthpiece back on its hook, he looked even more disgruntled. 'Anya.' He sounded as though he were talking to himself. He sounded unhappy. But every head nodded respectfully as he collected himself, and added, in a firmer tone, 'She says she's sorry she couldn't be here. We're getting the Yalta train tonight.'

'To Livadia,' Inna's companions echoed. Pistolkors even bowed his head, as if in the imperial presence.

Inna looked around the room: she hadn't been so wrong, after all, to imagine the peasant had been talking to the Empress, or someone close to her. Livadia was the Tsar's summer palace, down south in the Crimea. Inna knew that the imperial family had, after leaving Kiev, sailed on to Livadia for some autumn sunshine. She didn't know who Anya was, but it was clear that the peasant had been summoned to attend on the family, and that everyone here felt this to be a tremendous honour.

Their excitement made Inna feel an outsider. Not just a child, or a provincial, but something more extreme. To her, the Tsar was hardly real: just the stuff of the patriotic photo portraits held by those men, mumbling their talk in the puddles with their candles. Even when she'd seen the Tsar with her own eyes, that one time in Kiev, he'd still seemed more of a photograph than a living man, standing to attention in his box after the two gunshots, motionless, while the panicking crowd boiled below.

'I have to pack,' the peasant said roughly. 'You'll all have to go.'

Inna got up. As she did so, she realized she'd been so carried away by the group in this room that she hadn't thought to ask the peasant her favour. And now it was too late.

The others were slower to move. It was only when Munya went to the door with a basket full of rusks – more peasant food – that the crowd seemed, finally, to accept that it was time to go, and began fussing with coats and bags. Munya knelt on the floor, lacing the guests into their boots with a rapturous smile. The acolytes lined up to kiss the Father's hand, one by one, murmuring, 'Some rusks, Father,' and taking the burned bits of dry old bread as if they were Communion wafers. Some went on loitering outside, dragging out the wrapping of their rusks in scented handkerchiefs, hoping for a last glimpse. Felix stayed inside, smirking and watching Munya with enjoyment. Inna didn't think he was admiring his friend, though. There was mockery in his grin.

Inna was still half hoping for her own last private whisper with the peasant, so she hung around at the back. But the Englishman had glued himself to her.

'You're new, aren't you?' he whispered as they shuffled forward in the line. His Russian, though accented, was impeccable. 'Well, a word to the wise. When you get downstairs, leave by the back door. There were reporters out front when I got here.'

Reporters? Was that what those men waiting outside had been? But why? No, that was one question too many. She nodded.

The Englishman pushed her forward, and she took the rusk she was offered.

'What was it you wanted to ask?' the peasant said suddenly, stepping back to look at her. His eyes sharpened.

But the Englishman was there behind her, and she carried on moving, as if in a dream. It was too late. She'd failed.

The Englishman caught up with her on the stairs.

He took off his hat. 'So,' he said, without preamble. 'What did you think?' His voice was a discreet murmur, but his eyes were dancing.

Inna wasn't sure what kind of answer was expected of her. 'What do you mean?' she asked cautiously, before adding, because the Englishman's manner was so friendly and – compared with the other guests – he seemed so reassuringly normal: 'I only met him yesterday, on a train. I hardly know him.'

'I *see*,' the Englishman said. He nodded. 'Well, all the more reason to ask, if you're coming to him with fresh eyes: do you think he's a phony?'

She looked properly at him. The English weren't supposed to be so frank, were they?

'Felix does – my client, in there, Youssoupoff, you remember him? He's the one who's been bringing *me*, but I'm never sure,' he went on merrily. 'All dressed up in those absurd silk kaftans, I know, looking like a charlatan; and telling the acolytes off and making them eat eggs; but still' – he twinkled down at her – 'he's got *something*, hasn't he?'

'He wasn't like that yesterday,' she whispered.

'You weren't expecting *them*, I suppose,' he said, with a kindly understanding that she liked. 'The freaks.' Despite herself, she almost smiled at the description. 'I like them, personally, but then I've acquired a taste for the exotic, living here. I can see they're strong meat if you're new to them – and not least my client.'

He caught her eye. She thought, Why, he noticed I didn't like Felix Youssoupoff. And that surprising perspicacity, or just his interest in her reactions, warmed her.

He stopped at the last half-landing and pointed out the service door to the back courtyard. While she was still here, with this man who seemed so much a part of this strange, busy place with its rules that she didn't understand, she didn't feel such an outsider herself. She looked at the grey daylight outside the smeary glass. She didn't want to head towards the lonelier reality she'd managed to forget for the past hour or two.

'I'd walk you home myself, but I promised Felix I'd wait for him,' the Englishman added – a polite dismissal, she thought. 'And one has to look after one's clients. Oh, and by the way, I'm Wallick. Horace Wallick. We weren't introduced, were we? Never much in the way of formalities in there, I find.'

Dully, she introduced herself too.

'Will I see you here again?' asked Horace Wallick. She thought, though she couldn't be sure, that there was more than politeness in his voice.

The question brought her close to tears. She shrugged, struggling for words. 'I'm staying at Leman the violin-maker's,' she said eventually, 'for a bit . . .'

It was the best she could do to make it feel, or at least sound, as if their realities converged, but it wasn't really an answer.

Yet his face lightened. 'Anatoly Leman? Why, I know

him!' he exclaimed. 'I used to meet him at Repin's Sunday-night soirées. We're old friends. That settles it. We'll meet again, one way or another, either here, or there.'

Dumbly, Inna nodded and slipped away.

CHAPTER SIX

Inna walked the road home with dragging feet. I should carry on down Nevsky, she thought, and see it all while I still can. But she didn't have the heart.

She let herself into the building, but she didn't go into the Leman family flat. She thought they'd be having lunch, and she had no appetite. She didn't want Yasha staring at her bound-up hands, and she certainly didn't want any pitying or hostile looks. She went straight up the communal stairs to the attic, past the shoulder-high pyramids of crates on the landing, and shut herself in her box room.

To her surprise, she found her – or rather Yasha's – violin lying on her bed, with its bow placed neatly beside it.

Someone must have brought it up to her. Perhaps the Lemans hadn't understood that she'd deliberately left it downstairs, for Yasha.

She picked it carefully up. She'd have liked to play it. But she put it on the chest of drawers instead. It wasn't for her any more.

Then she lay down on the bed, still in her hat and coat, and pulled the quilt over herself.

It hadn't worked. She'd never be part of that warm, disorganized, laughing family downstairs.

At least there was no one up here to watch her facing defeat. At least here she could be alone.

But her solitude didn't seem a blessing for long. She listened to herself breathe, and watched the dust move. Then she stood up, and, trying not to panic or let herself feel the walls closing in, poured water out, washed and redressed her hands, so the two handkerchiefs looked as unobtrusive as possible.

At two o'clock, she went downstairs and slipped into the workshop through the back door. They'd asked her to clean up. She could keep a bargain.

The three men were sitting in three pools of lamplight, each busy with something. Marcus was whistling as he attached strings to a completed if still unvarnished white violin. Yasha had his back to Inna and she couldn't see his face or what his hands were at work on. Leman was holding up to the light a block of wood about the length of his forearm, scrutinizing it and marking it through some complicated template with a very sharp pencil. There was a tiny saw next to him, and two metal clamps waiting to be screwed to the workbench.

She'd never have been able to master all this anyway, she told herself. The walls were lined with tools whose purpose she'd never guess at.

They all looked happy and completely absorbed.

She stood, waiting to be noticed, letting the headlines from Leman's roughly refolded newspaper, stashed on the shelf next to where she waited, dance before her unfocused eyes: 'SR Bomb Factory Discovered in Yekaterinburg', 'Police Chief Killed by Terrorist Attack in Warsaw' and 'Holy Man a Murderer? Rasputin "Knew in Advance" that Assassinated Prime Minister Stolypin's Post Would Soon Be Vacant'.

Eventually, she went and got a broom and, without saying a word, began sweeping up the wood shavings.

No one greeted her. None of them even looked up.

'Personally I can never tell which of these holy fools that the Empress goes in for is which,' Leman was saying meditatively as he peered down and made another miniature graphite mark. 'Charlatans one and all, of course, I expect, but I can't for the life of me remember which one's notorious for what.'

'That's because you only ever read the arts pages, Pap,' Marcus said with a son's affectionate contempt. 'You've got to read the news to keep up.'

Inna walked a first pan full of shavings over to the bins. One bin was marked, bafflingly, 'For the chickens: shavings only, no prickly bits'. The others seemed to be half full of other things: wood offcuts, bits of wire, scrunched-up paper . . . Doubtfully she looked at the contents of her dustpan. Were some of those shavings too prickly for chickens?

Inna was beyond asking for guidance. She felt she was looking at this golden, contented world through glass.

'But this Rasputin who's in the papers today, for instance,' Leman went on, unperturbed. 'Is he the one who can make himself invisible by putting his hat on back to front?'

Inna heard laughter in Yasha's deep voice. 'No, that was the Frenchman, Monsieur Philippe, who kept predicting our poor German Empress would have a son, when she kept having daughters. He's back in Lyon now. She only had a son after he'd left; how he must have cursed. This one's Russian.'

'Siberian,' Marcus added.

Defiantly, she tipped the shavings into the bin. What did it matter? The chickens wouldn't notice any more than the men here.

'So is this the one with the withered arm, then?'

Another snort came from Marcus. 'No, that was Mitya Kozlovsky,' he said. 'I don't know what's become of him.'

'*This* is the one who's supposed to have seduced the royal nanny,' Yasha added. 'Today's man. Last summer, when she went on a train trip to his Siberian village with him.'

'I suppose we haven't been told why she did such an unsuitable thing as go to Siberia with him if she was really the pure vessel a royal nanny should be,' Leman replied, looking sceptically at Yasha over the top of his glasses.

She saw Yasha shrug; felt him grin back. 'I doubt there's a word of truth in any of it. Just newspaper lies, then and now. At any rate, she was fired; and he's still around.'

'Now I remember!' Leman cried, looking suddenly pleased, striking his head with his hand. 'This is the one whose adoring followers keep his toenail parings as trophies, and sew them on their fronts!'

He looked round expectantly. They all burst out laughing.

As the laughter died away, Marcus said, in a quite different, slightly shocked tone of voice, 'Why, Inna!'

At that, Leman's head swivelled towards her, as did Yasha's.

It was unnerving to have all those eyes on her, but it felt less lonely than before. She took a deep breath and said, trying not to gulp, '. . . thought I'd just start. You were talking . . .'

She could feel Yasha's eyes, even though she was avoiding his gaze. But she was also aware that he was trying, at least, not to look at her hands. She put them behind her back anyway.

'Working hard,' Leman said with warmth. 'Well done.'

'So quiet!' Marcus added eagerly. 'I didn't hear a thing. I nearly jumped out of my skin when I saw you.'

'It's cleaner in here than it has been since *he's* been working here, I must say,' Leman added, and Marcus fell silent, but his grin suggested he didn't mind the jocular rebuke.

Leman put his work down on the bench. He smiled at her over the top of his glasses. 'I tell you what,' he went on. 'Leave the sweeping up till the end of the day, why don't you – it's a boring sort of job – and come and look at this instead.'

Inna's heart was racing as she stepped forward. Now she was next to him, she could see Monsieur Leman had cut his block of wood into a rough approximation of the curve at the back of a violin's scroll – its head – and neck. It had none of the fluted elegance of a finished scroll yet, and the peg-box in the middle hadn't been hollowed out. It was just a question-mark shape on one side of a solid block of wood. When she took it and picked it up, it felt surprisingly heavy. It looked a primitive thing.

But a second glance showed her that he'd measured and drawn light markings on it – precise lines indicating the finer tapering that the back and top of the wood would be whittled down to, and dots, on each side, marking a snail-shell spiral which, she could see, would mark the parameters of the elaborately carved scroll shape itself.

'Looks nothing now, you're thinking?' Leman said. He

87

sounded amused. 'Well, you'll soon see a difference. We're about to bring out its shape. Make it beautiful for the future.'

We? She kept still, trying not to let either hope or fear show on her face.

'Get the clamp,' Leman was saying. Her fingers fumbled quickly for it. 'That's right. Now, screw it to the table top, with the scroll in it. Yes, like that: upside-down baby, head at the bottom . . . yes. First things first. We've got to saw away the sides of the peg-box before we can start carving our curves.'

She was trying to control the thumping of her heart. She told herself, I'm going to have to do the same as yesterday when he wanted me to play: empty my mind and just do it.

She'd barely had time to reflect on her musical performance yesterday, what with everything else that had been happening, but she was still astonished that she'd managed to play the violin so composedly for the family. At school, whenever she'd been asked to play her pieces at concerts, she'd always been so nervous that the trembling of her arm had stopped her holding the bow to the string; and she'd play such idiotic wrong notes that she'd subside in a shaky heap, unable to go on. So she'd avoided playing for other people. She didn't care, she always told herself; the point of music was to satisfy herself. It made no difference if no one else could hear her, did it? And then Monsieur Leman had pushed her yesterday, and she'd felt she had no choice but to try. And somehow she'd lost herself in the piece she'd chosen, and when she'd stopped and seen the admiration on their faces, she'd also felt the elation of success.

She squared her shoulders and took a deep breath. The cuts on her palm were stinging, but she screwed the clamp round the bit of wood anyway. If she could do it yesterday, when she had to, then today, too—

'She can't,' Yasha's voice said roughly behind her. She flinched and stopped tightening the clamp.

'Why not?' she heard. Marcus.

'She's cut her hands. Look, they're all bound up.'

She shut her eyes, hating him. She couldn't understand why he would want to do this to her, again.

'She'll be clumsy,' Yasha's voice persisted. 'She'll mess it up, with her hands in that state.'

The silence yawned on endlessly, or so it seemed to her.

'What did you do to them, Inna?' she heard eventually. The question she was dreading, in Leman's voice.

She opened her mouth to answer. But Yasha answered for her.

'Rough edge on the handle of her bag . . . infected . . . nasty.'

His voice was hesitant. She let out her breath a little. He hated her, but not enough to tell them what he'd seen her do.

'Does it hurt?' Marcus asked her. She was warmed enough by the concern in his voice that she felt able to turn slightly and shake her head in his direction.

'No,' she muttered, defiantly biting off her words. 'I'm fine.'

'Well, then,' Leman boomed, 'what's all the fuss about?'

She looked up. Leman and Marcus were gazing at her, eyes full of encouragement. She ignored Yasha, who, still somewhere behind, was saying, 'I just thought . . .'

'Come on,' Leman said, breaking into a grin. 'Yasha's a perfectionist, that's all. Very, very good at what he does, too. That's why. But take no notice.'

Yasha muttered: 'Better to let her heal for a few days . . .'

'Ach.' Leman turned back to the clamp. 'She can tell us herself if there's a problem, can't she? Don't be such an old woman, Yasha. Now, Inna, you're going to need that saw.'

Smiling her own shaky answering smile, Inna picked it up.

Monsieur Leman stood behind her, guiding her hands, murmuring encouragement as he showed her how to make the first cut, on one side of the block of wood, and then said, 'Now you do the other side on your own.' Her heart seemed to stop every time she made the smallest inroad into the wood, but, she soon realized, needlessly. He'd marked it all so clearly. All she had to do was follow his instructions. Soon they had cut the two outside lines of the peg-box just below the scroll, where, one day, once the wood inside the box shape had been hollowed out, the violin's strings would be attached to movable pegs for tuning. Then Monsieur Leman took a drill and, humming under his breath, made round peg-holes right through the still-solid future peg-box, while she watched.

'And *now*,' he said, as his kindly eyes sought her out again over the top of his spectacles, 'you're going to start shaping the scroll.' He picked up a second saw from the bench, this one no bigger than a breadknife.

But a scroll was one long sinuous curve, Inna thought, panicking; and how could you possibly cut such a thing with a breadknife?

'Saw-cut One,' he said, cheerfully. 'You cut it across by the throat . . .'

'". . . but don't cut its throat,"' Marcus quoted, smiling. Inna calmed down.

Leman must say the same words to all his apprentices. Apprentices?

She emptied her mind, not daring to think that word. But she couldn't stop the flicker of hope.

Just do it. Just obey. She clamped the scroll back down to the workbench, on its side this time. Leman showed her the pencil line she was to saw along, and, terrified of going too far, she moved the little implement carefully through the wood, towards the earlier lengthways cut Leman and she had made. 'Be braver,' Leman said, twinkling at her.

The relief when she'd cut far enough to join the first cut, and a neatly shaped sliver of wood came away in her hand, was indescribable. She turned the scroll over and re-clamped it, other side up. She was grinning as broadly as Leman by the time a second piece of wood also detached itself from the scroll without disaster.

'"Now, Saw-cut Two!"' Marcus sang out.

Leman showed her how. This even smaller cut would run from top to bottom of the side of the scroll, at right angles to Saw-cut One, taking off much less wood.

She was beginning to see now. These cuts would simply organize the wood into a shape ready for finer carving later: there'd be a series of neat right-angled saw lines, each taking away a smaller segment of wood than the last. They'd got the whole thing clear in their heads beforehand. With the unnecessary bits of the block cut away, the scroll would be easier to handle.

'Don't get too confident,' Leman warned, gently. 'Don't forget, we like you to be a little bit scared. Now, after this cut, you get rid of the wood you don't want by cutting in again, at right angles, at the back of the scroll. But, don't forget, don't

91

cut straight down. Your downward cuts must angle slightly away from the centre.'

She began, too boldly perhaps, for quickly he corrected the angle at which she was holding the little saw. Her heart seemed to stop. Had she destroyed everything? 'No, it's fine,' he reassured her. 'Keep going like this.'

When she'd recovered her breath and had made the two cuts successfully, she was left with more tools she didn't know – round and straight gouges, two little planes, and a scraper, Leman called them – first to shape the outside of the peg-box more finely ('"Flat across the width and slightly convex in the length,"' Marcus called, twinkling). Then, with Leman's help, she marked the width of the walls of the tiny peg-box and cut down the inside with a knife, angling the cuts towards each other so that the walls widened at the bottom.

Leman drilled out the wood between the cuts for her, leaving a rough empty box shape. 'Now,' he said, and her heart stopped again, though she was already beginning to understand that every new step was going to be the same sort of terrifying leap into the unknown, but that if she could only trust her teacher and wasn't too clumsy herself, it would come out right. 'Now, clean up the inside with chisels and gouges . . . you'll find the right ones over there, in that drawer . . . but be careful to leave enough thickness at the bottom.'

Leman was nodding comfortingly at her as he heaved himself up from the stool at her side. She liked the slow amusement in his voice. 'It's easy to go right through. So go easy, mind, especially under the top peg, where the bottom needs to curve up. Oh, and use a round gouge first at the throat.'

Ignoring the sting in her palms, ignoring the sting inside

at the thought of Yasha, so quiet at his place, Inna went to fetch the chisels and gouges from their drawer.

Soon, in spite of herself, she forgot the black knot of unhappiness in her stomach, and let herself get lost in her work. Her hands ached. The tools were unfamiliar. And without Leman's hands on hers, the wood in her golden circle of lamplight often seemed hard and resistant.

'Be braver,' he urged, from time to time. 'Don't be too scared to dig in – though just a bit scared is fine. I can see you can do it.' But otherwise he let her be. She'd never been so absorbed.

She didn't join in the fitful conversation, when it resumed.

'Well, according to the Stock Exchange News, he's as guilty as sin,' came Marcus's up-and-down voice. 'Went to Nizhny Novgorod three weeks before the assassination and offered the governor there the job of prime minister.'

She barely heard. She was too busy worrying at a stubborn outcrop of splinters in a corner she couldn't work out how to get at. She shifted her grip on a handle in her sore palm, trying to work out how to make the tool obey her.

'Ach . . .' came the rumble of Leman's voice. He sounded sceptical.

But Marcus persisted. 'And when the governor, who couldn't work out what some peasant was doing offering gentlemen government jobs, started joking with him a bit, saying, "Ah, but the Prime Minister's post isn't even vacant," do you know what Rasputin replied? "But it soon will be!" And then it was!'

Leman laughed it off. 'So? The Emperor is always appointing new ministers; and he's daft enough to send all kinds of odd bods off round the country to sound people out about whatever changes he's thinking about, too. This peasant might have been doing a bit of politicking on his own account, if he's so close to power. It doesn't mean he had a hand in the murder, though, does it?'

It was only when Inna felt a large hand on her shoulder that she came out of her dream. Leman was rumbling in her ear, 'We're about to see a birth.'

She looked up.

Marcus had the little unvarnished violin he'd been stringing up on his shoulder.

Tentatively he drew the bow across the strings. Then he played a line of a simple, sad folk song. He played just as he was, bending over the bench, with no vibrato and no dramatics.

The sound was thin and hesitant, innocent as a newborn's voice. And it was beautiful. Inna looked from Leman to Yasha. Both had their heads craned forward, and a joyful stillness on their faces.

When Marcus had stopped playing, and, to Inna's surprise, started unstringing the white violin again ('I'm going to start varnishing it tomorrow,' he explained, catching her questioning look), Leman came over to where she was sitting and picked up her scroll-in-the-making.

He held it up to the light. He turned it around, and the kindly smile on his face broadened.

'This is good work,' he said appreciatively. 'Neat. Elegant shapes. Why, look at the line she's made here, lads. Perfect.'

Yasha stayed where he was, doing whatever he was doing, but Marcus slipped round to her side of the workbench and took the future scroll, with the peg-box now hollowed out and shaped below it, and grinned at her. He said, agreeing with his father for once, 'Yes, deft fingers! We need girls in the workshop after all!'

It almost hurt, the pleasure she felt at their praise. Bashfully, letting down her guard, she smiled hazily back.

So she was quite unprepared when Leman, still admiring her scroll, said, casually, 'Pity we didn't get you started earlier. Where were you this morning?'

He meant no harm, she could see. But that question was enough to bring back Inna's memory of everything outside this warm workshop, where she now so wanted to belong. Once again, she experienced that black misery she'd felt in her stomach while she'd been walking back here earlier on, down the bleakness of Nevsky, through the biting salt wind.

She tried to be brave and disciplined, but she'd let down her guard too far. To her horror, she felt hot tears coursing down her cheeks even before she began to stammer out an answer. 'I went to see someone . . . a peasant holy man of my own . . . someone I met on the train . . .' She put her face in her hands and closed her eyes.

'Why?' she heard. Leman's voice was so soft.

'Because he said he had a friend who knew how to get residence papers for Jews,' she muttered, trying very hard to steady her tone. 'So I thought he might help me . . . because I so want . . .' She shut her eyes tight again, feeling humiliated. But tears squeezed out anyway. '. . . to work here,' she finished.

Into the silence came Marcus's question: 'Couldn't she just stay, Pap?'

It was as if Yasha wasn't in the room at all. He'd withdrawn completely. Well, she thought bitterly, *he* won't want Leman to say yes; that much is clear.

That combative thought returned a measure of control to

her and she opened her eyes. Leman was holding her scroll to the lamp again, looking at it, considering. There was a frown on his face.

'The thing is, your mother's worried that if I put a foot wrong I'll have the police on my back again,' he said, uneasily. 'You remember how things were after the revolution . . . back in 1906, when they shut down my paper . . .'

'But you won the day in court. They never managed to put you behind bars. Anyway, it was years ago; what can they possibly do to you now?' wheedled Marcus's voice. 'And she's good. You said so yourself. And you need someone else, you're always saying so . . .'

There was another long pause. Leman twirled the scroll absent-mindedly under the light. His eyebrows were going up and down, as if he were holding a long conversation with someone inside his head.

Inna watched through her fingers, barely breathing. Eventually, still uncertainly, he began to nod.

'Well,' he said. 'I expect I probably *can* square it with your mother for Inna to stay longer. But . . .'

Marcus whooped under his breath. Inna felt his hand grip her shoulder. Cautiously, not quite believing what she was hearing, she lowered her hands from her face.

'You'll have Yasha to help you settle in,' Marcus murmured to Inna. Over-optimistically, she thought. Yasha, just out of her field of vision, only grunted. 'Me? She doesn't need *my* help.' She ignored him. She was waiting for Leman's objection.

Leman was looking searchingly into her eyes. 'If it's on your own head entirely, that is,' he added, sounding stern. 'Let's agree this. You can do some work for me down here for your bed and board, but, since you're illegal, just don't say you're staying here, or that I know anything, or have helped you. Not to anyone official. Not to anyone. And if they catch you, you're on your own. All right?'

It was tentative. It was grudging. But it was something to work with.

Wordlessly, Inna nodded. She could already feel the dead weight inside her lifting and evaporating.

The clock struck six.

Everyone got up and started tidying away their work.

'Dinner at eight,' Marcus told Inna, unable to stop grinning. 'Do what you like till then.' Without looking up from the cloud of wood shavings – her own wood shavings – that she was sweeping up, she nodded.

Yasha hung back, behind her, as they left the workshop.

Inna turned to him, but he wouldn't meet her eye. Instead he started walking from lamp to lamp, needlessly pulling out plugs.

She waited at the door. 'Your violin's been put in my room,' she said eventually. 'Not by me.'

'Use it. That's fine. I've got a better one that I made here,' he said gruffly, still turned away. 'You're going to need it, aren't you? You won't be going out much, if you don't want to get caught without papers.'

Yasha waited till he could hear Inna's footsteps far upstairs before he left the workshop. Even then, he spent a long time fiddling with keys, locking up.

He'd done his best. He'd tried to stop Leman testing her out while her hands were still painful. He'd thought those cuts would make her too clumsy for the work and would turn Leman against her, but he'd been wrong. She was single-minded: determined not to let anything stand in her way. And what he'd said had come out wrong, too. He'd seen that accusing glance she'd given him when he'd mentioned her hands, as if she hadn't understood he was trying to help her. She hadn't understood, either, that he'd put his old violin in her room that morning by way of apology for his words the previous day, and so she'd have an instrument to play. Well, so be it. She didn't need protecting. She already had both Monsieur Leman and Marcus eating out of her hand, knife cuts or not. She didn't need him.

Upstairs, safely alone, Yasha got out his violin. It was a beautiful instrument. He was proud to have made it.

He ran the bow gently over the strings, thrilling to its richness of tone.

It was old Kremer who'd encouraged him to play the melancholy songs of the *shtetl*. At first, at least until Yasha had dismantled the walls of Russian-only snobbery that his parents' aspirations had built in his mind, he had heard in the poor-man's music only the alien-sounding wailing of other people's misery: a noise to be ignored. But now he heard the hope in it, too, and the prayer, and the learning, and the thousands of years of suffering. He understood how it spoke of Abraham, heavy-hearted on the mountainside, offering his son to God; of the taste of locusts and honey in the desert; of the creak of carts overloaded with pots and pans and blankets and frightened children, heading over the muddy roads of Russia, bound for Odessa and the Holy Land in far-off Ottoman territory. As he fingered the violin strings, he recalled old Kremer's voice, intoning 'Five million Jews in Russia, and a million of them gone in a single generation. Chased out by the Cossacks; scattered across the world.' The pity of it, the waste, the loss, infused his playing. He filled his versions of every melody he played with heartfelt, tear-jerking *dreydlekh* – 'Spins,' old Kremer's voice murmured pedagogically in his head, 'that is, musical ornaments,' – and *kneytshn*, and *glitshn*. (There were so many of these little musical renderings of feelings. 'But what are *krekhtsn*?' he remembered asking in bewilderment at the beginning. A laugh softened his teacher's rough prisoner's voice: 'Oh, a sort of weeping or hiccuping combination of backward slide and flick of the little finger high above the note itself, while the bow does, well, something . . . ach, words; useless; *nu*, just listen.' And he picked up the violin himself, and made it sob). Sobbing was what Yasha's violin had become best at, these days, however much he tried to keep in mind that these expressive melodies he was learning, so reminiscent of the human voice, were full of both tears and laughter, and that they were properly called Freilech music: happy music.

As he started to breathe life into a *nigun*, a mournful song without words, he heard the door of Inna's room click shut. She wouldn't know any of this, he thought, with sudden compassion. She was in the darkness, still, just as he'd been till he'd been taught.

Yasha hadn't been very good at the violin until old Kremer had put him straight about what kind of things he might enjoy playing. But now he'd got the feeling for it, he no longer felt guilty about skipping the hours of scales practice his parents had wanted him to do. That wasn't what mattered. It was putting your heart into it that counted, as he was doing now.

He played on; but a part of him was listening, through the thin party wall, to Inna moving around her room; putting things down; the creak of bedsprings; a scrape.

He was playing for her, he realized. Trying to play away her fear. Showing her the place they both came from, and that he could help her rediscover.

He swooped from one string to the next, losing himself in the melody.

All at once, he heard the answering sound of a violin from behind the wall: a long, quiet, open A, played alone, then with a D, which he could hear being carefully tuned, then the G, and finally the E.

He paused. He didn't remember that old violin sounding so pure. He hadn't done a bad job on it, considering how green he'd been. Not a bad job at all.

He was already feeling the beginning of elation.

His playing had encouraged her, but it was only when he heard the next sounds to come through the wall that he realized it wasn't going to be as simple as he'd imagined.

Inna began with a quiet, disciplined G major scale, a fluid run of quavers from the bottom to the top of the violin and back. He paused. Next, she moved up to A-flat major, then A, then B-flat. Her playing got gradually louder over the next few scales, up through D to E-flat.

She's not joining in, he thought, with disappointment. She's just drowning me out. Using music as a weapon. Making war.

E, F, she played, pressing on the strings.

He picked up his instrument again. He answered, with his own louder, more extravagant howl of pained catgut. Well, if that's what she wants, he thought, pressing as hard as he could on the strings in his turn, I can give as good as I get, any day.

But he didn't have Inna's stamina, or her technique, or her sheer breadth of repertoire. As Tchaikovsky and Wieniawski succeeded Rimsky-Korsakov from behind the wall, he felt as though she was marshalling an unstoppable, unforgiving Slavic musical army behind her. He finally gave up. He shook his head, baffled and defeated, put his violin down and slunk out, retreating to the workshop with the box of leaflets he still hadn't taken round to young Kremer's.

As he hurried down the stairs, he tried to empty his mind of everything but the leaflet he'd written. He had reason to be proud of it, he thought. It was a good piece of work that demanded a fair trial for a Jew accused of ritually murdering a slum boy in Kiev. Mendel Beilis's face – beard, spectacles; looking through and through the stolid brick-factory manager he was – stared arrestingly out from the front page. As young Kremer always said, how could you look at that face and believe for a moment that a person of such transparent, respectable dullness could possibly have lured little Andrei Yushchinsky into a cave and stabbed him thirteen times to 'milk' him of blood to bake into matzos?

Well, of course it was a ridiculous accusation. But that didn't mean Beilis wasn't facing execution. And the thought of that quiet, ordinary man, sitting in a damp cell in Kiev, staring at the walls, waiting for death, sent shivers that had something more personal than compassion in them down Yasha's spine.

But it wasn't just Yasha, or just Jews, who felt for Beilis. Oddly for a campaign of this nature – and hearteningly – they'd got support. Up here in the big city, Yasha now knew, there were more than enough liberals and radicals as disgruntled as he was with the creaking, brutal, hopelessly backward-looking autocracy and its crass police; people not unlike his own Monsieur Leman, who could really make a difference if they took a cause to their hearts.

Young Kremer had recently, on his uncle's advice, written about the case to a well-connected left-wing writer living abroad in Capri. This new friend, who signed his letters simply 'Maxim', was, it turned out, more than ready to help, and was already talking about lining up all sorts of the great and good to fight for Beilis: Rabbi Mazev, of course, but also all the most able counsels of the Moscow, St Petersburg and Kiev bars, not to mention the professors, even Glagolev, the Orthodox philosopher from the Kiev Theological Seminary. The important thing was getting other people united behind your cause, so they helped you achieve your aim. Inna, cutting away with her penknife as if damaging herself in solitude might somehow make her life better, had signally failed to understand that last night. (Though, Yasha thought, her embarrassment now, not to mention the charm she'd been showing Monsieur Leman earlier on today, might mean she'd now worked this out too.) If the Beilis case ever came to trial – if the prisoner didn't just die in his cell in mysterious circumstances, which still seemed the likeliest outcome – Yasha was beginning to think it possible that, whatever the police and the Black Hundreds alleged, he might, just might, get off.

And this leaflet might help.

Usually reflecting on this possibility energized Yasha. But tonight he was still sighing as he reached the workshop door and fumbled for the keys.

He remembered Inna's playing of that last Tchaikovsky waltz, upstairs. *She's* Jewish herself, he thought, yet she's probably also one of the people who looks at that picture of Beilis and thinks, No smoke without fire.

He squared his shoulders. He'd go to young Kremer's with his leaflets in a bit; after dinner, maybe . . . or perhaps he'd give dinner a miss? Suddenly he couldn't face the noise and bustle of Madame Leman's table.

CHAPTER SEVEN

It was early evening, and Lidiya Leman was deep in an armchair in the drawing room, exhausted from heaving round all the coats and boots for winter, daydreaming over a periodical with a fashionable cover: a nearly pornographic line drawing of a curvy art-nouveau Mother Russia being ravaged by a Satanic monster.

None of these images and ideas shocked her any more, of course. They were all so *used* to the end-of-the-world-is-nigh posturing by now. She'd let the magazine fall.

Instead she was gazing at the troubled sky outside – that thick, roiling, grey mass, so weighted with soot and filth that it seemed unable to explode the snow that needed to fall – and remembering the golden light of the garden at Vinnitsa all those summers ago, and the sweet, alcoholic smell of decaying fruit, and the drunken buzz of the wasps, and Masha the housekeeper shouting up the stairs, in her cracked voice, 'Madam! Madam! Christ has come for apples!'

How simple everything had seemed, back then; how alluring that golden fuzz of possibilities.

Masha's 'Christ' had been nothing of the kind, really, just a peasant from a village near Vinnitsa, a dear man with pink cheeks and innocent eyes and a slow, gentle burr. But he was a Christ to Masha, because he was the leader of the circle of peasants Masha worshipped with. This group used to hold evening prayer meetings in the Leman family bath-house down by the river, out of sight of Father Yefim. Masha, usually so strict, was soft as butter with her Christ, and always encouraging him to come up to the house in the summer and pick up the windfalls from the family orchard.

Lidiya Leman had never liked the bloated spiritual bureaucrats of the Orthodox Church. She'd almost gone and prayed with the peasants herself, one summer evening. But by the time she reached the cabin door, there was already nothing to show that Masha, or Dunya, or a dozen other women and three or four village men were inside – nothing but an echo of voices, singing. The grass had sprung back, hiding their trails in scatters of wild flowers. There were butterflies in the innocent air. Well, God bless them, she'd said to herself, equally peacefully, I won't disturb them; and she'd gone home.

Lidiya Leman knew more now. She knew that peasant groups like her Masha's met in secret all over Russia, hounded, everywhere, by busybody officials and offended priests. They didn't need church. They believed that modest goodness – celibacy and abstinence and repentance for past sins – would be enough to save them.

It was beautiful, Madame Leman still thought, that these innocents called their groups 'arks': secret ships of faith tossed on a sea of bureaucratic troubles; and that their gatherings were known, not as services, but as *radeniya,* or raptures.

Today, the newspapers said, there were hundreds of schismatic Christs in Russia. Every group had one, and a Lord of Hosts, too, just as every group had a woman known as a Mother of God. It was a peasant Trinity. But no one thought they were innocent any more, now that the peasant worshippers' recent brief moment as the darling of the city intellectuals had faded.

The novel she'd been so pleased to get out of the house, the other week, had made her see the whole thing in a nastier, dirtier light.

It told a story about peasant sectarians who, at first, reminded her of her gentle summers in Vinnitsa. But as she turned the pages, she'd read that the believers in the novel's fictional Brotherhood of the Doves had turned out to be evil. They had unearthly powers, all right, but they'd only used them to pervert the Russia she knew – to destroy the hope in it. The knowing, ugly, shaggy-bearded carpenter who led the sect had lured the book's gentleman hero away from his own life to sleep with the carpenter's pock-marked woman Matryona, in the clod-hopping belief that this unlikely pair's coupling would make a Christ baby . . . and when that didn't happen, and the carpenter got jealous of his handsome young rival, he'd ordered the sect to murder him.

Madame Leman now felt contaminated by the book, and so she'd lent it to the charming English jeweller, her Tolya's friend. She wasn't the only one troubled by it. Everyone in St Petersburg was reading it, and talking. And, of course, it had become deeply unfashionable to believe that Russia could be saved by godly peasants.

So perhaps it was no wonder that the papers were now full of these savage stories about the real-life peasant mystic, the

Empress's favourite, who was supposed to have known about Stolypin's death, or perhaps even been behind it. These days, it seemed, all you had to do to earn the frightened suspicion of the drawing-room classes was to be a peasant with a cross round your neck.

It was what Marcus and even her usually level-headed Tolya had been going on about when they'd come upstairs, making her feel a monster for not making that wretched girl from Kiev feel more welcome yesterday. 'She's so desperate she went to a peasant holy man for help!' they'd both kept saying. 'Some charlatan, of course . . . But she believed him when he told her on the train that he could get her papers! She's such an innocent! We can't, in all conscience, just let her wander off to dubious strangers begging for help. Who knows what might come of it? Really it wouldn't be any trouble just to let her stay . . .'

None of it made any sense, any more than Marcus going on about the girl having chafed her hands on a rough edge of her bag on the journey as if this was any reason to have her move in. Why, her hands would get better in no time. But however many times Madame Leman had said so, however high she'd lifted her eyebrows, however much she'd regretfully shaken her head, they'd just kept on begging. Until, in the end, half buried in coats and running out of reasons to refuse, she'd said yes.

She could see, as well as any of them, that Inna needed help. But even here, in the peace of her armchair, with the smells of dinner wafting comfortingly in from the kitchen, she still wasn't in the least sure it had been the right thing to do. Not that she really thought for a moment that Inna would get Tolya into trouble with the police, or that she'd turn into another nuisance guest like Yasha's Jewish revolutionary friend with the disgusting personal habits and body odour. And it was obvious she wanted to please. She'd looked so heartrendingly grateful, just now, when Madame Leman had gone up to her room to tell her, formally, that she could stay. But still, she could easily turn this whole family upside down.

Uneasily Madame Leman reviewed Inna's long, slender arms, floating back and forth over the violin; the flash of her green eyes under all that black hair; the slenderness of her waist, and the animated loveliness of her face whenever she forgot whatever misery it was that was eating away at her. Yasha, the most talented violin-maker they'd ever had in the workshop, was already looking so hungrily at her; her little Marcus, not so little now, was half in love; and even Tolya . . .

Madame Leman was shaking her head, and picking up her magazine again, hoping to dispel her worries with a bit more fashionably apocalyptic doom-mongering before dinner, when the doorbell rang.

A moment later, Agrippina stuck her tousled head round the door.

'It's the foreigner, Mama,' she lisped importantly. 'Mister Wallick . . . Papa's friend. I told him we were about to have dinner. But he says he's just dropping by for a moment. He doesn't want to disturb you. Won't even come in. But he wanted to tell me he's brought back your book.'

Madame Leman seldom minded if someone extra turned up for a meal (you could always stretch the food a bit further, couldn't you?), and even if she didn't really want that vicious novel she'd lent him back, she liked the Englishman very much. He was an artist just like her husband, someone who thought about the higher things, even though, with that job he was always laughing at himself for doing, painting hackneyed scenes from English life or miniature portraits on cigarette-box lids at Fabergé's, the court jeweller, he was also unlike Tolya in that he'd earned an entrée into fashionable society. That, she thought, must help him bring in lucrative commissions. So, thanking Agrippina and patting her bun back into place, she got up and went to the door herself to try and persuade Horace Wallick to stay for dinner.

He was standing in the doorway with the book under his arm, tapping his feet. He was looking up the communal stairwell with a wistful, delighted smile.

His awkwardness was his charm, Madame Leman thought, fondly: his legs were far too long for most rooms, his frame slightly stooped from politeness, but he had a lustrousness about the eyes that lit up what might have been stern features on a man of different personality. His eyes went down at the corners, and he had a big nose, lines down thin cheeks, and a strong cleft chin. He looked trustworthy, but also always ready to be amused. This was his attraction.

It was only when Madame Leman drew close that she realized what he was listening to. Inna was playing the violin up in the attic.

'You're keeping a nightingale in the attic, I hear,' he said, bowing over her hand. As ever, he had impeccable white gloves on, and a fresh flower in his buttonhole: every inch the English gentleman; and everything he said, in his beautifully modulated voice, was in idiomatic if exotically accented Russian. (Unusual, this, because so often, with foreigners, you had to struggle away in bad French; but he *had* been here for ten years, after all.)

He smiled at her as he swept back up. 'How lovely . . .'

Madame Leman smiled back, partly because you always did with Horace Wallick – his pleasure in life was so infectious – but partly, too, because of the voice in her head whispering, Now *this* could be the answer to all our problems.

'It's our new guest,' she said, in as light a tone as he'd used. 'Yes, she plays beautifully, doesn't she? If I could only persuade you to stay and eat with us – do say you will; I've made Ukrainian borshch; I know you like that – I'll introduce you. I was just about to call her down for dinner.'

In the end, Madame Leman didn't even need to eke out the food. Yasha, it turned out, had gone off on one of his mysterious errands, carrying a box of those Beilis campaign leaflets he'd written. So at the dinner table, Madame Leman sat Horace next to the empty seat that would be Inna's.

Carefully, if covertly, she watched his reactions as Inna came in. Inna looked fresh and pink-cheeked in a worn, but clean, dove-grey dress. She'd had the foresight to stop in the kitchen (you couldn't fault her on trying to please), and was carrying the soup tureen. She had her eyes turned modestly down, but she couldn't keep the beginning of a smile off her lips. She looked radiant; sparkling enough to make both Marcus and his father melt, at once, into protective answering smiles.

Quickly, she turned her gaze on Madame Leman. 'Do let me help,' she said eagerly. 'That soup smells delicious. Would you like me to serve it?'

But Madame Leman only waved her to her place, waiting for her to notice Horace Wallick, who was on his feet at her side, already half smiling, though with far more composure than either of the other men. He was looking at her as if he knew a joke he wasn't telling.

'Inna, this is . . .' she began her introduction.

Inna's eyes widened as she took in the newcomer, and her lips parted slightly. To Madame Leman's secret gratification, she then blushed and dropped her eyes. But it was Madame Leman whose eyes widened next, as Inna bobbed her head in a sketchy bow, and murmured, 'Why, Mi-ster Wall-ick . . .'

'You know each other already?' she couldn't help exclaiming.

'Why, yes,' Horace Wallick began, turning to her. 'We ran into each other this morning, at the *oddest* . . .'

His eyes were sparkling. He was clearly ready to tell one of his stories. He was a great gatherer of urban eccentrics, and good at witty descriptions of the latest oddities he'd found. The Lemans leaned eagerly forward.

But Inna had screwed up her face into a rueful, charmingly self-deprecating expression that Madame Leman hadn't seen her use before, and was shaking her head, just a playful fraction. 'Oh, please don't go on, Mis-ter Wallick,' she said prettily. 'You weren't to know, but I've alarmed everyone here quite enough already today with my stories of visiting peasant mystics. Please, let's forget it ever happened.'

Why, Madame Leman thought, not entirely happily, the child could be surprisingly sophisticated when she wanted to be.

Horace burst out laughing. 'Then our assignation this morning will be our secret, Miss Feldman,' he agreed with every appearance of delight. 'And by the way, do please just call me Horace. Everyone else here does.'

'Do sit down, everyone, or the soup will get cold,' Madame Leman called, and began to ladle out the borshch.

Horace was nothing if not a practised conversationalist. As soon as he'd unfurled his napkin, he set to amusing Inna with mocking stories about his master, Carl Fabergé, who was Swiss by birth and peppery by nature, and whose inability to suffer fools gladly made his relations with his most important client fraught with tension.

'There's never a problem with the Emperor, who makes no claims to artistic taste,' Madame Leman overheard Horace confide, and her heart swelled gratefully as she saw him leaning towards Inna, making it seem that the jewelled, sophisticated world he was talking about was hers, too. 'But the Empress is a different proposition. Her combination of a rudimentary notion of art and curiously middle-class stinginess often puts poor Monsieur Fabergé into the most tragicomic situations. She accompanies her orders with her own sketches, and sets the price in advance. And since it's impossible, both technically and artistically, to make whatever it is according to her sketches, all kinds of tricks have to be invented to explain the inevitable changes. Sometimes Monsieur Fabergé blames us, the masters, and says we misunderstood his instructions. And sometimes he says, as apologetically as he can, that her sketch got lost. There's no point in offending her, or charging her more than she's dictated in advance. But, oh,' and he laughed, ruefully, 'after one of these transactions, how well advised you are to get away for the afternoon.'

Madame Leman watched Inna dissolve into sympathetic laughter.

'Eat, eat, dear children,' she heard herself saying happily through the steam from the tureen. 'Dear guests, eat.'

CHAPTER EIGHT

It was late when Yasha came in. He stuck his head around the door of the yellow drawing room on his way to bed, just to be sociable. The Leman parents were in there, just the two of them, playing cards. There were several empty glasses of wine about the place.

'We missed you. We had a guest,' Leman said, following Yasha's eyes. He looked contented. So, Yasha saw with relief, did his wife. 'And a very entertaining evening.'

'The Englishman,' Madame Leman broke in, all smiles. 'The painter. He was very impressed with Inna's playing. Said she should be on the stage. Far better than half the girls you see giving concerts. Far prettier, too.'

Yasha barely took in Madame Leman's words. He didn't know what Englishman she meant (the Lemans often assumed he must know all their friends). No, he was noticing something else. Madame Leman had lost that watchful look he'd noticed earlier, and was back to her usual relaxed self. Her eyes were shining, and her hair, in rivulets of ashy blond, was coming loose from the precarious arrangement of pins she could never quite get to stay in place.

'Did *you* have a good evening, dear?' she added kindly. 'Did your friends like your leaflet?'

He nodded, scuffing his boots as he recalled the praise they'd showered on it, feeling a bit more that all was right with the world. 'Think so,' he grunted, and went on up the stairs.

Inna's door was closed, but she was playing again: a perky Strauss waltz this time. Yasha went into his own room and quietly shut his door.

All those things he'd been thinking about her earlier: well, he'd been a bit overwrought, hadn't he? At any rate, she wasn't marshalling any unstoppably Russian musical armies any more, just dancing in a Viennese ballroom in her mind, maybe, dreaming of the Blue Danube . . .

He picked up his own violin.

The wall between them was so thin that she might as well have been in here with him. He could hear everything. He could practically hear her breath.

As she went back into the waltz's refrain, Yasha joined in, first counting the three-four *dum*-dee-dee beat of the piece, then, very softly, starting to supply the playful staccato 'dee-dee' chords of the tune's accompaniment.

Through the partition, he heard her slow down. For a phrase or two, she played with her bow just touching the strings, very quietly and questioningly, as though trying to work out what was going on, but he just kept on duetting, in time with her, and just as quietly. He couldn't help smiling at the thought of her surprise or imagining her cheeks just touched with pink.

Then he heard her violin gain courage. She speeded up into the next melody till he could barely keep up. If we were dancing together now, he thought, following her tempo, we'd be whirling off our feet. He couldn't help imagining, either, what that might be like: pastel chiffon crushed against his chest, bare arms moving against his, shining hair, wafting scent, the beat of her heart . . .

Eventually the dance tune moved towards its magnificent resolution, with those final, flamboyant chords. There was no place for him in it. Catching his breath, he paused to listen, applauding in his mind – she was so technically sure-fingered with all that tricky double-stopping. And, as she slowed the tempo right down, so dramatically self-assured, too.

But, while she held the last octave A notes, rich with a vibrato that carried into the night, triumphant, yet poignant too with the small sadness of the parting to come as the dancers separated, he couldn't resist lifting his own fiddle for a final, jokey, whispered, 'dee-dee-DUM!'

As the music died away, he could almost swear he'd heard her laugh.

Yasha noticed that Inna kept her eyes down on her tea through breakfast, and didn't say a word to him. She practically jumped into the washing-up bowl, too. She was hard at it before Madame Leman even drew breath to ask her to help.

But once they were all in the workshop, and he started telling Leman about his outing last night, he knew she was following the conversation.

'What islands?' she asked suddenly.

They all turned.

Yasha had just said that he'd gone to the islands by the Samson Bridge, where there were fewer gendarmes.

Why, he thought, impatiently, how green she is! Doesn't she know anything?

'The St Petersburg islands—' he began, but Leman interrupted before he could say 'of course'. A moment later, with a hot rush of shame, he realized he was pleased to have been interrupted.

'"Oh, Russian people, oh, Russian people!"' Leman intoned in a playful sing-song. '"Don't let the crowd of shadows in from the islands! Black and damp bridges are already thrown across the waters of Lethe! If only they could be dismantled . . . but no, too late! . . . The shadows are thronging across the bridge . . ."' His expansive belly, pressed up against the worktop, was wobbling with mirth.

Marcus was grinning too. 'Take no notice, that's just one of his literary quotes,' he told Inna.

Seeing Inna's bewilderment, Leman laughed. 'The islands are the suburbs here. The boggy bits of land that really were just islands, once, when Petersburg was just an estuary. They're the places over the river. Beyond Palace Embankment.'

'Where the poor live. Where the factories are,' Yasha said impatiently. He didn't like the frivolous way Leman sometimes carried on. 'The rich, over here, all the brutes who make their millions out of the sweat of the factory workers out there, fear all those people like fire.'

'That's why the bridges are all drawbridges,' Leman added, twinkling at Inna over his spectacles in a proprietorial way Yasha didn't altogether like either. 'So they can be drawn up at night. So the great unwashed don't come surging in after dark. Naturally, the islands are where Yasha meets his revolutionary friends.'

Yasha hunched down over his work, sensing he was going to be teased, prepared to retaliate if she made some mocking comment in reply.

But she just nodded, big-eyed. 'I see,' she said, and got on with her scroll.

Yasha soon forgave Monsieur Leman because, a bit later, once he'd told them about what the lads at the meeting last night had been saying about his pamphlet, Leman turned to Inna again and said, with his admiration clearly audible now – no mocking undertones at all: 'Because you see, dear girl, here we are in our poor Russia, a country like a boiler, with the pressure mounting, about to blow, and no safety valve. Everyone held tight by Emperor and Church; made a mockery of by bureaucrats; the prisons heaving; the poor crammed into their flea-ridden dungeons . . . No wonder they throw bombs. And sooner or later that boiler's going to burst – how can it not? – unless energetic young visionaries like Yasha can change everything first. Which I think he can. He's a real firebrand, you know, full of the sterling qualities we need. And they must, if we're to be saved. Because if they don't . . . well, only God knows what will happen.'

Yasha didn't say anything. He just planed more energetically at his fiddle back, feeling the deadwood melt away as the curves of its true shape emerged, as he brought the future into existence.

But, a little later, while Leman was inspecting the final tiny Saw-cuts – Eight and Nine – of Inna's scroll, Yasha heard him ask her, absent-mindedly, as he fiddled with a stray shaving that might otherwise have broken the purity of the line: 'So what do you think of Horace's idea in the cold light of day?'

He noticed her quick sideways glance, too. 'What idea?' Yasha asked quickly.

'Our guest last night,' Inna explained in a rush – how quickly she'd learned to say 'our,' he thought uncomfortably – 'was very complimentary about my playing.' She looked down, blushing.

With a feeling of foreboding he didn't understand, Yasha waited. Yes, hadn't Madame L. been saying something about this last night? he thought. Now he could see the colour Inna had gone, he wished he'd paid more attention.

So Inna had brought her violin down, last night, and performed again? Was this why she'd been in such a good mood that she'd wanted to dance Strauss waltzes?

Yasha only breathed out when she went on, 'Even though he only heard me from the bottom of the stairs, while I was practising.'

Still, she was obviously excited. 'He was talking about taking me off to some artists' club, one night, to perform. He says it's very informal, people just get up and do a turn, but the whole of *la haute Bohème* goes.' She glanced up at him. 'But I couldn't, of course.'

'No papers,' Yasha agreed. He could see now that she knew the difference between dream and reality. Suddenly he felt relieved.

She bit her lip. 'There's that, too, of course. But mostly just because I'm no good at performing in public.' She paused. 'I know I played for all of you yesterday, but I don't, usually. I get too scared. I mess it up.'

'Oh, come now, dear girl!' boomed Leman. 'What nonsense!'

'You played so wonderfully for us!' Marcus squeaked.

She shook her head. 'I just don't like it,' she replied, very definitely.

Yasha's secret pleasure that she didn't, after all, seem to want to take up the Englishman's offer only increased at the thought of what neither of the others knew. She'd been happy enough playing with *him*, last night.

She put a hand on Leman's arm. 'But I did appreciate the thought,' she added, with more warmth than Yasha liked. 'It was so kind of Horace.' She turned to Yasha. 'That wasn't the only thoughtful thing he did, either. He'd seen me earlier on, you see, when I went out on my visit; and even though he was at that peasant's flat too he must feel the same way you all do about *my* having been there, because he actually thought to bring me round a novel about wicked peasant holy men – to warn me off, I suppose.' She smiled tentatively at him.

But Yasha didn't want to hear any more praise of this interfering Englishman, and he wished he could think of something dismissive to say about the club they'd been talking about. But he didn't know it. There was so much he didn't know about St Petersburg – not just about the white-gloved world of Nevsky high society, but even about the Lemans' circle of high-minded intellectuals.

'Well, he can't take you out anywhere when you haven't got papers,' he repeated, obstinately. It was only when he saw Leman straighten out the beginning of a private smile that he realized he'd have done better just to shut up.

*

Before going up to lunch, Yasha put out some of his pamphlets on the bench, so she could see them as soon as they sat down again to work; not just the much-discussed Beilis one, but a few of each of the others too, the calls for Jews to relearn Yiddish and Hebrew, and take back the culture they'd lost. She picked them up, with what he feared might be no more than polite interest (for perhaps all she was interested in was white gloves and bohemian nightclubs?). But when his fears instantly came true – when she put the leaflets down again, saying, coolly, 'I've never understood why anyone would want to learn Hebrew or Yiddish, even if their grandparents knew them; what would be the point?' – he didn't take offence, or start proselytizing. He just found himself taking the path of least resistance, and trying to explain the islands instead.

It wasn't just wronged Jews, or the students and radicals plotting over there, that Yasha cared about. There were more than a million people now in St Petersburg, he explained, and half of them were illegals, hiding on the islands, trying to escape poverty or the police in the tenements around the factories. He even pitied the prostitutes in the taverns where he met his political friends. 'Victims of the system,' he explained.

'How disgusting,' Inna said, quickly, to Marcus.

Yasha hoped that she just didn't know yet how to react properly. It was all so new to her, after all. She was just trying out responses. She didn't see that, in his mind, at least, she was almost like one of those victims herself. So he shrugged, and said in his best pamphlet-speak, 'But what are the poor souls to do? When all they have is the false freedom of destitution . . .' He leaned across the worktop. 'I'll take you, some day,' he said encouragingly, trying not to see her elegant nose wrinkling again.

After they'd finished for the day, and were all trooping upstairs, Yasha noticed Inna, half a flight of stairs above him, murmuring with Monsieur Leman. When he saw Leman quickly glancing down at him, through the banisters, before turning back to Inna to reply, he felt despondent enough to wonder whether she'd been poking fun at him. Then, nodding affably at the girl, the master took her off into the flat.

Not even a 'good evening', or a 'thank you for the company', Yasha thought as he trudged on alone up the stairs.

He flung himself on his bed. He wasn't in the mood to play.

It was ten minutes before he heard the click of the door, and a violin.

Miserably, he listened. Three low Es, then another, a long sob of a note, and then another piece with three beats in the bar, but as far as could be from the zany waltzing of last night: in a minor key, dreamily sad and reflective . . .

Wait. It was Jewish.

It took him a phrase or two more before he recognized the melody. Yes, it was the piece the Lemans had been so impressed with at that open-air concert last spring, wasn't it? Played by the thirteen-year-old wunderkind of the year, a new student at the Conservatoire, who'd drawn a crowd of twenty-five thousand and needed a police escort out afterwards to protect him from his screaming admirers; the Litvak boy who shared Yasha's first name? Heifetz, Yasha recalled; and the music, named 'Hebrew Melody', was by another young Jew at the Conservatoire. Akhron.

Of course. Leman had bought the sheet music as soon as Josef Akhron had published it through whatever the name of the St Petersburg society was that had been set up last year by Jews and anti-anti-Semites. It was just the kind of life-of-the-mind thing the Lemans did get involved in. It was called the Jewish Folk Music Society, he remembered, because the authorities had refused to register it simply as the Jewish Music Society.

He sat up, electrified by the realization that came to him next.

That's what she'd been whispering about with Leman.

She must have been borrowing the music, to play up here, for him.

It was the haunting music bringing this lump to his throat, he told himself now as he reached for his violin, and took it in his arms. But all he could do was cradle it, and shut his stinging eyes (dust, he told himself fiercely), and listen.

She must be sight-reading, he realized. But she finished the sorrowful first part of the melody not only without a false note but with such intensity of feeling, such depth of emotion, that it took his breath away.

It was only in the second, faster, more restless melody, full of rushed demisemiquavers, trills and sobs, high on the E-string, that her sureness of touch left her; only when she was at the peak of the cadenza, a wilder still improvisation on that second theme, that her tone roughened into hoarseness, and then, unexpectedly, went quiet.

In the sudden silence, he heard her open her door.

The sadness of that music might silence anyone, Yasha

thought, blinking. And it must bring back so much pain for *her*, especially, with the memories she must have.

Wrenched with pity, he got up, still holding his violin, and went out to the landing, half hoping . . .

But she wasn't standing there in the dark, needing comfort. She was flying away from him, down the stairs, four at a time.

Yasha hesitated. Then he put his violin down on a leaflet box.

What must she remember? he wondered as he stood in the dark. His parents hadn't had to tell him anything, in the end, because he'd learned how to find out for himself. He'd read the newspaper stories published in the foreign press, and translated back into Russian. He'd also read the survivors' accounts, gathered by old Kremer for a pamphlet. So he knew everything that had happened at Zhitomir, where her family had lived, from the first rumours that Jews had poisoned their Christian servant, to the mysterious appearance in town of a St Petersburg gendarmerie officer on the eve of Easter, to the printed handbills that started circulating, without interference from the police, telling people that an imperial ukaze had been published allowing the infliction of 'bloody punishment', and all the rest of the awful, usual story.

Whatever Inna might remember of those days, whatever her part in it had been, her memories now would be unbearable, he thought. His own painful childhood memories suddenly seemed trivial by comparison.

He put his hands to his face, overwhelmed with pity.

All at once, breaking into the calm of his breathing, something warm and heavy cannoned into his chest. He staggered back a step; then he steadied himself and looked down. Slowly he made out Inna, grimacing and picking at his chest. He hadn't even heard her come back upstairs.

It took him a moment to realize she'd just caught her hair in his buttons.

'Stay still,' he muttered. 'You're only making it worse.'

Obediently, she stopped and stood before him with bowed head, very close.

She smelled so innocent; of lavender.

Trying not to think how close she was, or how warm, or how full of turbulent emotion she must be, he got out a match and lit it, holding it away from her head, working out which button – one on his shoulder, he could see – her hair was tangled in. Then he held out the box, and – as calmly as he could, given this unsettling physical proximity – told her to go on lighting matches until he'd set her loose.

She reached for it. But she couldn't take it. She already had something in her hand.

'What's that?' he asked as she let it fall to take the matches.

He was looking at her face in the sudden circle of flickering light. There were no tears on it, he realized; no sign of upset; just frustration at being trapped.

'A mute,' she answered, sounding far more self-possessed than he expected, or felt himself. 'I wanted a mute for the next bit. I remembered there was one on the piano.'

'Oh,' Yasha heard himself say, not at all the decisive male rescuer he wanted to be.

She went on quite conversationally. 'Because the music was marked *con sordino*, in the next section, and I wanted to do it right. It's such a beautiful tune.'

'I thought that the music must have upset you . . .' Yasha

muttered, trying to make his hands gentler, 'reminded you of your parents . . .'

She turned up her trapped face, cautiously, so she could look at him. 'My *parents?*' she said, sounding astonished. 'Why would it?'

'Because it's Jewish music, and you sounded so sad.'

She laughed, awkwardly he thought. 'Oh, I'm afraid I don't really even remember my parents. Just Aunt Lyuba, who brought me up. And she wasn't Jewish at all. The flu took *her* off too,' she added, after a moment. 'I do miss *her*. But not when I hear Jewish music.'

It was Yasha's turn to stare. What did she mean, the flu had taken her aunt off *too*? Surely she didn't think this was what had happened to her parents, when everyone knew—

Suddenly the trapped hair came loose.

'There,' he said, his blood still pounding through him, and stepped quickly away from her flower scent, and the questions he couldn't ask. It was a relief.

She was free. She stepped back too, pushed open her door for the welcome lamplight, and stopped in the doorway, silhouetted in that square of light, so he could only see her outline.

'Why *did* you think I'd be upset by that Jewish tune?' he heard her ask curiously. 'They were never at all observant, you know, my parents. Aunty Lyuba said.'

He shook his head. 'I don't want to say.'

'Say *what?*'

She stepped forward, right up to him, so close that his senses were filled with flowers again.

He was so overwhelmed by the desire to take her in his arms that it made him angry. 'You must know what! They

125

died in the Zhitomir pogrom! I thought that the music might have made you think of it and caused you pain!'

She went still. 'What do you mean?' she asked, her voice a shocked whisper.

'You were nearly killed too,' he said softly. 'I heard about that pogrom all through my childhood. We all did. All the cousins, everyone – it terrified us! And my parents used to say . . . well, that's not the point . . .'

She stepped back. His body yearned to step after her, to keep her close. But he stayed where he was.

The light caught her stern profile as she came to rest against her doorframe. She stood there for a while, looking down at her hands, with the white bands across the palms.

'It sounds like a story from one of your Jewish freedom fighters' leaflets,' she said eventually. Her voice was quiet. 'If it were true,' she added, sounding more openly sceptical, 'wouldn't at least one of all those grieving relatives you're talking about have thought to get in touch – even if not to train me for your heroic fight for Jewish rights, maybe just to offer to bring me up? Because, you know, no one ever did. Aunty Lyuba was only a neighbour. She didn't have to have me. It was just that there wasn't anyone else offering.'

Her lonely logic defeated Yasha. No, he realized, miserably, of course they hadn't offered: they'd all have been too scared. For a moment, he almost spoke up for his parents, to remind her that after Aunty Lyuba had died, they *had* taken her in. But in the end he said nothing. Because even he could see that they'd only done it because they'd had a room free and needed a reliable paying guest. They'd taken her rent money, and left her behind when they ran off. How grateful would anyone be for that?

He blinked.

'No,' Inna was saying, insistently. 'The truth is that my parents died in the epidemic. It took off a lot of people in Zhitomir that winter. Aunt Lyuba's husband, too. So she took me in, and we went to live in Kiev. Kiev's the only place I remember. Aunt Lyuba was my only real family. What you were suggesting is' – and, for a moment, her calm broke and her face twisted in pain – 'politics.' She put her hand on the door-handle and stepped inside.

'Your mute . . . your rosin . . .' he appealed. They were still on the floor.

'I won't be needing them,' he heard before the door shut and the light vanished.

CHAPTER NINE

There was a woman screaming somewhere nearby.

Inna woke, full of dread, wondering where the noise was coming from, and found Yasha gazing down at her, very close.

It was nearly light, the soft grey of a winter morning. The reading lamp was still on, but its yellow was so weak that she couldn't make out his face – just the stubble on his chin, and the stare of his eyes. He was sitting on her bed.

At least the screaming had stopped.

She pulled herself up on to one elbow. 'What . . .?'

She didn't understand what was happening. He seemed to have his hands on her shoulders; and now his arms, in the striped blue flannel of a nightshirt, were tightening around her, and she was clinging to his chest, with her head full of his heartbeat. 'It's all right. It's all right,' she heard him murmur, as if she were a frightened child, though he was the one trembling. 'It was just a dream.'

It took her another long moment to realize the screaming must have been coming from her.

'I didn't mean to scare you,' she heard him say. 'I never thought you wouldn't know. I've been so sorry.'

She could feel his fingers on her scalp. He was stroking her hair.

She shut her eyes. She didn't have to wake up. All she had to do was stay here, in this dreamlike state, in the warm of her bed, against his warmth, being held . . .

She'd avoided talking to Yasha since that night. Not that she hadn't been aware of his stricken looks in the workshop, not that she wanted to quarrel with him, even though he was wrong. Because he had been wrong; he had to have been. She had no reason not to believe what she'd always been told, no reason to mistrust Aunty Lyuba, who'd been so good to her.

And now here they were, in something blessedly wordless. She felt the heat of relief go through her that the other thing had passed. His arms tightened; she moved closer.

She hadn't played the violin for days, either, and not just because she now felt that trying to meet him halfway by playing him a Jewish tune had been a mistake. Through the thin wall, knowing he'd be listening, it had all felt too intimate. She'd shut herself in her room every evening instead and read the novel Horace had brought her.

She caught sight of it now, half covered by the quilt: a green volume, with a silver dove drawn on the front. The peasant mystic book.

The part of Inna that knew that this new thing was happening, and knew, too, that somewhere beyond the tight control of her consciousness she *had*, after all, shown the weakness of a victim – *had*, shamefully, whimpered, and cried out, and woken Yasha up – latched on to that glimpse of book jacket with joyful relief. I've had a nightmare, she thought, because of the book.

Yes, that was it . . . She'd stayed up late, finishing it. She must have drifted away after finishing the murder scene, whose brutal last words she still remembered now.

In the sullen light of barely breaking dawn, the yellow flame of a candle danced on the table; in the cramped room stood sullen, unmalicious people, while on the floor Pyotr's body breathed in spasms; without cruelty, with faces bared, they stood over the body, examining with curiosity what they had done: the deathly blueness and the trickle of blood that oozed from his lip, which, no doubt, he had bitten through in the heat of the struggle.

Yes, it was coming back: how she'd gone to sleep with her head full of the fictional young man's terror as *they* closed in. And, even more, of how *they* had been afterwards. Her eyes had closed, last night, on the disgusted thought, Was that really how people would be, after . . . *doing that*?

'I shouldn't have been reading that book so late, that's all.' Her voice sounded throaty with sleep. 'It wasn't your fault.'

But, even as she looked at Yasha's face, so close, she also knew that it hadn't only been the murder in the book that she'd been screaming about. With another part of her mind, she could still, just, recall the dissolving fragments of her dream.

No, it had been something . . . else. Worse. In the dream, there'd been someone lying down, she vaguely remembered, lying in the dark, but they'd had a great red wet smile, one so dreadful you couldn't look at it without your gorge rising, without screaming—

And then Yasha's lips closed on hers. And there was no room in Inna's mind for anything except right now, right here.

'Yasha!' she heard, from far away.

His mouth left hers. He sat up.

It was Madame Leman.

'Yaaasha!'

She was coming up the stairs from maybe one floor down. Inna could hear her slow footsteps. 'I've got your laundry here – it's terribly heavy, too. Can you take it up the rest of the way, dear?' she called.

His eyes turned wildly to the door.

Inna could see him assessing what step Madame Leman would have reached by the time he got to the safety of his own room.

Then he bolted out on to the landing, running his hands over his head and patting at his nightshirt as he went.

Inna burrowed deep down inside the bed, under the blankets.

She could hear that Madame Leman was nearly at the top. She'd see where he'd been, there was no doubt about it . . .

The stair outside her door creaked. Yasha, she thought. But so did the top step. Inna screwed her eyes shut, expecting an explosion. 'Ah, there you are, dear,' she heard instead, right outside her door. 'Here, take this basket, do. It's breaking my back.'

She heard Yasha laugh, to her ears very uneasily, and his mumbled thanks. Then she heard him say, with new bravado, 'You're up early.'

But Madame Leman didn't seem to hear. 'And if you

wouldn't mind, dear, since you're up too, could you get dressed quickly and come and give me a hand downstairs? I can't reach the tops of the cupboards, and I'm spring-cleaning the yellow room. I need someone tall to fetch things down.'

It was only when Madame Leman was safely back downstairs that Yasha, now hastily dressed, tucking shirt into trousers under his shrugged-on jacket, stuck his head back round Inna's door.

She was doing up her skirt hooks, hurrying too. She looked up.

'Close,' he said, grinning conspiratorially.

Her panic receded, as the dream had before. Nothing bad had happened.

Slowly, she smiled back. Then he was gone.

CHAPTER TEN

Horace took off his eyeglasses and put down his tiny paintbrush on his worktable. The goggle-rings left on his cheeks and forehead chafed. Experience told him they would look red and painful if he bothered to go and check in the glass. He looked around him. The other dark-suited gents were still hard at it under the gleaming floor-to-ceiling polished mahogany shelving. Solemn and heavy as church pews, the shelves contained many, many jewelled and enamelled fripperies in the making. Horace's colleagues, straining their eyes through magnifiers at whatever precious tiny object they were working on, with whatever miniature instruments, were turning out more. There was an intent quietness in the back room: just the occasional mutter, in well-spoken English, or French, or playful Swiss-German. But the fine strokes of the latest layer of Horace's latest dreaming-spires Oxford scene needed to dry. And his eyes needed a rest.

A dozen silver cigarette boxes to finish by Christmas for Prince Youssoupoff's relatives, all with prettily idealized

Vanora Bennett

painted decorations of English scenes: the Radcliffe Camera
dome, autumn trees, mist. Who better than Horace, who'd
actually seen Oxford? Monsieur Fabergé had been pleased
with the commission from the richest man in Russia. But
Horace was doing them only slowly, between other orders.
It's dull doing the same thing, over and over again, he said
lightly; I'll spread them out. Anyway, he was also enjoying
the outings he went on with the prince each time he delivered
another box: a mystic one morning; a gypsy nightclub out
in the sticks for the whole night, after an evening meeting.
And then there was the time he'd sat for hours waiting for
his client in some raffish bar off Nevsky, alone at the table,
surrounded by packs of young officers drinking too hard
and laughing like hyenas, watching the beautiful swaying
singer, absent-mindedly admiring her pearls and décolletage
as well as her husky voice and sinuous dancing, wondering
what had become of Felix. It was only when the dark-haired
beauty strolled past his table and dropped a rose on it – and
winked – that he'd realized he'd been watching Felix all
along, onstage.

'If my mother only knew where her pearls had been,' Felix
murmured, grinning impishly, ten minutes later, when he
flung himself elegantly into the empty chair, dressed now in
impeccable gentleman-about-town clothes. 'Not to mention
her dress! I hate to think what she'd say.'

No, he didn't want to finish this entertaining commission
too fast.

Felix took the edge off the sometimes stifling respectability
of his job at Fabergé in which Horace painted very small
pretty things for stout generals' wives.

Unusually for an Englishman, Horace had spent his

entire youth in India; his father was a military surgeon; his grandfather had been a botanist who'd run the Calcutta botanical garden. His family hadn't had the finance to treat India, as most of the English did, like a temporary posting, with the children sent Home to school and their ayahs dumped on London street corners when their usefulness ran out. Home hadn't ever quite been home to the Wallicks; his grandfather, despite his accented elegance in English, had been a Danish Jew blown into English India as a young man by a change of political wind during the Napoleonic Wars. This meant there were no convenient aunts to die and leave them an inheritance to go Home on; no cousins with ramshackle houses crumbling under sprays of honeysuckle. So when Father had retired, there hadn't really been anywhere to go in England, except rented apartments in London, where there'd been good works in the East End for his more spiritually minded, dutiful sister while he'd watched the moths eat away at his parents' marriage after Father's bankruptcy. Even more painful had been the sight of Father, embittered by the world's ingratitude for his scientific researches, scraping around trying to re-establish himself professionally as a photographer.

The childhood life before that grey, pinched, outsider scrappiness was all so long ago now that Calcutta had shrunk to no more than a saffron-coloured cloud of dust in Horace's mind: hot, energetic, multi-lingual; with water glittering between the boats and exotic Himalayan plants swaying in the gardens and red-faced white men in military uniform and fabulous native grandees in bright silks. Horace felt oddly nostalgic for those dull, noisy colonels and peacock princes. He knew how to talk to them. True, he'd never be one of them, but he felt more at home with them than with the tepid rain of Home.

So he hadn't been able to believe his luck when he'd got to Russia ten years ago now, and found this other glittering, exotic empire, this brutal place of extreme contrasts and weathers, this splendid collection of oddities just waiting for him: where he could feel apart but also at home, again . . . at last.

His latest client, this charming, wicked, flamboyant mass of impossible contrasts, Felix Youssoupoff, was the living, breathing shorthand symbol of the Russia Horace loved.

Like the other delightful oddities Horace gathered else-where in his evening life, in the avant-garde circles he preferred to frequent (when his time was his own and he could sport the kind of dandyish coloured waistcoats and twirl the silver-topped canes that would have given the generals' wives of his daytime employment a heart attack), an occasional dose of Felix reminded him he was, really, an artist with a wild side.

Still, not tonight. He didn't think tonight should be too alternative.

He opened his case and got out the newspaper he'd been looking at over breakfast, to check the various concerts he'd ringed for this evening.

There was the new young English violin sensation, Elsie Playfair. Señor José, the violin-maker who'd introduced him to Leman during a visit to Petersburg two years ago, had written last week, saying he should be sure not to miss her recital. That might be just the thing. Though, hm, Mendelssohn . . .

He turned the page.

He'd given tonight a good deal of thought. But he still wasn't quite decided.

He wanted to make it exactly right.

'Oh!' Inna exclaimed, a few hours later. But then her voice faltered and her eyes clouded. She glanced sideways at Leman. 'But I can't. I'm sorry . . .'

Still in his hat and coat, already feeling warm in the heat of the workshop, Horace breathed in sawdusty air with his disappointment. He could see she'd been expecting him, as she'd had the book ready to return. He'd imagined she'd be pleased. He glanced at Leman, hoping for clarification.

But Leman just wiped his hands on his big apron. 'Why don't you stay to dinner instead, dear man?' he said, with, as it seemed to Horace, indecision mixed into his customary heartiness. 'The women have promised us cheeselets. Lidiya would be delighted to see you.'

Horace wasn't especially tempted. Greasy fried cream-cheese-and-raisin patties, topped with sour cream and sugar: highly indigestible. It wasn't really an aristocratic cuisine, the Russian one. And those naughty children, making their racket . . . Amusing, of course, but not at all what he'd had in mind.

But when he saw how Inna's face lit up at this invitation, he smiled assent. Slipping her apron off, she stepped quickly forward to take the coat he'd started unbuttoning. She *was* pleased to see him, then. He'd find out easily enough, over dinner, what the problem was.

*

'It's Inna's papers, that's the thing, you see,' Leman said indistinctly as he pushed himself back from his still glistening plate.

The question had hung in the air all through the meal.

Horace hadn't tried too hard to investigate. He'd just made maximum efforts to amuse and flatter. There wasn't much he could do with the surly assistant, a tall good-looking dark youth who scowled silently into his plate all through dinner. But he'd tipped both the children a rouble, to their loud glee. He'd agreed with earnest young Marcus that both the Yugoslav princesses, that pair of troublemaking sisters married to grand dukes, should be banned from court or otherwise prevented from meddling in politics, or else the latest Balkans crisis would certainly end in war. He'd laughed not unsympathetically at Leman's vaguely socialist musings about Russia being a powder keg, though his answering comment had been a wry one to the effect that, true though all that undoubtedly was, he still found evolution easier to contemplate than revolution.

Horace poured Leman another glass of Crimean champagne.

'Ah, yes, papers,' he murmured, shaking his head understandingly. 'A nightmare, dealing with *chinovniki*. Why, it took me *months* when I got here.'

He paused, enquiringly, noticing the quick glance between Monsieur and Madame Leman. Inna's face was turned down. The sour young man was sighing in an attention-seeking way. Horace ignored him.

The young man, visibly provoked, put his glass down, with a thump. 'She doesn't *have* any papers,' he said loudly. 'You can't take her out to any concerts.'

Horace watched, astonished, as every head drew a little lower; every face bowed. Then, collectively, in scandalized tones, the family hissed, 'Shh!' And, 'Yasha!'

Only Inna raised her head. Her face was scarlet (and, Horace thought, even lovelier for it). Defiantly, she said, 'He means I got here on someone else's. I left mine behind.'

Horace was privately pleased to see the flash of anger in her green eyes directed at Yasha.

'So we thought it would be best she stays in for a while, out of trouble,' Monsieur Leman explained hurriedly. 'You know how the police are. I know *you* won't say a word, of course, dear fellow, but still . . .'

Horace smiled reassuringly. Personally, he always felt a bit impatient with this dreadful Russian fretting over documents. He'd worked it all out during his long years here: if a policeman started giving you a hard time about your papers, you just slipped him a rouble; there was never any more to it than that if you were a foreigner.

But being Jewish, here, was different; of course she'd be at risk. He rather admired the bold act of pinching a passport. She knew what she wanted, clearly.

'So,' he said, to Inna, 'you do have a document, even if it's not your own, that you could take out, just in case – if you *were* to go out?'

'Temporary,' Yasha supplied.

'Valid till?' Horace asked, addressing himself only to Inna.

Addressing herself only to him, she whispered, 'End of the month.' He could see the hope in her eyes.

'Tomorrow,' he said, triumphantly, turning to Leman. 'In which case, we might as well put it to good use while it's still useful, don't you think? It's too late for the concert, now, but I'd be delighted to take Inna to the Stray Dog before her purdah begins.'

The children giggled at that. How brisk he was sounding.

Leman again began to expostulate, but Horace over-rode him.

'Let's agree this, dear fellow: we'll go by cab (no policemen hide in cabs that I've ever heard of); I'll bring her back by one. You know, no one ever does ask many questions of a foreigner. She'll be quite safe with me.'

Leman might have gone on fretting, but, suddenly, Madame Leman reached over and patted her husband's hand. 'All right,' she said decisively. 'If Inna is willing to take the risk, she should go.'

An hour later, they were sitting in the dark, just the two of them, gazing around. Inna was wearing a rather loose black evening shift, borrowed from Madame Leman. Horace was topping up her glass, and making a point of not noticing her astonishment at the more outré habitués of the Stray Dog.

Brilliant tropical flowers and birds decorated the cellar walls. There was a candle on their table, and icy dew on the Chablis glasses. Someone had been playing jazz earlier on, and there'd been a ballerina. Right now, over by the piano, a man with a bass voice was reciting a poem. You could hardly see him through the blue smoke.

There was a ripple of applause. The poet bowed, and Inna clapped, wide-eyed.

Horace had been waved into the club without paying. Bohemians didn't have to pay, he'd explained casually. Only autograph-hunters, or the respectable – dentists in frock coats

– or the vast rabble of nouveaux riches infesting Petersburg. He grinned, feeling a proper artist himself again, here. 'We call them the Pharmacists.'

Now he was watching her watch the tall stubble-headed man lying across a table, banging mockingly on the drum he was holding every time a monocled Pharmacist came in. Horace could imagine what she was thinking: Well, he must be Someone. You wouldn't go out wearing a yellow and black striped smock unless you were. And people kept buying him drinks.

'That's Mayakovsky,' Horace murmured. 'The Futurist.' He rather enjoyed Inna's blank answering look. She was such an innocent. Why, she'd only just heard of Symbolism, which had been all the rage for as long as she'd been alive, though it was now out of favour with the avant-garde assembled here. Even if he were to introduce her to every last poet and painter here, she wouldn't have the faintest clue who they were. Well, there was time for all that.

'What's next on the programme?'

He dipped his head courteously closer to answer. 'There's no particular programme,' he murmured, in her ear. 'People just get up and show whatever they've been working on. This is somewhere to try things out.' He twinkled down at her. 'There'd be nothing to stop *you* getting up and playing, if you felt like it.' But she only shook her head.

Horace wasn't quite sure how to bring about the idea that had hazily been forming in his head ever since he'd heard her play: Inna in a wonderful dress, arms flashing over her violin . . . him at one side, cheering her on . . . and the rapturous applause from all these people, not least for him, for finding her. He knew, deep down, that although his foreignness wasn't really an impediment to fully belonging here, and nor was his day job (not really), the combination, along with his lack of an all-consuming furnace of a talent, would always keep him somehow on the fringes of everything: welcomed, always; enjoyed, certainly; but not embraced. But what if he had a lovely wife with an all-consuming furnace of a talent? What if he could play Osip Brik to Inna's Lily, proudly twirling a monocle as she won the hearts of the world?

For a moment he was too entranced, again, by that vision to realize she was saying something. She'd cut her hands. Look. She was showing him; making excuses. It would be impossible to play till they were healed.

Hastily collecting himself, he took one outstretched hand in his – how soft her skin was; how slender the fingers – and shook his head over the cut palms.

'In the workshop?' he asked, tenderly. 'You must be careful.'

She glanced uncertainly up at him, and his heart twisted when he realized what she was stammering out next.

'A new *lifeline*?' he asked, and his fingers closed protectively over the slim fingers lying in his palm.

Horace thought many things at once: that any Symbolist would love the desperation of that gesture; that she must have been scared stiff on that train up here; and that she must feel even more of an outsider than he often did.

Then he saw the shame in her eyes; the awareness of what she'd done. She wasn't that scared child any more, he realized. She was already learning how people did things in this new, busier, more sophisticated, more tolerant city environment, where being Jewish made so much less difference: watching with bright eyes, taking it all in. He'd been aware of her doing it all evening. It would be crass of him to dwell on the other thing any further. 'Well,' he answered lightly, 'I can only wonder what future you've made for yourself. I must say I hope it will include performing. Because you play unusually beautifully; you'd be a sensation if you ever *were* to go on stage.'

Resisting the temptation to go on holding her wounded hand, he gently relinquished it and refilled their glasses.

She took her glass and cradled it, thoughtfully. Sipped. 'I mean, I can play all right at home, but on a stage I just can't . . .' She shook her head.

'What, a person with your presence of mind?' He paused, and then added, casually, 'Your friend, who didn't want you to come out tonight – why was he so angry?'

She shrugged. 'I think he was worried that I might get the Lemans into trouble,' she said cagily. 'But I won't, will I?'

Horace was reassuring her when new people came, laughing, to the next table: a young woman, and two young men fussing around her chair. The woman had dark hair in a severe bun, a fringe cut high on the forehead, and a tall, very slender shape wrapped in an embroidered Chinese dragon-shawl. She was a little older than Inna, in her twenties, but their bearing was not unalike. She had strong features, not exactly beautiful: jutting cheekbones, hooked nose.

Horace leaned forward in the pleasure of the moment. Here, at least, was someone his young guest would almost certainly recognize. For surely all young girls loved Akhmatova.

'Why,' he heard Inna say to her, 'you're Anya Gorenko, aren't you? From Kiev?'

Everyone at the neighbouring table turned to look at

143

them as Inna hurried on, 'I remember you. You were at the Fundukleyevskaya Academy. You wouldn't remember me. I was small then – just starting when you were taking exams. But it *was* you, wasn't it?'

At last, Akhmatova – Horace knew the exotically Tatar name to be made up – inclined her head: 'Yes, it was.'

'My name's Inna,' Inna stuttered. 'Inna Feldman.'

Horace caught surprise in Akhmatova's eyes.

'My sister was called Inna, too.' Akhmatova's voice was soft and low, with a tragic catch in it. 'She died,' the poetess added. Then, equally simply, 'Won't you join us?'

Now the minutes flew by. Horace, who'd delightedly recognized one of Akhmatova's male companions as the new poet Leman had been reading the other day, found a tactful way to whisper to Inna how illustrious her schoolmate Gorenko had become in the past couple of years. Inna's eyes widened in instant, open adoration.

Akhmatova only replied, with grave modesty, 'Oh, fame; it embarrasses me. It seems indecent, as if I'd left a bra or a stocking on the table.'

Inna laughed in surprise.

Bryusov, in the black garb of the decadent set, with a scarab bracelet, was the next performer to take the floor. His voice was loud, and felt louder when he started declaiming straight at Inna:

> 'You're Woman – you're the witch's brew!
> It sets on fire as soon as touching lips . . .'

He bowed to her, very deeply, when he'd finished.

Inna bowed back, looking only a bit flustered. She had

savoir-faire, Horace thought. He'd wanted to thump the man. But it was only when the applause was over, and Bryusov had sat down again, that Inna, discreetly, wiped her cheeks.

'What did you think of his poem?' Akhmatova asked Inna.

'I don't know if I understood it,' Inna replied, searching for words. Horace saw she knew she was being tested. 'It was so high-flown. But then I'm learning violin-making, and violin-makers are practical. We make something useful – beautiful too, but basically useful – music from a piece of wood. That's honest. But that poem felt different. Like being . . . *drunk* . . . with words, without knowing what all the emotion meant, or what it was for.'

Horace breathed out. He hadn't quite realized how nervous he'd been for her.

'Bravo,' said the quieter young man.

'Yes, I'm tired of all this bloated mystifying, too,' Akhmatova agreed. 'Symbolists, decadents: it's all too much.'

'She plays the violin,' Horace told them, proudly, after a companionable pause. 'Very well, too.'

And, soon after, Inna let herself be persuaded to join one of Akhmatova's two companions, playing for the room.

She might not have, if Horace hadn't quietly explained that Sasha was going to sing a poem of Akhmatova's that he'd set to music himself.

'It would be a mark of respect,' Horace prompted gently. 'Everyone would like it.'

'Really?' Inna said, looking doubtfully from one to another.

Horace could see her assimilating Akhmatova's nod as she tuned up by the piano, and Sasha, perched on the piano stool, played the melody very quietly through for her and showed her the words he was going to sing. As Sasha whispered, Horace could see Inna slowly forgetting to be nervous and instead getting that expression he knew musicians always got when they were listening intently, moving her head very slightly to the imagined beat, with a faraway look in her eyes.

It was a melancholy ballad, of course, with the sparseness of all Akhmatova's work. A husband, on his way out to his night shift, telling his wife that the grey-eyed king has been found dead in the woods; the wife, in pain, listening to the poplars whispering, 'Your king has gone,' and waking her little daughter, who has grey eyes too.

Looking suddenly lost again as the room went quiet, Inna played just one tentative opening chord, gazing at the floor. Even through the smoke, Horace could see how painfully she was blushing. For a moment, he was so full of nerves himself that he had to shut his eyes. But, he realized, opening them again an instant later, it didn't matter. Sasha was a professional, and his voice, soft and tender though it seemed, was strong enough to rise over Inna's wavering sound and carry on solo, creating the impression in the audience that her uncertainty was just part of the mood of the music. At the end of the first verse, Inna, giving Sasha that intent, faraway look again, lifted her bow and, still hesitantly, joined in. Horace caught the graciousness in Sasha's slight nod to her, that hint of an answering smile on her lips as she took heart.

By the time the ballad approached its emotional peak, with the wife imagining her little girl's grey eyes, Inna had so far forgotten her nerves that she even picked up the tune herself, and improvised a haunting, lovely cadenza of her own for a few bars, while Sasha and the rest of the room listened. Horace felt tears in his eyes. He looked around as the clapping began to see Akhmatova, opposite, sitting quite motionless, still listening inside her head. But the sombre poet beside him was smiling, with faraway eyes.

At the piano, Inna, now looking both relieved and excited, was putting down the violin while Sasha grinned up at her and said something. A knot of other people approached to congratulate them, and Horace hoped she was thinking, I've walked in and made friends; I've played in public; I did it all myself. She had, too; she hadn't really needed him there. After that one moment's panic, she'd performed without a sign of fear. But, he also thought, with the melody of that wistful ballad still in his head, she'd enjoyed his company, and perhaps had seen him, at least a little, as her guide. That was enough, for a first night.

'How did *you* come to live in St Petersburg, Horace?' she asked with her new poise, after the modestly received applause and the farewells, in the cab.

He didn't know quite where to start: the art-school years in Paris? That first commission to spend a summer here, 'repainting' a family picture for a gentleman who'd been losing a bit too heavily at cards, and wanted to quietly sell the original?

Or . . . Wera?

He caught himself on that thought: Wera, with *her* zest for life, and green eyes, and dark hair. With her Russian mother; with the Fabergé trinkets, gathering dust in South Norwood, talking to seventeen-year-old Horace over the fence. That was really the answer, wasn't it?

147

'Oh,' he replied, lightly. 'The usual. A girl . . .' He paused. She waited.

'It was all very long ago,' he added, dismissing the memory with a laugh. 'I'm not one to dwell on the past. I much prefer thinking about the future.'

The cab stopped with a jingle and the man got down to open the door. She jumped down, too, before he'd even managed to brush the back of her hand with his lips. But she looked alertly back up at him, and she was smiling.

'Yes,' she said, as if he'd said something wiser than he had. 'Me too.'

CHAPTER ELEVEN

Inna let herself in.

She almost went up to the attic, before remembering that Madame Leman had moved her down, that morning, to take Marcus's old room inside the flat.

For a moment, she almost went up anyway, so she could tell Yasha about the wonderful evening she'd had with Horace.

Might it be possible that, after all, she did have buried somewhere within her the desire to actually want to make people stop talking and listen to her playing? Might Horace really be kind enough to want to help?

Suddenly pleased that the change of room meant she didn't have to have this conversation with Yasha, who had, after all, been so against her risking going out, she let herself in through the flat's front door.

But Yasha was in the lobby before she'd hung up her hat. She could see he'd been waiting up.

'You're all right then,' he said gruffly.

'I was fine,' she said calmly, unbuttoning her beaver collar.

He engulfed her. She smelled tweed and sawdust and soap as he pulled her close.

'I was worried,' he said.

Horace would never sound so awkward, she thought. But she knew too that this moment felt more deeply right, more natural, than anything about the enchanted evening she'd just spent in town, and that she wanted nothing more than to go on hearing Yasha's quick heartbeat through his jacket.

'I didn't want you out running risks with that bourgeois lecher slavering all over you and plying you with champagne.'

Why, he was jealous! She did raise her face now.

'You don't mean Horace, do you?' she whispered, looking Yasha full in the face, feeling suddenly, overwhelmingly happy. 'Because you've got it all wrong if you do. Heavens, he's just very kind – and interesting, too, a real man of the world. You should see the people he knows. And he wants me to play the violin in public.' She added, not without pride: 'He says I could make a career of it, even. He goes to concerts, he's seen everyone, and for some reason he thinks I'd be good enough.'

Yasha looked mulish. 'He was just softening you up. Waiting to pounce.'

She laughed, feeling more and more in control. 'I promise there was nothing. He didn't even kiss my hand.'

She could hear the Lemans talking in the yellow room, just a few feet away. So she smiled, waved as she retreated down the corridor, and shut her door.

She was still smiling to herself as she undressed.

Tomorrow I'll start to practise more seriously, she told herself. She wanted to believe this golden, carefree happiness was because of that applause in the Stray Dog.

But it was Yasha who was in her mind as she turned out the light.

Daylight the next morning – grey, with a threat of snow – dissipated Inna's excitement.

There was no one to tell about last night; at least, not at much length. Most of the family was going out.

Leman took himself off after breakfast on his weekly trip to the ministry, weighed down with forms and a bottle of cognac ('My little sacrifice to the bureaucrat-gods,' he said wryly as he left). Marcus was taking the children, who had a day off school, out to the Field of Mars to watch a parade. And Yasha wasn't there at all. Between squeals at Barbarian and Agrippina, Madame Leman said briefly, in a way that suggested this was no business of Inna's, that he'd had letters to deal with, and had come down early to ask for a few hours off.

Her ask-no-questions look reminded Inna, uncomfortably, that she didn't think Madame Leman would be at all happy to find out that Yasha and she—

'And when is Horace coming next?' Madame Leman added, with a friendlier smile.

'Oh,' faltered Inna, realizing she hadn't asked. 'He didn't say.'

Trying not to feel downcast, or lonely, or claustrophobic at the thought that even her stolen passport had expired and, unlike everyone else, she couldn't go out, Inna finished her tea and made her way down to the quiet workshop.

She cheered up, though, when she got to her bench. She already had a recognizable violin form under her hands. The rough wooden mould she'd chosen had the outline of a 1715

Stradivarius: delicate and narrow-waisted. She'd planed slim strips of maple down till they were scarcely thicker than paper, and bent them, over a hot iron, to the exact shape of the mould's side-curves. Then she'd glued the strips to six stout corner blocks of spruce. These would be the sides of her violin, one day – or, in luthier's talk, the ribs, because violins were little human bodies in the making.

She'd cut the back and the front of her instrument, next, from slim wooden wedges: hard, fierce, tiger-striped maple for the back, and soft, splintery, vibrating spruce for the front. Her baby: with outward curves for its shoulders and belly, and inward waist curves in the middle, and, at the top, the beginning of a rudimentary neck. These two violin shapes were still just a matching pair of silhouettes. The three-dimensional contouring they would acquire – the gentle lines, like the subtle swell of stomach and back, that would one day make these dumb pieces of wood sing – had yet to emerge. She didn't know how, yet. She didn't have to. She just had to trust.

A banging on the shop door stopped Inna moving – the front door, the one that opened on to the street. It wasn't just a single knock, but a volley of loud blows, then a great jangling at the bell. She looked up fearfully.

Because she was alone, the door was bolted, behind the lace curtain obscuring its glass panes. You couldn't see in through the display cases in the windows, either, any more than she could see anyone in the grey murk outside.

For a moment, she crouched, just listening, and then she clamped her fingers over her scarred palms. Why be frightened? she admonished herself. Defiantly, she went to the door, ignoring her racing heart, and turned the locks.

It was Yasha: red-cheeked, bright-eyed and excited. There were sleet flecks on his shoulders and scarf.

Relief filled her, but only briefly. He cried, far too loudly, 'Come quick!' He stared wildly past her, as if hoping for one of the men; then, seeing no one, he pulled her – just as she was, no coat or anything – out on to Moscow Prospekt.

Shivering, she resisted. 'What . . .?' she exclaimed. Icy water was seeping into her flimsy slippers. Had he lost his mind? 'It's freezing!'

'Just here,' he shouted, oblivious, and dragged her – out of the slanting wet wind, at least – into the alleyway at the side of the building. There, he stopped, at her side and a little behind, protecting her against the weather. She was aware of her resistance melting away as his arm came across her shoulder, and she leaned into him.

There was a man slumped in the alley. He was not a tramp, not in that great mass of snowy fur. There was no smell of drink or filth either. Just an expensive silver fox from neck to toes, and a tall tube of an astrakhan hat, above. He was clutching at a puffy, half-closed blue eye socket, with a deep cut below, and muttering 'Lord God in Heaven' as he rocked back and forth, oblivious to everything but his pain.

Shivering harder than ever, Inna looked more closely at the man. He seemed quite small under all those skins. And his chin was covered by the wrong kind of facial hair for the smart coat: the straggling beard of a peasant or a priest.

As if only just becoming aware of onlookers, the man looked up, held out bleeding, ungloved hands to them, and mumbled, 'Help me . . .'

But, instead of helping, Yasha was hissing something into her ear.

Impatiently she shook her head. The man had been mugged. They should be getting him inside. Then she stared. Why, she could swear . . . wasn't that . . .? It was the one eye that was, more or less, open, that did it: the pale-blue gaze that went right to your soul.

'Father Grigory,' she said, with sudden tenderness. She'd remembered him bigger and simpler. She took his freezing fingers in her hands. 'Is it you?'

'It's Rasputin,' she heard Yasha say in triumphant counterpoint. 'The Empress's—'

They turned towards each other, startled.

'The Empress's—?' she asked.

'You *know*—?' she heard, again at the same moment, like the other part in a mocking duet. There was no time for argument. Whoever he was, he needed help.

'Let's just get him into the warm,' Inna said.

As they heaved him through the door, the peasant kept tight hold of her hand. 'You're a good girl,' he muttered pitifully.

They sat him by the blessed warmth of the stove, in a chair. He slumped down, looking stunned, and shut his eyes. Yasha, looking almost as stunned, went at a run for Madame Leman and the medicine chest. Inna, meanwhile, got out of her soaked slippers, grabbed one of the dry coats hanging up and shrugged it on, rubbing life back into her own sleet-lashed hands. She could see she'd need all her strength for what was to come.

Trying to quell the quiet dread inside, she bent over Father Grigory, saying, 'Let's get you out of this coat.' She began unbuttoning it. He muttered something inaudible back, but to her private relief kept his eyes closed.

154

She could hear the whispers as the feet rushed downstairs – 'What do you mean, she *knows* him?' – or if she couldn't, she could imagine them.

But when Yasha and Madame Leman did join them, it wasn't in the recriminatory spirit she'd feared.

Yasha went straight to the peasant and dropped on one knee to survey the damage visible now his coat was open. Yasha took in the red-and-blue hands, the damaged face, the blood on the collar. 'Yes, you're in a bad way, brother, and no mistake,' he said straightforwardly. 'Let's see what we can do for you.'

His voice was rough but warm. He put an arm round the peasant's back and heaved the trembling older man up. With Madame Leman at the peasant's other side, and Inna hanging back, they struggled up the stairs and into the kitchen.

There Madame Leman told Inna to bring hot water, and briskly bathed his cuts, put liniment on his eye and bound his knuckles. Her hands were gentle, and when he tried to speak, Madame Leman cut him off, saying practically, 'Let's just get these dressings on, shall we?'

When he was all cleaned up, Madame Leman eased off his coat – it was far too hot for furs in the kitchen – and settled him in the wooden armchair by the stove with a blanket over his knees. She got down the bottle from the shelf, and poured him a big glass of vodka.

'Medicinal,' she said briskly, sitting on a stool and holding it out.

But he only held up a bandaged hand, and shook his head.

Madame Leman looked surprised at that. Impressed, too. Inna thought he might take food, so she cut a few pieces of bread, and some cheese and pickled cucumber, and knelt down before him with the plate. But again, he didn't touch it.

Yasha was the only one left standing. Inna was surprised, and impressed, by the softness of his voice as he said, 'That's better. Now, what happened?'

They found it hard to understand Father Grigory's story (Rasputin's story, Inna told herself as he spoke; but she couldn't altogether believe it). He stammered. He broke off and started over. He'd come to town for the Holy Synod meeting next week, they understood that much. And this morning his friend Iliodor had called by to take him to visit the bishop – a good man, Iliodor, an old friend, his dearest friend. (Inna noticed Yasha flinch at that, though she didn't know why.) And Bishop Hermogen, he was a good man too, Father Grigory muttered, with difficulty, a benefactor. He and Iliodor had taken a cab to the bishop's rooms at the Yaroslav Monastery. Father Grigory had been happy at the idea of a reunion in that lovely place. He'd spent some time at the monastery, once.

It was the next part they couldn't understand.

He'd got into the bishop's rooms, all right.

And he'd been beaten up.

But what he seemed to be saying was that he'd been beaten up *in* the bishop's rooms, by the bishop, who'd come at him with a big jewel-encrusted bronze cross and given him one across the head, and then another. And by Iliodor, the good man Yasha didn't seem to like the sound of – whoever he was. And by someone called Rodyonov, who'd threatened him with a sword (Sword? Inna wondered). And by another man called Mitry, who'd grabbed him by the neck.

'He says – Mitry, that is – he says . . . well, shouts, more like, howls, like a wolf, "Ah, ah, ah, you are a godless person, you have done wrong to many mamas! Sleeping with the Empress! Scoundrel! Antichrist!'"

At this proof that he really was Rasputin, *that* Rasputin, Inna heard Madame Leman's intake of breath.

As if he couldn't do anything else to give expression to his own utter confusion, Father Grigory began shaking his head, though very slowly and carefully, with a hand cupped protectively over his bandaged eye.

"'Antichrist . . .'" he repeated. 'Me? . . . Why?'

'But,' Madame Leman said, gently yet firmly, 'please tell me, what had you been talking about with them *before* all this began? What set it, them, off?'

Inna could see she was baffled too.

'Nothing.' Father Grigory's voice came weakly, but lucidly enough, from the swollen lips. The long, pure 'o' sounds of his slow Siberian speech seemed stronger than Inna remembered. 'That's the thing. In the cab, all we talked about, Iliodor and me, was the imperial palace at Livadia, the new one. I've just come back, you see. It was fresh in my mind. I was telling Iliodor how beautiful it was. Papa himself showed me around it, I said, and then we came out on to a porch, and gazed at the sky for a long time . . .'

Papa, thought Inna numbly; he means the Tsar. He was standing on a porch looking at the sky with the Tsar. It seemed so unreal that this ordinary man with his Siberian singsong could have been doing that. Yet he said it so innocently. He wasn't lying, or boasting. Had his talk just made the other man, the friend, Iliodor, jealous? But even if it had, what were all those others doing lying in wait too? A bishop?

'That's why I don't understand,' Father Grigory added

plaintively from inside his hands. 'There was nothing, nothing. And yet there they were. My friends. Men of God. So hateful, God forgive them. I ran away, because they wanted to kill me. I felt it. But not before they'd made me swear, on the Bible, with hands at my throat, to leave forever. Never to see Mama and Papa again . . .' His voice broke as he lowered his head on to his waiting arms.

Over his head, Inna could see Yasha and Madame Leman nodding at each other, as if they were beginning to understand. 'The churchmen going after the favourite,' Madame Leman mouthed at Yasha. 'There's no one left to keep them in order, now *he's* been bumped off.' She must mean the dead Prime Minister, Inna thought, after a moment. Yasha nodded. 'Everyone jostling for a place at the trough.'

Madame Leman turned back to Father Grigory, laying a soft hand on his forehead. 'Do be careful, don't dislodge the dressings, my dear.' Her voice was tenderer by the moment. She believed him, Inna could see. 'Are you sure you can't manage a taste of bread and cheese, or some tea, maybe?' Madame Leman patted his shoulder. 'With plenty of sugar. Sugar helps against shock.'

But Father Grigory didn't raise his head.

In the silence that followed, Inna stole a glance at Yasha and Madame Leman. She'd feared Yasha might look condemning. But, she thought, her heart swelling with gratitude, he just looked sympathetic. 'Well, don't you worry about it for now, brother,' he said softly. 'Let's get you on the divan, lie you down for a bit. I'll get you home later.'

Father Grigory started pushing himself up. 'Oh, no,' he said, very low and hasty. 'Though I'm grateful, I'm grateful.

But I can't be lying about all day. There are things I need to do, right away.'

He'll never get up, Inna thought, horrified at the pain in his face. But he did. And Yasha, looking appalled, helped him.

'You don't want to be going out just yet,' he remonstrated. 'You're in no state . . .'

But they could all see now that Father Grigory urgently wanted to get on.

So Yasha pulled him up by one arm, and Inna went to his other side and gave him her arm. As the three of them shuffled forward, step by painful step, back down the corridor towards the front door, she was aware of Madame Leman clumping breathlessly around the kitchen behind her, scrabbling for things on the shelves, and of Yasha's left arm, very close to her own right shoulder, and how warm and strong it was.

No one spoke until they got to the vestibule, and Madame Leman proffered the coat she'd put over her arm. She had something else, too.

'I thought . . .' Madame Leman said, hesitantly, and there was something Inna didn't understand in her voice, '. . . you might need some food. Please, take this.'

It was a wicker basket. She'd bundled into a napkin the bread and cheese Inna had cut. There was more food below – a layer of big, sharp-scented apples.

When Father Grigory bowed his head over the basket and lifted his free hand to make a clumsy sign of the cross she saw with astonishment that Madame Leman was acknowledging the devout old-fashioned gesture with a bob of her own. And that Yasha, too, had respectfully lowered his head.

Madame Leman had put the peasant's astrakhan hat down. Father Grigory reached a hand out to the table for it now.

It was lying on a box. One of Yasha's, Inna supposed.

As Father Grigory picked up his hat, his good eye fixed on the leaflet beneath it.

Peeping down sideways, following his eye, Inna could see just one sentence, in capitals: 'CRITICAL REMARKS ON THE NATIONAL QUESTION'.

But Father Grigory could clearly see more. Slowly, he mumbled, making out the words with difficulty, '". . . is an enemy of the proletariat, a supporter of the old and of the caste position of the Jews, an accomplice of the bourgeoisie . . ."'

Yasha went crimson.

'Ah,' Father Grigory said, much more clearly, 'revolutionary talk, I see.' He shook his head. 'The kind of dangerous nonsense that's destroying the land. You don't want filthy thoughts like that in your home.'

Inna saw Yasha's mouth open.

'I tell you what, brother,' Yasha started, heatedly. 'It's not the socialists destroying things in this country. It's filthy anti-Semites like your so-called friend Iliodor: filling people's minds with hate. Not to mention all those rich idiots at the court, doing bugger-all to look after the poor they say it's their God-given duty to rule.'

Yasha was red-faced and furious, but, to Inna's astonishment, the peasant didn't look angry, just slightly surprised. And he was nodding.

It was all too much for Madame Leman. 'A cab, Father, you'll need a cab.' She rushed him out on to the landing. Like

Inna, earlier, she was still in her indoor clothes and slippers. Her passport was lying forgotten on the table.

Yasha, meanwhile, grabbed the box, and fled back into the apartment.

When she and the peasant reached the half-landing, and turned, Madame Leman looked back up. She made a sympathetic face. But, 'He's just a bit upset,' she said to Inna. 'He's had a letter from his parents. He'll be all right.'

But Inna had seen Yasha's expression.

She stepped back inside, among the coats and hats and boots of the vestibule, wondering whether she dared go to him.

She didn't need to. As soon as the outside door banged shut down below, Yasha emerged again. His coat was buttoned up; hat on. The leaflet box was in his hand as he barged past her.

'Where are you going?' she called.

He didn't reply. She heard footsteps rushing down the stairs.

Moments later, Inna was also in her coat and boots and, by the time the outside door slammed again, she was slipping out of the flat after him, with Madame Leman's passport in her pocket.

CHAPTER TWELVE

Yasha strode out of the city across first one bridge (over which, Inna saw, he hurled the box he'd been carrying), then another, and on into a shadowy unknown of deserted island streets running between looming factories, foul with the muddy leavings of the afternoon's sleet. He was going so fast that Inna was frightened of losing him and being left alone in the thickening moon-shadows. Half-panicked, she was out of breath as she trotted, and sometimes ran, to keep him in sight.

It was already almost night-time by the time he turned into an alleyway, where Inna saw a shadowy gaggle of poor folk hanging around the doorway of a hulking prison-like building.

By the time she finally came close enough to cry breathlessly out to him, 'Slow down, can't you?' she was red-faced and wishing she hadn't come.

But as soon as he turned and she saw his delight; when he put big, warm hands on her shoulders and muttered, 'What the Hell are you doing here? No papers or anything. Alone.

Insane . . .' with a mixture of pride and solicitousness, she suddenly didn't regret a thing.

'I wanted to see you were all right,' she whispered. 'You looked . . .'

'I needed a walk,' he replied, suddenly cagey. But he kept his hands where they were. 'I had things on my mind.'

He didn't mention Father Grigory. She thought, Well, I won't ask about the letter, either; or his parents. Not yet.

'I have a friend here,' he added after a moment's thought. She glanced doubtfully at the ragged shadows moving behind him. Was Yasha really . . . *friends* . . . with these people? She straightened her back. She didn't want him to sense her fear. 'They're going into the poorhouse,' he explained, which didn't exactly answer her question, but she nodded anyway.

'They'll open the doors in a minute,' he added. 'For the night.'

He'd barely finished speaking when a door cut into the big gates swung wide to let in the night's newcomers. There was a creak like a cry of distress and a man stepped out: the man in charge, Inna could see. His fat was disintegrating in alcohol, falling off the bones in sagging pouches. His lantern cast shadows into the crevasses of his cheeks.

Peeping out from under Yasha's arm, Inna was transfixed by the crowd shuffling towards the light. The man in charge was taking the beggars' kopeks silently, but he looked askance at Inna.

'No women, mate, you know that,' he said. 'Round the back for her.' But Yasha muttered in his ear. A coin changed hands. They were in.

The consumptive at the door coughed blood on the flagstones as they passed. He wouldn't last much longer,

Inna knew, and she was filled with a desperate longing to do something for him. But Yasha was already pulling out another coin. 'Here, brother. Get yourself some food,' he said.

They stopped in the echoing hall. Yasha was searching for someone in the slow-moving crowd.

His friend wasn't one of these victims, then.

'Trust Kremer to find a cosy berth,' Yasha muttered, pulling Inna forward again. He must have seen his man. It took Inna a moment more to identify him. A short, squat, gingery young man in a relatively respectable, if ragged, coat was standing in the doorman's office, just down the hall. There was a stove and a lamp in there, and he was nursing a glass of steaming tea. His face lit up at the sight of Yasha. But he started looking suspicious as soon as he saw her.

'We'll only be a minute,' Yasha said to Inna. 'I've got a message for him, that's all.'

Still holding on to Inna, Yasha put his free right arm around Kremer, pulling them all into an unlikely, unwelcome near-embrace. Hastily, both Inna and Kremer shuffled away from each other. Yasha looked from one to the other, then shrugged – with a slight, surprising twitch of the lips – and let go of Kremer.

Kremer immediately put an expectant hand out to his friend, and Yasha put a banknote into it. Ten roubles, Inna saw: a good whack for a journeyman luthier.

Kremer pocketed it and looked expectantly at his friend. Yasha muttered into his ear.

'It won't be ready till Monday,' Inna made out. When Kremer's face fell, Yasha just looked impatient. 'Look, I'll bring it, don't worry. But you'll just have to hang on till I do.'

Inna turned her head away and went back to gazing at the dispirited shadow-mob still streaming in. Her heart swelled at the misery of it as she remembered how she'd sneered at some story Yasha had told, in the workshop, about the beggar-women from the starving villages. If only she'd seen this first.

And then, unexpectedly, a new sight met her eyes: one so strange that it drove every other thought from her mind. Near the back of the crowd trudging through the door were three tall, young, handsome beggars. They were dressed in ragged britches, true, but their limbs were as slender and well muscled as if they'd been raised on a refined diet of meat and greenhouse fruit and fine wine. Their heads were not bowed like the others, either; instead their eyes darted about, half fearfully, half pleasurably, as they took in the other poor souls' appearance. They were rich boys, surely? They didn't even look drunk.

She touched Yasha's arm, but he was still whispering furtively with Kremer. '. . . not my fault you're in this mess . . .' she heard. By the time he turned, and said briskly to her, 'Right, let's go,' the three young men had vanished into the murk of the sleeping hall.

There were so many questions Inna wanted to ask Yasha. But what she was most aware of as they came out of the alley and began walking back through the black and silent streets leading to the Samson Bridge was the way she'd started leaning into his side. How self-assured he'd been with everyone. How good he was with the needy, and how well he'd handled everyone today, Father Grigory – Rasputin – included.

'Kremer's not a pauper, but the police are after him.

165

He's got to get out of town. I'm getting him travel papers, but they're not ready yet. I told him to doss down at the poorhouse while he waited. They like me there. I usually give them a bit of my pay, so they ask no questions,' he explained, and she heard confidence in his voice. 'It's a good place to lie low. No one asks for passports and there are no name checks. It only costs a few kopeks a night, too.' He laughed. 'It's not luxury accommodation, true. He's not happy about it, but it's his own silly fault he's there.'

I had no idea he knew all this, she thought in a daze.

'Why are the police after Kremer?' she asked, respectfully.

He didn't answer for a minute. 'He got himself mixed up with some Socialist Revolutionaries, the bloody idiot. You know – the bombers,' he replied eventually.

Perhaps he heard her intake of breath. '*I* don't have any truck with them. No one in their right mind does,' he went on angrily. 'No bloody judgement, that's his problem. He was just letting them keep their buckets in his cellar, but he didn't count on the janitor getting nosy and blowing himself up. There's nothing against him, but he was the only Jew in the building. Of course they came after him.'

Inna had no idea what to say to this. So I was right not to like Kremer, she thought. He'd killed some innocent old man with a tub of explosive? Well, he *should* be arrested, shouldn't he? Kremer's crime only confirmed all the worst things she'd ever thought about politics, not just about the terrorists on its fringes: it was all violence, really, all threat, wasn't it?

Yasha was continuing, possibly aware of her unease. 'I owe Kremer a debt, you see. He has an uncle . . .' and a whole torrent of stories about the Kremers poured out: about old Kremer's strength, and the years he'd suffered in Siberia for what he believed. How different he was from Yasha's father, who couldn't even protect his ten-year-old from a gang of thugs. How important it had become to Yasha to stand up firmly for what he believed – to be brave, like old Kremer, who'd had the defiant word 'TOMORROW' tattooed on his arm on his first day behind bars.

Yes, Inna thought, remembering Yasha's parents' fear while she'd been living with them, and the hasty way they'd left. Realizing, only now, that it had been a betrayal to leave a schoolgirl alone in a town so full of danger. 'Yes,' she said. 'I can imagine that; they didn't look out for me much, either.'

His hand tightened on her shoulder, and then slipped down around her waist.

'I got word from them today. They're in Haifa. They got cleaned out on the boat, and were too broke to go on to Jerusalem. Mama's found work scrubbing floors, and they have a room. Papa's not well. I wired them some money. But it makes you wonder where all their Russian conformity got them in the end: a bedsit and a cleaning job in an Ottoman port.'

'I see why you'd want to stand up and be counted, too,' she said softly, and she could understand, now she'd looked at some of those faces, how much there was to fight for. 'But all those poor men,' she went on breathlessly. 'Why does no one help them more? And how did they get like that?'

'They're victims of the factories, most of them,' Yasha said with bitter compassion. 'They lose a limb, and they're no good for a sixteen-hour shift any more. So that's the whole family, out on the street. Goners.'

Inna glanced up at him. His profile was stern.

'And no one gives a damn. Nevsky is so close, stuffed

with plutocrats' wives buying lobster, but they might as well be on the moon. There's no one much helping. Just the factory committees, and a few socialists with hearts but no money. We give all we can, but it's nothing compared with the need.

'It impressed the Hell out of me, suddenly seeing you out there,' Yasha added gruffly. His voice vibrated through her ribcage. 'Leman's always talking about the islands, but he's not actually brave enough to come.'

She took her hand out of her pocket and touched his hand, which was resting just above her hipbone. His skin was freezing, so she drew it into the warmth of her pocket, closing her fingers around it.

She could feel the length and strength of his arm, a stripe of heat across her back, and was fully aware of her gesture as an invitation.

'The morning,' she heard him say. 'In your room. I never should have – I mean, we were only seconds away from Madame L. coming in.'

He was looking at her, not quite meeting her eye. Joyously, she saw in that snatched look that he was memorizing her face, the line of brow and cheekbone, the cast of eye and lip, just as she so often did, stealing her glimpses of him.

'I didn't mind you being there,' she whispered, smiling shyly, and when they walked on again through the factory yards, she noticed with relief that Yasha's urgent pace was slowing to a relaxed saunter.

Until, suddenly, he stopped. A moment later, Inna felt it too: a prickle of the skin. Her heart started thumping as he turned his head, keeping his body still, scenting danger.

He'd heard something. Behind.

'Footsteps,' he breathed.

He pushed her into a black alley between two factory yards. They crouched behind crates and watched as the men approached.

Knives? Sticks? Inna felt sick with helplessness. Yasha was nearer the street, to shield her.

The moon came out as they appeared. As they walked by – not even looking into the alley – she could see them clearly. No weapons, no bottles. Three ragged youths sauntering by, laughing. It was the boys from the poorhouse, Inna saw, with a rush of relief.

She could hear their loud, confident voices, swearing prettily in the playful half-French of the aristocracy. 'God . . . absolutely *freezing* . . .' one said, hugging himself with limber arms, rubbing his hands fast against his skin. '*Merde* . . .' Another boy, a dark one, looking disgusted, was shaking his head and frenziedly scratching. 'I don't care,' he answered, petulantly. 'I'd rather be cold now than itching all night.'

His face was turned towards them in the moonlight. He was unusually dark for a Russian, Inna saw. Above his torn britches and wadded workman's jacket, he had the delicate southern cheekbones of a Tatar, with his olive skin and almond-shaped eyes. His face was lovely enough for a girl.

I know that face, she thought.

It was the prince. Horace's friend. Felix.

Shakily, Yasha pulled her out. 'Who the Hell . . .?' he was muttering. 'Who were they?' He looked at her, baffled. 'Didn't they sound . . .?'

She nodded, but kept her eyes on her hands. Best not to reveal she'd seen the dark one before, she thought. Best not to say where, either. It would only confirm, in his mind, that she'd been an idiot to go visiting Father Grigory: that mixing with him, and even with Horace (who of course would have no idea that his friend went out on dubious mock-the-poor missions like this, late at night), had been the worst kind of naïveté.

'Mmm,' she murmured, wondering, suddenly, if she *had* been naïve, 'like tourists in the underworld.'

He looked surprised for a moment, and then snorted out his held breath with laughter, or relief; she couldn't tell which. 'Come on,' he said, holding out his arm to her. 'They gave me the creeps. Let's get out of here too.'

They tramped on, faster, through the grimy black of the Petersburg Side, over Samson Bridge, into the equally miserable Vyborg Side and down Artillery Embankment. At least, she thought, breathless again, his arm was back around her.

It was only when they got to the stately Alexander Bridge and saw, over the water, the city of the novels – the longed-for iron lacework of palace gates guarded, on the ground, by shivering men in gold braid, and, on the rooftops, by eyeless statues – that they breathed easy. A car roared away, somewhere nearby.

The sky was heavy, the wind sharp again. But at least there were no policemen: no one at all, save the occasional drunk tottering home and once, in the distance, a noisy party of smart young men in evening clothes, singing. They fell silent, down Liteiny, each one listening to the rhythm of the other's breath and footfalls. Both tired.

'I've been wondering' – he spoke quietly – 'why am I telling people, Jews, to stay in Russia and demand their rights, when my own parents . . .?'

She could see the pain in his face as he looked at the square, at the litter twirling and flapping in the salty wind.

He brought his other arm around her.

She swung round, unresisting, aware of many things besides the tumult of blood, the giddy spin of it all: the snowflake melting on his eyelashes, their buttons clashing, heat . . .

He was trembling again, she thought tenderly.

'Your hair smells of flowers,' he whispered, before his lips found hers.

Inside, there were no sounds. The family was in bed. The lights were off.

Except in the kitchen where, in a pool of warm yellow light, Leman was half-asleep by the stove. He rubbed his eyes and stood up as Inna and Yasha sprang guiltily apart. He's been worried, she realized, with a pang; not about Yasha, but because he didn't know where I'd gone. Surprise and delight mixed with her contrition.

'Ah,' he said, without the anger she thought she deserved. 'Here you are.'

Inna was hoping desperately he didn't realize the enormity of her offence – not only sneaking out with Yasha till nearly dawn, but also 'borrowing' his wife's papers. Her face burned.

'We thought you'd be back in time for midnight tea,' Leman said, in a voice carefully bleached of disapproval. 'Horace came. He left you a note. I forced the children to leave you some cake. The tea will be cold, though. Forgive me if I don't sit up with you.'

Inna wasn't hungry, but it gave her shamed eyes

171

somewhere to turn. The apple *sharlottka* was covered with a napkin, against which an envelope had been propped up.

Trying not to compound the offence she'd already given, she hesitated before picking it up. Cautiously, she asked: 'What's this?'

Leman didn't look round. 'What we were celebrating,' he said as he left. 'Your temporary residence permit.'

CHAPTER THIRTEEN

Inna woke in a tangle of limbs to the slamming of grey wind and sleet against the window, to the warm stillness of a bed containing their two bodies.

Yasha was asleep. Looking at his peaceful face made her heart swell. She remembered how, last night, they'd lingered at the doorway, clung together, full of the glorious unknown, before . . . *here*; how he'd laughed a little as they shifted towards, then away again from his room; how he'd whispered, 'I thought you were beautiful right from that first moment, when I opened the front door, and there you were.'

She ran her hands down his chest, marvelling at the newness of everything she now knew, at the happiness suffusing her, aware of the stir of his flesh.

'Don't,' he whispered sleepily, taking her hand in his.

She kissed his ear. 'Why?' she breathed.

'Because . . .' he said, turning his head, opening his long dark eyes. Kissing her nose. 'Because it should be you who goes downstairs first.'

She felt sudden heat on her cheeks and not unpleasurable coyness as the world beyond this nest of bedding came rushing back. Of course. Downstairs: the children; Madame Leman, perhaps already boiling up tea and making batter. She should get away from up here before Marcus got up, next door, in her old room. They didn't need to know about this; not yet.

'Your papers,' Yasha prompted. How deep and relaxed his voice was. 'You don't want to look ungrateful.'

Of course! The papers! She scrambled up, hastily buttoning her crumpled blouse. Why, she hadn't even opened the envelope – it would still be lying where she'd dropped it on the kitchen table, untouched.

Mercifully the kitchen was still empty when she got downstairs.

Inna stuffed the envelope hastily into her waistband while she whisked back into her new room. She changed her shirt and linen, went into the kitchen again, lit the samovar and the stove and mixed *blini* batter – a penance; something Madame Leman would appreciate – before she allowed herself to examine it.

Not bothering with Horace's note on the outside, she tore open the envelope and flicked down to the date on the document inside. Three months: she was here till the end of the year!

'Your eyes are popping right out of your head, did you know?' said a loud treble voice. She heard a giggle behind her and turned round.

Two blond heads were in the doorway: Barbarian and Agrippina, in nightgowns, staring and prodding each other and wriggling.

Behind them, bustling footsteps could be heard in the corridor. It was Madame Leman, who followed the children into the kitchen. She didn't, to Inna's relief, look angry, just relieved to see her.

'Wherever did you two get to last night?' she asked.

'You see, I was worried about Yasha,' Inna said to placate her. 'He rushed out in such a rage, right after you. I wanted to calm him down, but he was going so fast I couldn't catch up. And then I got lost, and he went on and on for miles – all the way to the islands . . .'

She stopped, thinking she was babbling, and guiltily saying far too much.

'The islands!' Barbarian cried rapturously. 'Really?' His eyes were round.

'And did they all have green faces and creep through keyholes out there?' Agrippina asked slyly. Inna laughed and shook her head. 'Or whisper socialism in your ear?' Agrippina dropped her own piercing voice to a mocking whisper and quoted her father quoting whatever novel it was he was always quoting.

Still grinning, Inna nodded: Yes, a bit.

'Well, you must be careful, dear,' Madame Leman said, stirring the batter and checking for lumps. 'We were worried for *you*. You didn't even have papers.'

Inna looked down. She felt obscurely pleased at the idea Madame Leman had been worried for her. 'Yes,' she said as Madame Leman got out the frying pan and put it on the stove. 'I'm sorry.'

She still had the document in her hand, and started to say, 'But now I do,' intending to thank Madame Leman, but she didn't get a chance, because the children swept noisily on, in chorus, 'And is it true that you had the Empress's holy man to tea?' (Agrippina); 'Putnik, Rasputnik?' (Barbarian); 'Mama said he'd been hit on the head by a bishop?' (Agrippina).

Head bowed, feeling her cheeks redden, Inna nodded again: Sort of.

'It's so unfair. Everything interesting always happens while we're out,' Agrippina said, exchanging envious glances with her brother.

There was a hiss as the first spoonful of batter went into the pan.

'Horace thought it was funny that you didn't even realize, the other day,' Madame Leman said, 'that it was Rasputin you were visiting.' Her voice was unemotional. She was concentrating on her *blin*, which went wrong, as they always do, first time. With pink cheeks, she scraped it out of the pan.

'Mam's embarrassed to admit it, but she rather liked him,' Agrippina informed Inna. 'Rasputny.'

Madame Leman smiled faintly at the pan. A pin tinkled out of her hair. 'Horace thinks he's got something, too,' she admitted.

The arrival of Leman and a very silent Yasha, with the morning papers and some fresh bread, not only spared Madame Leman's blushes, but also gave Inna a chance to try and make the pretty thank-you speech she'd been failing to start on with Madame Leman.

Without looking at her, Yasha sat down at the kitchen table and opened the paper. Inna was laughing inside at their secret, as he must be. She couldn't look at him, either.

'Oh, don't thank me,' Leman said breezily before she'd got more than a few words out.

She stopped, sensing Yasha's alertness behind the *Stock Exchange Gazette*.

'Thank Horace,' Leman went on, twinkling at her. 'It was all his idea.'

Yasha lowered his paper as Madame Leman turned to smile at her from the other side of the kitchen. The children were giggling.

Uncertainly she looked down at the residence permit, still in her hand. What could it possibly have to do with Horace? Surely she'd seen the Lemans' address written down?

But as soon as she looked further down the page she saw that, although she lived here, she worked, according to the document, as a decorative box-maker for Fabergé.

'He said that was the way he got his own papers sorted. After months of trouble from the ministry, he just got a letter from Fabergé,' Leman was explaining, 'which smoothed everything out at once. It's sometimes easier for foreign firms, he said: the ministry men are scared to stick their noses in. He said it was worth trying with you, too – as soon as he heard about your troubles. He sent me round the Fabergé standard letter the very next morning, and very impressive it was, too: "Give this honoured craftsman your best help on his/her visit to St Petersburg," with red stamps, the lot. And see? It worked like a charm.'

Inna's eyes were as wide as Barbarian's had been earlier.

'Why,' she murmured, so overwhelmed with gratitude towards the Englishman that she thought she might cry. 'How terribly kind of him . . .'

'It's only temporary,' Leman said. 'But it gives you a breather.'

'He's a very good man,' Madame Leman agreed,

lifting out half a dozen *blini* from the pan. 'And now, shall we eat?'

A few minutes later, Yasha put down the paper he'd been hiding behind. 'The newspapers don't think your Rasputin is a very good man,' he said, scowling at Inna.

Looking over his shoulder, she saw that article after article featured the attack on Rasputin – and not just in that paper but in the ones the Lemans were reading, too. There was no sympathy for him, or anger against the violent bishop, for the churchmen (or someone) had struck again with an anonymous pamphlet that offered 'proof' Rasputin was the Empress's lover. Every article was dripping with poisonous malice, or so it seemed to Inna.

There were enough facts, just, to get the viciousness started. Rasputin was reported to have run straight from the bishop's palace to the Central Post Office (though no one knew he had dropped off at the Lemans' on the way) and telegraphed the Tsarina to denounce his attackers.

But it was the other stuff they were printing that defied belief. Yesterday's Duma budget debate had been upstaged by the roughly copied anonymous pamphlet that started circulating in the streets before nightfall, containing what purported to be letters to Rasputin from female members of the imperial family. The lines the papers had quoted, with most evil-minded pleasure, were from the Empress. 'I wish only one thing: to fall asleep forever on your shoulders, in your embrace . . . Will you soon be back by my side? Come back soon. I am in torment without you.'

Inna's heart sank. Surely the letter was a forgery? Then again, any of the acolytes she'd met might easily write to Father Grigory in that hysterical vein. They'd think it displayed their exemplary spirituality. And why would the Empress be any different? She was an acolyte, too. But Inna could also see why the papers would prefer to call it a 'love letter', and link it to his enemies' accusations that he had physically seduced the Tsarina's untouchable imperial person.

The talk was that his holy-man rival, Iliodor, had written the pamphlet, and tried to blackmail the imperial family through the Empress's lady-in-waiting, Anya Vryubova; but she'd walked away. So he'd passed it out among the buzzing parliamentarians in revenge.

There was another rumour that the pamphlet had got out after being given for safe keeping to the fashionable Tibetan healer, Pyotr Badmayev, whose usual job was supplying drugs to the upper classes, but who hadn't been able to resist a little extra mischief on the side.

And there was more, much more. So much more that it made Inna almost weep with the sheer nastiness of it. A denunciation of Father Grigory, signed by a man called Novosyolov, asked the Synod how long they were going to tolerate 'that sex maniac, Whipper and charlatan, and the criminal comedy that has victimized many whose letters were in his hands'. Articles headlined 'Rasputin and Mystical Debauchery'. A malicious confection called 'The Confession of N' featuring a lady seduced by a lecherous religious peasant. And everywhere vicious cartoons of Rasputin, gloating or drinking or, in one, playing the pipes while the cuckold Tsar squatted obediently and kicked out his legs, Cossack fashion, dancing to the peasant's tune.

'I'm going to him,' Inna said. She couldn't get the picture of Father Grigory, *her* Father Grigory, bruised and defenceless at this table, out of her head. The Lemans had all been murmuring what a shame it was, but no one was actually suggesting action. And she was burning with indignation. 'I want to show my support.'

'But you can't,' Madame Leman said quickly.

'Why?' Inna asked, all ready to wave her passport.

'Didn't you see Horace's note?' Leman said, rather chidingly.

Slowly she reached for the envelope, still lying on the table among the newspapers.

'He's coming by to take you out to lunch,' Madame Leman said, more gently. 'To celebrate.'

Inna bowed her head over the spiky writing with all the hard and soft signs of the Russian alphabet charmingly muddled. Of course, she owed Horace. That should come first. She could go to Rasputin later: after work, maybe, or tomorrow.

A few hours later, Inna was sitting opposite Horace in the Astoria restaurant. Looking around, she thought she'd never seen so much starched, folded, draped and pleated white linen. It hung on tables and on the haughty waiters' arms and rustled solemnly in her lap. Or cut glass, come to that. On the table in front of her, wine glasses and champagne glasses and water glasses sparkled among the flash of jugs and the glitter of chandeliers above.

There was ruched muslin at the tall windows, and heavy gold silk, too. The great array of cutlery was polished bright silver. And there were diamonds at every female throat.

The champagne was French, like the murmur of conversation all around.

'Ah, the widow; I love the widow,' Horace was saying, smiling to himself as the waiter poured. And now there were bubbles in her glass as well as stars etched on its edges.

She would watch carefully when the soup came, when the tiny birds in their pastry cases came, and when the flambéed pancakes came too, to see which eating iron Horace picked up.

She was glad Madame Leman had lent her that crisp pin-tucked blouse, because everyone at the tables around them was dressed in uniform, or in silks and chiffons. There was gold braid everywhere, and medals winked in the daytime candlelight. The ladies seemed indescribably beautiful, and most had tiny dogs on their laps.

Horace lifted his champagne glass. Looking very kindly at her, he said: 'To your future success, my dear.'

With beating heart, she lifted hers too, and sipped.

She quickly forgot her nerves, and soon they were talking animatedly about the Stray Dog evening, and Bryusov's demonic philandering, and what Anya Akhmatova had been like when she was Gorenko the schoolgirl; about Monsieur Fabergé's caustic tongue; and about Horace's childhood in India.

When the cheese came, she even felt confident enough to broach the Rasputin scandal in the newspapers. 'The Lemans said he'd been to you, right after the fight?' Horace replied, sounding intrigued. He laughed at the idea that Madame Leman, and possibly Yasha too, had fallen at least partly under Rasputin's spell. 'It's a dreadful mess, all of it. I feel for him, poor fellow.'

She wanted him to come with her and visit Father Grigory

after they'd eaten. But he said, 'I think we won't; I hear the Tsar's personally ordered police put at his door, for his own protection; and he'll have the fools all mooning about, anyway. He doesn't need your support. And your papers are too temporary to bear much examination. You have too much at stake, and too much to do, I think.' It made her feel so considered that she acquiesced.

'What do you mean, I have too much to do?' she asked, leaning forward.

'Well,' Horace went on, and he was twinkling now, just as Leman had been earlier, 'I have a suggestion, you see, and if you like the idea I imagine you'll be pretty busy in the next few days . . .'

Horace's plan, explained over tiny cups of sweet Turkish coffee, was this: that Inna should use the three months' space the temporary passport had won her to start violin lessons with Leopold Auer, the greatest master of the instrument that the city could offer.

'You know of him, of course?' Horace asked. 'Oh, my dear girl . . . He's the first violinist to the orchestra of the St Petersburg Imperial Theatres: the Ballet and the Opera, Peterhof, the Hermitage. He's the man all the composers write the violin solos especially for: Pugni, Minkus, Drigo, Tchaikovsky, Glazunov.'

Nodding, and pleased that her ignorance hadn't condemned her in Horace's eyes, and that he was explaining everything so kindly, she eventually broke through his stream of praise and asked, 'But surely such a great man would have no time for teaching? Let alone teaching *me*?'

Horace's voice was full of excitement. 'Ah, but he's one of the great teachers, too. That's why Anton Rubinstein wanted him here, originally – to teach at the Conservatoire, back when Rubinstein was still setting the Conservatoire up.'

The great thing about Auer, Horace said, was that he took students from everywhere: there was Mischa Elman, a poor klezmer's son from somewhere down south, now off touring America and world famous; Efrem Zimbalist, the child of a minor conductor from Rostov-on-Don, who'd started with Auer at twelve and was now acclaimed in Berlin and London and Boston; and his current star, Jascha Heifetz, the twelve-year-old who'd done that outdoor concert here last summer that had made the whole city go crazy for the violin.

Horace grinned. The maestro could be severe, he said. A rib-prodder, he was liable to snarl in the middle of the lesson, 'Give it a bit more blood, can't you? More blood!' and he'd been known to eject pupils physically, throwing their music out into the corridor after them if he thought their playing too anaemic.

But Auer loved his better pupils like his children. He helped them get scholarships, patrons and better instruments. Horace looked intently at Inna.

'And, of course, he uses his influence to get residence for his Jewish pupils . . .'

Her mouth opened.

'Permanent residence permits,' he stressed.

'Is Auer a German name?' Inna asked. But even as she said it, it seemed a foolish question. Heifetz, Elman, Zimbalist. 'Or a Jewish one?'

'Well, it's one of those names you can never quite tell with,' Horace replied, looking amused. 'Like yours.' He smiled. 'And mine.'

Her eyes opened wider. But he only shrugged, as if having Jewish blood was of no importance to an Englishman; which, she reflected, perhaps it wasn't.

Still, there was a new softness inside her as he went on.

'Auer took over at the Conservatoire from Wieniawski, at a time when ladies like the dear creatures here' – Horace waved his hand at the neighbouring tables – 'were all still startled at the very idea that you could use the uncultured Russian language, not civilized German or French, for teaching music. "Teach music in Russian – why, what an *original* idea!"' he mimicked.

'It was the notion of Russians thinking about music that shocked the élite here; not Jews. It's really only secret policemen and peasants down south who are so frantic about the Jews, don't you think? No one in St Petersburg cared where the musicians came from. I suppose they thought, what did it matter, if you could play the piano as wonderfully as Rubinstein did?'

He leaned closer still. So did Inna. Their faces were nearly touching.

'Do you know what Rubinstein wrote, about his origins?' he murmured.

She shook her head.

'"Russians call me German, Germans call me Russian, Jews call me a Christian, Christians a Jew. Pianists call me a composer. Composers call me a pianist. The classicists think me a Futurist, and the Futurists call me a reactionary. My conclusion is that I am neither fish nor fowl – a pitiful individual."'

They both laughed.

'So we're agreed,' Horace said briskly, handing her a

bubble-like glass of Armenian cognac. 'Auer's class would be a good club for you to belong to.'

'But how would I ever meet him?' she whispered, sipping.

When she looked up, pink-faced, she could see the delight in his eyes.

'Oh, he's a friend of Repin's, too,' Horace said airily, yet she could see what an effort it was costing him to sound casual. He waved at a waiter for the bill. 'So Leman and I both know him a little. And Leman's written to him, this morning, asking him to dinner. You'll most likely meet him in the next week or two.'

Afterwards, while they were talking about what she might play, Horace took her for a saunter around St Isaac's Square. They walked down to the gardens by the grey river to gaze at the tiny golden ship on top of the Admiralty spire ('Like an English country church, only more beautiful,' he murmured). Then he said that, although he wasn't working today, he had to pick something up from the shop.

'Oh,' Inna said, smiling into the fur of her collar, warm from the cognac and the plan. She felt so safe with him, so treasured. 'I'd love to see Fabergé's.'

He bowed. She could see the pleasure in his eyes.

Fabergé's was round the corner, on Great Sea Street: a square stone shop front with carriages stopping outside to deposit silk-and-fur ladies with their uniformed gentlemen.

A uniformed doorman bowed as he ushered them through into the shop itself. Inside, gloriously dressed customers lingered over great glass-fronted cabinets in the shop, or talked to men in dark suits in French.

Inna wanted to stop and stare at them too, but Horace

whisked her on, with the dignified adult courtesy that slightly overawed her, through a door to a much bigger room behind, where the craftsmen, gentlemen from Switzerland and France and England, in neat dark suits, sat at individual desks, looking through magnifying glasses at the unbelievably small and intricate *objets* they were working on. All round, smooth brass measuring tools gleamed.

He stopped at an empty polished mahogany desk and opened a drawer in it. Inside, she glimpsed tiny paintbrushes and small jars, arranged very neatly.

'Aha,' he muttered, and picked something small out. 'Here we are.'

He put the little bag he'd found in his pocket, glanced at Inna, and then hesitated.

But Inna couldn't restrain herself. She so wanted to see it all. 'May we take another look at the shop?'

Smiling, Horace took her arm and led her back into the front of the shop.

The dark carpet on which the clientèle walked (in the indoor shoes they'd never had to take off, because they travelled everywhere by carriage) was so thick and soft you couldn't hear footsteps.

An imperious barrel of an old lady caught her eye. She'd got out of a carriage directly in front of them as they came in, Inna remembered. Now she was standing in the middle of the shop floor, eyeing the various jewellers as if picking her victim.

'Ah, Monsieur Fabergé,' she said suddenly in a loud, deep voice, plucking at his neat, navy lapel, not bothering with greetings. 'I haven't come to buy, I just have a question. Have you got any ideas yet for the design of next year's Easter eggs?'

'Watch this,' she heard. Horace, ever diplomatic, had bent so his whisper would reach no further than her ear.

Monsieur Fabergé – slim, neat, thoughtful, fine-featured, bald on top, but with a fine grey beard above his striped shirt, dark waistcoat, and perfectly knotted sober tie – paused, clearly considering his options. He couldn't get away from her as she had his jacket between finger and thumb. He scratched his pepper-and-salt beard and pushed up his spectacles.

'Well, dear lady,' he said solemnly. 'It's a secret, but I know if I tell *you* that it will go no further. This year, we're working on *square* eggs.'

The lady blinked as she assimilated his words, and let go. Bowing, Fabergé moved on. 'You're the soul of discretion, I know . . .' Inna heard him saying. 'Promise me, now . . .'

Not a muscle of Monsieur Fabergé's face had betrayed him. But Horace was smiling broadly, and Inna had to look down at the dark carpet so no one would see she was laughing too.

'That will be all round town in an hour,' Horace breathed. 'Just wait and see.' But she already could, because, as the doorman helped the old lady back into her coat, she was still muttering, 'Square eggs! Well, I never!'

Inna could have stayed for hours longer. But soon the door-man was back at their side, saying the cab Horace had asked for was waiting. Once inside, on its scuffed leather seats, watching the streets move by, and the officers in their braid turn back into salesmen and hawkers, a silence fell between them.

Inna felt, a little awkwardly, that the silence might be

her fault. Perhaps she'd committed some error of taste or judgement that, in her inexperience, she wasn't even aware of. Horace had an important job, after all. She might have taken up too much of his time. Perhaps he hadn't liked it that she'd wanted to gawp at the grand customers. Or perhaps he'd wanted her to look at his work (but his desk had been so very bare?). Now he looked a little distracted, as if he might be worried about getting back to work. He was sitting very straight on his side of the banquette.

How foolish Yasha had been to think Horace might have taken advantage, Inna thought suddenly, turning towards him, trying to get him talking again.

'I don't know how to thank you,' she said. 'You've been so kind.'

But she felt his answering nod had embarrassment in it, so she stopped and looked out of the window, uncertain how to proceed.

It wasn't until she was getting down from the cab that Horace, looking startled, clapped his hand to his pocket and started digging about inside it.

She turned from the street to wave goodbye to him, and smile, hoping she hadn't bored him; hoping he would kiss her hand, at least.

But instead he pressed a little package into her hand.

'It's to bring you luck,' he said quickly, not quite meeting her eyes; then he nodded the driver on before she could respond.

The cab was already creaking off across the Hay Market when she got the midnight-blue suede bag open. It was the one he'd been looking for in his desk.

She drew in a quick breath. Why, this was at least as

generous as any of the things he'd been saying that his Hungarian teacher friend did for his pupils . . .

Inside the bag was a tiny Fabergé charm: a silver violin on a chain.

CHAPTER FOURTEEN

It was late evening by the time Yasha got in. He walked into the kitchen, hoping to see Inna before she went to bed. And there she was, sitting between the mistress and Monsieur Leman. They'd been talking for hours, he could see that, and had got carried away. The supper was long gone cold and the greasy dishes, still littering the table, had been forgotten. There was a pile of music on the table, some of it held open with spoons and glasses. They were choosing something. Leman had been singing, in his cheerfully out-of-tune voice, tapping along in time with a spoon. He could hear the children fighting noisily in a bedroom.

He didn't like the hush that fell when they heard him come in.

'Look, Yasha,' Madame Leman said. She held up what seemed to be a little chain.

'What is it?' he said. His voice sounded gruff and suspicious, even to his own ears.

'It's nothing really,' Inna said quickly – too quickly, as if she felt guilty.

'It's the Fabergé jewel Horace gave Inna,' Madame Leman said, smiling so widely she seemed to Yasha almost to be baring her teeth. 'Isn't it pretty?'

He'd gone down to the workshop quite soon afterwards, not bothering with supper, and was working off his resentment by planing the great stretch of a cello's back, putting his whole back into the energetic movements. Around him, screeds of wood shavings flew to the floor.

'I've got the keys.' He turned round. Inna was standing in the doorway. 'It's late. I told them I'd lock up.'

A part of him was appeased by the idea that she'd come down here specially to look for him. She couldn't go up to the attic any more, now Madame L. had got her sleeping downstairs. Not without inviting questions. So here, in the workshop, was probably the only place they could meet unobserved.

'Leave them,' he said gruffly. 'I'll do it. I've got stuff to finish.' Turning his back, he pounded away at the wood. 'Kremer's driving me crazy. I have a new pamphlet to write. And I've no time, no time for anything,' he said, desperately, and far too loud. 'I shouldn't be doing this at all. I shouldn't be keeping the bourgeois in musical playthings. No. I should be out there, doing what my heart tells me, leaving all this behind. I should . . . vanish into the night and leave you all behind.'

'Please,' she whispered, from just behind him. 'Don't be so angry. It's a lucky mascot, that's all. It's nothing special to him. He works for a jeweller.'

He felt her hand on his shoulder. Tentative though her touch was, he felt it burning through his skin.

He stopped planing. He didn't look round, though; just blew at the wood in the sudden quiet to get the shavings

191

away, and made a point of feeling the curves that he was beginning to bring out in the cello's elegant back.

'What do you need a lucky mascot from Fabergé for anyway?' he said after a while, hating himself even as he spoke. And then he remembered that nincompoop of an Englishman, all togged up in his white gloves and gold watch-chain, all bows and scrapes and imperial flim-flam; and old, old, with grey in his hair and pushing forty. Yet there he was, taking her swanning round the fleshpots, turning her head.

He could never give her a jewel.

'He wants me to play for a friend of his,' Inna said. She was almost whispering, but Yasha couldn't help hearing the damped-down excitement in her voice. 'He wants me to meet a music teacher. And if *he* likes me he thinks he might teach me, and get me proper papers, because apparently he's got pull with the people that give them out. And that's what we got so excited about at supper, why we got all the music out, because if he *can*, why then . . .'

Yasha's head was still spinning from all the 'hes'. But he turned a little, just enough to look at her over his shoulder without dislodging her hand, and he saw her eyes beseechingly on him. And suddenly he understood what she was excited about, and it *wasn't* that stupid little violin which she hadn't even put on, any more than it was that old idiot of an Englishman Englishmanovich, with his eager-to-please smile. No, this was about finally getting her permanent residence papers, and in a dignified way, too, through music. He'd been unfair.

He took a deep breath.

'. . . you'd be in,' he finished for her.

*

'I want to stay,' she whispered, in what seemed a different lifetime, though it must only have been a few minutes later.

He pushed her back, liking the way her hair was all mussed up and her body, utterly yielding under her skirts, was moulded to his. His own body was all nerve endings, all desire.

He didn't know whether she meant 'stay down here in the workshop for a while longer', or 'stay in St Petersburg'. But he did hear the unspoken 'with you' that went at the end of either idea. He could see that thought in her eyes.

He blew out a long sigh. He wanted her to stay, too. But he released her. It almost hurt to step away. 'Go,' he said. 'Go and practise.'

Yasha watched her practise like a demon all week. When any of the Lemans were around, she'd fret with them about her programme, or ask Leman endless questions about this Auer, whom it turned out he knew a bit. And whenever Yasha came across Madame L., she was fretting about what to cook on Sunday night, which was when old Auer was going to show his face, just casually, for supper.

All week, too, Yasha had to struggle to remember that jealousy demeaned him. It wasn't easy to force himself out of the house before or after work to chase Kremer's papers, or to tell the brothers that they'd just have to put off their meeting till next week, whatever the rabbi had written yesterday about Beilis, because this week he was busy with something else. However hard he tried, though, it was almost unbearably tempting to fall into the despicable cycle of feeling jealous, then hating himself for it, then being furious that his passion for his other, secret work was being dissipated by all this sitting around fretting about Inna, which he'd promised himself he wouldn't let happen.

But somehow he kept the jealousy at bay because, between those long blinding volleys of tiny notes, and all that fretting, she'd come down to the workshop and tell him, in a hasty whisper, whenever no one else was around, that she was so grateful he understood. She'd say that she needed those papers more than ever now, and then she'd drop her eyes and come to a confused halt. And he'd smell flowers on her hair and imagine the brave green glow when she lifted her face up to his, and think if she *did* get the papers then they could really start to imagine being together for a long time.

But when she did look up, he could tell, she'd already be thinking about playing again, and how did he think the Prelude had sounded last night? It was all so confusing, so he'd just squeeze her hand back, kiss her, and whisper, 'You sound beautiful. You *are* beautiful. You'll play beautifully.' And hope.

It was Sunday morning, and Yasha had made his own big plan for the day.

First he walked to the watchmaker's just down Moscow Prospekt, whose nephew had been supposed to deliver Kremer's forged travel papers more times in the last week than Yasha had fingers and toes for, but had failed to show up every time. He was all ready to be exasperated with the hunched-up old man, who in previous meetings had peered apologetically at him over his pince-nez, blinking like a tortoise, mumbling out excuses. He'd thought of quite a few frank things to say to him. But, to his astonishment, this time the man was scuttling across the floor almost before Yasha got to the door, and had pressed an envelope into his hand as if he wanted rid of this looming presence in his crowded workspace as much as he did of the compromising document.

In no time at all, Yasha was out on Moscow Prospekt with the envelope flapping in the wind, feeling almost cheated by his success. The contemptuous call-yourselves-activists-you-lot-couldn't-organize-your-way-out-of-a-paper-bag-*if*-you-had-a-map things he'd been going to say were still in his head, with no one to say them to.

Uncomfortably aware that even possessing this document was a crime, Yasha stuffed it inside his coat, down the torn lining. He didn't want to schlep it around for too long. But, having not really expected it today, Yasha hadn't planned to spend his day walking all the way to the poorhouse to deliver it to Kremer in person, either.

Kremer had taken up quite enough of his time already. Kremer could damn well wait.

Hunching his shoulders, Yasha set off towards the offices of the newspaper edited by a certain Yermansky. He'd had plenty of time to think in these past few days, and had gone round and round his painful thought like a dog trying to make a comfortable sleeping-place from a lumpy blanket. And, in the end, he'd managed it. He'd thought it all through. He loved old Kremer; the man had been like a father to him. But old Kremer had gone, and he was fed up to the back teeth with the rest of the brothers. Young Kremer was the biggest idiot of the lot. Some poor old bloke had died as a result of his exploding buckets, and now everyone was endangering themselves trying to get him out, and never so much as a sorry or a thank you; just me, me, me, when are you coming next? But then, Yasha had decided, they were all fools, the Bundists: not just because they were fighting a losing battle, but because they were so bad at fighting it. They were just playing at rebellion.

Yasha wasn't sure whether it was his parents leaving Russia that had opened his eyes, or Inna's instant dislike of young Kremer. All he knew was that, sometime in the early hours of one of those long nights this week, as he lay awake listening to Marcus snoring, he'd decided to leave Kremer and his friends in the Bund. Inna was right to say you should be fighting for the whole of the underclass, not just the Jews. It was only here in the city that he'd really understood how many people needed to be saved. The struggle was bigger than the Bund and so was he. He'd join the socialists instead.

Today was the day. It had to be now, because he wanted to have something to tell her, something as important as her music test today, so they could both be proud by tonight, and each have something to admire in the other. That was the thought keeping his jealousy at bay; keeping it from demeaning him.

He'd known for a long time how you joined at least one group of socialists. Old Kremer had told him. You just went to Yermansky, who'd be at his newspaper office, and you told him you were *one of us*. And Yermansky took you in hand, and showed you the rest.

Inna picked up her violin.

She could feel the social smile set on her face, the nervousness of it.

She could half see the two bearded heads together on the sofa: Leman's dark, with its handsome grey frosting; the other, thinner man's a sable grey under a glistening, freckled bald pate. They were facing towards her, but chatting quietly to each other. They had eaten dinner, and Horace had gone to help Madame Leman open some French champagne. Marcus was in the kitchen, grinding coffee beans. (Everyone was still pretending they always ate and drank like this. Everyone except the children, that was, who'd been sent to bed. 'Delicious grapes, Mam,' Agrippina had giggled. 'I like the Yeliseyevsky pineapples better, though, as a rule. Can't we have one of those tomorrow?')

How hot she was. How fast her heart was beating.

Yasha would be along any minute, surely. It was nearly eight already. She couldn't think why he hadn't got back in time for the meal. But she couldn't think about this now. He knew, surely he knew, for he'd been present at every single strategy discussion all week – and every breakfast, supper and tea break had been a strategy discussion – that now, this after-dinner moment, was the one that counted.

Very quietly, she started to tune up, playing a long A, twisting the sticky peg to change the pitch. Her bow arm was shaking, bouncing like a skimming pebble on water. She couldn't keep the bow lying flat on the string.

It wasn't as if Monsieur Auer was *expecting* a concert, she told herself. It wasn't as if it mattered, to him, one way or another. As far as he knew, this was just going to be a little after-dinner music. She could even pretend he wasn't there. She could play over here, and not look at them, and tell herself she was practising, as usual, alone in her room.

It wasn't even as if Monsieur Auer, or Monsieur Leman, or even Horace had taken much notice of her. They'd talked exclusively to each other all through dinner, swapping anecdotes about Conservatoire luminaries unfamiliar to Inna. There'd been a lot of talk, for instance, about the arrogance of a piano pupil who'd only scraped through the Conservatoire composition class, and, quite unabashed by failure, was still churning out new works with names like Sarcasms, works so scandalously chromatic and dissonant that the audience had actually walked out of one première, saying things like, 'The cats on the roof make better music!' They all laughed at that.

For a moment, Inna let herself imagine what it would be like if Leopold Auer *were* to fix his solemn attention on her.

She lifted her bow arm a little higher, to play the D and A strings together. One step at a time . . . She made her arm heavy and slow. But the legato sound she expected didn't come, and her bow just skittered off the strings altogether.

They hadn't noticed. But they would if she started to play properly.

She looked around. No, no one was coming through the door. Any minute now, she'd have to begin. She tried to call the Prelude to mind, but she was too breathless to be able to remember it. She couldn't think of anything except the shallow, hurried air coming through her nostrils; the panicky sickness inside; how her muscles had turned to razorblades, and how her hands would not stop shaking.

Horace took both her hands in his.

He could barely see her face, bowed away from the lamp, with her long back drooping like a wilted flower. She'd retreated to the sofa at the back of the yellow room as soon as Leman had taken Auer out for an after-dinner smoke before her musical interlude. She'd been like this for, oh, maybe, fifteen minutes, though it felt an eternity. But she was letting him hold her hands.

'It isn't important, the fear you're feeling,' he said gently. 'However crippling it must seem now, it's temporary . . . it will pass.'

She turned her head. 'Do you think so?' Her voice was hollow.

He squeezed her hands, which were still and dry and cool as paper, wanting to transmit some of the warmth he could feel in his own flesh.

Leman had noticed the colour Inna had gone straight away, and had taken Auer downstairs, chuckling in a fat after-dinner way, 'Would you like to see where our real work happens?' and was showing him the workshop and loitering down there, or in the courtyard or the stairwell, with him, over a quiet cigar.

They might yet come back and find her, upstairs, playing merrily away as if nothing had happened. Auer might just hear her on the stairs – a nightingale in the attic – as he had, himself, a few weeks ago.

Horace flattened out her hands to trace the scar lines she'd marked across her own flesh. 'Look,' he whispered. 'What do those scars tell you? What future did you write in your hands?'

She was wearing an innocent, girlish scent: he could smell roses in it. He glanced across at her, hoping she was about to give some positive answer about how she'd chosen to be the kind of person who would seize this opportunity for salvation. But all he could see was the shadowy line of her profile. Eyes cast down, gazing soundlessly at his fingers stroking her palm. Motionless.

And then the door squeaked, and Inna's eyes turned towards it, and Horace could see how hopeful she suddenly looked.

Horace felt a flicker of irritation. The last thing he wanted now was for her head to be filling with thoughts of escape. He'd asked Madame Leman to leave them, because he thought, even now, that he could persuade her . . .

But it wasn't Madame Leman. It was the cousin, who hadn't been at dinner. Tall and slightly menacing, he advanced on them.

'What's going on?' the cousin said. His dark eyes were flashing angrily. For an unpleasant moment, Horace thought he was going to make a scene about the way Inna's hands had been in his. But he wasn't touching Inna's hands any more: she'd leaped up as soon as the cousin's head had poked round the door and run straight towards him. When she got close enough, the cousin put his hands on her upper arms, as if to catch her and stop her disappearing out of the door altogether.

'Yasha,' she was saying desperately. 'You should have been back hours ago. Where have you been?' and then, 'I can't do it. I can't.'

From where he was standing, Horace could no longer see Inna's face. But he could see the cousin nodding. After a bit of apologetic mumbling about 'trying to find a man called Yermansky' and 'I didn't mean to be late' and 'I gave it up in the end, till later', he started to say things that were more to the point, like 'stage fright, eh?' and 'butterflies in the tummy?'; all quite lightly though, as if he didn't really understand that this was important, and her fear was nothing much out of the ordinary. Yasha had kept Inna's upper arms in that tight grip, an arm's length from himself. None of it seemed the right approach to Horace, yet, as he watched, it seemed as though the strength was flowing out of Yasha and into Inna, who stopped stammering and fell quiet. 'Come on, now,' Yasha added, after another moment, taking no notice of Horace. Horace could see his face was lively and encouraging. 'It's not so bad if you're not on your own, eh? Why don't I get my violin out too?'

Guessing that Inna was at least considering this thought – if for no other reason than because she'd stopped saying, 'I can't, I can't,' and her back looked less rigid with terror – Horace felt a glimmer of hope.

'What an excellent idea,' he said, addressing Yasha over the top of Inna's head with much more enthusiasm than he'd expected ever to feel for the young man. 'Yes indeed. It would be very helpful if you would warm up together.'

Horace wasn't sure whether Yasha had even heard him, because he didn't take his eyes off Inna. But the young man nodded, at least, and then he moved his hands down from Inna's forearms, took her hands, and squeezed them quite hard. 'Come on,' he said bracingly. 'We can do this. Strauss.'

Yasha Kagan would never be a violinist, Horace thought, a few minutes later, but he was definitely having a good effect on Inna. They were playing a Strauss waltz together. Young Kagan had taken the lead part, which he was massacring cheerfully while capering about the big bright room, grinning at his shy fellow-player. Inna, meanwhile, was playing the simple 'dee-dee' accompanying line. She was all fingers and thumbs, still: wild-eyed, biting her lip, looking pale. But she was calming down.

At the end of that first attempt, when they'd scraped right through the whole piece once, somehow, wrong notes, wildly missed slides, jumpy bows and all, Horace saw Inna grin, impishly, as, after young Kagan crashed disgracefully through the final chords, monstrously out of tune, she suddenly played a final, jokey, 'dee-dee-DUM!'

Looking up at each other, both players burst out laughing.

'Again!' Yasha cried, quickly, still smiling at her, but turning the manuscript over on the stand before she'd had time to think. 'With you on top this time!'

Horace could only admire the boy's aplomb. Why, she'd lost her fear entirely, he thought, astounded at how little time it had taken to shake off that pinched, hunched look she'd had before. Now, as she picked up the top line of the waltz with all the panache he'd known her to be capable of, he saw that her lips were parting into the beginning of a smile, her cheeks were flushing pink with the exertion, and a bit of black hair had escaped her severe bun to twine along her long neck, over the high collar and crisp pin-tucks of Madame Leman's borrowed best blouse. She looked utterly beautiful again, Horace thought. She looked happy, too, he thought, a moment later. This second thought was strangely disconcerting. He watched more attentively. Her green eyes were dancing as they followed Yasha, who was still jumping around her like a court jester, making her laugh as he plonked out the rhythms of the accompaniment. Her long frame was half dancing too, swaying to the tune as she played, rotating on her toes to follow her partner's perambulations, lifting an eyebrow above her smile to indicate when she was about to playfully draw out a phrase for what would feel, to real dancers, an agonizing eternity longer than nature intended, then leaning forward to speed up again to the breathless drama of those last chords.

Well, of course they'd be like that, Horace told himself. They were two musicians, playing together, following each other's leads, a lifted eyebrow here, a lifted bow there. It was natural enough. But, however much he tried to explain it away, the fact remained: she was lost in Yasha's eyes, and he was lost in hers.

Horace became aware that he was no longer tapping his toe.

'From the top!' he heard Yasha cry, again, very cheerfully, and as Inna began the gentle teasing of the introductory notes he also became aware of Madame Leman slipping into the yellow room and coming to stand beside him. He turned to her. Her eyes were all lit up with relief and excitement. 'Isn't she playing well now?' her eyebrows signalled.

With automatic graciousness – graciousness that would, at least, help keep at bay the misery in the pit of his stomach – Horace bowed deep to his hostess. He opened his arms. Madame Leman smiled, bowed her head and stepped forward. Between the armchairs, bumping into occasional tables, the pair of them started to waltz.

Horace heard Inna laugh. For a moment, he hoped she might turn and meet his eye with that same pink-cheeked, back-from-the-dead pleasure with which she'd been looking at Yasha.

'Faster!' Yasha cried, and instead she turned towards her cousin with a graceful curve of the neck. 'Come on, Inna, make them run!'

It was only several minutes later, when she reached for the music to turn a page, and the paper slipped between her fingers, fluttering to the floor, that the music stopped. Yasha paused with his violin still up; his bow raised above the strings and his eyebrow lifted in that strain of comic enquiry that, to Horace's stricken eyes, signified possession. Inna retrieved the manuscript, smiling back at Yasha as if to signal that yes, as soon as she could get it back on the stand, of course they'd go on . . . But Madame Leman laughed breathlessly and stepped back from Horace's arms. 'You sound lovely, children, but, heavens above, that was energetic!' she said.

'Thank you,' Horace said to his partner, making sure he kept the smile on his face as he bowed.

And, as they all disengaged, Horace realized that Leman and Auer must also have come unnoticed into the room while they'd been dancing, because there was more laughter – male, this time – from the doorway.

'Very charming, *Kinder*,' Auer said. He twinkled at Horace. 'As you said, dear man,' he added, 'Your protégée does indeed make a beautiful sound.'

For a moment, Horace allowed himself to hope that, even if Inna hadn't yet performed solo, hearing her duet with Yasha had, in itself, been enough to persuade Auer to take her.

But it took only that moment for Horace to realize he was deluding himself. The truth was that Auer had heard enough – perhaps even that comically bad first attempt at the duet, with Yasha on top – and *wasn't* taking her. For, politely but with finality, the maestro had turned to his hostess. 'Do carry on . . . I just wanted to make my farewells to Madame.'

Horace broke through the genteel consternation that followed: the Lemans, hovering anxiously; the oh-but-what-about-the-champagne? and not-even-a-little-coffee? questions.

'I'll come down with you,' he said smoothly, 'and find you a cab on Hay Market.'

Horace kept the conversation going through the disconsolate handing over of hats and buttoning up of coats. The Lemans hadn't understood, one way or the other, what the decision was. Inna might not understand either. It was all-important, Horace thought, to be elegant about this; to observe the niceties; to only ask Auer his frank opinion once he'd got right out of earshot of the family.

It was only once both foreign gentlemen were outside in raw night air that hit the lungs like a stab, looking round for a cab, that Horace re-opened the topic of Inna's talent. He murmured persuasively, 'One day I'd love you to hear her properly; today, of course, there was her cousin as well; but I was delighted that you heard, even in this evening's informal setting, the astonishing sound she makes.'

Auer sounded very polite indeed, as he replied, 'Mm, yes, and Strauss, a delightful composer; a very pretty girl, too,' though that didn't sound, to Horace's ears, quite like a compliment, or an answer.

And then a cab appeared, and the two men ran after it, and began haggling over prices with the drunk coachman. It was only after all that was agreed and Horace had settled the other man inside that he returned to the question of Inna. He ventured, 'I was wondering whether perhaps, one day, when you're next holding auditions at the Conservatoire, you might agree to put Mademoiselle Feldman on your list?'

Auer smiled, but he shook his head. It seemed to Horace that there was pity in that smile.

'Charming and talented though Mademoiselle undoubtedly is, dear fellow,' he said in his Mitteleuropean growl as the coachman applied the whip to his beasts, 'she and her partner are clearly in love. I make it a rule not to take young girls in love for my pupils. Whatever would be the point?'

Sometimes the most important thing is not to lose face. By the time he reached the yellow room, Horace had more or less decided how to save Inna's.

Inna seemed at least partly aware that the hope and potential of the evening had fizzled out, he thought as he entered the room. She was sitting in an armchair and had folded her arms around her instrument as if it were a baby. She was looking, not wounded, especially, or hurt, just distant.

To Horace's relief, at least she wasn't looking at Yasha, who was sitting quietly in the armchair beside hers. Horace let his own eyes slide past the young man, concentrating on his desire to spare Inna the crushing blow of a rejection based on Auer's mistaken impression. (It had just been the way two people are when they're playing, he told himself, again. And look, Inna was paying her cousin no attention at all, now it was over.)

'Well?' Madame Leman said.

'There are auditions, twice a year, for the Conservatoire,' Horace stammered, and then, plunging into the lie direct, with a brave smile, 'He said, "Why not try?"'

Slowly the Lemans nodded, trying not to look deflated. They knew that for Auer to have mentioned the regular auditions meant he hadn't been overwhelmed, but hadn't closed the door altogether. What they didn't know was that Auer hadn't even said this.

Horace glanced over at Inna. She understood, too, he

could see, though she was trying not to show disappointment. Quietly, he watched the dance of fleeting expressions on her face. His heart was full, feeling her imagined distress. Now an eyebrow went up a fraction; now he caught the ghost of a smile. Horace had never loved her with such breathless tenderness as in this defenceless moment.

He ignored the tall dark shape behind her. Unlike everyone else, Yasha was not even trying to take the disappointment lightly, but was frowning. Scowling, more like. Well, Horace thought irritably, the boy had never had any pretensions to finesse, had he?

'Well!' Madame Leman said, rather too cheerfully. 'Let's not let the champagne go to waste, anyway. We'll drink to Inna's success at the auditions when they come round, at least!'

Horace was beginning to feel he'd made a mistake by bringing in Auer, and stirring up feelings he'd have done better to leave untouched. So he was more grateful still when Lidiya Leman first handed him a fizzing glass and then, putting an arm round him and smiling very wide, began making a speech of thanks.

'I know Inna will feel this more than the rest of us, so perhaps I'm speaking out of turn,' she began, loudly and with far too much emphasis. Horace sensed the reproach to Inna in her words, but Inna just nodded with that vague, unsettling half-smile. 'But we are so very *grateful* to you, all of us, dear Horace, for your *tremendous* generosity of spirit, and above all for your *great* kindness to Inna, for all the *wonderful* opportunities that, out of *sheer goodness of heart*, you've been making available to her . . .'

Horace, bobbing and grinning and keeping his eyes fixed

on the smiling Lemans, was nevertheless horribly aware, as he might be of a throbbing toe inside a polished shoe, of Yasha looking thunderous at these words.

Out of the corner of his eye, he saw Yasha put an apparently casual hand forward and touch Inna's arm, as if to cut her off from Madame Leman's flow of thanks.

Then, to his relief, something seemed to change. Out of the corner of his eye, he saw Inna move very slightly away, out of her cousin's reach. She, at least, didn't intend to be rude. Instead, she turned towards Horace.

'Madame Leman's quite right,' she said, though her face was still empty of all but the vaguest of feeling; her voice too. 'I have so much to thank you for, Horace. I don't know where to begin.'

'The jewel alone!' Madame Leman enthused, with a level of excitement that, after Inna's words, struck Horace as embarrassingly false. 'Your good-luck gift – that little violin! Why, I was looking more closely at it, after you'd gone, and the *quality* of the workmanship – those little strings, and the bridge, and the F-holes, all so tiny, yet so perfect. It absolutely takes your breath away!'

Leman nodded. 'Yes indeed,' he said. 'It's a very beautiful thing.'

Horace bowed his head, feeling that, even if Madame Leman was trying far too hard, this evening's events were beginning to go at least a little his way, at last.

With exaggerated curiosity, Madame Leman added, playfully, 'Inna, dear, can't we take another look?'

Obediently, Inna put a finger to her neck and pulled the fine chain up from under the blouse's high collar. She held out the tiny violin in one hand, while still holding the real violin in the other, and both parent Lemans came close and began exclaiming over the jewel.

Madame Leman began an arch question. 'So where, Horace dear, are you planning to take Inna . . .?'

At the same time, Inna opened her mouth. 'Yes,' Inna said quietly, and she did, finally, meet Horace's gaze now, and gave him a small but definite smile. 'I think it's lovely, too.'

'. . . next?' finished Madame Leman, looking flirtatiously at Horace.

Horace relaxed, but only for a moment. Because suddenly, Yasha, looking and sounding like an aggrieved child, had pushed past the Lemans and was standing in front of Inna.

'You wore it!' Yasha hissed.

Her eyes opened wide. She shook her head. The gesture clearly meant: Stop, stop. 'Yasha,' she said quietly. 'Please.' But she dropped the silver violin, which came to rest, winking as she breathed, against her pin-tucked chest.

Appalled, Horace watched both the Lemans' faces turn down, their shoulders hunching defensively about their ears. He'd never seen them so embarrassed.

'Of course I wore it,' Inna was saying in a placating tone that was only just above a whisper. 'Heavens, Yasha, why wouldn't I? It's the loveliest thing . . . and after all the help Horace has been so kind as to give . . .'

'We've all been helping!' Yasha persisted. 'Haven't we? Haven't I?' He grabbed her by the shoulders, staring straight at her, as if he were imitating a jealous lover from a comic opera. 'But it's all, "Horace, Horace, Horace", tonight, all "Where are you taking her next?" What about *my* help?'

Horace saw Inna close her eyes. He liked the way she kept

her emotions small in public – something her tempestuous relative could usefully learn, he thought – but, for a moment, she looked openly exasperated, or worse.

For a long moment, Horace saw Yasha look hungrily at her face, and observe her closed eyes and the weary anger in her expression.

Then the boy was off, flinging out of the apartment, at a run.

Motionless, they listened to the crashing and snatchings of his retreat.

Inna's eyes remained shut.

'Well, really!' Madame Leman said – wholly inadequately, Horace thought – long after silence had fallen. Her embarrassment was turning to indignation. Her cheeks were pink.

'Mmm, an absolute symphony of slamming doors,' Leman said, raising a mocking eyebrow and beginning to grin. 'He's surpassed himself tonight, our Yasha. God knows where he can fling off to at this time of night, though. He'll be back soon enough.'

Still with her eyes shut, Inna said, 'He was going to see a man called Yermansky, I think.'

Leman shrugged that off. 'Well,' he added merrily, 'all the more champagne for the rest of us, at any rate.'

But Inna shook her head. 'Will you excuse me?' she said, politely but distantly. 'I'm very tired.' In the doorway, she stopped and said, still in that small, remote voice, 'Thank you again, Horace, so much.' But she didn't look up.

CHAPTER FIFTEEN

It was December before Horace took Inna out again. She was still recovering from her long bout of influenza, which had been so severe that, at one stage, it had seemed she might not recover.

He'd chosen the opera, thinking that the opulent blue-and-gold cylinder of the auditorium, the swaying ladies in their silks, the bowing cavaliers in their medals, and, in general, the ritual flavour of the solemn pleasure, would be so far from the life Inna usually led in St Petersburg that they would cause her no pain.

The performance that night happened to be *Eugene Onegin*. For a while, at work, as he stared through his magnifying glass at the lid he was painting, Horace allowed himself to worry about whether Inna might miserably compare herself to its heroine, poor Tatyana, who as a helpless young provincial falls in love with the dandy Onegin, and, after an agonizing baring of her heart in the moonlight, is rejected.

It had cut Horace to the quick to realize how exactly the timing of Inna's illness coincided with her young man making off into the night to manufacture bombs in the provinces, or wherever he'd gone; but it hadn't surprised him, exactly. Not after that last evening, performing for Auer. Auer had been right, he knew, however hard he had tried to convince himself the maestro had misunderstood the situation. Horace could still remember the pain he'd felt, watching the way they were looking at each other as the music drew to a close, when he'd begun to realize that she was in love. But he could also tell, without needing to be told, how humiliated Inna must then have felt that her cousin had just upped and gone, without a word. What he didn't know was whether there was now any reason for *him* to think there might yet be hope.

By the time Horace had finished putting away the second to last of the Youssoupoff Oxford boxes in his desk drawer, and had cleaned up, he'd calmed himself. As he got the other little square box out of a different drawer in his desk, he told himself firmly that the end of the opera – in which, seeing that Tatyana has successfully grow into a sophisticated, married lady of the world, Onegin regrets having rejected her and tries to seduce her again, but too late, for now she rejects him – should give Inna encouragement, and him, too, perhaps. He slipped the box into his pocket.

It was Inna's first evening out after her illness, and Leman would be bringing her, by cab, to the outside of the glorious mint-green bubble of a theatre building.

It was a windy night, and a little below freezing. Horace walked the hop, skip and jump from Fabergé's to the Mariinsky. It was one of his favourite places in the city, that magical palace of fantasy, with its Botticelliesque nymphs dancing round a sky-blue circular ceiling, three-layered chandelier glittering with the fire of a thousand crystal pendants, and layer upon blue-and-gold layer of loggias and boxes piled gorgeously one on another. Horace wanted to feel composed when he met Inna. It had been – what? – a month since the Auer evening had gone so wrong, and so much needed to be said. The fresh air would do him good.

She was so thin that Madame Leman's winter fur coat hung off her bones.

He kissed her hand, noticing that her wrists were so translucent and brittle that they felt snappable. She smiled, wanly. How pale she was. It wrung his heart.

Leman winked encouragingly at him as he straightened up.

Had he looked discouraged? He wondered briefly about this before nodding back.

'Would you like to join us?' he asked Leman politely. 'I'm sure I could get you another ticket. And there've been wonderful reviews.'

But Leman just grinned and gestured down at the stained, sawdusty clothes they all knew must be covering his large body, just one layer below the big bear of a fur he was wearing. 'Civil service gents in medals!' he said, in a mock-piteous voice. 'I know, I know: Chaliapin singing Gremin – marvellous, of course. But not marvellous enough to put up with an audience of stiffs. Spare me that, dear man. Spare me that.' He roared with laughter. 'Enjoy yourselves, my friends,' he said, blowing them a kiss from above his black beard and turning away.

Horace was grateful for the overwhelming nature of the opera, which gave them very little time to talk about anything. They could use it to get used to each other again.

213

Inna's eyes turned from one golden marvel to the next, taking it all in. When the curtain came down for the interval, she sighed. 'Poor Tatyana.'

'Let's get some champagne,' he replied nervously, fussing with opera glasses.

It was only during the interval, when, like hundreds of others, they took their glasses of champagne and went promenading along curving corridors, between fronds of tropical palms, up and down gilded staircases hung with clouds of white and swathes of pale blues, that he plucked up his courage and slipped his arm through hers.

Her arm, painfully thin under her dark clothing, was soft and unresisting.

'How very well you look, already,' he said, willing that to be the truth.

'I was lucky,' she said, and, for the first time she turned her eyes – huge, now, and shadowed, but still that arresting shade of green – directly on to Horace. 'Both my parents died of influenza.' She smiled a bit wider, and Horace was relieved to see the old Inna still there. 'But here I still am,' she added. 'I must be made of sterner stuff.'

Cautiously, they re-established subjects they could discuss, and negotiated their way round the shadowy areas they had no words for. Of course, they both avoided mentioning the disappearance of Yasha.

The boy had never come back after he'd stormed out on that Auer evening. Obviously there was no point in going to the police; that would always be more trouble than it was worth. But Leman had subsequently told Horace how he'd discreetly asked various old journalist cronies where young Kagan might have got to, in case the boy was in trouble of some sort. Inna thought he'd been going off to see Yermansky, which, as Leman knew, was probably code for joining Yermansky's secret socialist group. He'd discovered that Yasha had indeed been out looking for Yermansky, but he'd never actually made contact. However, the boy had recently, and separately, collected false travel papers from a revolutionary group connected with the Jewish Bundists. He'd had these papers made out for a young man of twenty-five, but in Leman's name. He must have used them to vanish into the night, Leman said. It wasn't just a spontaneous fit of jealousy. The fact that he had them at all suggested that he must have been planning to do a flit for some time. Horace, seeing on his friend's face how betrayed he felt by this cavalier use of his name, and by young Kagan's disappearance, had just nodded sadly. There was nothing more to say.

So there would be no mention of Yasha Kagan tonight. But it was fine to talk about how good Madame Leman's nursing had been, how keen Inna was to get back to the workshop tomorrow, and how snowed under Leman was with orders in the run-up to the Christmas season. She told him how much she wanted to help, to repay the Lemans' kindness.

Horace knew there were only a few weeks to go till the temporary papers he'd got her in the autumn ran out. But he couldn't find the words to ask what she would do next. And she didn't say.

One of the many conversations Horace had imagined them having, when they met again, was about whether she would like him to make another appointment with Professor Auer. He'd even pictured himself pointing out the Conservatoire, just across the square from the theatre, as an inspiration. But now he saw her here, so quiet and effortful, he couldn't do that either. Whatever had caused her illness, it had been real enough, Leman said, with raging temperatures, sweats, the lot. She wouldn't have touched her violin for a month. She'd need to convalesce. She'd need to practise and get back on form. And, even then, would she have the nerve to play on her own? Horace blinked and set aside the thought of the duet that had come unbidden, painfully, into his mind.

So, in the second interval, he just told her society gossip about the possible engagement of the Grand Duchess Olga, and tried to make her smile.

The Rasputin scandal was still getting worse, he continued. Every paper, every day, was full of extraordinary diatribes, as if one peasant really could be responsible for all the ills of the age. The man himself, Horace said, was desperate to get back to the quiet anonymity of his Siberian village, but the Empress wouldn't let him go. Still, the Emperor would probably soon have to put his foot down, because there wasn't a soul in St Petersburg who wasn't wondering whether Rasputin might really be the Empress's lover. The secret police surveillance team whom the Tsar had detailed to protect the peasant had given his most faithful female followers code names – Bird, Dove, Owl and Crow – and these had been leaked to the papers.

Inna smiled at that. 'Which follower is which?' she asked.

Encouraged, leaning a little closer, Horace replied, 'I don't recall exactly, but I think Munya is Dove . . .'

'I wouldn't want a bird name,' Inna said. 'I wouldn't want to be written about like that.'

Rather sadly, Horace nodded. 'I don't imagine Rasputin likes it much either. It's vicious, what people are saying about him. As if his just being here, breathing the same air as them, enrages them.'

Inna nodded, looking straight at him for only the second time that evening. 'Yes,' she said, with more vehemence than he'd expected. 'Father Grigory stands out too much in the city. He should go to his village, and his family: where he blends in better, and seems ordinary, and people don't notice him, so he's safe. Where he can be innocent. He should go home.'

The night air was gentler when they came out, muffled in their furs. And it was snowing: the first real snow of winter, falling soft and quiet and thick.

White drifts were piling up on caryatids, wrought-iron balconies and bare branches. Drivers spurred on the vehicles and horses thronging the square. No one wanted to be caught out when their carriage's wheels began slipping and sliding on the uncleared roads. But an almost reverent joy crept into the faces in the crowds embracing, bowing and moving away. There was hope in every tired, happy voice, a quiet faith that this snowfall would mark the natural end to the dark, gloomy, rain-lashed, miserable weeks that follow the golden-leaved autumns of Russia, and the beginning of the crisp, blue-skied, sparkling-white, crunchy-underfoot, invigorating real winter of everyone's dreams.

Hope, and hush, everywhere: Inna took her hands out of her muff and turned her face skywards.

'Oh, let's not get a cab,' she said, with sudden vivacity. She turned to him, and the animation in her face tugged painfully at Horace's heart. 'I'd rather walk.'

*

This would be the perfect moment, Horace told himself, fingering the little box in his pocket that contained the ring he'd brought out with him. He had one arm through hers, and she was leaning slightly against him. They were on Nevsky, walking past a store front gleaming with pyramids of foie-gras cans, towards the Hôtel de l'Europe. The street was teeming with other people with lit-up faces and pink cheeks, out venerating the snow. Inna looked so happy, Horace suddenly thought, that she'd become beautiful again. Snowflakes sparkled in the clouds of dark hair under her hat.

There'd never be a more romantic place or time.

He'd already asked her to a poetry reading the next night at the Stray Dog. Inna had said yes. But tomorrow there'd be a crush, with friends everywhere, and eyes, and it would be even harder to get up the courage. Whereas, if he were brave, he could just take out the ring, right here, right now, and ask her. Get it over with.

He was still fiddling with the ring-box, undecided, by the time they got to the corner of Nevsky and Garden Street, outside the Merchants' Yard covered market, where you could always find a few newspaper-vendors, puppy- and kitten-sellers and demagogues on soap-boxes.

Even tonight, there were a few political activists who were too interested in their all-enveloping vision of the future to be put off by anything as temporary as snow. One man was selling an anti-Semitic gutter paper of some sort – these were closed down, often enough, but whether they were called *Today*, or *Tomorrow*, or *Morning*, or *Evening*, you could tell straight away what they were from the big front-page cartoons of hook-nosed, grinning men sitting on moneybags. Horace pushed straight past him, hoping Inna hadn't noticed the paper, and paused instead by his rival, a man of identical scrawny build, identically muffled in an dark ankle-length coat and balding rabbit hat, who, a dozen paces on, was selling some parallel sort of fringe left-wing publication – there were so many of these, even more than there were leftist groups, whether anarchists, Social Revolutionaries, Social Democrats or the quarrelling sub-groups that each one spawned so regularly. This paper had a long name made up of the words Socialist and Banner and People's and Future, and the slogan 'Proletarians of the World, Unite!' under the title.

Horace caught the man's eye. He delved deeper in his pocket for a coin.

'Oh, don't,' he heard. He looked down in surprise at Inna, who, he saw, was suddenly ablaze with impatient indignation. 'You're not going to buy that paper, are you?'

He paused. He was aware of the newspaper-seller, standing so close.

He'd only meant to divert her attention from the other man's paper. It hadn't crossed his mind that even this small act – more or less an act of charity – might remind her of the cousin who'd gone off to make the new world.

'It's just some rag, spouting on about the revolution to come,' Inna said bitterly. 'Why waste even a kopek on that pack of lies?'

Horace nodded understandingly, and the newspaper-seller moved away. Inna tightened her arm against Horace's and pulled him forward, down Garden Street, faster than before.

'So you don't think that they're just doing what they can to build a better world, those people?' he asked, amused.

'Oh, I hate the whole thing,' she answered robustly. 'They're all the same, revolutionaries: fanatics and crackpots, dishonest through and through.'

'You know, I think you're really on the mend.' Horace smiled. Tomorrow, he told himself. I'll definitely ask her tomorrow.

The snow had stopped by six the next evening when Inna left the workshop and, wrapping herself up in her winter hat and muff, went straight into the centre of the city. She walked quickly, surprised at how capable she suddenly was of admiring the stars between soft grey drifts of snow cloud, and at how exhilarated each cold-champagne breath she was drawing in left her, and at how full of anticipation the piles of Christmas luxuries in the Nevsky shop windows made her feel. As if the snow had magicked away more than the drizzly sleet of outside; as if it had brought her back to inner life too.

One of the many benefits of the strolls Horace had taken her on around smart Admiralty District, between Nevsky and the river, around the Astoria and his workplace, was that she now knew who lived in which tall townhouse mansion.

She knew exactly where the Golovin mansion was, for example. But, even if she hadn't remembered its neo-Renaissance front and the duck-egg-blue of the façade, the clutch of journalists outside would have been a clue. Father Grigory – she found it difficult to think of him as Rasputin – must be there.

Once, not long before, she would have felt intimidated by the very idea of marching up to the front door of a house like this and ringing the bell. Once, not long before, she might also have felt intimidated by pushing among these young men with old eyes, who were stubbing their butt-ends out in a patch of snow they'd already tramped into grey-brown ice.

As she shouldered her way through, she felt a flicker of gratitude for Horace, her teacher. *Why, I've become a real Petersburger.*

It was only when the tea ran out, and Munya scuttled off to ask for the samovar to be refilled, that Inna got her chance to speak to Father Grigory one to one.

Looking frail and irritable, he was complaining about the crowd of journalists outside, about his enemy-in-chief Novosyolov and various other hostile reporters. 'Don't they have anything to write about except me?' he muttered. His eyes were flickering around the room, as they had been all afternoon. 'I'm a nobody. A fly! I don't understand why they won't just leave me alone.'

Inna leaned forward. Cutting across his voice, she said, urgently and emphatically, 'Father Grigory, you shouldn't be here.'

She wanted to look him in the eye. She needed to be sure he was listening. She wanted to convey to him her sense that this city was as dangerous for him as being down south had been for her. She'd been lucky to find a refuge, even if it wasn't yet a permanent one, in these streets. She'd found welcome invisibility among the canals and palaces, where her Jewishness – for now at least – no longer had the power to define her and offend others. But it was the opposite for him. He stuck out among Petersburg people. He offended them as surely as she, simply by being of her race, had offended people down south. But she didn't like the pleading note creeping into her voice as she added, 'You can see that, can't you?'

It seemed to get his attention. With relief, she saw that the deep-set eyes he now fixed on her were as attentive and intelligent as she remembered.

Then he said, in a quite different, more alert voice, 'Go on.'

'Don't stay here, Father Grigory,' she repeated. 'This city isn't good for you; it's not safe to be near people who hate you. Go home to your family. Go back to your innocence.'

He nodded, and smiled, rather sadly. 'Oh, I've tried. Don't think I haven't. I'm always trying. That's all I want.' He sighed. 'But they're always pulling me back here. They're such unhappy souls, all these poor little rich folk. They need me. It makes no difference whether it's the ones who love me, or the ones who hate me – none of them will let me alone.'

This was true enough, Inna knew.

'I just don't understand *why* they're all so obsessed with me, when all I want is to live in peace,' he added, plaintive again.

This was exactly what Inna had come to tell him. She'd even brought her copy of *The Silver Dove* with her. Now she got it out of her bag and held it out to him. He didn't take it, only looked at it in puzzlement. She knew he barely read. They said his followers had had to write down his prayers and homilies for the pamphlet he'd published.

But, Inna thought, he ought to know what people were talking about. She put it down by his glass of tea.

'You should read this if you want to understand why they're all so hysterical with you.'

He shook his head, dully.

'Look,' she said, trying to sound patient, 'people have got this idea in their heads that there's a great darkness waiting to engulf us all, do you see? And some of them think all that will save them is a man of God, someone pure from the peasantry – someone like you. While at the same time there are plenty of other rich people who think they're about to be destroyed by someone just like you – a poor man who'll lead the poor against them. And it's all in here, or enough to see, in this book.'

He seemed almost frightened. 'What, you mean journalists are writing whole *books* about me now?'

'Not journalists; and not really about *you* – that's the point – but a kind of imitation; you'll see when you read it. What you need to realize is that they *think* that's what you're like. The truth won't ever matter.'

'But I'm not one for books,' he said. 'I never have been.'

Inna sighed. 'Well . . . it was just an idea. I simply wanted you to see. The point is, they've written you, over and over again, every possible way they can think of. Or they think they have. So they'll always ignore the real you, whatever you say or do, because they can't see you for all the imitations. All they can see is the monster, or the saviour, whom they've created in their own heads. And so it seems to me that it can't be any easier being you, here, living with their expectations, than it was being that harmless brick-factory man in Kiev who everyone was convinced had killed a child to make his Passover matzos, just because they believed that was the kind of things Jews did. Which is why I think you need to watch out for yourself. And go away.'

She nodded at him, willing the man who'd helped her reach her safety to take her advice on finding his.

Father Grigory was looking back at her, shrewdly, as if he had indeed begun to understand, when Munya rushed back in with a jug of water, and started refilling and relighting the samovar herself.

Well, Inna thought, she'd done her best. Said her piece. She could only hope he'd take her advice. She got up to go.

'Oh, do stay,' Munya breathed. 'Mama will be down in a minute. And I've sent the maid out for some proper country black bread for you, dear Father.'

'And you,' Father Grigory said, finally, so gently that Inna felt they were speaking to each other's souls, 'what about you, now you're here? Are you safe?'

A part of her wanted to respond, in a warm rush, by telling him all about the violin she was making, and about the Lemans, and the children with their Roman names, and the bedroom she slept in, right among them, which she'd made so charming, and Madame Leman's kindness while she'd been so ill.

But instead, because there was so much else she didn't want to think about, or mention, she just nodded.

His face softened, as, slowly, he nodded, too. 'Yes, you've got people who love you to protect you. I've seen that. That's good . . . good. And do you have someone *you* love?'

Inna blushed. No one had asked her that before. And then she surprised herself by replying: 'I do.'

The lines around his eyes crinkled and deepened. 'A good man?' he asked.

'A craftsman.'

It was only as she said this that she realized she wasn't certain whom she'd meant. Gentle, witty, kind, peaceable Horace, who'd asked for nothing, but who'd devoted so much time to her; whose company she so enjoyed, even though she'd thought him too sophisticated to feel more than compassion for her, but who, she was only just beginning to realize, might have been waiting for her to notice the feelings behind his great kindness? Or idealistic, impulsive, handsome Yasha, whom Rasputin had seen her with; Yasha, who Leman said had vanished into the revolutionary underground, without a farewell word?

No, she couldn't have meant Yasha, she told herself. Not possibly. Why, Yasha wasn't even a craftsman any more. He'd given up music, given up violin-making, and chosen to be a revolutionary strongman instead. Marcus had told her what his father had found out. Yasha had chosen conflict over love.

Her heart ached.

'I must be off,' she said hastily, fussing over her bag. 'Heavens, the time . . .'

But Father Grigory was still looking at her with that gaze of his. 'Yes,' he said slowly. 'You've changed, I see that. You've found your way forward. You haven't found perfect happiness, maybe; though who does, in this vale of tears? But you've chosen peace.'

He stood up and put his hands on her shoulders. She felt the brush of whiskers on her cheeks as he kissed them. 'And I should too,' he added. 'You're right about that. There's nothing keeping me here. And how I miss my home: my village, my family. There's a train tonight. I could just go.'

But the phone started ringing again when Inna was in the hall. She stopped and looked round.

Father Grigory was striding energetically to the vibrating

instrument of torment, clearly ready to give the next nuisance caller a piece of his mind.

'What do you want?' he rasped into the mouthpiece. He didn't hold the instrument close enough to block out the answering sounds.

Then, unexpectedly, as he took in what the disembodied voice at the other end – a court lady's voice – was saying, he smiled. 'You won't know me,' the tinny miniature voice was saying. '*Fascinated* by the Unseen . . . *enthralled* by the schismatic movement . . . your mastery, wisdom . . . I obtained your phone number from a friend . . . wondering . . . *such* an honour . . . pay you a visit?'

'Why, of course,' Father Grigory said, and Inna, from the doorway, saw Munya relax. 'Tomorrow . . . Eleven.'

He was dictating his address by the time Inna slipped away. So he wouldn't be taking a train tonight, after all. His curiosity had been tickled by a new admirer, his vanity flattered. Inna sighed. It wasn't just the Emperor and Empress who had him shackled to their side.

CHAPTER SIXTEEN

It was late, but not quite late enough at night for the theatres to come out, so the Stray Dog hadn't yet come to life. No one was ready to perform. Horace liked the quiet. He liked being able to see the carefree shabbiness of the place, and to have it confirmed in his mind that people didn't come here for smart chandeliers and slick waiters and imperial grandeur, just interest in all the unusual, free-thinking other people they'd meet in this rare place.

And Inna would be along in a minute.

He poured himself a drink, but didn't touch it. He liked the cheerful expectancy in the atmosphere as the waiters prepared for the rush. He hoped that coming into this vibrant, imaginative place again would help Inna regain some of her old energy.

He sat, nursing the glass, remembering that other happy place, the Botanic Garden in Calcutta, planted with Himalayan ferns, palms and rhododendrons, by Grandpa Nat. It was known as Wallick's Pet, and was always full of picnickers, with bright cloths, chapattis, cucumber sandwiches, laughter.

How different from England. He recalled his father, stuck in that little house in South Norwood, desperate to have his oceanography papers read out at the Linnaean Society – all those travels in the Atlantic, so many notebooks filled – but never getting anywhere, because they only wanted Darwin, now. He recalled the frustrated, petulant twist to Father's chin, the disapproving Kentish servants, and Marmaduke and Collings, his brothers, drifting around not sure what jobs they were suited for back home, wondering listlessly whether to take themselves off to Canada, or Australia, and start again. And his sister Beatrice, the only one to have found a niche in England, married to a vicar, living in a Warwickshire rectory with seven children, so far away. He loved her, but if he went back, would he ever even see her?

He hadn't meant to reminisce about Wera, in the house next door at Springfield Road, but this melancholy train of thought always led back to her. She had been the only life in that whole dull place: energetic, green-eyed, undisciplined, scrambling up the tree between their gardens with her favourite ornament in her patched apron pocket, grinning down at him. Her bird cry: 'Come and see!'

He'd never seen anything like that ornament: a glittery egg-shaped pendant, striped in gold and pink-and-white enamel, with a chain attached to its top and its bottom end studded with a tiny diamond. On each side, the curly letter 'W' – once for 'Wera' and once for 'Wiensienska', he supposed. 'Faberrrgé,' Wera breathed, with her exotic accent, those heavily rolled Rs. 'Papa bought it when I was borrrn.'

Poor Wera, who'd been so bursting with vitality. She'd been nothing like his family, the Wallicks. She hadn't been lost at all, however disconcerted she might have been expected to feel by all her mother's marriages and moves, by all those half-sisters from all over Europe, by all those financial crises. She'd just made plans – her endless plans – with bright eyes. Parrris! Arrrt school! Escape!

He didn't like to think of the quiet marker in the churchyard; all that was left of her. Today, it was easier to think how thrilled she'd have been to know he'd made it here. And how happily she'd have laughed to see him with his client of this morning, Felix, that supremely elegant young man with the hooded eyes of the Tatar princes of old. Horace had flattered him that morning into giving him a tour of the family palace overlooking the Moika canal, and Felix had shown him one treasure after another, with a characteristic mocking twist of the lips and careless flick of the cuffs. He could almost hear Wera's voice, trembling with pride: 'Akh, you'll never be borrred in Rrrrussia.'

No, he wouldn't go back – not to South Norwood, or anywhere else in England. Not at the age of thirty-eight, after living away so long. And not now that he'd found another young woman with that same green-eyed, electric will to live.

He looked up.

'I'm sorry I'm late,' Inna was saying hurriedly. 'I ran all the way.'

He stood to kiss her hand and quickly memorized her image, there in front of him, before, keeping that mental picture in his mind's eye, he bowed his head.

She still looked too thin, and anxious, but more alive than yesterday at the Mariinsky. She met his gaze and, even if it was only because she'd been hurrying, she had pink in her cheeks again.

'Not to worry,' Horace said reassuringly. 'As you see, nothing's started yet.' She was beginning to move easily between worlds, he thought. They might, if she would only agree, do well together. He raised his glass.

But even while he was admiring the colour in her face, his thoughts were still partly in that magnificent, absurdly overwrought house on the Moika that he'd visited this morning. Even the servants there had been exotic: Arabs, Tatars and Kalmuks with olive skins, wearing multicoloured costumes. Even the basement – a labyrinth of rooms lined with sheets of steel, with a device for flooding them in case of fire – had been packed with fine wines, plate and china for receptions, and what seemed hundreds of spare objets d'art for which there was no room upstairs.

Gorgeous, unashamed excess: it was why he loved Russia.

Felix Youssoupoff lived on the second floor; his mother on the first. But it had been his father's floor, the ground floor, which Horace had been shown. The apartments were ugly, but crammed with valuable curios: old masters, miniatures, porcelains, snuff boxes. In one showcase alone Horace had examined a Buddha cut from ruby matrix, a Venus carved from a huge sapphire and a bronze Negro holding a basket filled with precious stones.

One of the cigarette boxes making up Horace's commission from Felix was a present for his father. Horace thought, turning over the Venus, that he'd have his work cut out to impress a man who lived with this. He'd better make it good.

Next to the father's study was a Moorish room. When they'd gone in, Horace had seen mosaics, a fountain, marble columns, divans voluptuously draped in Persian fabrics.

'Copied from the Alhambra,' Felix said languidly. He

watched Horace shiver. 'Though with rather different weather conditions,' he added drily. 'When I was a boy I was very taken with this room. The perfect place to play sultan, don't you agree? I only stopped after the day my father caught me, wearing all my mother's jewels, lying on the divan, with one of our Arabs at my feet, raising a dagger as if to stab him . . .' He shook his head. 'Oh, how angry he was. Wouldn't let me back in for years.'

It wasn't Felix's father who'd collected these treasures, as it turned out. It was his grandfather, the late Prince Nikolai. Felix's father was a simple army man who liked shooting and drinking. Horace had been relieved. It wouldn't be so difficult to impress a man of that kind with the quality of his dreaming-spire scene.

It had been Felix's grandfather who'd bought the violins stored in a third room in the suite, too. 'They're sleeping in deep peace, as no one ever practises or plays there,' Felix had cheerfully remarked. 'Would you like to see them?'

Horace had declined – he wouldn't have understood what he was looking at – but not without wondering whether, one day, if he continued to be on such familiar terms with Felix, he might bring Leman, or even Inna, to see them.

Felix hadn't been offended. 'A pity,' he'd said lightly. 'My mother took it for granted that I'd inherited my grandfather's talent. She insisted on my taking violin lessons with a professor of the Academy of Music. Even the Stradivarius was brought out to encourage me, but all in vain. My career as a violinist soon came to an end. The instruments are quite forgotten, now.'

He'd laughed, and Horace had laughed with him. People were always saying young Youssoupoff was a spoiled playboy, too busy with dubious pleasures to settle down. But Horace couldn't help enjoying him. And now they'd also started saying, about town, that he was going to get married. Marriage would change everything for Felix, Horace thought optimistically. It would give him that centre of gravity so lacking at present.

Yes, Wera would be pleased if she could see him today, Horace thought, with the box in his pocket, and, inside, the ring. With Wera, he'd never got that far. Just dithered, and put off the moment of decision – should they study first, should they live in London, should they . . .? Until, suddenly, it was too late.

He'd learned his lesson. He had the ring. Was this the moment?

His heart beat faster. But then he hesitated, as he always did. As if he lacked Inna's energy, and the will to act that had made her cut a new lifeline through her flesh. As if he didn't know the road home.

Stop dithering, he chided himself.

The doors opened and half a dozen people came in. Men. He could hear more footsteps on the stairs behind. The after-theatre crowd; too late, then. He looked down. His heart was still racing.

He was ashamed to think it might be from relief.

'But . . . that's the police!'

Horace heard the panic in Inna's hissed whisper. 'Surely not,' he said, calmly, before looking up and realizing she was right.

The men were in uniform, and they were shutting the club doors behind Inna.

*

The policemen took the passports of Inna, Horace and the other half-dozen early birds. Then the Stray Dog clients were shepherded upstairs to wait in the courtyard for the theatre-goers who'd come any minute to swell the numbers, while the police turned up the lights in the cellar, moved tables back and arranged themselves to question the club members in due course.

Everyone who came into the courtyard – and a couple of dozen newcomers did, within minutes – had their passports taken, too.

Panicky knots of artists hung around the courtyard, whispering. Soon, everyone knew what the police were here for. Some boy who'd taken to coming here recently – one of that silly dancer girl Sudeikina's lovelorn moon-calves – had blown his brains out, far away, in his regimental barracks in Riga. The mother was claiming it was because he'd seen Sudeikina with another man, here at the club.

'How very sad, but nothing for us to worry about,' Horace said to Inna, who'd gone absolutely quiet. He could see she was clenching her hands into white-knuckled fists at her sides. 'A few routine questions, and they'll be off.'

Inna nodded, but she didn't relax.

What drama addicts Russians were, Horace thought as he watched the histrionics on all sides: doomily lowered heads, trembling hands.

It wasn't the first time he'd thought this. It was one of the things the Western Europeans at Fabergé's laughed about among themselves. Ask a Russian with a cold how he felt and you could be sure he'd never answer, 'Oh, not too bad,' or 'Can't complain.' Oh no. What you always got here was lugubrious eye-rolling, followed by a mournfully exaggerated wail of something more like, 'I'm dying!' That was Russians for you. No balance. No restraint.

You'll never be bored here, Horace repeated to himself, not without irony. Though, if you're English, you might sometimes feel a little exasperated.

Young Osya Mandelstam was being especially melodramatic. He paced up to Inna and Horace, radiating despair. 'We're all so selfish, so self-absorbed. We play our selfish little games with love, tormenting the innocents who don't know how to play, like that poor boy. This is *our* punishment – our richly deserved punishment.'

How he's hamming it up, Horace thought, almost laughing. It was a suicide the police were looking into, after all, not a murder. There'd be no punishment for anyone.

'Why, they don't want *you*,' he said, trying to keep the English pull-yourself-together briskness out of his voice. 'They'll want a quick word with Sudeikina, that's all.'

But when a policeman emerged from the cellar, with a pile of open passports in his hand, it was Inna he called for.

Horace squeezed her arm. Inna squared her shoulders and stepped forward matter-of-factly enough. He was proud of her composure.

At least, he was until he saw her look over the policeman's shoulder down the stairs. And then he saw how white her face had turned; how dread was written all over it.

He stepped forward, suddenly anxious.

But she'd started downstairs already, slow and straight-backed.

She'd been down these stairs before.

But this time, with the policeman giving her that hateful

smile, Inna felt dizzier with every step. As if she was going back into an earlier time; as if she was sleepwalking into danger.

She was in the dark, with her nostrils full of smoke, struggling to breathe. She knew what the people reaching for her would say. Words and leers filled her head. She could almost see the other great wet red smile, the one she couldn't bear to recall; if she only turned her eyes, it would be there again, and then she'd scream, which she mustn't do, because if they remembered her they'd turn on her. *Hey, Abramovna, see this?* She could almost hear the tearing of clothes, the desperate, silent scuffling in the corner, and the glint of firelight on silver uniform buttons. The guffaws as they all closed in on that corner, while she crept backwards towards the door and the safety of the stairs.

Stairs . . .

She stopped at the bottom step, overwhelmed.

She said to herself, You're just remembering a nightmare. An old nightmare. You can't panic now.

She knew how important composure was. Look them in the eye; keep your chin up. Be proud.

She pulled at her collar, gulped in air, and entered.

Nothing the two men inside actually said, once they'd got started, was half as frightening as the dream-image. But the look in their eyes was the one she'd almost forgotten since she'd been here, the one she'd grown up with in Kiev. They meant trouble.

'*Venyaminovna*, eh?'

'*Feldman*, eh?'

'Jewish by nationality, then?'

'It's in my papers,' Inna said through tight lips.

'Just want to know where we stand, don't we, when there's funny business going on,' the fatter policeman said. 'Because you so often get Jews mixed up in funny business. So you were born, where, now . . . Ah, I see, Zhitomir. Down south. An incomer.'

The thinner one began picking at her passport with a cracked thumbnail; testing stitches and glue. He held it under the light. He stared suspiciously at the flowing copperplate writing and the red stamp-marks, and the dates.

'Forged?' he asked, before eventually putting it down and shaking his head. He looked disappointed.

'Now then.' The fatter one moved on to a new tack. 'Were you . . .' he paused for emphasis, and bared his teeth, in a way that looked to her more snarl than smile, '. . . *intimate* with the deceased?'

'*Me?*'

Inna asked, in a stupidly small voice, cursing her breathlessness. Surely they knew which woman that poor boy had been in love with; surely they knew who Sudeikina was?

At least, that was what she thought she'd been thinking.

So she had no idea, looking back, why the next thing she remembered was rushing up the stairs, sobbing, and colliding with Horace, who was coming down four steps at a time.

But she remembered him catching her, all right. She remembered him murmuring 'there, there' and 'calm down' and rocking her until she could breathe again.

And she remembered the two police – who now looked less like tormentors than naughty boys caught red-handed in some small misdemeanour – watching nervously from the doorway at the bottom of the stairs.

They flinched when Horace brought Inna back down, for what Russian policeman would want to be questioned by a tall, elegant person of visibly high status; someone wearing a well-brushed coat and starched collar; someone with a gleam of watch chain at his front and a flash of gold at the wrists; someone from the unbullyable classes?

And they cringed at the command in his voice when he snarled, with fury on his face, 'What the Hell's going on?' and, 'This is a disgrace!'

Inna leaned into Horace's side, trying to slow her tearful gulping as he berated the policemen.

'No wonder Russia has the barbaric reputation that it does!' he barked. 'Have you people absolutely no idea how to conduct an inquiry? I will personally ensure that your behaviour is reported to the very highest authorities and that you are punished!'

A calm part of her couldn't help admiring Horace's upright bearing and confident turn of phrase. He knew exactly what threats and tone to use to terrify these bullies who'd so terrified her. His English accent was no problem in this kind of rant; it was his menacing connectedness to power that counted. Half the aristocracy spoke Russian no less imperfectly than him, with some kind of French or English twang.

It was only during his final growl of – 'BECAUSE I KNOW MY RIGHTS!' – that he slipped on a case ending. Which exposed him, she suddenly saw, as the kind of real foreigner whom every thieving bureaucrat in Russia would love to fleece.

He stopped, looking shocked, and she felt his arm tighten protectively around her.

It was the first time Inna had seen Horace at a loss.

I should be really frightened, now, she told herself. But what she actually felt, stealing a glance sideways and seeing that unexpected vulnerability on his face, was something quite different. A soft, magical tenderness was stealing gently through her, like warmth; and, close behind it, a dizzying first inkling of the possibility that the answer to all the questions she'd been asking, all these months, might have been here, right under her nose all along.

Trying to lend him strength, she leaned closer into his side.

The fat policeman was staring meekly at his toes, still overawed, but the one with a face as long and bony as a sturgeon's snout raised his nose.

Sniffing weakness.

'What's it got to do with you, anyway, Mr Englishman?' he said after a long moment's silence. 'What do you even know about the troubles we Russians have with our Jews and revolutionaries?'

His tone was pugnacious. Hearing it, his colleague raised a hopeful head.

'This has nothing to do with Jews and revolutionaries, for God's sake!' Horace snapped, but if Inna could sense he was rattled now, then so, surely, could the policemen. 'You're investigating a suicide in Riga, and you're in an artists' club in St Petersburg. There are no revolutionaries here.'

Inna held her breath.

'Ah, but that's never quite true, is it?' the thin policeman said. 'Whenever there's trouble, it always comes down to just two things, as we all know. Jews and revolutionaries.'

Horace's eyes opened wide at this idiocy.

Don't give up! Inna implored him, in her head. Taking hold of his hand at her waist, she squeezed it encouragingly.

For a moment, he looked down at her. His gaze expressed no clear, single emotion. But his hand squeezed hers back, very hard.

Then, letting go of her, he stepped forward until he was right in front of the thin man, eyeballing him. Horace was a head taller, and now there was real threat in his face.

For a long moment, nothing happened. Then the policeman pulled back.

'Don't give me that bigoted nonsense,' Horace said. 'You've wasted enough of our time. Just let Mademoiselle Feldman sign a statement saying she knows nothing about this suicide, and has never been to Riga, and let her go. Do it now – right now – and I'll drop my complaint.'

Inna, standing to one side now, reached out again for his hand.

After another long moment's eye-lock, the thin man gave in, and flicked a dispirited arm at his subordinate, who sat down at the desk and started scratching away on a form. Inna stood beside Horace, keeping hold of him, of the hand that was anchoring her here in this world.

'It's all very well for foreigners to go on about bigotry,' the thin policeman grumbled. 'Here today, gone tomorrow, what do you care? When we're the ones who get left behind with the revolutionaries, long after you've swanned off to Paris or Baden-Baden. We're the ones who'll be blown up or have our wells poisoned or our children's throats slit. By the Jews and Reds.'

'Just give Mademoiselle Feldman the statement,' Horace said coldly.

The fat policeman handed Inna the scrawled statement.

She took it with her free right hand. She put it on the desk and signed.

Then she turned back to Horace, breathing out a big sigh of pent-up air, signalling, with all the poise she could muster, 'Can we go now?'

Horace's eyes lit up. Their answer was 'yes'.

It was his right hand she was holding. But now she was facing him she saw what he had in his other hand: a small velvet box with the looping word 'Fabergé' on the outside, the size and shape declaring unmistakably what article of jewellery it contained.

Her heart pounding, she began to lead him towards the door.

But the thin one was still glaring at Horace. 'I mean,' he continued, resentfully, 'what's this particular Jewish female and her trouble-making going to be to *you*, sir, once you've gone off home to your England?'

Horace shook his head, as if he had nothing more to say to this man.

But Inna answered. Stopping in the doorway, turning back to the two policemen again, she raised her chin. 'He won't be going back to England.' Her voice shook just a little. 'He'll be staying here with his wife.' And now she could feel Horace's hope. 'With me.'

PART TWO

1916–17

CHAPTER SEVENTEEN

It was a beautiful December morning, cold in the startling and brilliant way of real winter. There'd been the first proper snowfall earlier in the week. Today's blue sky was spotted with pink clouds.

'Friday, so it's your night away at the hospital . . .' Horace said as he opened the pale-gold curtains. Inna sat up, stretching. She nodded sleepily.

On Fridays, nowadays, she took a day off from her job at the Lemans'. Like many other good-hearted city wives, she'd taken to doing a little voluntary work nursing the poor soldiers wounded in the war. Like many city aristocrats, Prince Youssoupoff had turned one wing of his palace into a hospital (though, unlike most, he hadn't actually gone off to fight), and, like many craftsmen, Horace had wanted to cement his ties with his wealthiest patron. So he'd suggested that his wife become one of the Youssoupoff palace's lady volunteers, and now Inna did whatever she could for the soldiers lying in cots crammed into a former ballroom, for one evening and night every week, and made up the time to the Lemans by going on there on Saturday morning, and working till evening.

'And you'll be going straight on to the Lemans' in the morning,' Horace sounded absent-minded, but then they both knew their timetables too well to need reminding of them. He must be working round to something else, Inna thought.

Horace was dressed already in the austerely tailored dark clothes he wore to Fabergé's. In the hand not occupied with tweaking back the curtains, he was carrying a cup of tea on a tray for Inna, with a sliver of toast and marmalade (she liked the exotic Englishness of that sharp orange taste; it made her feel genuinely foreign to breakfast off it). He put the tray down on the bed beside her and sat down behind it on the oyster satin quilt. Inna looked up at Horace, and beyond him to the austerely high ceilings, dark wallpapers, stiff curtains and curlicued dark furniture of their rented apartment. Along from their bedroom, the drawing room was her husband's territory, full of the scribbles and scratches of the avant-garde art Horace was interested in at the moment. But she'd done what she could to make the rest of their apartment a home for them by covering everything ugly with quilts and lace and cushions in soft warm colours, which she'd piled up like snowfalls on the bed and sofa and armchairs till Horace started indulgently calling the place 'Inna's nest'.

He raised an eyebrow. She loved the way he always did that, just a bit, when he was about to make a request. 'I thought I might dine out with my dear old boy from the City Duma, tonight, since you won't be there? I know you find him dull . . .'

Sitting up straighter herself, Inna wrapped the pretty lace

peignoir he'd given her on her birthday about herself and reached for the teacup. 'Of course, *darling*,' she said with a smile (using the English word for 'darling', which she knew made him laugh). 'You'll have a lovely time talking politics together. Much better without me.'

Monsieur Shreider, the white-bearded mayor of Petrograd – and Horace's client, who, like all of them, must be wined and dined every now and then – was a decent man, she knew: full of solid, good-hearted, bourgeois virtues, and a mine of information. But she did find him dull: not just because of his clunking gallantry (all those toasts to 'the ladies, God bless 'em!') but also because of his wartime talk about turning more factories over to make munitions, and the corruption of the big tycoon class, and the rest of it. And she couldn't abide the restaurant they went to either. These days Sadko's was all profiteers and red plush and beefsteaks and too much dark wine and brandy. It was characteristically sensitive of her husband to spare her. She wrapped her hands round the delicate china of the cup and breathed in the steam, scented with heady Assam leaves (she'd developed very English tea-drinking habits, too, since marrying Horace).

'I particularly want to see him . . .' Horace was saying as he leaned over to kiss the top of her head: an affectionate, low-key gesture. She felt his lips on her hair. '. . . because there were such extraordinary new rumours at the club last night. Shreider's my most political client, and I *would* like to find out if there's any truth in any of it.'

Inna sipped. She was aware of his slight tension but not especially worried, because there were always rumours. Of course there were. Russia had been at war with Germany and Austria for more than two years. The generals were hopeless, and the Germans were advancing. The Great Retreat last year, as the foe moved forward, meant the city was now packed with hundreds of thousands of extra angry, hungry people: deserters from the army (the men who'd refused to go into battle without boots or guns), the limbless (the ones who hadn't refused), and the landless (the peasants whose villages were now in German hands). They joined the jobless (the former workers of all the factories not making munitions) massing in the streets. With so many people in town, starving so near the plutocrats and wartime profiteers, and with the papers censored so hard that they conveyed none of the reality, rumours were only to be expected.

If it wasn't rumours, it was singing: while the destitute marched angrily through the streets, the poor who still had something left to lose complained through song. All the doormen at the Youssoupoff palace, all the salesmen on Nevsky and all the urchins in the gutter were, this week, singing the same sarcastic song, putting words in the mouths of the spoiled city rich, who were getting richer while they starved:

> 'We do not take defeat amiss,
> And victory gives us no delight;
> The source of all our cares is this:
> Can we get vodka for tonight?'

There'd be a different snide, hateful song next week, Inna thought, because the government was as hopeless as the generals. Beyond patriotically changing the German-sounding city name of St Petersburg to the more Russian-sounding Petrograd, back when hostilities started (the German embassy had been ransacked, too, and German Christmas trees burned), and beyond silencing criticism in the newspapers, what had any ministers achieved? It had been left to good-hearted individuals to set up a bit of a hospital here, or organize some charity supplies to the soldiers there, because no one official was doing anything. Not that it was all the ministers' fault, either, since, while the Emperor was off at military headquarters, making a mess of running the war, the Empress had been here in the city, making a mess of running the country. She'd been dissolving parliaments – they'd had three Dumas in just a few years; a fourth one was sitting now – and banning papers and people, and changing ministers every few days or weeks, till no one knew who was in charge of what, or why, and everyone just whispered, all the time, trying to make sense of things.

Sometimes people said the Empress was interfering so destructively in government on purpose, to weaken Russia, because she was German, and, to her, the Kaiser was Cousin Willy. Because, secretly, she wanted the Germans to win.

How confusing everything was. Inna put her cup down, rubbed her eyes and stretched, letting her descending arm sweep down Horace's head and back. Horace called her his Sleeping Beauty on these late Friday mornings. She'd sleep again when he'd gone, as she'd need to be fresh for the hospital tonight; because it was only then that she was confronted with the disturbing misery of outside.

Inna often felt pleased she didn't have to look too hard into the swirling darkness outside any more, or try too hard to understand what was going on, or plan several anxious moves ahead, now that she had the dusty calm of this rented flat to retreat into, and the safety of her husband's foreign name. And, of course, there was kind, knowledgeable, unflappable Horace, who would always keep them both out of trouble, and who thought every problem through so intelligently that they could live without fear, or as close to it as anyone could hope for nowadays. Horace had held her close in the night, last night as so often, tenderly attentive to her body's needs; and she'd felt the protective softness she always did when she heard his groan of pleasure at the end, when his breath eased as he held her and whispered about love. Horace knew everything, from how to deal with the authorities to when not to make love to avoid having a baby. This was marriage: shelter from the storm; a warm cushioned nest; this great, shared kindness. Horace would look after her, however frightening the world beyond their door. Horace would keep her safe.

'There are always rumours,' she said now, picking up the toast and nibbling at the nearest edge.

'But this one was about people we know. They're saying Felix Youssoupoff is planning to assassinate Rasputin.'

Inna didn't stop eating, although she felt uncomfortable even hearing that name. The Rasputin who was written about so scandalously in the papers all the time in 1916 seemed nothing like the commonsensical Father Grigory she'd known long ago. But, she thought – letting her mind slide away from wondering how Father Grigory had become so different, because the man he was now had no place in her comfortable life with Horace – people do change. She certainly had: she'd become sleek and loved and well cared for.

Their paths had diverged, but she'd heard a lot about Rasputin over the years. People claimed that the Empress was flailing about in the dangerous way she was because she was so under his influence. They said he knew secret country ways of easing the inherited blood sickness her little boy suffered from: *gessenskaya bolezn'*, the Hessen disease; her German family's curse on Russia. So the Empress couldn't say no to Rasputin. And perhaps it was Rasputin, more than the Empress, who wanted the constant change, the leapfrog of ministers, because he was evil, and corrupt, and hell-bent on the utter destruction of everything.

Not all of what Inna had read and heard was bad. Inna had privately rather liked the argument that had made Rasputin so unpopular with the aristocracy back on the eve of the war: that he was opposed to fighting over the Balkans. He'd apparently told the Empress for years that it would never be worth shedding a single Russian peasant's blood to protect other, lesser Slavs living under Austrian rule. But he hadn't been around to dissuade the Emperor from rushing to war with all the patriots of Europe in the summer of 1914 after that assassination in the Balkans.

Rasputin hadn't been around because he'd been in hospital in Siberia, fighting for his life.

That was the moment Inna had stopped being able to understand Rasputin's strange and frightening story, beyond knowing that it was not for the person she was becoming.

Rasputin had been in hospital in Siberia, fighting for his life, because he'd been stabbed in the gut by a religious maniac. The maniac was a syphilitic woman with no nose, a follower of his religious enemy, Iliodor, who'd run after him with a bread knife. Afterwards she was locked up (though Iliodor somehow got papers and left Russia for America; people said the secret police had helped him go).

Rasputin had told people the war might never have happened if he had been well enough to talk to the Emperor, in person. But he was too late. By the time he came back to Petrograd, months later, bitter, ghost-white, with black-ringed eyes, the war was already raging. That was when he seemed to have changed. He'd taken up women, they said: street women, society women, gypsies, orgies . . . And drink, because, as he took to growling in the restaurants he spent his nights in, 'Why not? I am a man like any other.'

Perhaps he was drinking to suppress his fear – fear of the murder plots that the police only ever seemed to foil at the eleventh hour, the bombs, the poisoners and the cars poised to crash into him. But he was a nasty drunk, who got into fights in restaurants. And he was always drunk.

Inna didn't believe *all* the things the papers said, even now, from inside the silken cocoon she inhabited. She wasn't sure, for instance, that she really believed that this new, bribe-taking, malicious, whoring, Madeira-swilling Rasputin dined so regularly with a Jewish banker known to spy for Germany. But still, as people were always saying, there's no smoke without fire.

And now the latest rumour going around Horace's club was that Prince Felix Youssoupoff had gone to the Duma building and told the parliament's chairman that he and a group of friends were secretly planning to do away with Rasputin, thereby rescuing the Empress's reputation and saving Russia from the revolution of discontent that her catastrophic friendship with Rasputin was threatening to bring about.

'Felix actually asked the chairman to help, can you believe?' Horace said. 'And that absurd MP, the Jew-hating one, Purishkevich: *he's* been in the Duma press room, too, sounding off about it. He's been saying he's going to help, and intoning, 'Remember the date, brothers: the sixteenth of December.' That's next week! And: 'We're going to kill him like a dog.' So not much of a secret! It was all anyone was talking about last night.

'Of course the chairman said no, but apparently Felix has got a whole team of other helpers as well as Purishkevich. His friend' – here Horace wiggled his eyebrows, to indicate the athletic grand duke who was Youssoupoff's closest ally, Dmitry Pavlovich – 'and some other officers, and, I heard, the English secret service team who live at the Astoria. Oh, and even his wife. The princess.'

Here Horace had the grace to look ashamed, and laugh in slight embarrassment. Inna smiled too. It sounded so absurd: Felix Youssoupoff's *wife*?

'All right, that part I'm not so sure about,' he admitted. He let out a long sigh. 'Well, it's probably *all* just hot air.'

'People say your Felix is scared of blood,' Inna said cautiously. She didn't want to belittle her husband's worry, but how could he be taking such lurid talk seriously? She hoped that by recalling another popular rumour – that the prince, as a boy, had been so appalled by the blood that came out of the first and only rabbit he'd ever killed that he'd never touched a gun again – she could put Horace's fears to rest.

Horace nodded. But the worry lines were still there, between his brows.

Inna put out a hand and laid it on his. She knew he was short of good commissions – the gangsters making fortunes from the war didn't want miniature scenes from English life when they went to Fabergé, they wanted gold lumps and diamonds like hen's eggs and pearls the size of fists, made into giant ropes of glitter to hang on their molls. And she'd seen how delighted he'd been when Felix Youssoupoff, who'd been away a lot with his wife since getting married, had placed a new order this autumn. Felix was recently back from his estates in the south, while his wife and their new baby daughter enjoyed the last of the Crimean warmth. He wanted to give them both a lavish Christmas gift of toiletry boxes decorated with flowing pre-Raphaelite nymphs in the manner of Rossetti and Millais. Inna remembered how encouraged Horace had been, and Fabergé had been pleased, too. Horace needed his prince.

'You mustn't worry,' she said.

'He's still a wild boy, you know,' Horace muttered. 'Marriage hasn't changed him.'

Inna could privately agree with that. She'd spotted Felix Youssoupoff herself, every now and then, on her Friday nursing trips to the hospital corner of his palace this autumn. He was still tall and elegant and disdainful: the last smart young man left in Petrograd not to be in some sort of uniform, fighting for the Motherland – which didn't seem to embarrass him in the least. She disliked him, because, oh, he was vain. You could see that from the swashbuckling photograph of himself in Tatar fancy dress, fur-trimmed turban, daggers, jewels, the works, that he'd had hung at the entrance to the ballroom-cum-hospital for the nurses and doctors and dying men to contemplate.

Morality didn't bother Felix Youssoupoff much, Inna thought now. He had graceful manners, and a lisping, clever way with words, and he always bowed politely to her, and exchanged a few pleasantries; but you knew straight away, from the shameless mockery in his eyes, that he was still the vicious child who'd played cruel jokes on servants. He hadn't changed with marriage. He'd always been only interested in his own pleasures; he always would be. But you couldn't imagine him ever actually *doing* anything.

Inna lifted her husband's hand and kissed it. 'Why are you worrying so?' she asked curiously.

He made a small, uncomfortable sound: half laugh, half sigh. 'Well, because of the silliest detail. Because of what I heard about *how* he was saying he'd do the murder.'

He paused, gathering words. She waited.

'Do you remember that novel we all read a while back? *The Silver Dove*? The murder story with the evil peasant mystic?'

Inna nodded.

'Well, in the book, you remember, the peasant offers his woman to the young gentleman, saying that the three of them will form a Holy Trinity and give birth to a Christ child who will save Russia. But then the peasant gets jealous, and gets his followers to murder the young gent instead?'

She nodded again, feeling suddenly uneasy too. 'Well, a man at my club had it that Felix has got it into his head to borrow the plot of that book – but, of course, turn it upside down, so that it's the peasant who gets murdered, not the gent. The idea being to lure Rasputin to his home by pretending to offer him his wife – and telling him they must form a sectarian Holy Trinity, and that Rasputin must father on the princess a Christ child, who will save Russia . . .'

'He'd be excited . . . He's vain enough to say yes,' Inna said, almost to herself.

'And then, once he's in – well, we both know what happens next.'

CHAPTER EIGHTEEN

When Inna left the hospital the next morning, her head was still full of the frightened boy she'd sat with for half the night, who hadn't had the lucky escape he'd hoped for from the gangrene that had set in while the generals failed to get their wounded out. She was remembering the clutch of his hand, and the sobbing; the smell, which had only really turned her stomach after he'd gone; and the quiet answering anger in the eyes of the doormen, out in the hut at the courtyard gate, when she'd gone to say they'd need to move another body.

But as she came out on to the pretty embankment road by the ice-clagged Moika River, past the yellow-and-green palazzo façades, under a sky thick and low with unfallen snow, the rumour Horace had been talking about was also still with her.

So she wasn't altogether surprised to realize that the man getting out of a motorcar on the otherwise empty road just up ahead was Father Grigory himself. It was just part of the unreality.

He was clearly still lost in the night before, just as she

was. But his night had surely been different. He was holding unsteadily on to the door.

He was Rasputin in her mind, by now, more than Father Grigory. She recognized him from the pictures so often published with all the scandalous stories, rather than from her memories. What she saw, above the silver fox fur, was hair that was long, black and greasy, a matted, shaggy beard, and eyes that were deep-set and (as they were always described) piercingly, sinisterly blue. He was scowling and swaying.

He was drunk.

So this is what it looks like to have lost your innocence, Inna thought, staring with horrified fascination.

The virtuous wife she'd become should walk anonymously by. But now he was actually here, so near, she couldn't resist the chance of one more conversation.

She started walking towards him.

He should have taken my advice and got away long ago, she was thinking, taking in the shaking hands, the pitted, blotched skin. Just look at him, and what he's become.

'Oho,' he slurred, after a first startled glance at Inna. His tone, though vague, became jocular. 'Whom do I see here?'

He had teeth missing, Inna noticed. She could smell the Madeira (so that part was true). She stopped just out of touching range, and bobbed her head.

'Been a long time,' he said, still holding on to the car door, but making an effort not to sway too much. 'Many summers, many winters.'

She couldn't help compassion creeping into her heart. The eyes in that ruined face, now gazing into hers, were still human.

Vanora Bennett

'What's happened to you, in all these years?' he mumbled.

'Well, I got married,' Inna began, but then doubt made her voice trail off. He hadn't even said her name, after all, and people said he was a monster with women nowadays. He could just be talking to her because she was young and female . . .

'To a good man,' Father Grigory supplied helpfully, 'whom you loved; a craftsman, you said . . .'

Inna nodded, surprised and reassured.

'And spirited,' Father Grigory added with blurred approval. His eyes were a blaze of blue. 'Not that I liked his politics, but he's young, and the young are always a bit wild. But I could see right off he was a man of integrity. The kind who'd always be true to his beliefs.'

He nodded several times, wistfully, as aware of how he himself had fallen. But the confusion Inna had felt when he'd started praising her husband was now turning to something nasty in the pit of her stomach.

He wasn't talking about Horace at all. He was remembering something else: the box of revolutionary leaflets in the lobby, the shouting in that tiny enclosed space, on another winter day, long ago.

She took a deep breath and shut her mind to the memory. 'Ah,' she said, with the kind of thin social smile she had learned for evenings with the gentlemen of Fabergé. 'A misunderstanding, I think? Because that young man went off to fight for revolution.' Making an effort, she broadened her smile. 'My name now is Wallick,' she finished, with an attempt at brightness that sounded hollow, even to her.

Father Grigory gazed at her for a moment, as if he hadn't understood. Then he burst out laughing. 'Oh, you married

256

the *Englishman!*' He rocked forward against the motorcar door and wiped his eyes. But he was still smiling, eyes travelling down her body, taking in her button boots and well-cut coat. 'Well, well; now *that* will have got the police off your back.'

Inna swallowed hard. She didn't want him to see how his laugh had stung, or how disturbed she felt by the suggestion that she'd married only for papers, and had lost her innocence just as surely as this wreck of a man standing too close to her.

She shouldn't be talking with a dissolute drunk, she told herself, with something close to panic.

'I'm so sorry we can't talk more, but I'm in such a hurry,' she said, beginning to retreat, in tiny steps. She was aware of a flash of fuddled surprise in Father Grigory's eyes – those still honest eyes, unchanged, despite the ruin of his face.

As she edged past the car, and nearer the safety of the street corner, she added, in a small voice, 'Well, goodbye,' before walking, straight-backed and as tall as she could make herself, round the corner.

But once she knew he couldn't see her, she realized there *was*, after all, something she should have been saying to him back there.

She should have warned him about the rumour Horace had heard. He'd helped her, once, after all. Even if there was nothing else left for her to say to him now, she should have said that.

She clenched her fingers into her palms, inside her glove, a gesture she often made, but whose origin she'd all but forgotten. She squared her shoulders and turned back.

But she only got as far as the corner.

Father Grigory was still there, leaning heavily against the

open motorcar door. But there was someone else tipping out of the other side of the vehicle, making a second door creak: another man, younger and leaner, wild-eyed and bare-necked and giggling, clearly still in night-time dream-world too.

It took her a moment to recognize Felix Youssoupoff, mostly because his hair, usually slicked down so neatly above his dandyish, tailored clothes, was standing up like a scarecrow's.

Inna drew into the shadow of a doorway, trying to make her fogged mind work normally. If it hadn't been for the rumour, she might not have found it so strange that these two had been out drinking together, because Munya had introduced them once, hadn't she? Thinking back, she felt briefly sorry for Munya, who must have assumed that Father Grigory's virtue would rub off on to Felix. Looking at them now, you could see that it had all happened the other way around.

Inna hesitated, not wanting to rush back now she had seen Felix, so she saw the stumble as Felix staggered around the car, saw Father Grigory guffawing, then leaning down and hauling up his drinking-mate, then slipping himself, into the same yellow-grey pile of pavement snow. They were too drunk to care. She heard the princely whinny of laughter, and then she saw Felix pushing Father Grigory's head back against the wheel of the motorcar, and bringing his own face close; saw the older man's acquiescence, the straggle of hair, the rough hand wavering on the slimmer, smarter back. And she also saw the chauffeur's shoulders, inside the car, rigid with embarrassment. He'd been there all along.

She turned away, hating Felix Youssoupoff, the triumphant

possessor, the casual corrupter, the robber of virtue, but also relieved that the latest rumour had been so wrong, and that it was kissing, not killing, that she'd been witnessing. She felt relieved, too, as she started lifting and lowering her feet to plod carefully, winter fashion, through the brown city snow towards the Lemans', that she now had something else to occupy her mind instead of that disturbing laugh of his, which, just for a moment, had made her so unsure about the way her own life had turned out.

Madame Leman was knitting in the yellow room, under her husband's portrait. She was sitting by the window, for the light, such as it was, but she also had a lamp pulled up close. There were balls of white wool everywhere, spilling out of her knitting basket and on to the chair and floor. She had a knitting needle skewering up her carelessly piled ashy hair.

She didn't get up when she saw Inna – she wasn't as nimble on her feet as before – but her eyes and face wrinkled into her familiar warm smile and she broke into talk as quickly and eagerly as ever. 'You poor darling. You look exhausted. I do admire you. Was it a harrowing night? Marcus is downstairs already, but stay a minute. There's tea just coming. Agrippina is bringing it.' She patted the cushions, and Inna slumped down beside her, glad of the still heat of the room and the soporific flash and click of the needles, on which another tiny matinée jacket back was taking shape.

But when Madame Leman got to the end of the next row, a moment later, she put her work down in her lap and reached into the basket to pull out a bundle wrapped loosely in tissue paper.

She held it out to Inna with a different kind of smile – one

259

in which Inna couldn't help seeing a vulnerability she didn't remember from the old days, a helpless, wordlessly imploring hope.

It made Inna's heart sink. There'd been more and more of this, recently.

Gently, she took the package from her, unwrapped it and shook it out: a fluffy white baby blanket, knitted in a complicated lacy pattern.

'It's beautiful. However did you do it so fast?' she said, trying to infuse her words with enthusiasm, while picturing in her mind the increasingly packed drawer of baby knits she already had at home, knowing too that the hope Madame Leman could only express in white angora was all she had left to sustain her, now that her beloved husband was dead, and Marcus, back from the war, was limping around on one leg, trying to make the business work with only Inna to help.

Madame Leman wasn't to know that the angora made Inna's soul itch, because Inna wasn't planning to have a baby, and was grateful that Horace understood her hesitation; agreed, even.

At the beginning, in fact, when Horace had still wanted her to train as a professional violinist, he'd been the one to say they should wait until she'd had a career. 'You're so young,' she remembered him saying. Even now, the memory of his voice echoed tenderly in her heart. 'You need time to live life for yourself before you give yourself up to caring for others.'

Horace had only slowly given up on trying to make a violinist of her. For months he'd hung around with a dreamy look on his face whenever she practised in the quiet of the evening, until, feeling oppressed by his attention, she'd stopped playing unless he was out. After a while she'd all but stopped taking her instrument out at all, even when she was by herself. Though she didn't like to say this to him, she had no real desire to turn herself into yet another freakish *Wunderkind* – that cliché of the concert halls, a talented young Jew escaping the *shtetl* through music. But most of all, playing the violin – and *that* violin in particular – reminded her of a time and a person she didn't want to go back to.

By the time the war came they had reached a tacit agreement about her playing. It had been an easy decision then not to bring children into a world that was turning so dark. Look how love for their son has turned everything inside out for the Lemans, she'd said, and Horace had nodded. During those first months of the war, when Marcus had gone off and volunteered for the army in spite of – maybe because of – his father's years of laughing at soldiering, Inna had seen how distraught the Lemans had been; and how even more utterly beside themselves when they'd read in the newspaper that his entire regiment had been killed. Walked into a marsh by their idiot general, who hadn't checked the lie of the land and, when the German planes came with their machine guns, slaughtered. Almost every soldier had sunk into the swamp under the strafing and never been seen again – except, as it turned out after days of frantic visits to ministries, and influential acquaintances, and telegrams, and telephone calls, Marcus. He'd hung on to a bush and, by a miracle, limped out that night with only a minor leg wound. It should have been a story with a happy ending, but it had taken weeks to get him off a station floor to a field hospital behind the lines, and weeks more, as winter fell, to get him here. And in that time, the gangrene had taken hold and spread.

261

But Marcus was lucky, Inna reflected now. He could have been that other boy, last night, dying, in fear, away from his family, in a hospital cot. Marcus had lost a leg, but lived.

Yet it was agonizing to remember Monsieur and Madame Leman shrivelling and ageing so fast in those dreadful months. Their fear for their child kept them so busy that no one even stopped to wonder why Monsieur Leman's belly was shrinking so fast, and his appetite going, and he had those pains in the gut all the time, until it was too late. By the time Marcus finally got home, his father was dead and buried. Madame Leman – whose frivolous pre-war fondness for séances and spiritualist gatherings had gone, replaced by grim attendance at soldiers' mothers' protest meetings against the criminal inadequacy of the authorities – took one look at the gaunt son who pegged in through the door, unannounced, and fainted.

Even now that Marcus was home again, there was no time, or space, or money for babies. Work was sporadic. Musicians still played, but in these hard times they thought twice before having their instruments expensively repaired, and no one bought new ones. But when work did come in, you absolutely had to be available to do it fast, and well, and cheaply. Inna couldn't leave Marcus on his own, at least not until after Barbarian finished school next year and they could start getting him trained too. They needed her in the workshop, not having babies and changing nappies.

There's a lot in what you say, Horace would always reply when she said this to him. He went along with everything. Sometimes, Inna thought, he sounded relieved. Perhaps he enjoyed cosseting her as if *she* were a child. Maybe it felt easier for him, too. Would he be able to go on enjoying the life of the mind if he became a father? Even though the Stray Dog had closed its doors forever, and the war had taken away so many of the artists she'd once known there, he still went out with Marcus to meet the very youngest generation of avant-garde writers and sculptors and artists whom Marcus had gone to school with, and came back laughing over their audacious experiments. He bought their radical works of art to decorate the apartment: nonsense poems by Futurists and Supremacists pinned to walls, stick-men drawings, and his favourite (Leman's favourite, once) the sacrilegious red and black square in the icon corner. Might he not be scared too of the changes to his playful life that a baby might bring?

She liked to think her decision not to have a child was simply because she so enjoyed being babied by Horace that she wanted to stay suspended for as long as possible in this moment, enjoying the tenderness of their life as a couple; enjoying the certainty that she would never be alone again.

She didn't want to think there might be something else holding her back.

She never mentioned Yasha. No one did. And if, sometimes, when Horace was out, she did get out her violin, and, very softly, play a Strauss waltz, just to herself, and cry a little, it wasn't for Yasha, because her life today was complete without him. The melancholy sense of emptiness that came over her at these rare moments was the sadness that had come into everyone's lives. It wasn't personal.

'It goes with the little bonnet I made last week, do you see?' Madame Leman was saying. 'It's the same wool. I was so lucky to be able to buy so much of it, so cheap.'

Inna leaned over and kissed her cheek, privately thankful that there was so little of the wool left. 'Soon, maybe,' she said, in answer to the question in the other woman's eyes. 'It's all in God's hands, isn't it?'

This was a deceiving phrase, as Inna both knew and chose not to know at the same time. Perhaps she *had* lost her honesty; perhaps she *was* morally compromised.

By the time the tiredness kicked in, the dawn encounter with Father Grigory seemed almost a dream. She told Horace about it while they were walking home in the grey dusk, her head on his shoulder.

At least, she told him about part of it. She left out the conversation they'd had, especially what Father Grigory had implied about her marrying him for papers. Horace might misunderstand.

When Horace heard about the drunken kiss, he shook his head, rather sadly. He said, 'They call it "making mistakes in grammar" at court, you know, those young men's follies. But I thought it would all stop when he married.'

It was an effort to keep her feet going as they turned off Nevsky, away from the ragged, resentful crowds, on to the long sweep of cavalry exercise ground that fronted their building. She was aching with fatigue. 'Anyway,' she sighed wearily. 'You should be pleased, with all the other things you were fearing.'

Horace laughed, and held her tighter in his one-armed walking hug. 'I tell you what, though. I'm going to hurry up and finish that last box I'm making Felix for his wife's Christmas present before he gets into more trouble. And I'll take payment, too!'

He turned her into their courtyard, swung her towards him, and closed his other arm around her. She breathed in the scent of him, and laughed softly back, trying to forget. They'd be inside in a moment, sinking into quilts in golden lamplight. This was what she'd chosen. This was what there was. It was enough.

The fears she'd set aside only surfaced again when, the next Friday, sitting in the ward in the middle of the night while the men in their rickety cots tossed and groaned, Inna heard the crack of breaking glass and shots out on the street, loud and close enough to startle her out of her doze.

It's the sixteenth, she thought with the confused dread of someone not sure whether they're waking or sleeping. Horace's face flashed into her mind, with the expression of foreboding he'd had when he'd told her about the fat MP singing in the Duma press room, 'Remember the date, brothers.'

But when she ventured out to see what was happening, no one else was stirring. All she could hear, from somewhere far away in the palace, beyond the hospital wing, was the distant sound of dance music on a gramophone. She'd heard the English words of that chirpy song before: 'Yankee Doodle'. Whoever was playing it must like it a lot; it had been repeating for hours. Still, no one seemed to mind. The night watchman was asleep in the ward corridor.

And, although at later moments during that night – while she changed wet sheets, and mopped bloodied floors, and held boys' bandaged hands, and told them they would be all right, and get home safely to their mothers – or, sometimes, that she would be with them, right here, whatever happened – she had the vague sense that there were more motorcars outside than usual, revving and backfiring and rushing about, and more people shouting and banging on doors down in the street.

She looked up at the vast chandelier, with its hundreds of crystal drops, imagining it lit and blazing above a crowd of alternately dark-shouldered and bare-shouldered dancers, all jigging elegantly in time to the perky rhythms of 'Yankee Doodle'. So many things seemed so unreal, so often, in this dreamlike place, inhabited only by people suspended between peace and war, death and life, between the howling darkness outside and the calm stillness of home.

CHAPTER NINETEEN

Horace kept the newspaper he'd been reading open as he came through the workshop's street door.

'Look,' he said, urgently. He jabbed his finger at the little paragraph of late news.

Of course you couldn't understand a word of it. The censors had been at it.

All you could tell from this paragraph was that *something* had happened.

A certain person visited another person with some other persons. After the first person vanished, one of the other persons stated that the first person had not been at the house of the second person, although it was known that the second person had visited the first person late at night.

Horace wanted to see how the others reacted without putting ideas into their heads. He was half hoping someone would come up with a different, better explanation. He wanted to be wrong. Inna must know what he was thinking:

last night had been 16 December. Inna had been at the Youssoupoff palace. If anything unusual had been going on there, she'd have said, wouldn't she? And she wasn't saying anything. She was just yawning and rubbing her red-rimmed eyes – she was always so tired by this time on a Saturday. She shook her head, as if she didn't want to think.

Marcus, though more alert, looked mystified too. 'No, I've no idea at all what that's about,' he said. 'But Mama will. Now she's got so political, she's always good for a guess.'

When Madame Leman responded to her son's yells up the stairs and came down to take a look – she was so small, these days, Horace thought, with her dark clothes hanging loosely off her – she burst out laughing as energetically as if she hadn't been sitting for hours on her stool in the bread queues, chanting near-revolutionary chants with all the other disgruntled housewives.

'You have to admire the censors,' she said. 'A masterpiece of obscurity, that. I don't know what it means either.'

She called Barbarian down, and sent him out to buy all the papers.

'They can't stop *everybody* telling the truth,' she added with the grim satisfaction of the investigator.

The *Stock Exchange News* – Monsieur Leman's favourite, in the good old days – had been as brave as ever today. A single paragraph in bold type at the bottom of page two read: 'Death of Grigory Rasputin in Petrograd.'

Madame Leman read it out loud. '"This morning at six o'clock, Grigory Yefimovich Rasputin passed away suddenly at one of the most aristocratic houses in the centre of Petrograd after a party."'

All Horace was aware of, in that first moment, was Inna closing her eyes. She was swaying slightly on her feet.

'It's true, then,' Horace said, putting an arm round her waist, surprised by how dejected he felt. 'The rumour I heard about Youssoupoff and his friends. They've done it.' He shivered. How utterly pointless. Rationally, he knew that the killers would have simply fallen into the Russian error of refusing to believe their all-powerful Emperor could be ruling them wrongly, and so blaming those around him instead. Horace had always laughed at that over-deferential frame of mind, encapsulated in the Russian saying: 'good Tsar, bad advisers'. Killing Rasputin would make his assassins feel better, Horace thought, but it wouldn't change the way the Emperor reigned over Russia, or make the generals efficient, or stop the Empress wreaking havoc. It would do no good.

In that newspaper snippet, Horace also heard an entire millennium of reverence for simple religious men of Grigory Rasputin's type shiver and shrivel to dust. This killing signalled the end for a land which, since time immemorial, had defined itself as Holy Rus and had been crisscrossed by those bearded men of God with innocent peasant eyes; the schismatic Christs, the superstitious pilgrims in their dusty bast shoes, the wandering *stranniki*, the otherworldly *yurodiviye*, the hermits and holy beggars and simpletons . . .

And what effect would this murder have on the other Russia, *his* glittering urban Russia, this home from home he'd made for himself among the artists and princesses and sophisticates in this extravagant place where Easter eggs were made of gold?

Horace sighed, trying to hope Youssoupoff *wasn't* involved.

'What heroes,' Marcus said ironically into the silence, quoting the favourite lines of the right-wing press: '"Saving Russia from Rasputin. Saving us all from *rivailooshun*."'

'They've destroyed him, then, those aristos,' Madame Leman said. 'He wasn't a bad man, you know, not until they got their hands on him. He was a man of the soil, once, a man of God. I saw that myself, in his eyes.' Her voice rose in the shrill lament of the bread queues against the powers that be. 'And what I want to know now is, what's to become of us all if *they* feel free to just go round exterminating people as the fancy takes them, putting them down like dogs – who's going to save Russia from *them*?'

She sounded ready to go and man a barricade herself, Horace thought. How many other respectable ladies would also react like this when they found out that the wealthiest young men in the land were just a pack of murderers?

'Mam,' Barbarian said warningly, looking full of adolescent embarrassment. Marcus, in turn, gave his younger brother a quelling look.

In the silence that fell again, Horace noticed Inna blinking and curling the fingers of both hands in against her palms, making loose fists. Touching her scars. She used to do that, he remembered, to give her courage.

He waited for her to say something – anything – about the previous night.

But she kept quiet.

There were a lot of people gesticulating excitedly to each other on Nevsky, and a lot of newspapers being pored over as they walked home. Horace heard faint hoorahs coming from the inside of a smart café. The story was clearly out.

Inna held on to him, clutching his coat as if she needed support to stay upright.

'Did you hear anything, in the night?' he asked her finally. 'At the palace?'

A quiver of uncertainty went through her.

'I don't know,' she whispered at last. 'Maybe.'

He looked down at her, raising an enquiring eyebrow.

'I mean, I heard some cars, some people in the street, a bit of shouting.'

Horace became aware that a tear was coursing slowly down her cheek. Then more. She didn't do anything to wipe them away.

'He still talked like a countryman, you know, all slow and gentle,' she said. 'Poor Father Grigory. You know, he still had goodness in his eyes . . .'

It was natural for her to sound so fond of him, Horace told himself. She'd met him when she first came to the city, after all, and it was at Rasputin's home that the two of them had met, too. At that, Horace had a sudden clear memory of Inna on that day: so young, still, with no idea yet of how beautiful she was or why all the other people in the room were looking at her, with her angular stillness and heartbreakingly brittle poise and big, scared, watchful eyes. And yet, even as he felt this long-ago memory warm him, he was also starting to wonder, with the beginning of fear, how well she had actually known Rasputin, both back then and later. Yet he didn't like to ask. Instead he put his arm around her waist and they walked on.

In the long silence that followed, with nothing but the

sound of her footsteps to distract him, Horace went back to the anxious thought that had been bothering him since before they'd left the workshop.

It was about his pay. He'd worked out weeks ago that his commission for the Youssoupoff order would be enough to pay a three-month block of rent, as well as an expense Inna didn't know he had promised to cover, the school fees for next term for Barbarian and Agrippina. The Lemans couldn't keep themselves afloat without him. Everyone needed him to be earning well. Probably nothing would happen to young Youssoupoff – if he were the killer – as a result of this escapade, as Russia wasn't a place where the mighty could easily be punished. But Horace needed to be paid for the boxes before things went further, just in case.

'I'll take you up and settle you in,' he said, once they'd reached Great Cavalry Street and paused for breath in their courtyard. He was digging in his pocket for his keys. 'But then I need to go out for an hour or two.'

She turned hurt eyes on him. 'Now? Why?'

'To drop something off with a client,' Horace said vaguely.

'With who?' But she already knew. He could see it from the accusation in her eyes.

He hesitated. 'Youssoupoff. I need to collect payment for those boxes I'm painting for him.'

She didn't reply. But he was aware of the ominous nature of her silence, and of the way she held herself so as to avoid his touch as they walked upstairs. She took off her outdoor clothes as soon as she was through the front door, then stalked into the drawing room and buried herself up to the neck in one of the hillocks of silky quilts and pastel-coloured cushions she was so given to piling up on sofas everywhere, as if making them into fortifications against him. Horace didn't bother taking off his boots or hat, but, hoping she wasn't as angry as she seemed to be, went to his desk for his briefcase.

'I'm sorry about the floor,' he said, turning back and seeing that he'd left a trail of footprints of melting black snow right across the parquet.

She didn't reply. She was staring at the far corner of the room, but her chin was up, and her lips pinched tight.

Well, there was nothing for it but to go. Briefcase in hand, he began to step carefully back through his slushy traces towards the front door.

Her voice, when it came, was like a whiplash.

'I can't believe you're really going to that murderer's house – now.'

Horace stopped. She was looking straight at him, at last, and her eyes were harder and colder than emeralds.

He lifted his shoulders, Faced with that contemptuous gaze, he didn't know how to explain.

'How could you even think of it?' she pursued. 'How could you sink so low?'

Horace barely recognized the hot white feeling that lifted him on his feet and speeded up his heartbeat. 'Look,' he said, very quickly. 'We don't even really know what's happened yet. When has anyone ever been able to trust anything they hear in this town? And we need the money. I have to go.'

There was an answering flash of green from above the quilts.

'Well, let me tell you something,' she said harshly. 'There's more to life than money-grubbing—' Her voice was getting louder and crueller.

'Let *me* tell *you* something,' Horace broke in, outraged by the injustice of what she'd said, but still trying to keep his voice under control, to steer them back towards compromise. 'If I went about refusing to take payment from anyone in this town whom I thought less than perfectly moral, we'd both starve in no time, and so would the Lemans, children and all. You must know that.'

'—at least there is for anyone with any sort of claim to integrity.' Her voice topped his, furiously, as she sat up so straight under her quilts that a few satiny cushions slithered unnoticed to the floor. 'You'd know that yourself if you believed in anything, or stood for anything.'

Even after he'd gone back out into the treacherous sharpness of the evening winds, he couldn't get the sick dark look she'd given him as he'd turned away out of his head.

He wanted to hurry. But he hadn't reckoned on the tyranny of winter. Once there's snow-covered ice on the streets, there's no more running. To avoid slipping and breaking a limb, you have to remember to put each foot down carefully, with your weight directly above, shuffling like an invalid learning to walk. So Horace's haste had to take clumping, laboured form, puffing out white clouds as he stomped into the wind, ignoring the joyless wartime shop fronts and crowds of frostbitten beggars. He cursed his cautious feet and the gleaming black threat under the churned-up snow.

He could be back in an hour if he was lucky. Fifteen minutes to the shop, to pick up the box. Fifteen minutes to the palace on the Moika. Fifteen minutes for presenting his compliments and taking the money. Fifteen minutes home.

But Felix Youssoupoff was not at home.

Horace was admitted to the palace all the same. He looked

around at the marble floors and chandeliers, the servants in national dress. Everything seemed reassuringly as usual in Felix's part of the palace.

'He's spending a few days with his father-in-law, your excellency,' the Tatar butler explained impassively, taking receipt of the box and handing Horace an envelope containing his payment. Once Horace had counted out the notes they both signed the household book to prove payment had been made.

Horace half wanted to ask what had happened last night, and whether Rasputin had been here. He knew the butler a little, after all. But his nerve failed him. What if the man said yes?

On the way home, relieved to be able to finger that warm, dry paper in his pocket, Horace, feeling calmer, didn't risk his neck on the snow by even trying to hurry. There was no point. Inna would be asleep by the time he got there.

She wasn't.

She was lying in bed. But the lamp was on, and she turned red-rimmed, accusing eyes on him as soon as he entered.

'I hate to think of you touching that man's money,' she said.

He only grunted, and went into his dressing room. As he hung up his jacket, he was thinking: How can she have any idea of the kind of people who come into Fabergé's these days to spend the money they're making from the war? How can she have any idea of the financial reality confronting us all? He wanted her to feel loved, protected. And if her harsh words were the price, well, then he'd just have to bear it. Her coldness would pass.

But when he came out and lay down next to her, she didn't

roll towards him and entwine her body with his. They slept turned away from each other, huddling on opposite sides of the bed.

The chill in the Wallicks' bed in the apartment on Great Cavalry Street persisted through the between-worlds weeks that followed – both of them going to work as usual in the morning (though Inna didn't go to the hospital the following Friday, or ever again), and plodding home again in the evening, and eating, and talking perfectly amiably until bedtime about this and that, but, at night, pulling apart and huddling far away from each other under the covers. It felt strange to them both, but neither was willing to break the silence and talk about something that felt so full of danger to them both.

Everyone in town had learned the truth about that Friday night once Father Grigory's corpse, dumped over the rotting wooden bridge to Krestovsky Island at dawn, was finally fished up, frozen solid, but with head and upper body horribly battered, one eye almost out of its socket, stab wounds to the arms, deep rope-marks on the wrists, a bullet wound to the head, two more in the back, and God knows what other damage that would now never come to light, because the Empress, who couldn't bear the idea of an inquest being performed on her holy man, had stopped it midway with the words, 'Just leave the body of Father Grigory in peace.'

The Wallicks kept their distance from each other while the princely assassins jaunted around town for a few days, to standing ovations at the opera and cheers in officers' barracks everywhere, and their exalted families pleaded with the Tsar to pardon them. They were sent into exile anyway, when the sovereign angrily refused, and the imperial family broke into quarrelling factions.

Inna and Horace went on sleeping as far as possible from each other, despite the brutal cold that gripped the city as Christmas came, even after the muted celebratory meal at the Lemans'. (The family tried to make merry over cabbage soup and meat patties and the last of the bottled mushrooms and summer berries, along with an old bottle of brandy: the only things Madame Leman, for all her standing in line, had managed to muster for the table.)

Not everything changed. They even dressed up one evening towards the end of February and went together to the première of *Masquerade*, the great glittering Meyerhold production that *le tout Pétersbourg* had been waiting for through years of rehearsal (Horace was good at getting tickets).

Like everyone they knew, they'd wanted to see what the 300,000 roubles had been spent on. And yet, on the night itself, like so much else for Inna (and perhaps Horace too, now), the performance seemed alternately trite and grotesque. Onstage, an imperial capital's élite made merry while rushing to their doom; in the gilt loggias all around, Inna saw, were the élite of another imperial capital, gawping through opera glasses, guzzling ice cream and champagne; with nobody listening to the ominous crowds outside, calling for bread and freedom.

As they and the rest of the jewelled audience swept out, Horace said something so quiet that he might have been talking to himself (though if he had been, Inna thought, why would he be talking Russian? No, it was for her): 'So close to the starving . . . all this frenzied luxury. What is this: the Rome of the Caesars?' She didn't reply.

They couldn't find a cab to take them home. There were shots further up Nevsky. Machine guns were set up on rooftops. None of the coachmen wanted to go in the direction of the shots. One indignantly told Inna, 'Young lady, I have a wife and two children.'

So they linked arms and walked, in the silence that was becoming habitual to them. Then, as now seemed usual, they slept facing away from each other.

They woke up like that, far, far apart, when the future began the next morning: when the cold snap ended, and the women in the bread queues and the men in the marches finally lost patience with the avoidable shortages and fear of famine that the bureaucracy's inefficiency forced them to live with, and took matters into their own hands.

CHAPTER TWENTY

A band of grannies with linked hands pushed in front of Inna in the surging crowd. A low head whacked Inna in the mouth. She let go of the arms she was holding and clutched at her face. A little old woman looked up briefly and grinned at her. 'Sorry, dearie, sorry,' she mumbled, before turning away to join her group's next excited mass yell of 'bread! Bread! Bread!'

It was the first sunny day of the year, in February, and the tens of thousands of women who made up the bread queues were out on the streets of Petrograd. With the sun so unexpectedly on their faces again, they'd stopped to talk, for once, instead of just plodding miserably to their lines. And soon they'd started gathering in clumps, which coalesced, and grew, and were now moving together towards the centre of town. There were gales of defiant, raucous laughter. Women sang rude songs, and waved their empty baskets, and mounted the great hippo of a bronze horse on which the memorial statue to the last Emperor was seated, and cackled and cheered and egged each other on.

'Don't get separated, that's all; just hold on tight,' Madame Leman had said when they'd set out together to try and buy bread – because obviously, however excited she was at the latest turn of events, Madame Leman couldn't go out alone in those crowds, and Agrippina was too young to protect her. Anyway, they'd all wanted to see what would happen today. 'We'll be fine as long as we can feel each other's elbows.'

But now Madame Leman and Agrippina were being pushed one way, and Inna another. She could see their heads, bobbing up and down, further and further away; she could see Agrippina's anxiously energetic waving.

'Excuse me,' Inna kept saying to the women bearing down on her as she struggled to get back to them, 'excuse me.' But no one seemed to hear.

Of course Inna had wanted to come and see this. Throughout these last weeks of reproaching herself for having let Horace decide the course of their lives for so long, while she just sat inside that stifling apartment – 'Like a slug in silk cushions!' she'd been angrily telling herself – she'd been longing for the chance to do something brave and honest, to put things right with her conscience. The knowledge that Horace, locked away at his desk making trinkets for the rich, would certainly disapprove of this outing had put rebellious colour in her cheeks as she strode out. But she didn't like crowds, and, from the moment they'd set out, she'd also been scared of exactly this: that she, Madame Leman and Agrippina would be separated.

Yet now she was out in the street, with the sun glittering on windows and golden snow, with the sky so blue, and the air so bright, and with everyone so good-tempered in the crowd, and excited, and full of songs and stories, the panic she'd thought she'd feel was less overwhelming than she'd expected. After a while, she gave up and let herself go with the crush. There was really nothing else to be done.

She was slowly tugged by the human tide right across the curved Imperial Army General Staff building at the back of Palace Square, past the arch leading back on to Nevsky, nearly as far as the embankment on the other side. She was close enough to see the iced-over Neva behind the Admiralty Gardens. Every bit of that vast space was full, full to cracking, of bodies, not just women any more but men too: striking factory workers and the refugees who were always going on protests. Both women and men were shouting and laughing and shouting again, whether it was whatever slogan they believed in, or stories they'd heard. Blood had poured from the revolving door of the Astoria this morning! The mob got in there last night and drank the cellars dry! Respect for waiters: call us *vy*, not *ty*! The Fortress is open: they've let the prisoners out! Soon Inna began to enjoy herself.

And then something changed. She didn't know what, at first. You couldn't actually see anything way back where she was: the speeches were all up at the front, outside the green front of the Winter Palace. Back here, the mood of the people around her suddenly began to turn fearful.

'Cossacks,' she heard, a whisper that seemed to come from everywhere at once. 'The Cossacks are coming.'

It was worse than dismay, what she felt. It was a blackness. She couldn't think, yet she could feel her limbs poised to run. The problem was that there was nowhere to shelter. Just thousands of people, packed tight, looking at each other with the same dread.

She scanned the sea of faces around her.

One particular pair of eyes fixed on hers, belonging, she could see, to a very tall, gaunt, wild-bearded man in a shabby worker's wadded-cotton jacket, who'd made himself taller still by climbing on to the base of a street lamp.

It made her uncomfortable, that stare, which she went on feeling for a few long seconds more as she looked along the embankment and round towards the palace. It sent prickles down her spine. She turned back for a second look. But the man had gone; slipped down off his lamp base and been swallowed up by the crowd. She must have been imagining him staring at her.

The whisper started again. 'Cossacks, Cossacks.'

And then someone touched her – someone with an emaciated shoulder and back and a long straggly black beard.

Above the beard, a pair of dark eyes stared straight at her.

'Yasha,' she whispered.

His jacket smelled of mould and sweat and tobacco, but *he* still smelled, wonderfully, just as she'd remembered. 'I shouldn't be surprised to see you here, I suppose,' she said, breathlessly, feeling herself tremble as his arms enfolded hers. 'I mean, you left me for the Revolution, and here it is.'

She didn't dare meet his eyes any more; not now she'd named the terrible thing he'd done to her.

He turned her head with his hands, so he could see her face.

'What are you talking about?' he said, with none of the sugary tenderness that she'd added to her memories of him over the years. 'I didn't bloody well leave you for the Revolution.'

She opened her mouth to protest.

'I was in prison,' he went on roughly. 'I've just got out. We

282

all have. They opened the doors.' He jerked his head over the river, towards the Fortress. 'Look.' There was a tattoo on his neck, with a number. 'That idiot Kremer – remember him? I got him papers. The police found them on me the night I ran out.'

His voice softened. How deep it was; how soft. 'Didn't you know?' she heard him say.

Suddenly, deafeningly, just behind her, a man began yelling, 'Hoorah!' and then they were all at it: a new sea of sound. The panic seemed to have disappeared as quickly as it had come.

'Come on,' Yasha said in her ear. 'Let's get out of here.'

The crowd was fluid now. There were just as many people as before, but things had eased so you could walk again. Yasha was making for the Triumphal Arch that would take them back on to Nevsky, from where they could duck into the back streets on the other side and get to the Lemans' – or anywhere else – safely. They slipped out between families and friends, all hugging each other, half-hysterical with relief, and under the arch they saw the reason for the change of mood.

A detachment of Cossacks had dismounted and put down the rifles and sabres that might have killed half the crowd. They were being mobbed by a throng of new admirers, who were clapping them on the back and cheering. One snub-nosed youth was grinning bashfully and carrying a bunch of red roses as if he didn't know what to do with such a thing. His horse's reins were in his other hand, and there was a girl in his saddle, a street-trader girl in a wadded jacket like Yasha's and a ragged dog-fur hat. She was grinning round at the whistling crowd, waving and blowing kisses.

'Just walked up to them, she did, with her basket of roses,' the man next to Inna said. 'Sweating a bit, she was. Brave as anything. I mean to say, they had their rifles pointed. They was all ready to charge. But they didn't. He took her flowers, that bloke there. And then they all got down off their 'osses. And now look at them.'

There were women pinning red ribbons on the Cossacks' uniforms. There were men calling out to each other, all around, a phrase something like the old Easter greeting, 'Christ is arisen!' only without the Christ: 'Russia is arisen!'

'Russia is arisen!' the unknown man said to Inna, and kissed her.

She kissed the stranger back, 'It is risen indeed!' she answered, feeling Yasha's arm around her, feeling the joy of this new world in which everything was possible. Red: the colour of revolution. Red roses: the colour of hope.

A courtyard, somewhere, with no one around, and his hand still in hers . . . There were too many things to say. Where to begin?

'What do you mean, they opened the doors?'

Yasha grinned. He stopped walking. She did too. How close they were standing. How abruptly he spoke. Perhaps that was prison. She didn't know him very well any more.

'We were in the yard, maybe two hundred of us. Then we saw the door open. Just like that. The guards were all gone, and there was the street, and, just round the corner, the bridge . . . Well, I mean, we knew there was trouble in town. But still. I thought: Maybe it's a trick? Get you through that gate then shoot you. A few of us started sidling up towards the gate, casually, like they'd just slip through on the quiet. But no one said a word. A few actually went through. Then the first one who'd got through, a bloke called Mitrofan, was walking over the cobbles out there. He got a good way off, then looked round. Slowly, like he couldn't believe his luck. And then he turned back to us, and started yelling. "Come on, you idiots! There's no one here at all! Get on out!"'

They were both laughing now; Yasha still disbelieving, his laughter with a hysterical edge.

'And you did,' Inna finished.

'Ran like fuck; hundreds of us.' It was so dark in the courtyard that she could only see his eyes, crinkled up. 'And I ran straight into you; it's a time of bloody miracles, I'm telling you.' And then his eyes shut, too, and the kiss began.

It was only when his hands moved to her blouse, crushed her breasts, and started a clumsy quest for buttons and hooks that she came to, and pulled back a fraction.

'Yash,' she whispered, dizzily, right into his ear, because she couldn't move away from his skin or smell, not altogether; it was magnetic, overpowering, this need to touch him; and surely she was demonstrating virtue enough by stopping the kiss? 'Yash . . . I'm not your wife.'

He nuzzled at her neck, not wanting to know anything.

'I thought you'd gone,' she whispered. He ignored that too. 'I married Horace.'

It overwhelmed her, the cosmic injustice of it, the stupidity: that she could feel all this for Yasha, but belong elsewhere.

But Yasha didn't sound bothered. 'Did you now? Well, we'll soon see about that,' he murmured, as if she'd told him a joke he wasn't all that interested in laughing at, because he had something better to think about. He grinned down at her. 'Time of bloody miracles. Didn't I say?'

*

The Lemans were still all out, except Marcus, who was down in the workshop, when Inna and Yasha tiptoed into the apartment, quiet as thieves.

Inna's mind was clear as she worked out what to do, her body full of almost religious thankfulness for that first communion of their bodies in that blocked-off courtyard with what felt like the whole city singing and laughing out in the streets. She took the key for the attic room from the hook in the kitchen and gave it to Yasha. The Lemans would be glad enough to have him back, wouldn't they?

'Show me my room,' Yasha whispered in her ear. 'Mrs Wallick.'

And they both laughed.

She laughed later on, too, when she saw on what unlikely chests red ribbons had sprouted: on Madame Leman's and Agrippina's and Barbarian's, of course, but also on the scrawny chest of Aunt Cockatoo, the genteel séance-holding neighbour, who'd spent a miserable winter last year standing on street corners selling her trinkets for food, and this winter, more profitably, selling the moonshine vodka she'd taken to brewing despite the ban. That evening, excitedly talking over the day's events over whatever-you-can-find soup in the Leman kitchen, Aunt Cockatoo declared herself as sick of the imperial family and the corruption all around them as everyone else. 'Who needs the life to come, or the Emperor, come to that, when our life on earth is turning into such a festival of freedom?' she said. 'There'll be no more crime now we've got the Revolution: or *chinovniki*, or bribes, or drink . . .'

Who needed drink? They were all drunk on happiness.

They all laughed over Yasha's tales from the Fortress: the

lice, the idleness, the cold, the prisoners whispering in the cells. Yasha, now clean-shaven again, and shining-eyed, was dressed in one of Monsieur Leman's old country shirts, with the buttons up the side of the neck and a strip of country braid on the cuffs, and with a pair of very baggy, but too short trousers, held up against his long lean length with a belt.

'How happy we are to have you back, dear boy,' Madame Leman kept saying, and Marcus kept clapping Yasha on the back. Inna just watched, keeping to herself her memories of the afternoon up in the attics, alone together, and what had happened between finding the clothes, and the combs; what they'd done together as the dust rose from the old mattress, making them both sneeze.

Inna even laughed in acknowledgement, though it was thinner laughter, when Horace turned up to take her home. Horace wasn't laughing. Her husband came in looking strained and breathless, and went straight to Inna. When she didn't get up, he swooped down and kissed the top of her head. He didn't even see Yasha.

'I've just seen someone shot on Nevsky,' he said. 'Right beside me. Some young woman with a red ribbon handing out leaflets dropped down dead on the pavement. Just like that.'

'That will have been a sniper,' Marcus replied knowledge-ably. 'And I expect everyone ran away, which will be what they want, to spread fear and keep everyone inside. To regain control.'

'Who?' asked Aunt Cockatoo, in her splendidly grating voice. Her yellow eyes blinked double-time above her little hooked nose.

'The police, of course! The Tsar's police!' Barbarian said.

Madame Leman tut-tutted at him. But as Inna reflected on the possibility that a fat man with silver-gilt buttons might indeed still be sitting on a rooftop, watching her down the sights of a rifle as she went to sit in the bread queue, or find a paper, the hilarity went out of the evening. Everyone else was probably having the same quiet spasm of dread she was, she thought; they'd all be imagining the alleyways and courtyards and stone colonnades they might cut through to avoid main roads, if they were to live.

'I was thinking that perhaps,' Horace began, 'dear Lidiya' – he nodded at Madame Leman – 'in the circumstances, we might stay the night here?'

Inna winced. She couldn't even begin to imagine staying in one garret room with Horace with Yasha just on the other side of the partition.

She glanced up at Yasha, on the other side of the table. She'd avoided looking at him all evening till now, especially since Horace arrived, but he just shrugged and grinned insouciantly – the picture of revolutionary dash. 'Just make sure you don't stand around giving out leaflets on Nevsky, Wallick,' he drawled. 'That's how to keep your hide intact.'

It was rude, but the children laughed.

Inna tried to stifle the queasy guilt she felt at their laughter. Well, he *is* only worried about keeping his hide intact, she told herself sternly. And he took that man's money.

Horace blinked. Then, rather uneasily, he laughed, too.

'Kagan – Yasha, isn't it? Delighted to see you back, young man. Delighted,' he said. 'And I can see you think I'm fretting needlessly. Well, you may be right.' He nodded self-deprecatingly and gave one of those meaningless little English half-smiles. 'But I do want to be sure I've done all I can to protect my wife, whom I will, after all, be walking home tonight.'

Inna and Horace walked home by a cautious route, along cross streets, through courtyards and service doors, down deserted places where there were few footprints on the snow.

Looking at the occasional places where earlier sets of footprints blurred, trying not to remember that other nearby courtyard where she and Yasha had come to a halt, earlier on, or to shiver with pleasure as she recalled his urgent breathing, and the lift of fabric, and the hand that had held both hers above her head, in the attic, Inna kept very quiet.

'Kagan looks well,' Horace said.

'He's just out of prison,' she countered. 'Madame Leman is letting him sleep in the attic for now. And Marcus is pleased. He'll be around to help in the workshop.'

'Maybe you can stop working there, then.'

'Stop? But I love it there! I don't want to stop!' she said, too loud and too fast.

But Horace didn't seem to notice her vehemence. He only nodded.

The police – that last vestige of the Tsarist order, now exiled to the rooftops with their guns – were the last to give up their vain hope of retaining power. People carried on collapsing unexpectedly in city crowds for weeks, as February became March, causing a panicky scattering of those around them whenever the tell-tale trickle of red appeared on a coat on the ground. For weeks, too, people carried on dragging down from one rooftop or another some die-hard sniper who'd been taking pot-shots at innocent civilians.

But the Emperor went quickly and quietly enough. They said he'd abdicated internally long before he agreed to step down. Smoking (he was always smoking) with the smoke rising silently past his beard and empty eyes.

What people started saying was that the riots of February, and, to a lesser extent, the new provisional government that replaced the former Emperor, were bringing about the moral resurrection of the people. February became known as the festival of freedom, and the patriots who had torn down the double-headed eagles of the Tsars as the restorers of Russia's virtue.

Throughout March, having told Horace she was quite safe and, in this new, more elevated, moral atmosphere on the streets, didn't need to be walked home from the Lemans' after work, Inna quietly went upstairs to Yasha's every evening at six, a minute or two after he'd left the workshop.

He'd come to his door half-naked, and pull her to him. She'd stopped being shocked at his burning prison gauntness by now. She'd just sigh into him, and then one of them would breathe 'shh' with a hint of a laugh, and click the door shut. After that there was nothing in their shabby secret world beyond the two of them: the kiss inside the wrist, the feel of skin, the tautness of stomach, the slow entwining of limbs. Sometimes they never even reached the bed.

She hadn't realized you could have love without the trappings she'd become so accustomed to, without candles and little kindnesses and breakfast chat. She'd never realized it could be this simple: this ache, this heat, this catch of breath at a touch.

At seven, she'd dress and somehow take herself out of the room, pulling away from the mouth exploring her neck again, from the longing and melting, from the teasing whisper, 'Oh, not yet.' An hour was only a moment. But the memory of him stayed with her all through the night and day that followed, the smell and taste. She was languorous with love, drugged with it. It was everything else that was a dream.

At seven, Yasha also had to go striding out, taking whatever bit of bread and onion he'd saved from the midday meal, to the halls where he now spent his evenings discussing the future. At seven, too full of memory for guilt, she'd go home to her husband.

CHAPTER TWENTY-ONE

It was a bright cold Sunday afternoon in March when Prince Felix Youssoupoff sauntered into the drawing room of the apartment in Great Cavalry Street, behind a hovering, anxious-looking Horace, and bowed to Inna.

There's no sugar to offer him for tea, was her first panicky thought. Even after the Red Revolution, you still needed to queue all night to buy basics at dawn: one night for bread, one night for meat, one night for oil, one night for sugar, and so on. The only difference in the queuing since February was that now you queued with hope. But it was still dog-cold sleeping on your stool on the street, even under wadded blankets, with your pillow. If she and Horace didn't have sugar, it wasn't because they didn't have the money to pay for it, or that the queuing was too onerous for her, because Horace did alternate nights, sitting up with the women. They'd simply agreed weeks ago to give up on buying sugar, since what was the point? They never had guests at the apartment, and they'd be better giving Madame Leman their sugar money instead, so she could use it for her family.

Inna thought next, There's only a tiny bit of tea, too. Then anger replaced her panic: Why has Horace even let him in? What's Felix Youssoupoff doing back here, anyway?

Youssoupoff didn't belong in this revolutionary Petrograd as Inna did. She loved the happiness of now: the self-congratulatory victory salutes in the street, among perfect strangers who suddenly felt themselves all together as part of the brotherhood of man, in this great new beginning. The provisional government had, among many other good things, abolished the Pale of Settlement down south and granted Jews full civil rights, at last. It was a triumphant end to the campaign that had started by getting Beilis freed. Inna would never need to feel less than equal to anyone again. ('We're free,' Yasha said, whenever they were on their own, 'as well as equal. Both of us.' She knew he meant, 'Leave Horace.')

Yet, however exciting February had been – and however her private life had been secretly transformed – Inna was well aware that there was a lot that hadn't yet come right in the Revolution.

Horace still had money. Even if he didn't get paid very regularly, he still went to work, and Fabergé's was still rich, and he didn't complain of being short of cash. He had savings, she thought. And they never went hungry, even though it was hard to buy food in the shops to cook. But everything could be had, even in this new land of virtue, if you were willing to pay the price in the formerly fussy restaurants where you could still find uncertain meats in mysterious stews as well as enigmatic alcohols in grand bottles.

Yet Madame Leman only waved her arms indignantly whenever Horace suggested she and her family come with them to these restaurants. 'What, take my children to sit with those vulgarians? Profiteers? Pimps? I'd sooner starve! We all would!' Inna wished she would be less indignant about their invitations, because it was obvious the Lemans were feeling the pinch. You had to eat, after all, and, if they weren't actually murderers, who cared who was sitting at the next table?

And Marcus was miserable, cooped up in the workshop, chafing to be out and away like Yasha, longing to be cutting a dash among the crowds of men in long overcoats arguing in smoky meeting houses every evening; but forced, by his crippled leg, and the snow, and the responsibility of being the master of the family, to stay at home.

Freedom was what Yasha talked about; but what Horace said, with one of his cultured English smirks, whenever the conversation turned to the Revolution was, 'Fine words butter no parsnips.' And he was right. Inna couldn't help noticing that Madame Leman cooked soup for midday, on good days, if there were cabbages or potatoes on sale. Otherwise they made do with tea and bread. Inna had no idea how Madame Leman was managing to pay her rent, or the children's school fees.

Still, whenever Inna felt downhearted at the various shortcomings of life after the Revolution, she let herself be sustained by remembering – with a certain pleasure – that at least Youssoupoff and his murderous friends, who'd wanted their killing to stop a revolution before it started, had failed. She'd enjoyed imagining the prince cooped up at his father's estate, and his grand duke lover kicking his heels in a barracks on the Persian border, contemplating the rebellion they hadn't managed to prevent. Feeling their power ebb.

They'd be off abroad soon, she thought. They'd never come back to Petrograd.

Yet here he was, in a fine brown suit, handsomer and more pleased with himself than ever, if that were possible. Twirling a stick.

Of course, she realized, after a moment's rage at the smugness of the man. The Emperor who'd exiled him was gone. So the prince had come skipping boldly back – freed, like everyone else, by the Revolution.

She stood up, but didn't extend a hand. She wasn't going to shake hands with a murderer.

'Citizen Youssoupoff,' she said, coolly: today-speak. You weren't allowed to call the mighty 'your excellency' any more, and she didn't choose, either, to call him 'Felix Felixovich,' the well-bred way of addressing him as an equal.

She saw Horace wince, noticed the way his back bent a little more (he was a good head taller than Youssoupoff) as he started murmuring, with a fussy courtesy she found achingly hypocritical, 'Felix Felixovich, do sit down, please.'

'I'm afraid we've no tea,' Inna said.

Youssoupoff only smiled wider. She got the uneasy feeling that he understood her discomfiture, and was enjoying it.

'Ah, yes, the new nomenclature,' he said lightly. 'You're quite right, *Citoyenne* Wallick. We must all get used to it.' He made a point of tweaking at his trouser legs as he sat down, so as not to bag the perfect cut. 'My apologies for dropping in unannounced. But – as I was just explaining to your husband outside – I may not be in town for long. I'm just here to arrange the restoration of some of my art collection.' He spoke as if nothing had changed; as if he hadn't even noticed the Revolution. 'Including my grandfather's violins.

Beautiful instruments, I'm told, though sadly neglected. Also . . .' he paused, delicately. 'How to put this in a way that won't give offence to a master maker of your renown?'

Inna glanced in astonishment at Horace – she wasn't in the least renowned. Whatever had he said about her to inspire this piece of blatant flattery? Almost imperceptibly, from behind Youssoupoff's chair, Horace shook his head: nothing to do with *me*.

'. . . the violins are a little, shall we say, battle-scarred?' Youssoupoff looked at his hands, adding, with composure, 'Because I'm afraid my brother and I didn't treat them with much respect, as boys. In fact, we used to fight duels with them.' He laughed.

Inna didn't laugh back. She could almost see those two beautiful princelings, yelling and scrambling over the backs of sofas as they carelessly whacked each other. She could just imagine those dozens of layers of slow-drying varnish, each sanded down to no more than a fine glow by some craftsman with painfully bent back and failing eyes, cracking and splintering. She shut her eyes. Hadn't Horace said that one of Youssoupoff's violins was a Stradivarius?

'Reprehensible, of course.' She heard the prince sigh. 'So there we are. One of them is damaged, and, naturally, as soon as I looked them over and realized how badly it needed repair, of course I thought, *at once*, of you.' He bowed, and then looked expectantly at her.

She didn't respond. She just kept her eyes turned down, staring at her own twitchy fingers knotting and reknotting themselves.

He resumed, with exquisite patience, 'That is, to make myself perfectly plain, dear *Citoyenne* Wallick, may I offer you a commission to come to me at my home on the Moika River and put my Stradivarius in good order?'

For a moment, she was tempted. She'd never worked on a Stradivarius, never even seen one . . .

But then she remembered who was offering her this work.

Decisively, she shook her head. 'I'm afraid I couldn't possibly,' she said. Her tone would have been firmer if she hadn't looked behind Youssoupoff to Horace for encouragement, and seen that, far from nodding quiet approval at this high-minded rejection, he was looking agonized, and nodding, frantically. *Say yes*, his eyes were saying.

For a moment, she couldn't understand what Horace was doing with his hand. He'd turned it over, palm up, and was rubbing his fingers urgently together.

And then it all coalesced. The ten pounds of flour they'd bought, way back when, to stave off famine, had now been reduced to a loaf or two and a few rusks. The jar of oil was half empty, and when had they last seen milk, or yellow butter, or eggs? Last autumn's mushroom pickles and cranberry jams, given them by Madame Leman, were almost used up. The shrunken sack of tea, the empty bag of sugar, the many evenings out in restaurants, and Horace's reluctance to say what the meals actually cost, and Madame Leman's face as she brought out the glass jar with her housekeeping money in, every day, and counted the diminishing piles. (Because, even if you had the time to stand in the queues all night and all day, what was the point if you didn't have enough money to buy the pitiful amounts of food on offer once you got to the front?) And when was the last time the workshop had been paid? Or Horace, come to that? They'd been rejoicing, only that morning, over the parcel from Horace's sister in

297

England – dried blackcurrants! Raisins! Coffee! – but how long could they sustain both of them, let alone the Lemans, on Beatrice's raisins and coffee?

Doubtfully, she went on looking at Horace, wondering suddenly what other expenses he was silently paying. The Lemans' rent? The children's school fees? Wondering, too, how much he still had in savings. Yes, she could see what his gesture meant, now: they couldn't afford the luxury of principles.

But if she took this job, she'd be no less of a money-grubber than the man she'd married.

Hesitantly, she started to speak again. 'I couldn't possibly,' she repeated. 'Possibly . . .' She took a deep breath and looked Youssoupoff in the eye, firmly shutting out everything except what was necessary from her mind. '. . . do a job so delicate, except in the workshop, with all the proper tools.'

She heard Horace sigh with relief.

She squared her shoulders. 'I'll come to you, tomorrow, and take a look at the damage,' she added. Because the palace on the Moika was only a place, after all: a geographical point, a pile of bricks and mortar. There was no point in getting the horrors about a place. Whether she went there or not wouldn't change what had happened within its walls. Nothing would.

'I can't make any promises, mind.'

She heard another sigh, behind. She sighed too.

'Not till I've seen it.'

Perhaps it was only because of her secret with Yasha – that snatched other life with her lover, experienced in minutes and whispers and kisses in that room, in the dust and dark, by lamplight, which she hardly dared call to mind here in front of her husband – that Inna could even begin to understand that, in a different way, she also, secretly yet profoundly, desired that Stradivarius of Youssoupoff's.

So while she told herself that she was helping save the Lemans by getting a well-paid job in for Marcus's workshop, putting meat and sour cream on the table, what she really wanted to see was that most beautiful and glamorous of musical instruments, a violin that in the normal run of things would have been out of her reach. I just want a glimpse, she told herself, just to prove to myself that I've really been offered it. That's not so bad, is it?

A vanity, she then admonished herself, sternly. But a powerful one, because she already half knew that, once she'd seen it, she'd be unable to resist the temptation to go further, to touch it, know it, work on it, to try to save it, to make it hers.

Hers and Yasha's, because in her mind she'd begun to move on to the next step, and was imagining them sharing the task of making that damaged beauty whole; and seeing the excitement of the work binding him closer to her.

In the last few weeks, this had become overwhelmingly important to Inna.

At first, in all the shock of rediscovering Yasha, it had been magical enough just to be alone together for a time in that familiar old room: the creak of the bed; his skin against hers, his eyes on her nakedness; the hardness of their bodies; the softness of their voices, afterwards . . .

Maintaining the shell of secrecy had felt attractive too: the life lived in two parallel universes, one of which no one else could see, except herself and the man she now knew she'd always loved. She'd been enjoying the kindly power, conferred on her by love, of saving others from hurt by shielding them from reality.

And this was where she'd got stuck. Horace might have faded in her mind in these past weeks, but even to think of the conversation she might begin with him, the one that would destroy everything – and annihilate him – was too agonizing. If she tried to imagine it she felt sick. She couldn't do that to him, or herself; she couldn't imagine life without Horace there in the background. So she was stuck in the tainted, muddled here and now, clinging on to both her radiant secret love, and her weary married habits. She was nostalgic sometimes for the simpler way things had been, before Yasha's return; yet all she wanted was to be with him, and she could not bear Horace hanging forlornly around, making her feel cheap and guilty.

Yasha had started to ask what she thought was happening between them. It had been an innocent enough mistake, her marrying the wrong man, Yasha kept saying; he could see how it had happened, but now they were living a deception. And he didn't like that. It was time to clear things up. She was free to leave; there were no children. Life was different now, he said; she should liberate herself from a contract made in error. He'd find a place to live. She should go and live there with him, after telling Horace frankly why she was leaving. She could go on working for the Lemans, and Yasha would work there, too, as much as Marcus could pay him for. He'd also spend a lot of time at meetings, he said, with the straightforwardness she loved in him, because this revolution was only the beginning. There was so much more to do.

Otherwise . . .

Well, he hadn't said what, otherwise, but she'd seen, from the play of his eyebrows, that he was thinking that he might just go. And that possibility was unbearable.

Yet she still hadn't said yes.

Maybe it was the idea of sitting alone in some shabby room, waiting for a husband who never came home from those all-night revolutionaries' meetings. Maybe it was just that she couldn't bear the prospect of hurting Horace, who so visibly loved her. Or maybe it was her fear of shocking the Lemans with her ingratitude for all that her husband had done for her. Whichever it was, Inna couldn't be sure she wanted what Yasha was suggesting. Not now, not yet.

And so she told herself that taking this violin and making it whole, with Yasha, would give her a breathing space. Because if Yasha would only wait until it was done, surely she'd know more clearly what was in her heart.

Reverently, Inna stroked the instruments on the marble table, fingering the glow of the wood, the old, lovely Cremonese varnish, and wondering how to heal the cracks and breaks. She'd been gazing at them for hours. As well as the Strad, there was also an Amati, and a strange jewelled and heavily inlaid violin with half its gemstones missing (but a bag in the case containing some of the loose ones), which the prince had said had been made for the French Sun King, centuries earlier, and a Strad-shaped viola that the prince didn't know was a viola, let alone whether it was a Strad, though the papers with it said it was a Vuillard copy of one. Even broken, they were all so beautiful. And, when the Strad's mangled loveliness was repaired, she could see it would sing with the voice of an angel.

Looking at them, Inna had almost forgotten why this job was ugly.

It was only the Strad that she was being asked to repair. It was the only one of the four instruments that had been really damaged by being treated as a child's weapon. Its back had a great open gash in it. (Had they whacked it down on a spike? Or stabbed it?) Its front was badly scratched. There was a rattling inside, as if the sound-post had gone, along with the vanished bridge. The scroll had a bite taken out. And a peg was missing.

The other instruments had scratches and gashes and missing strings and broken bridges, but, locked up in their cases, could safely travel abroad. And that was clearly what the prince was planning. One glance round his rooms showed that he was taking stock. He was packing. There were boxes and bags of jewels and trinkets out on tables everywhere. There were carpenters banging and sawing, too, building shelves into alcoves in every room: secret storage to hide the bigger valuables behind the walls. There were piles of movables being readied so he could stuff them in his pockets for a quick getaway, if there was any more revolution.

That was all these violins were to him, she could see: portable wealth.

Inna was glad Youssoupoff had taken himself off to read newspapers in the library, and stopped lurking around, chatting. She needed to concentrate.

She'd disliked him more than ever today: boastful and skittish, talking too fast with the pupils of his eyes turned into great black pools. He'd offered to give her a guided tour of the cellar where *it* had all happened before showing her the violins. Even when she'd refused that pleasure, the prince had told her the long, strange, gleeful story he told everyone about Rasputin, full of that Satanic strength of his, refusing to die, even after eating enough cyanide to fell an elephant, fed to him in little pink cakes (as if, Inna thought, locked into her defeated silence, any friend of Rasputin wouldn't have known he'd always hated sweet things).

Refusing to die, again and again, even after first Youssoupoff then the MP Purishkevich shot him. Rising up, again and again, roaring. 'Like a hairy black bear,' Youssoupoff reminisced, enjoying his ghost story. 'Or a mad bull. Terrifying.' His story ended with Rasputin refusing to die even after they'd bound him, and put him in a sack, and thrown him through a hole in the river ice. Which was what everyone said – that his arms were out of their ropes by the time they'd dredged him up, frozen solid; he'd been trying to get free, even under water.

As Youssoupoff took her upstairs to the study where the violins were, she was thinking of all the other stories, the ones Youssoupoff didn't tell. There were people who said it was his friend, Grand Duke Dmitry Pavlovich, who'd actually shot Rasputin dead, or dead-ish – since he was the only one who could shoot – and that Youssoupoff had just taken credit for the killing to shield his more royal friend from the Emperor's anger. There were people who'd said the killing was a plot by the English secret service, who'd urged Youssoupoff and Purishkevich and the others to murder so Rasputin and the Tsarina wouldn't make a separate peace with the Germans . . . Oh, all kinds of whispered stories. Inna had even heard that Rasputin's daughters were accusing Youssoupoff of falling, insane with rage, on their father's body, and of castrating his corpse . . .

Now, as she stroked the Strad that Youssoupoff had so nearly destroyed, trying to make a list of what she'd need to do to put it right, she thought, I'll never know Felix Youssoupoff's real secrets; I don't want to.

She'd take the violin, anyway. She'd bring that, at least, back to life.

Back at the Lemans' shop, she set it out on the worktop.

Marcus was only too ready to be enchanted.

They were both gazing softly at it, like adoring parents watching a sick child sleep, when Yasha came in. Inna's heart lurched.

'You're joking,' Yasha said, when Marcus told him. 'Mending *his* fiddles?' Still in his coat, with his wet hat in his hands, he grinned, ready for the laugh.

'Just look at it,' said Marcus. 'It's the most incredible thing. A Strad, Yash, in our workshop.'

The cheerfulness was fading from Yasha's face as he looked uncertainly at Inna and Marcus, clearly wondering why they weren't smiling.

Inna kept quiet.

'We have to eat, Yash,' Marcus pleaded.

Yasha grinned his wolf grin. 'You don't get much bread for thirty pieces of silver.' But he did at least step up to the battered fiddle box, which was covered in undistinguished pigskin. Inna held her breath. Because surely, once he'd looked, he'd see the magic too.

He looked inside and reached out a hand to feel the biggest of the gashes across the front, and to touch the damaged scroll. He sucked in a long breath through his teeth.

'That savage,' he said, softly. 'Did he *eat* it, or what?'

Inna watched as, very gently, Yasha lifted it out, and, with nurse's hands, turned it over, to inspect the gash in its back. She could only hope the sheer splintered beauty of it would make him want its loveliness more than his revolutionary principles, as she and Marcus both already did.

He was shaking his head, now. 'A one-piece back,' he said thoughtfully, stroking the beauty of the tigerish stripes running diagonally across the wounded wood. 'There's some maple in the store with a grain not unlike this, isn't there?' he added, looking up, and Marcus nodded.

Marcus, Inna could now see, was also, if for more practical reasons, longing for Yasha to bring his skill to this difficult work, to help the workshop make a success of it.

'It'll be quite a job,' Yasha said at last. His eyes were still on the violin. 'It'll take us a while.'

Inna's heart lurched again.

'When do we begin?' he asked.

CHAPTER TWENTY-TWO

Sometimes, Horace imagined himself saying to Inna, 'You talk about Yasha a lot these days,' because of course he was alert to the negative possibilities of young Kagan's reappearance in their lives, especially at a moment when things had somehow gone so awry between them. He had been aware of the danger from the first. And now the pair of them were whispering away all day in the workshop over Youssoupoff's violin; and Horace couldn't help but be aware of Marcus's embarrassed grins when he saw Horace watching him, or of the furtive happiness Horace kept glimpsing in his wife's eyes.

It wasn't really Yasha she talked about, to be precise, any more than she ever mentioned Youssoupoff's name. It was the violin. But Horace heard Yasha hiding in all Inna's excited explanations. She said that they were approaching the repair from two different angles. She said she and Marcus were working together to make replica curved wooden shapes to patch into the existing violin. Yasha, meanwhile, was making a whole new violin of the same pattern – a very late

Stradivarius design, from 1730 – as a control. If repairing the existing pieces of wood failed, their back-up plan was to cannibalize Yasha's copy, taking it apart and using the back or possibly the scroll from it to replace the broken part in the real violin. They were also intending to experiment with varnish on the new instrument Yasha was making, to be sure they had a recipe, and a method, for reproducing the colour and depth of the original varnish as precisely as possible.

'Thank God we've got Yasha to work on it; he's the only one of us with anything like the experience you need. He's a wonderful luthier.' One way or another, she kept saying, they'd have the best possible version of the Strad mended, and playable, by the end of the summer.

Even if the Youssoupoff payment for the violin would tide them all over for several months to come, Horace knew that it had been a mistake encouraging Inna to take it. He wished, now, that he'd just let her say no.

As the cold months of winter turned into spring, then early summer, part of him wanted to succumb to raging, helpless, pointless, jealousy, but he'd never known how to rage. He was better at working out carefully how best to proceed.

To the relief of the staff of Fabergé, a new day of anti-war rioting that might have brought further, more extreme revolution fizzled out in the heavy rain of July.

Horace had been bringing in the papers every morning, and telling the Fabergé foreigners who worked in the back room, sheltering among the mahogany shelves as if behind circled wagons, what was in them. And this particular piece of July news suddenly seemed, as he read, like an opportunity.

What the failure of the latest action by the left seemed to

have brought was a swing back to the right. In the aftermath, triumphant, preening, vain Alexander Kerensky took over government at the Tauride Palace and booted out the trouble-making workers' deputies of the Soviet, who until now had been meeting there too, to hold their interminable smoky, shouty sessions at a girls' boarding school on the edge of town. As Kerensky began planning to move the former Emperor and his family away from Tsarskoye Selo to somewhere less volatile, in the remote interior, the tiny extreme-left Social Democrat faction known, ironically, as the Majority, or *Bolsheviki* – vociferous in its demands for peace at any price – was also kicked out of its cosy city headquarters. It was reported that the foul-mouthed bald leader of these Bolsheviks had scuttled right out of town, for fear of arrest, and was now sleeping in haystacks somewhere, wearing a blond wig.

He was an almost comically unlikeable character, this Lenin, as Horace told his fellow workers at Fabergé. He'd lived abroad until April, and hated all the home-grown revolutionaries he'd found here on his return, and wanted to steal their triumph from them. His head was polished smooth like a billiard ball, who called everyone he met bastard-blockhead-bugger-cunt-shit, and who hated music because, he said, it made him want to say kind, stupid things, and pat people's heads, when what you had to do nowadays was beat them round the head, beat them without mercy.

Well, never mind the losers. It was who was winning that mattered. The diktats coming down now from on high, with their retreat from revolution towards a more usual kind of authoritarianism, felt very familiar.

Some Bolsheviks were hanged – their Lenin hadn't been

wrong to be so scared – and the death penalty was brought back at the Front. Soldiers were banned from joining Soviets. In the city, the eight-hour factory day was abolished. And, by night, the Black Hundreds were out again, beating up Jews.

'So *that's* the way things are going now, *hein?*' Carl Fabergé said with satisfaction after Horace read out that last snippet, once the other men had started moving off to their desks. Not that he especially wanted Jews beaten up, Horace knew. He just wanted normality back, as they all did. And, in Russia, the Black Hundreds, and their authoritarian masters, had always been normality. '*They* can always sniff out the lie of the land, those ones.'

Gently, Horace shook his head, because he didn't believe this state of affairs would last for long, or lead to normality. The revolutionary genie was out of the bottle for good. It had vanished for a moment, but it was waiting, and it would reappear, all too soon, in some new shape. He should talk to Monsieur Fabergé; and now, he hoped, was the right time. 'I wonder, sir, if you and I could have a word in private?'

If Horace admired the carefree ways of his wild young artists, it was perhaps because he planned his own life with such caution. His thinking today ran along these lines. Fabergé, as a jeweller, had a safe, which in these uncertain times had been enough to turn him into an unofficial banker. Half Petrograd kept something in Fabergé's safe: their jewels, or their savings, because Fabergé's was believed to be safer than any of the real banks. The clients were all certain that, if there were another, worse revolution, one that obliged them to leave the country in a hurry, they'd be safe from runs on the banks if they'd left their movables with Fabergé. They'd just drop in, pick up their things, and be off. But what, Horace had asked, if this Kerensky who was in power now was toppled in his turn? Who else might be out there, hiding in haystacks, plotting a return? Could Fabergé be sure that his safe would really be safe?

'It would be like a form of insurance, you might say,' Horace finished.

He was pleased to see Carl Fabergé thoughtfully stroking his beard.

'You may be right, *mon vieux*,' the jeweller said.

Another man living with Fabergé's awful anxieties – his factories turned over to munitions, his order book collapsing, and so many mouths to feed – might have had bloodshot eyes and a blue-stubbled chin. A drink habit, or worse. But then that's what being Swiss did for you, Horace thought, admiringly. Fabergé just kept slowly nodding, and stroking his beard. You could only see his worry in the flicker of his eyes.

They wrote a contract, just the two of them, right there and then, and got a clerk to witness them signing it. 'For form's sake,' Fabergé said apologetically. That piece of paper wouldn't help either of them, in law, if things went wrong, Horace thought. This was a question of trust. But he, too, welcomed the illusion that a contract still counted, and signed with respectful pleasure.

Then the two gentlemen went to the safe, together, and, as if this were a perfectly normal thing to do, took out about a third of the little boxes and bags, loaded them into a crate with their own hands, then found a boy to wheel the closed crate out, and put it, and Horace, into a taxi.

'Wait,' Carl Fabergé said, once Horace was in the carriage.

He came out a few minutes later, with a canvas bag. 'You have thought of everything else. Allow me to have thought of this first. Inside: one large chisel, and one hammer.' He grinned, as merry as a boy to be sharing his burden.

He'd had that look in his eye, earlier, when Horace had first said: 'After all, who would ever think of looking for your treasures in a run-down attic in Dostoyevskyland? It's the safest place you could possibly keep them!'

'They're for getting up the floorboards,' Fabergé added, now.

Naturally Horace did not tell Madame Leman that he would be jimmying up her attic floorboards and stuffing them with Fabergé jewels and keepsakes, to keep them safe from any socialists who might come trying to requisition the jeweller's safe.

Instead he told her, as soon as the July trouble on the streets had died away, that it was getting too expensive to keep on his flat on Great Cavalry Street, and that he would like it if Inna and he could move into one of the attic rooms at the top of the Lemans' house. If Yasha were to leave the other room, he added, he'd take that too. There were many advantages to living together. Horace would pay rent – less rent than before – to Madame Leman, not to an outsider. She, meanwhile, could feed them all. And Inna wouldn't have to walk across town twice a day to get to work. She could spend all the time she needed in the workshop, Horace said robustly (ignoring the twist in his heart).

And even though he had till now worked purely on commission as a miniaturist, he told Madame Leman that

311

Monsieur Fabergé would in the future also be paying him a separate, small, regular stipend, in return for which Horace would help any colleague who might wish to leave Russia to arrange papers to do so.

'Which, I might add, is just making a virtue of necessity,' Horace added, with a rueful laugh. 'Because there's precious little of my kind of painting work about any more. Fabergé's really only being kind, paying me a regular bit extra to be ready to help people get stamps on their passports, in case there is any more revolution. Though of course I'm grateful. Every little helps.'

Madame Leman was nodding enthusiastically. The words 'regular stipend' had gone down particularly well, Horace noticed.

'We'll introduce you to Maxim,' she said quickly. Maxim, Horace remembered, was one of her husband's old socialist friends, sometimes talked about in the Leman apartment as a benefactor who'd helped the family with one problem or another. This Maxim, who'd come back from exile in Capri shortly before the war, was no doubt just waiting now for the next wave of revolution. 'He'll help, for sure, if you do need to start getting people papers; he's a socialist and knows all these new people . . .'

'And I'll go in to the shop, every day, of course, for form's sake,' Horace added, diverting her from the undesirable fantasy of a socialist future back to the point. 'But basically I'm here. I'll help with anything.'

Madame Leman looked relieved. She felt her responsibilities, Horace knew, and her age. She wanted an older man about the house; someone to rely on.

*

On a tray, Madame Leman brought up two jugs of water for the washstands, and a spray of lilac in a vase. She put the flowers on the little table between the two armchairs at the end of the room. 'You can sit and read here together,' she said, fondly. She sat down in one of them herself.

They were just getting back their breath, looking admiringly round at the transformation – 'So *sensible*,' Madame Leman was saying. 'Why didn't we think of this before?' – when they heard footsteps on the stairs.

'That'll be Yasha,' Madame Leman said comfortably, leaning back in the armchair in the corner. 'It must easily be six. They'll have finished.'

But Horace could hear there were two pairs of feet.

He could also hear the silence as the people outside saw all the changes on the landing.

The betrayal was in that moment's caution, he thought, not in Inna's brightness when, a moment later, she looked around their door.

'So we've moved, it seems!' she said. Still standing in the doorway, not coming in, she glanced around the room, taking in her cushions, and quilts, and brushes, and the lilac. 'Well, you *are* good to have done all this by yourself, so fast,' she said, not looking him in the eye. 'It's just like home.'

Yasha must be standing right behind her, Horace thought.

They must have exchanged startled glances, out there. And how long had they been coming up here alone together after work in the evenings?

'You knew what I was up to, then?' he couldn't resist asking.

Inna smiled. 'Oh, Madame Leman said, so I came straight up,' she replied breezily.

Horace was aware of Madame Leman stirring awkwardly in the armchair behind the door, out of Inna's line of sight; of how she wanted to cover up the unpleasant nakedness of that moment's untruth as much as he did.

'Isn't it *pretty* now?' Madame Leman called, very brightly.

'I mean Marcus said. And I couldn't wait to see,' Inna corrected herself. Then she came round the doorway, and kissed first Madame Leman and then Horace.

Horace was aware of the other shadow moving, out on the landing, and of Yasha's door shutting.

'I'll leave you, then, darlings,' Madame Leman said, getting up and going downstairs.

Horace could see Inna didn't know what to say to him, once they were alone together. He could see she wasn't sure if he'd noticed her lie, and thought – in a way he felt grateful for this – that she wanted him not to be hurt. But he could see, too, that she was as aware as he was of the silent third, next door.

She twisted her hands. And, for a moment, he wondered if this hot faintness he was feeling – he had the sense he was walking a few inches off the ground – might be anger?

'I bought us a housewarming present,' he said, pulling the cloth off the top of the plate on the little table with a flamboyant gesture.

It was a pineapple. An exotic, spiny pineapple, in all its expensive glory: its top, from which the fatly luscious, spiky leaves grew, neatly decapitated; and two rings cut and peeled, ready for eating, balanced immediately underneath.

She stared at it. Yeliseyevsky food. Luxury food. How fascinated she'd been by pineapples when she came to live in Petersburg. Horace remembered how she'd gazed, and prodded, and sniffed the air of the shop to draw out the tropical scent when he'd first taken her there to see them. He'd bought one for their wedding night, and they'd eaten it with champagne, sticky with happiness. 'The food of the gods,' he'd said. And only after that, when every trace of fear at what was to come had gone, had he laughingly drawn her to the divan, murmuring, 'Ah, the smell of the south, so delicious . . .'

She turned to him now, looking pained. It wasn't the same any more, as her eyes seemed to be saying. She wasn't a child. They didn't—

They hadn't, for six months or more, Horace thought, hotter and lighter than ever. Seven.

I am a man like any other, he told himself.

Ignoring her look, and pushing her against the party wall more roughly than he'd meant to, he kissed her.

He wasn't going to ask difficult questions; he was going to stifle any confessions with his lips and his tongue. He could see how disorienting it must have been to have the man she'd once been in love with come back from nowhere, just like that; he wasn't going to blame her for letting her feelings get the better of her. He could, almost, understand, and, almost, feel sorry for her in this predicament, which she must find ugly. He just wanted her back.

For a moment, he almost believed she'd just surrender to him, and everything would go back to how it had once been.

But she didn't. He could feel her muscles tense. And there was such a startled look in her eyes when he opened his that he let her go.

She flung herself down on the bed after that, all right, and hard enough to make fountains of dust and symphonies of squeaking springs, but not in the way Horace had been hoping. She'd rushed for the far side of the bed, and now she lay there with her back to him, curled up, with her arms protectively around her shoulders, and one hand covering her eyes. She reminded him of a bird fluffed up, with its head down, against the winter wind.

Horace had known this would be difficult, but he hadn't realized until now how painful he was going to find her unhappiness at being alone with him, here, when Yasha was so close. He took a deep breath. Then, careful not to alarm her further, he sat down on the other side of the bed and stretched out a hand. 'I didn't mean to startle you,' he whispered. But her back stiffened in rejection of even this touch.

'Inna,' he said bleakly, and, not knowing what else to do, he lay down too, in another grind of bedsprings, leaving the hand she'd rejected stretched out towards hers across the great empty space in the middle of the bed. 'Please.'

She didn't turn round.

But, after a few moments she did at least speak.

'I had no idea you were thinking of this, you see,' she said, very low, but with a brittle attempt at everyday tones. 'It's been such a surprise.'

She shifted, with another creak of bedsprings, and for a moment Horace tried to draw some sort of bleak comfort, or at least humour, from the idea that Yasha, next door, might be finding the sound agonizing. He could see a little of her face now, in the half-light. She was looking at the pineapple. Her cheeks were wet.

It was almost a relief to hear Yasha's door closing again: a quiet click.

As Inna heard Yasha go, she bit her lip.

Those footsteps outside became less disciplined as they went downstairs: two at a time, then three at a time, then four. Then a door downstairs slammed so hard Horace could feel the walls quiver all these flights up. Despite the misery inside this room, he couldn't help a quiet moment of self-congratulation.

'It must be nearly suppertime,' Inna said in a small voice. 'Do you think we should take the pineapple down to share with the others?'

The pineapple went well with bread and tea. Barbarian and Agrippina gobbled it up.

Inna looked at the empty chair, but didn't ask.

'Where's Yasha?' Horace said.

'He won't be back till late,' Marcus said, looking uncomfortably down.

Did they *all* know? Horace wondered. Or guess, at least?

Then, making an effort, he let go of that flash of resentment. After all, it wouldn't be hard to guess there was something wrong. Inna hadn't said a word since they'd got downstairs. She'd just put the fruit down on the table and let the younger members of the family exclaim over it. She'd accepted a slice, but left it uneaten on her plate. And then she'd sat, white and quiet, at her place, while they ate, looking at something no one else could see.

Now Horace reached out and took Inna's hand, laying it across the top of the table, under his, in full view of everyone. Then he tightened his grip on it by pushing his fingers between her unresisting ones.

Madame Leman got up. She started gathering plates.

But, before she left, she looked down at the Wallicks' interlaced hands, on the table, and gave Horace a quick, approving nod.

Know what you want to achieve, Horace told himself. The picture in his mind was clear: insects in the killing-jar. Alive and scuttling one minute. But shut in, deprived of air; they're dead of claustrophobia before you know what's happened.

Morning in the bedroom: fumbling footsteps from next door; the rattle of piss in the pot outside. Eyes in the crowded dark of the landing washbasin. Water splashing. Yasha, in baggy old underwear, was already lathering his chin when Horace, doing up his sleek dressing gown, followed him out.

'Ah, Kagan,' Horace said, trying to sound as calm and even sunny as possible, as if he hadn't spent what felt like all night lying awake while Inna cried in silence. 'Pass my bag, there's a good fellow.'

He'd gone to sleep in the end. He must have, because when he'd opened his eyes Inna had gone. She must have dressed and crept downstairs at dawn, to avoid any morning conversation. But at least Yasha didn't seem to know.

Yasha, looking surly and averting his eyes, stopped and unhooked the new bag from the towel hook.

'Give me five minutes,' he grunted, going back to his shaving. 'All right?'

There wasn't really room for two at the washstand.

Horace ignored him. He planted himself just beyond the path of Yasha's elbow, but still too close for comfort, checking things in his bag, pulling out the shaving brush, combing through his copious dark hair, ostentatiously waiting for Yasha to get out of the way.

And, all the while, he hummed, tunelessly but very cheerfully, hoping that Yasha was remembering whatever it was he might have thought had happened between Inna and Horace last night, and was suffering too.

'Good evening out?' he said, after a while.

He didn't mind when Yasha slouched back inside without replying.

Before Horace left the apartment for Fabergé's, he dropped in at the workshop to say goodbye to his wife. However badly things were going, he knew he had to keep up appearances.

He was pleased to see that Yasha wasn't there. Even if Inna only looked vaguely about her when Horace praised their progress, Marcus looked delighted. They were doing well with Youssoupoff's violin. The scroll patch, which Marcus had carved, was in place, like a white new ear on the side of the instrument's head. Inna's back patch, also still in the white, was visible behind the clamps gluing the violin together. It didn't look, after all, as though they'd need to use the 'spare' violin Yasha had been making. That was lying forlornly on one side, by its maker's abandoned place.

'Now it's really just a question of the varnish,' Marcus eagerly told Horace. 'We've settled on oil varnish: we made up a big lot of it yesterday, out in the courtyard, because it can be an explosive business. Boiled linseed oil, with pale yellow rosin and Venice Turpentine and mastic . . .'

They were going to take the varnishing slowly, Marcus explained, as Inna, with her head bowed, began tidying away the spare violin. It was better for the wood to darken naturally, from exposure to sunlight; the summer was doing that naturally. They were leaving both instruments by the back window, to catch the light. But tomorrow they were going to add a very light stain from a tea solution, too.

Then the ground: the first coating on the wood, a key for the varnish film, Marcus said.

'Egg white,' Inna said, more understandably, and, even if there was nothing very romantic about those words, even if she wasn't facing him as she spoke, Horace was delighted to hear her voice at all.

The ground would be sanded down, Marcus added, very fast; then another layer of egg white; one coat of clear varnish and more sanding; another layer of varnish, this time very slightly warmed with colour extract, to help build up the desired matching rich golden-brown glow . . . and so on.

'Fascinating,' Horace said, mildly. 'Fascinating.'

Marcus added, pleadingly, as if this explained everything: 'Luckily Yasha is a genius when it comes to varnish . . .'

Horace nodded. 'I understand,' he said. He could see Inna sidling off with the violin box to put Yasha's violin away somewhere at the back. There was a store out there, he thought. He asked Marcus: 'By the way, where is Yasha?'

'He's gone to have another look at the room he might take,' Marcus said. 'If he moves out. I think.'

Horace saw Inna's back stiffen and her head half turn. Then she hurried out through the back door.

He didn't think she'd known that either.

That was enough to persuade him that he was perhaps winning – at least until they didn't come up at six.

He'd put them successfully out of his mind for hours, while he first visited Fabergé's, then queued successfully for bread, then returned to the apartment to compare notes with Madame Leman, who'd queued successfully for sugar.

He sat in the yellow room, alone, and read the paper. At six, in stockinged feet, he went out of the apartment, on to the staircase.

Work was over. He could hear Marcus inside in the kitchen already, talking to his mother. The others would be up any second. Horace hovered just outside the front door of the Lemans' apartment, on the landing.

He was rewarded, eventually, by overhearing the whisper at the bottom of the echoing stairwell: 'But where can we go? There's nowhere left . . .' He tried, unsuccessfully, not to feel punished, just to deaden himself, when he realized those yearning words had been said by his own wife.

Should he have rushed downstairs and hit Yasha, as part of him wanted to? Or faded away, and left the lovers to whisper? He did neither. He just hovered, ingloriously, trying not to imagine them twined about each other at the bottom of the stairwell, not wanting to eavesdrop, but unable to do anything else.

'Please, let's not even think about it till the violin's finished,' he heard a few moments later. A female whisper. Inna.

'It practically is finished,' was the angry male answer.

At least they were just talking. But he didn't like what he was hearing. Because those words were inevitably going to lead up to what he heard next.

'Surely it's simple,' Yasha's voice said from far away, through the blood in Horace's head. 'Leave him.'

'Shh,' hissed Inna. 'It's not that simple. You must see that. How would I explain?' Her voice was stubborn, as if this conversation had happened many times.

He couldn't make out Yasha's reply. He could only hear the exasperation.

'Because,' she capped the other voice, 'with him living here, where would either of us work? How would we survive without jobs?'

Silence.

'Look, come and see the place I've found, at least,' Yasha said. 'It's far away, but it's not bad, and—'

'I can't,' she said, and Horace heard she was crying. 'You know I can't.'

'If you won't come with me' – Yasha's voice was getting harsher – 'I'm going anyway. You know that, don't you?'

'"Because the Revolution needs me," is that it?' came her tearful attempt at a taunt. 'It's only your politics you're really in love with, isn't it? If it were me, you'd never even have thought of saying such a thing. You know how hard this is for me. You *know* I don't want to hurt Horace . . .'

How *that* hurt.

After that all he could hear was sobbing.

Even in retreat, Horace kept his wits about him. After going back into the flat and sticking his head back through the kitchen door to tell Madame Leman in clipped tones that he was feeling a little tired and would not have supper, he went quickly up the main staircase to the attics, alone. There were no more whispers from the bottom of the stairs. They'd gone.

It was only when he'd shut his own door behind him – quietly, because he wasn't a man to vent his feelings on bits of wood – that he gave way to emotion.

He stumbled over to the unmade bed. It still smelled faintly of her flower scent, and the smell made him suddenly horribly aware of what he was doing to them all. He threw himself on to the mattress, remembering the hopeless sound of her tears downstairs. Once he was lying down, he clamped a hand tight over his eyes, so tight he saw flashing lights inside his eyelids. He breathed as slowly as he could, but nothing could shake off the panicky sickness he was feeling. He was supposed to be the one with the poise, who knew how the world worked and could offer solutions. But he didn't have the least idea what to do now.

He wanted an hour of quiet, without the thoughts that were torturing him, to rest his frantic mind. He'd barely slept last night. But there was no peace.

It would demean him to look in her cupboards and see whether she'd taken any clothes out with her. It would humiliate him to look for her bag, in case it had gone. But he longed to do that because, he thought with sudden desperation, she just might have. She might never be back.

There was no sound from Yasha's room next door.

Horace took his hands away from his eyes. All you can do is wait, he told himself. So he lay, open-eyed, on the bed. Trying to keep his mind from buzzing relentlessly round the same awful possibilities, he watched the sky lose its luminosity. He saw the first faint prickle of the evening star, and the moon.

Below, he heard the people in the different flats, including the Lemans', go in and out of their apartment doors, to the courtyard dustbins or out for an after-supper walk or a smoke or a chat on the stairs. He heard Aunt Cockatoo's grating voice talking for quite a long time. There was something reassuring in its ordinariness.

It felt as though that evening went on forever.

When it was quite dark, and he started hearing the sounds

of bolts being drawn and shutters being closed downstairs, he wondered whether to bother with his own shutters, or with getting undressed. He was surprised to find, as he shifted position on the bed, that his cheeks were wet.

It was later still, and silence had fallen on the building, when he heard her footsteps on the stairs. It was so late, in fact, that he couldn't be sure whether they were real or a dream. But then the door opened, and for a moment a stripe of fainter darkness from the landing became visible.

Yasha wasn't with her.

Horace shut his eyes, pretending to be asleep. She tiptoed in with her shoes in her hands. Without getting undressed, she lay down on the bed. She was as far away as ever, across the mattress, but at least she was here beside him.

In the blazing sunshine of the next morning, Horace went out to make the acquaintance of Maxim, Leman's old socialist friend, whom Madame Leman had suggested would be a useful contact if he did ever need to help Fabergé employees get papers to leave Russia. Horace laughed out loud when he caught his first glimpse of the man, setting out copies of his paper, *New Life*, on the newsstand on the corner of Garden Street and Nevsky where the speakers shouted about the future. Maxim was unmistakably a friend of Monsieur Leman. He had that same wry smile and the same taste in side-fastening country shirts.

The usual crowds were out, stamping around Nevsky, picking over the pamphlets and papers that were sold nowadays instead of food, talking, explaining, protesting, arguing, shouting, revelling in their new freedom of language, using all the pent-up words they'd never dared speak before

– as if, as Maxim said, grinning under his droopy Slavic moustache as soon as Horace had explained who he was, someone had waved a magic wand over Petrograd and transformed it into the Latin Quarter in Paris.

Horace let the sun warm his back, feeling more optimistic than he'd done for months. There were always new chances, and new friends, and new ways forward.

He picked up one of the pile of *New Life*s that Maxim had set down at the table. It was characteristic of Maxim that he would come and talk to his readers and buyers, out here, in person, whenever he could.

'I'm your biggest admirer, these days,' Horace said sincerely. It was a good, honest paper, after all. Maxim raised an eyebrow, but seemed pleased with the compliment.

'Well,' Horace added easily, 'we're all for the Revolution now. Young Kagan at Leman's workshop – he's always talking about you.'

Maxim's eyes narrowed. 'Young Kagan, eh?' he said. His face was serious. 'You must be worried about him.'

Horace leaned forward, suddenly interested. 'Why?'

'It was just like the bad old days: some Jew-bashers caught him in my courtyard at dawn with a load of papers. They started yelling at him for being a Jew and a Bolshevik, and then they whacked merry Hell out of him. He's at my place, covered in bandages. Broken arm. And look at what this lot in government's doing now – turning back the clock to the days of reaction, that's what. Mark my words, we'll soon be back in the same mess we were in before.'

Horace shook his head. 'Ah, but who knows when the pendulum won't start swinging the other way?' He was glad Inna was safe at home if there were murderous thugs out Jew-bashing again. But he was also thinking privately that he'd never felt so grateful to a bunch of Black Hundred reactionaries as he did now to Yasha's attackers.

'What was the boy doing at your place anyway?' he asked.

He was imagining Yasha heaving great piles of newspapers down to the delivery cart at first light. That sounded as though he'd been working off anger after a quarrel. Inna hadn't said this morning why she had come home so late, or mentioned Yasha's new place. She'd just woken up with a look of set, dazed misery, and gone quietly downstairs to the workshop. Precisely what the quarrel between the lovers had been about didn't matter, Horace told himself: whether she'd hated the idea of living in whatever room he'd found, or simply lost her nerve on the way to see it, or had realized she wanted to finish the violin, or not wanted to say goodbye to the Lemans, or . . . He couldn't formulate the rest of his thought. Detail was only detail. The important thing was that she was home.

Maxim shrugged. 'Woman trouble, I think. He asked to sleep on my sofa. I don't like to ask.'

'Well, keep him safe, eh? Couldn't you encourage him to get out of the centre of the city, if he's not safe here? Surely he could find a room out where they've moved the Soviet – near that school, Smolny? He'd be happy enough, close to the action, wouldn't he?'

Maxim nodded thoughtfully. Knowing better than to labour the point, Horace picked up a paper and set off back to the Lemans.

There was a spring in his step as he turned the corner. Maybe, just maybe, it would work out in his favour after all.

CHAPTER TWENTY-THREE

You go on living, however much your heart aches. You go on getting out of bed, dressing in something or other, eating food that tastes of sand, and nodding when the people around you are talking, so they think you're part of their conversation. You stand in line for bread and flour and sugar, go to the woods for mushrooms and berries, join in all the pickling and preserving and jam-making you can to stave off the hunger of the winter to come. You follow everyone else's fretting about politics as the tide turns, and the Revolution, which had faded in the summer, comes back into fashion in the autumn, though its hapless current leader doesn't. *What, the Bolsheviks siding with Kerensky against the army! What, the military coup failed! What, Prime Minister Kerensky a drunken womanizer! A cocaine addict! A Jew in woman's petticoats!* You even laugh out loud, one day, when your husband comes in to tell you he's just seen a slogan on a wall, praising an obviously Jewish revolutionary just out of jail who now kept getting his name in the papers; a slogan reading, 'Down with the Jew Kerensky! Long live Trotsky!' And, generally, you carry on with something that looks, from the outside, almost indistinguishable from your life before, only with the joy subtracted.

That, at least, was what Inna found as the summer drew to a close and the days got sharper and greyer, and her misery – which she'd explained to the Lemans and Horace as illness; a reason to stay alone on her side of the bed – shrivelled down to scepticism. It wasn't as if Yasha had gone that far away to work. Smolny was just across town, wasn't it? It wasn't as if he couldn't have come back and visited if he'd wanted to see her.

It was true that the last time they'd talked they'd had one of those excruciating discussions about whether she could leave Horace, and that she'd been reluctant even to let him persuade her out to see the room he'd half agreed to rent. They'd got as far as the embankment together. They'd hovered on a bridge, kissing and crying and arguing. But the place he wanted to go was much further off, and she found, when she looked at the grey currents rushing below, that she couldn't cross the water to look at a possible future waiting on the other side. So you won't go to the islands any more, Mrs Wallick? he'd said. It's not that, she'd stammered, wondering if he really thought her so shallow as to be frightened of the poverty over the bridge. Surely he must know that she was more afraid of the not coming back than of the going there? Cut to the quick by his easy injustice, she hadn't been altogether surprised when he'd flung off alone. She just hadn't expected him to be gone for good.

He'd never even said goodbye, just got Marcus to pack up his stuff and take it over to him, along with the still-white copy of the Youssoupoff Strad that he'd made but not yet varnished, for something to work on in the evenings. She could see that a part of him might have been scared, after being beaten up. But she couldn't altogether excuse him because of that. However many anti-Jewish mobs might have been prowling the courtyards of central Petrograd over the summer of reaction – and she didn't see many, especially as the tide turned again, and revolutionaries again displaced the Jew-hunters on the streets – all he'd have had to do would be to turn his coat collar up. If he'd really wanted to persuade her, he'd have come. He'd have tried.

No, Yasha had made his choice. She wouldn't go chasing after him: that was her choice. But that didn't mean she didn't go on agonizing about it. She couldn't be sure, even now, that if Yasha were ever to turn up saying he'd chosen her over his politics, she wouldn't choose him over the safety of life with Horace. It was just that this now seemed so unlikely. He was gone.

They finished the varnishing by the end of summer, Inna and Marcus. They hardly dared draw a bow across the violin's strings to hear the magic of its voice; instead they locked it away, under two other violins, behind the wood stack in the storeroom. Felix Youssoupoff would send for it when he was ready. For now the Strad filled her with such sadness that she could hardly bear to look at it.

Once it was locked up, things got a little better.

Horace's kindly presence – the way he'd say everyday things in a gentle voice, his knack of keeping life on an even keel – began to lift the fog of heartbreak that surrounded her.

One day, Inna saw Agrippina – really saw her, skulking in the shadows with a shawl clutched round her, as she always seemed to be these days. She looked dreadfully uncomfortable.

'Oh, Agrippinochka,' she said, suddenly realizing that the girl's developing figure was crammed into a tired child's dress, with tears up the bodice seams hidden by the nasty old shawl. Of course – there was no money for new clothes. 'You need a better dress. Let's get you something of mine.' She was surprised how pleased Agrippina's grateful, if embarrassed smile made her.

One moment of domestic insight bred others in the following days. She was aware of Marcus grinning to himself when he saw her tutoring young Barbarian in varnishing, just as Horace smiled when, one evening, she and the young Lemans started teasing Marcus about a girl. He'd taken to going out on Thursday and Friday evenings to meetings of the Union of Youth avant-garde art group, which this girl attended. Inna even laughed when Agrippina, clearly feeling more confident in her pretty, cut-down, dark-green dress joked, 'No secrets, brother: we can guess what she looks like already. We know your type: tall, thin, black-haired?'

That night, alone together upstairs with her husband, Inna rolled over in the bed towards him.

Horace was graceful enough not even to show surprise. He just enveloped her welcomingly in his arms, and smiled a great joyful smile as she wound her legs around his. She could feel his desire.

When they surfaced from that kiss of reunion, the first in so long, and he murmured, 'How I've missed you,' she saw from the tenderness in his eyes that it was *all right*, and everything could be as it was before. Only then he didn't, as she'd imagined, shift her on top of him, with a great groan of want.

Instead, he blinked and, obviously remembering the bucket and rags on the landing, whispered, in that practical way of his, 'But we should wait a week, shouldn't we?' That was their agreement: how not to have a baby.

She wriggled against him, suddenly desperate to move on from the impasse in their lives and create something, someone, new: another life to face the world with the pair of them. 'We don't have to wait, do we?' she whispered back. 'We could *choose* . . .'

'It's not the time for children,' Horace said sadly, though his hands were still moving over her skin. 'Not yet.'

If Inna was disappointed, she couldn't help but see that Horace had reason on his side. She couldn't help, either, being impressed at how adroitly her husband sidestepped the growing difficulties of getting money, as the autumn turned to brutal sleet, and the Germans got closer, and the queues and demonstrations swelled. At how he handled the gentlemen from Fabergé who, as he spent less and less time at the shop, took to dropping in at the apartment instead to chat quietly in English or French. Or at the small amounts of money on top of his stipend that Horace magicked up for the communal pot. And at his practicality, repeatedly moving around the furniture on the top landing and experimenting with the placing of the bookshelves he'd made to add to the comfort of what was now almost a second apartment.

Horace, still sauntering around the city with his linen ironed and his chin shaved, still dropping in on the many acquaintances he'd made here and there, managed to find

331

jobs for everyone, too, which brought in a few extra roubles. He teamed Madame Leman up with an English journalist called Ransome, who'd started employing her, a couple of days a week, to translate the Russian newspapers for him. He found Barbarian and Agrippina little evening jobs: one preparing paints for a group of wealthy amateur artists over on the English Embankment, where the foreigners lived; the other turning pages for pianists at the Philharmonia.

Horace's jobs were a cut above the employment Barbarian had briefly found for himself as an evening janitor at a peculiar medical museum round the corner. He guarded glass jars of bobbing body parts pickled in alcohol and came back with pockets jingling, and furtive glee in his eyes. They had Revolution sausage (don't ask what meat) for three or four meals. But it only lasted a fortnight, and he finally confessed what he'd really been up to: emptying the alcohol from the jars, pouring in water instead, and selling the murky pickling liquid in the market to sailors. 'It's all gone now,' Barbarian said, rather wistfully. 'There's no point going back.'

In his quiet way, Inna realized, her husband was taking charge of all their efforts to muddle through and survive. And, against all the odds, they – a widow, a cripple, two children, a Jewess and a foreigner – were still getting by without too much hunger or too many quarrels. It wasn't perfect – far from it. They were all outsiders now. But the cautious optimism in the household reinforced her hope that, maybe, everything would turn out all right.

'Horace?' she said, one night, in the yellow room.

'Mm?' he said vaguely. He was reading the paper.

'Marcus says he's heard of a society paying musicians to give concerts at working men's clubs.'

'Mm?' He looked up from his newspaper. His eyes were kind.

She took a deep breath, wondering whether she would get over her nerves and actually come to enjoy doing what she was about to suggest. 'If I started practising again, do you think they would want me?'

By October people were saying that the Provisional Government was so scared it now held its sittings standing up. Out in the Hay Market, at dawn, they were saying the Bolsheviks would attack the Winter Palace tonight. Horace and his new friend Ransome had dropped in for a bite in the restaurant near Palace Square that had become the correspondents' stamping ground: 'For the ringside seat,' Ransome had said, 'all the reporters will be going.'

They had come in after an evening at the Mariinsky Theatre, in theory enjoying ballet, but really just watching the evening newspapers floating, like swans, along the rows from one buzzing member of the audience to another, as rumours, wilder by the hour, spread through the *parterre* and the *belle étage*. Ransome needed light relief, he'd said, when he ran into Horace on Theatre Square. And his newspaper would pay for the whole evening. Who would say no?

Horace would have gone even without the promise of food. He enjoyed curiosities, and Ransome was certainly that: an unathletic man, soft-muscled, who suffered from stomach ulcers, but all buoyed up tonight with the strange high spirits of newspapermen in extreme times. (Madame Leman said Ransome was enjoying the unrest for an extra, private reason: because he was sleeping with the secretary of one of these now-fashionable Bolsheviks, Leon Trotsky, the squat, wiry-haired brute who, Horace now knew, had been running things since their real leader Lenin had fled.)

They were finishing their soup when the waiter came up and asked if Messieurs wouldn't mind moving into the other dining room, at the back of the hotel, for the second course. The management was expecting shooting, the waiter said uneasily. The mob attack on the Winter Palace was supposed to be imminent, and they wanted to put out the lights in this room, which was too close to Palace Square, and very exposed.

Ransome grinned cheerfully and got straight up. Horace too. As he followed the tweed-backed journalist into the other room, he wondered whether Ransome's Yevgenia was really the rouged-up hussy Madame Leman made her out to be, which sounded intriguingly un-revolutionary. He couldn't help but recall what Fabergé had said that morning: 'No one in their right mind wants the Bolsheviks, but no one will bother to go out and fight for Prime Minister Kerensky either.'

Horace didn't believe there'd be more fighting in the street, even though the German army was so near to the city; even though he'd seen the barges full of ministry paperwork and treasures from the Hermitage floating down the Neva every blustery day, the first signs of the evacuation that must surely come soon; even though every street corner seemed to be manned by a ragged orator, yelling, 'The rich have lots of everything; the poor have nothing; everything will belong to the poor,' and it now took a bagful of worthless new paper roubles to buy salt, or candles, or bread. People were too busy just surviving to rebel any more, weren't they?

Still, he wanted to know what Ransome thought.

Ransome had been at the Winter Palace in the afternoon, interviewing the 'defenders of the palace' – as it turned out, just a few hundred Cossacks and schoolboy cadets, and two hundred bedraggled women known as the Women's Shock Battalion of Death, who'd been drafted in to save the Prime Minister from the hungry mob. He'd been laughing at how Kerensky's motley crew of defenders had got so depressed as the light faded that most of them had quietly gone off into town to lift their spirits by finding some supper.

'Just like us,' Ransome said easily, waving at the other reporters eating at nearby tables; all, like him, lit up with electric excitement.

'So,' Horace deduced, hopefully, 'you don't think anything will actually happen after all?'

Ransome had picked up his spoon, ready to return to his soup. But he stopped at that, and looked brightly across the table. The un-English fervour of his gaze, Horace thought, sat very oddly on his tweedy academic shoulders.

'Oh no,' he said. 'I *do* think it will. You see, Lenin's on his way back.'

But not that night, it seemed.

It was eleven before Horace set off for home, merry on Château Latour, leaving his new friend with an American colleague, swapping stories. What did they know? There'd been no shooting. Nevsky was deserted. The night was quiet. The city seemed dead.

Yasha was polishing his fiddle left-handed, alone in his room near the school at Smolny, thinking of the way Inna had looked as she worked on the Strad. She'd had the same expression on her face whenever they were alone together, too – except for that sweet first moment, whenever he closed the door on the world and took her in his arms, when she'd sigh as if all her cares were lifted from her, and shut her eyes.

Yasha's thoughts ran naturally on from this to why he'd left the Lemans' house. He couldn't explain this satisfactorily to himself. He didn't like to think that he'd been successfully squeezed out by Horace, or had been rejected by Inna, who wouldn't come with him, or that he'd just cut his losses and given up on her. He'd found he preferred to tell himself that it was fear of the thugs who'd beaten him up that had forced him to clear out, however much he hated to believe that he was a person who could be governed by fear.

Well, it was true, he had been scared. Even now, out in the safety of Smolny, with his arm nearly healed, he still felt black sludge in his gut whenever he remembered those three brutes closing in on him – the empty look in their eyes, as their fists and feet crashed into him, as if he wasn't a person at all, just vermin to be exterminated. And he had nightmares he still woke up sweating from, however often his bony revolutionary flatmate Fanny slid into the bed and rocked him in her skinny arms. (She wasn't a bad sort, Fanny. Not maternal exactly, and not really a lover either, except for the occasional bleak fumble, but at least someone who, after all she'd gone through in all those prisons, really understood fear, and he clung to her like one terrified kid hanging on to another.) He was ashamed of having felt that fear. But he was more ashamed still of using it to avoid thinking about how defeated and outwitted he'd felt by Horace, even before the men had laid into him. Gradually, as his bruises and broken bone began to heal, and the layers of varnish went on, he began to tell himself that, soon, once the violin was done, perhaps he might take it back, and find Inna, and explain. As the weeks went by, he found himself believing she would listen, and forgive him his fear, and take him back.

Now, as he put the violin back down on the table, wrapped in the ragged scarf he'd been polishing it with, he caught a glimmer of movement on the street.

He glanced out. Two men were walking very quickly towards Smolny: short, unimpressive men. Coat collars up, noses stuck forward under workers' caps, eyes flickering furtively round; one very blond.

Nothing odd about that, except that it was nearly midnight – the time people left Smolny, usually.

He was just about to get up and take off his clothes, ready for the rumpled bed in the corner, when he saw a gust of wind outside lift the blond man's cap off his head. It lifted his blond hair, too, revealing the bald pate gleaming underneath. The man grabbed at it, and steadied it back on his head. But Yasha couldn't miss the black beard, which popped out from inside his coat collar.

With a prickle of excitement, he recognized the missing Bolshevik leader: the man who'd been on the run since July.

Immediately his fatigue vanished. Lenin had come out of hiding! Something really was up. He grabbed at his coat, flung himself down the stairs, and began to race back towards the crowds at the doors of Smolny.

It was only that night that Yasha finally knew for sure that, of all revolutionary groups and beliefs represented here at Smolny, it was the Bolsheviks who would win, and it was their leader alone whom he could support with all his heart. What swayed him was the fearless, doubt-free way that Lenin walked into Room 36 and announced, 'Comrades! We need to start the seizure of power now!'

Yasha's heart swelled. He'd found his truth. Most people were ground down by prison, exile and violence. Even he had been, a little. But now it felt as though all those distortions and impurities were being burned away, for here, at last, was a man stripped of the personal and immune to the stupidity of emotion. Impervious to fear.

When Inna and Horace and Madame Leman went out at dawn the next morning to join the bread and groceries queues, shivering and yawning, it was to discover that the palace had, to Horace's astonishment, already been overrun. Young men with pails of glue were slapping up posters telling them Kerensky was gone and there was a new revolutionary government: the Soviet of People's Commissars.

Inna and Horace and the Lemans didn't really understand how it was that the tiny Bolshevik group, in the days that followed, so quickly took control of everything, although Horace's friend Ransome described how the rest of the revolutionaries from the Soviet, the Mensheviks and Left SRs, who were outraged by the lawlessness of the night seizure of the Winter Palace, went to the packed Soviet Congress to denounce it as a criminal venture which would cause civil war, and then walked out, leaving only the Bolsheviks on the podium. It had been political suicide, Ransome said, recalling how Trotsky had howled after them, 'You're finished: go where you belong – into the dustbin of history!'

It soon became clear to Inna, though, that they were in ruthless hands, and just how ruthless became apparent right from that first grey morning in October. There was shouting, somewhere in the crowds on Hay Market. Horace drew Inna and Madame Leman into a doorway as a pack of men in some unrecognizable sort of hand-me-down soldiers' uniforms came noisily by. They were dragging a skinny youth towards the canal. He was covered with blood; his face was smashed and one eye was out. There were children running along shouting beside them: high-pitched cries of glee.

When the group had passed, the three of them stepped out of their doorway and began, quickly, to retrace their footsteps home. 'Best away from this,' Madame Leman muttered, white-faced, pulling the others between the frozen bystanders. Still, they weren't quick enough to miss hearing the return of the crowd to the square, and the elated soldiers chanting, 'The People's Judgement!' and the children's bright cries behind, 'Sunk him, drowned him!'

What could you do, Inna thought, if you were ruled by men who seemed to encourage lynch mobs and hatred? Just shut yourself in at home. What other choice was there?

CHAPTER TWENTY-FOUR

They'd boarded up the Leman shop front, Yasha saw a few weeks later as he stood outside in the bitter cold of December. With the violin box under his right arm, he banged and banged at the door, wondering which of them had gone out to hammer those nails so roughly into the window frames.

No one answered.

Well, they were wise to take precautions, he thought. The mob had got into the Emperor's cellars, and the crowds everywhere were still drunk and would be for weeks more. Ruffians were waving bottles of Château d'Yquem as they shuffled along Nevsky; ragamuffins were sitting on walls draining bottles of vintage cognac; courageous drunks were breaking shop windows to get at the merchandise behind. You stepped over puddles of half-frozen Armagnac and vomit through a fumy, swaying world.

After a while Yasha gave up and went round into the courtyard. He still had his key, so he let himself into the stairwell, then the apartment. In the vestibule, he stopped, took off his hat and smoothed down his hair in front of the glass. He fiddled with the collar he'd gone to the bother of ironing this morning. He'd shaved, too. The reflection staring back at him looked sickly pale.

How quiet it was. Unnerved, he ventured on to the kitchen. They were still living here, he could see. There was a newspaper on the kitchen table by a cup of cold tea. But there was no heating, and the stove was out. No one was in the yellow room, or the bedrooms.

He hesitated. Slowly, he returned to the vestibule. For a moment it came into his head to go up to the attics, just to see . . .

Then, thinking better of that, he squashed his hat against the fiddle box under his arm and went down to the shop the inside way.

Perhaps it was better if no one was home.

They were all down in the workshop, right behind the boards they'd nailed the windows up with, and they'd made a nest: a tight little fug of family warmth around the stove, that, for a moment, made Yasha's heart yearn shamefully for the cosy, intimate ordinariness of it. There were six wooden chairs drawn up in a near-circular huddle, with cushions falling off them, a mess of books and writing things and chess and knitting and mending on the floor all around, two old oil lamps shedding a shaky golden light (the electricity must be off). The samovar was on the workbench, next to a violin and bow and some music.

Instead of sitting down, though, they were standing up, very quiet, staring straight at him as he came through the door in a frozen tableau. The men, to left and right of the women, were warily holding chisels, and Barbarian, the only one moving, was jigging from foot to foot in front, with his

341

pocket knife out. In the middle of the women was Inna, thin and still, with dark-ringed eyes, but as painfully beautiful as ever.

Madame Leman broke the silence.

'Why, it's only Yasha,' she said. By the time he'd registered that there was no great warmth in her voice, the rest of them had also unfrozen. Agrippina sat down, rather heavily, on her chair, then the others, one by one, fiddling with cushions and setting things straight, also settled themselves back down.

He moved further into the room, letting his eyes adjust to the false golden evening they were living in, created by shutters and lamplight, forgetting the harsh salt and fierce white-blue of the wind and light outside, forgetting the hot stink of rhetoric, the catch of brandy in the nose, the tinkle and ripple of glass breaking everywhere.

'I didn't mean to frighten you,' he said awkwardly.

How old and worn and sick they all looked, he thought; even the young ones were pale about the jaw and sunken-eyed, and Barbarian had spots erupting between the unruly new fluff on his chin. He looked again at Inna, who was swaying just as she had when she'd first walked into the apartment; her skin was so pale it was almost ghostly, and her eyes huge in a diminished face.

He didn't expect his heart to contract the way it did when she moved closer to her husband, who put his arm around her shoulders.

Yasha turned away to put his violin down on the workbench.

He was hoping they'd find him a chair; ask him to sit down; offer him tea; get the samovar going. But no one said anything.

Well, he thought, trying not to be discouraged, perhaps there was just no tea. He opened the box.

'I finished the fiddle I was making for you,' he said, addressing the box while he composed himself, because the dusty air was tickling his nose and making his eyes water. 'Before all this . . .' He gestured to indicate the tumult of outside, the tide of events that had engulfed them all, and that, he now saw, might have separated them, perhaps forever. 'It's yours, after all. I brought it back.'

He'd thought, until he got here, that they'd be pleased with the generosity of this gesture. They wouldn't need parts from this violin for the Youssoupoff commission any more, he knew, since they'd managed to repair the real Strad so successfully before he'd left. The prince must have been pleased with the job they'd done. But times were hard. They'd want this one back anyway. Yasha recognized that this was a time when ordinary people – the kind who wanted bread for their children now more than they wanted the bright tomorrow when personal possessions didn't matter – still wanted to hang on to everything they could. And the Lemans might, even now, find someone willing to buy it.

Without looking, he was aware of Inna's small shake of the head. She stayed where she was, but Yasha's words brought Marcus forward, at least. The younger Monsieur Leman – Comrade Leman now, Yasha supposed – limped towards him, perched one buttock on the workbench and picked the fiddle up. He turned it this way and that, nodding; finally, still cradling it, but looking shyly at Yasha – as shyly, Yasha thought, stricken, as if he'd forgotten all those years they'd sat together at this bench – said, 'You've done a good job, all right. It looks just like the Strad in the store.'

'Why's the Strad still in the store?' Yasha asked, surprised. 'I thought *he* wanted it by September.'

'Youssoupoff left,' Horace Wallick said in carefully neutral tones. 'About the same time you did. He was scared there'd be another revolution.'

'He didn't pay,' Marcus added, nervously; then, too fast: 'I know I owe you a month's wages. But I can't pay you. We have no work.'

'Fabergé's has closed down too, of course,' Wallick explained. 'The Bolsheviks requisitioned everything in his safe.'

The silence deepened. Yasha could feel the blame in it now.

'I didn't come to ask you for money,' he answered stiffly. 'You don't need to worry about that. I have a job now. A Party job.'

This was true, though he hardly knew what it would entail. He'd been approached, only last night, at a Party meeting, by a tall, elegant, bearded comrade with a Polish lisp in his voice. He was a friend of old Kremer's, who, Yasha had been happy to hear, was still alive and now a Bolshevik, enlisting Jews to the broader cause in the confusion of the south. Young Kremer had vanished into the Siberian prison world at the time of Yasha's arrest, but perhaps he too would now soon be found and released. The conversation had felt as warm and friendly as if Yasha were rediscovering a long-lost family.

Being short of funds himself in the here and now, and with the landlady on his tail, he'd eagerly accepted the offer of a wage to join some committee to stop sabotage and keep the Revolution going. So he didn't need to grab the Lemans' last kopek. He might even, in due course, be in a position to help them out. He was just starting to imagine how Marcus or Barbarian might gratefully join him, their benefactor, in some future office, shuffling files, when he saw the look that Wallick and Madame Leman were exchanging.

'Yashenka,' Madame Leman said, suddenly soft and anxious, reaching for his arm and looking tenderly at him. 'Darling, don't you *worry* about where all this is taking you?'

They didn't understand, Yasha realized. Perhaps they never had. He was the outsider here, the one who didn't belong. Not Inna, who still wouldn't look at him, or her soft English husband, whom Inna had chosen over him. At last, he could admit that to himself.

It was too much. Yasha could feel himself losing control.

'Me?' He could hear his voice trembling with the awful disappointment of this encounter, which was going so differently from how he'd imagined it. 'Me? *He's* the one who should be worried about where everything's taking him, isn't it: Englishman Englishmanovich, a smart bourgeois gentleman with gold cufflinks?'

It was only when these words were out that he realized how wrong they were, here, however right they might sound among the comrades. All the eyes on him now were shocked, even Inna's.

He got up. Trying to sound casual, he mumbled, 'Anyway, I just dropped by to see how you all were, really.' He was hoping, even now, that they'd stop him, but all they did was watch as he put his hat slowly on his head. 'Mind if I take a look at how the varnish turned out on the Strad, since it's still here?' he asked, 'So I can compare it with my one?' To the torn collar of his own coat, he addressed a

345

final plea. 'Inna, would you open up the store for me, and let me see it?'

But Inna just ducked her head towards Marcus. Marcus, equally quickly, nodded towards his mother. 'Mam?' he said. 'You've got the keys.'

So it was Madame Leman who led Yasha out to the back, into the lock-up cupboard that gave on to the courtyard, that familiar little room with shelves full of half-finished instruments, finished ones in a variety of cases, and neatly sawed cake-slices of wood, ready to be made up.

He put down his violin case on the floor, breathing in that familiar smell, knowing this would be his last visit.

'Let's have a look at that Strad, then,' he said to Madame Leman's back. She turned round, but she was busy pinning up a falling strand of hair, and smiled without meeting his eyes.

'Of course,' she replied, pointing to the pile of wood the case was stashed behind, then swaying to squeeze past him, in this confined space, without touching. 'I'll leave you to it.'

Whistling bravely, Yasha got the Strad and his own fiddle out as soon as she'd gone. He laid the two bodies out, side by side.

He'd done as well with his work as Inna and Marcus had with theirs, he told himself. He was pleased to see how closely the two pale gold backs matched. Only a master would be able to tell them apart. He could see subtle differences, of course: his F-holes and C-curve corners and purfling didn't have quite the sharp perfection of the master's, the delicate waist of the original had come out fractionally thicker on his copy, and his violin's tone, sweet and powerful though it was, wouldn't be imbued with all the uncanny golden magic of the Italian one. Still, if these two instruments weren't quite twins, they were, at least, close relatives: as similar in appearance as he and Inna, with their dark heads, and long, lean arms and legs, and strong, straight features . . .

All at once he was overwhelmed by a memory of her sitting on a stool at the workbench, leaning over this extraordinary work of art, with a strand or two of black hair escaping and wafting against the wood, concentrating as she worked; the beauty in the line of her cheek and neck mirroring the loveliness of the violin.

The pain he felt then came on like an ambush; a blow in the pit of the stomach. There was nothing he wanted more than to take both the violins back into the workshop, show the others, compare, get them talking the way they used to. No, not that: just go back, go to *her*, talk to *her*, and find a way to make things different between them. No, not that, either . . . Just to be alone with her again, in that little attic upstairs, murmuring love talk in her ear, dreaming of nothing more profound than how to get the next order in for the workshop, and pay the rent, and suck up to the next idiot in a top hat who wanted a present for his violin-playing daughter. It wasn't that Yasha hadn't always enjoyed making violins and known he was good at it, but he'd had no qualms, before today, about setting it aside for the higher goals in his life; it was just a job, after all. Yet it now seemed, as he writhed with the agony he hadn't known was coming, that that tradesman's life, petty and blinkered and closed in though he might have found it, a life in which he made no attempt to improve the world, might also have been his only chance of happiness. He closed his eyes as the pain rolled through him.

He wrapped his hands round his gut and rocked back and

forward. With his eyes shut, he breathed slowly in, then out, trying to get control of himself again.

By the time he stopped rocking and opened his eyes, expelling a sharp whoosh of breath, he'd regained his grasp on reality. He could even smile, a bit shakily, at the way he'd just been carrying on. He could feel the pain lurking nearby, but he wasn't going to let it return. One burst of stupidity was enough. He couldn't turn the clock back. If the Lemans didn't want him around, then so be it. He had important work to do. He wouldn't even go back into the workshop to say goodbye. You're just tired, he told himself. Tired having been up half the night with the comrades.

He picked up the violins by their necks, one in each hand, ready to put them both back in their open boxes and hide them behind the wedges of violin-making wood, to confuse looters.

But then he paused. Hardly knowing what he was doing, or why, he put the Strad down again, and quickly put the copy he'd made back into the real Strad's box.

Fumbling at the catches, he closed both boxes, piled them up against the wall, the empty box under the full one, and arranged the wood blocks in front.

The Strad was lying on the shelf where he'd left it.

Taking off the big brown leather bag he always carried round his shoulder, Yasha eased open the thongs at the top and slipped the fiddle in.

It was only when he was shutting the storeroom door again, from the outside – very quietly – and standing in the fetid courtyard, with rubbish overflowing everywhere, cradling the bag in his arms, that he could begin to think what he was doing.

I'm liberating it to give to the Revolution, he promised himself, tiptoeing towards the archway on to the street. It's not doing any good just lying there, is it? Youssoupoff's forgotten all about it. That savage doesn't deserve it anyway. And just think how many hungry workers a priceless thing like this would feed, if you turned it into cash: why, hundreds. Thousands.

That was a good enough explanation, for now.

But he also knew that he might not do that yet. He might keep it a while in his room, just gazing at its beauty – because with beauty, at least, if not with the life of equality he and his political comrades were fighting to create, there were hierarchies, and this was at the very top. And it would remind him of Inna, too.

It was the only memento he could take. He wouldn't be going back.

Yasha didn't know why there were tears burning down his cheeks as he went out through the arch into the roaring street: into the drunken, shambling, brutal chaos of a today which, after this visit to his past, suddenly seemed so very far removed from the bright tomorrow he still wanted to believe was coming.

PART THREE

1918–19

CHAPTER TWENTY-FIVE

On a crisp, frosty October afternoon in 1918, Mr and Mrs Wallick, with darns in their coats and moth-eaten bits of rabbit skin at their collars, joined thousands of other shabby comrades walking through Petrograd. The Bolsheviks had turned the city into a People's Art extravaganza to mark the first anniversary of the Revolution. Palace Square, now called Uritsky Square after a comrade, was festooned with giant posters, as were the Hermitage, the Admiralty and the Academy of Sciences. 'Hero City!' and 'Cradle of the Revolution!' the posters screamed. Arm in arm with Horace, Inna stared up at the soaring Alexander Column in Palace Square, which was enclosed by a giant red and orange Cubist-style rostrum, whose jagged planes looked like flames. It seemed to be blowing the column into the sky.

'It's not so bad, you see!' Horace kept exclaiming, his stubbly face lit up. Inna knew that he loved all the strange, angular, athletic art of this new life. He'd sat up till all hours last night with Marcus and his poet girlfriend, Olympia, drinking in their fanciful talk about the explosive beyond-sense language the young were now experimenting with, the language of the birds, or of the gods, or of the stars; a language beyond time, the speech of the future; or was it the lost aboriginal language of the time before? Inna couldn't keep the doubt off her face.

It was 365 days since all this began. In that year, so many other people's resistance to the new order had been overcome. The bank workers who'd refused to open their safes for these grubby new masters had given in after the Bolsheviks held guns to their heads. The surly ministry doormen who, a year ago, had tried to turn away the first Bolshevik Commissars had, likewise, changed their minds. The actors in the imperial theatres, who'd come out on strike against the new regime, were back on stage. But Inna wasn't reconciled.

It wasn't all bad, true. Inna had been impressed by some of these new Soviet rulers' odder, more idealistic new laws. She oohed and aahed like everyone else when they abolished the two weeks that would ordinarily follow 31 January, making the next day 15 February instead of 1 February, and bringing Russian time, which had for centuries lagged two weeks behind the West's, bang up to date. She marvelled when they did away with all the old-fashioned glitches in Russian spelling and killed off a couple of useless letters, turning the written language into a logical modern construct.

It was true, too, that the war had ended (though it was best not to think about the terms).

Still, Inna was less willing than her husband to be charmed by the posters. Their defiant brightness reminded her of all the things that had gone wrong this year; of the darkness underneath.

Lenin had moved the Soviet government to Moscow in

the spring after someone had taken a potshot at him. There'd never been anything to keep this boggy city going but the machinery of empire, and now the innumerable government offices and functionaries had gone. So Petrograd was dying all around them: and those people who hadn't already left were starving. The White resistance, down in the south, was crystallizing into civil war. The Bolsheviks had a secret police of their own called the Cheka, as terrifying as the Emperor's secret police had ever been; worse, maybe. Since someone else had taken another potshot at Lenin in August, in Moscow – a girl this time – the Cheka were stamping out opposition to the Revolution. But you didn't get details of the Red Terror from the papers, which were as empty as ever, just from whispers in queues: stories that the Romanovs had all been killed, from the former Emperor Nikolai Romanov, shot with his wife and children and servants somewhere in the Urals, to every insignificant cousin in every remote corner of the land. Shot, stabbed, dissolved in acid baths, dropped down mine shafts.

There was the everyday terror you saw whenever you went out, too: gloating servants turning on every grandee they'd ever felt slighted by, yelling, 'Time to start looting from the looters!' as they emptied the houses of the rich. Everywhere eyes glinted with hate.

And then there was the hunger. Pavlov, a Nobel scientist, growing his own carrots and potatoes; poor old Professor Gezekhus, blown up with hunger like some African famine victim; or Nastya, the teenage daughter of the family upstairs, who'd taken to hanging around outside on the street, not with the icons and pearl brooches and leather-bound books and woollens and boots that took other gloomy ladies out to the market, but with cheeks boldly rouged and a pinched look on her face. How long before Agrippina went the same way? How long before she herself . . .?

So walking about this festival of revolution in Petrograd this afternoon didn't delight Inna. It just made her feel dizzy, especially when she thought about the future. No wonder the sky was so cheerfully blue. Why would there be clouds, when the factories had all stopped working? Weeds sprouted from the Merchants' Yard walls, and the wooden pavements were rotting.

So there was bitterness in her voice as she replied, 'Not so bad, no. And who cares if people heat their apartments by burning their books, and eat dogs and cats?'

'Do you mind if I quickly drop something off?' Horace asked casually a little later when they got as far along Nevsky as Yeliseyevsky's. She could see the strip of open ground just beyond, marking the turning into Great Cavalry Street and the apartment where they'd once lived. Inna shivered. The great black skeletons of the trees there, beckoning bonily in the sharp wind, seemed to be calling her back.

She nodded agreement. She didn't want to be walking around on her own any more, and she definitely didn't want Horace doing so. Lucky his coat was so shabby, she thought, because it wasn't just thieves being killed on a mob whim any more. They were catching officers too – anyone in smart clothes – and administering revolutionary justice from the nearest lamp-post. That's why Madame Leman had sewn these mangy old rabbit skins on to everyone's collars. She'd started with Horace's, Inna guessed, because he was the one street boys were likeliest to stop and point at, squealing in their high, innocent, dangerous voices, *'BUR-ZHUI!'*

Horace's upright carriage and kind, gentlemanly air meant he could easily be taken for some vestige of the old orders, or simply recognized as a foreigner who must therefore be a bourgeois, and punished accordingly.

'Where are we going?' she said. But she'd half guessed already, even before they set off towards their old home. Franz Birbaum from Fabergé's still lived in the same building, with its view of the avenue of tall trees and the green-and-white classical temple where the Finnish Lutherans prayed. He was the last of Horace's colleagues left.

'I won't be a moment,' he said, not answering her question. She glanced at him: at the lines – laughter lines – round his eyes, and those other lines, down his cheeks and across his forehead, which could only be worry. With sudden concern she thought, How careworn he looks.

He kissed her forehead when they'd pushed through the unlocked downstairs door (no doorman here any more). 'You wait downstairs.' That excitement she'd seen in him outside seemed to have evaporated, as he plodded up the stairs.

She stood, pleased to be out of the wind, remembering the dusty smell of this place, and the wild wind soughing in the branches outside while she'd lain in her cosy bed with Horace beside her. Refusing to dwell on the anguish of those last few weeks here – the creeping about, the deceit – she remembered instead the warmth of the rooms, the electricity, clothes and food plentifully available at shops round every corner. She remembered laughing and eating with Horace on her wedding night, and the peace they'd shared. Yes, they'd been good times, here, she thought.

She'd liked Monsieur Birbaum, too: a precise, fussy, good-natured old gentleman, who'd learned passable Russian for a foreigner. And Horace admired his stubbornness in staying on, mending watches and gold chains, as he waited for the Whites to win the Civil War and the good old times to come back. Inna knew that Horace felt solidarity with him, when so many other foreigners were giving up and slinking away. They all came to say goodbye. These days, Horace seemed popular among foreigners whose names she'd never even heard until they came to shake his hand as they left; though, after they'd gone, he sometimes called them faint-hearts, and laughed a bit.

'What are they running *to*? That's the question they should be asking,' he'd say, shaking his head. Carl Fabergé himself had gone, she knew, but Birbaum hung on. And, though she hadn't been back here for several months, Inna knew that Horace still dropped in on him every now and then.

Why didn't he ask me up too? she wondered, but without minding. They'd want to talk English or French, she supposed, and reminisce about old times.

Horace was as good as his word, and was down inside five minutes.

She didn't understand why, when he reached the bottom of the stairs, he embraced her as if they'd been parted for years, but she didn't mind that either.

'How's Monsieur Birbaum?' she murmured into his shoulder.

'Packing.' She heard tightness in his voice. 'He's leaving the city tonight. The Housing Committee wants his flat.'

Inna could just imagine the grim requisitioning party of men with old coats and hard eyes, working out how many people could be crammed into Birbaum's living space and where the partitions should be.

'They've scared him off. He says I should be going too. It's all over here for the likes of us, he says.'

He looked down at her. His eyes were wet. She'd never seen this before.

'Oh Horace,' she whispered, holding him close. 'I'm sorry.'

He told her the rest out on the street as they walked under the heaving trees. Birbaum was planning on taking the route most people were leaving by, now the city was emptying out. He'd go south, through Kiev, down to the Black Sea at Yalta. Yalta, behind the White army lines, was where the White sympathizers were, the aristocrats, and plenty of less aristocratic people, too. Even if you hadn't liked the way things had been before, life for anyone remotely well to do had certainly felt safer under the Emperor. At Yalta, you were poised for onward flight, if need be, to Constantinople or Jerusalem or beyond, though no one wanted to leave Russia altogether unless the Reds broke through. Inna had heard that the White sympathizers were enjoying their long sojourn in the pretty seaside resort, under the bougainvillea. Felix Youssoupoff was among the many Fabergé clients down there, or nearby, at his family estate in the Crimean peninsula's hills, Horace continued, waiting for all this to be over, and for normality to return.

'Perhaps we should go too,' Inna said cautiously, watching her toecaps kick up, one after the other, under her coat. Horace had never wanted to leave before, and he didn't answer now. Perhaps the wind had blown away her words? Inna thought, forgiving him.

'What were you dropping off, anyway?' she asked, when they were nearly home.

He stopped, and Inna was aware of the sudden carefulness

359

in his eyes. 'Well, it's all over now – like Barbarian's adventure with the pickling alcohol, I suppose,' he said reluctantly.

Out of his pocket he took a roll of money she hadn't seen before, carefully cupped in his hand so that the ragged passers-by wouldn't be able to see it. Even in the debased currency of the day, with a bag of flour now costing five thousand roubles, she could see it was enough to help for a while. Once she'd seen it, he stuffed it away again.

'It's for travel papers,' he said. 'People pay me and I get them from Maxim.'

Inna blinked. Horace had gone out early this morning, true, and come back with a copy of *New Life*. But he hadn't said he was going to see Maxim. And what did Maxim have to do with getting travel documents, anyway? His newspaper was always in trouble with the authorities, for being so critical. But then again, the new rulers were still supposed to be fond of him, personally, for the support he'd given them in the past, and he knew all the socialists and was close to many Bolsheviks. He could have a word in anyone's ear. He was connected. So, yes, perhaps he would be a good man to go to, if you wanted documents for getting away.

She blinked again. Was *that* why all the foreigners came to see Horace?

'I've been storing things for old Fabergé customers – things they used to keep at the shop, in Monsieur Fabergé's safe. Gold is better than money, with the inflation,' he went on, very low.

She let it sink in – how had she not known? Or had she half known all along? She nodded, slowly. 'You kept them under the floorboards,' she breathed. 'Of course. Under those bookshelves you keep moving round . . .'

'I knew they'd rifle the safe in the end,' Horace confirmed jerkily. 'I said, better to take precautions than just wait for the worst. I wanted to help people leave with their belongings. That's what my stipend was for. And Birbaum's been paying me that, too, over these last few months. But now there's no one else left.'

Inna nodded again, more bleakly this time. So the stipend would stop too. All they'd lived on, at least in the early months, before Madame Leman had got so good at sourcing government ration parcels, would come to an end.

Suddenly overwhelmed, she wrapped him in her arms again. 'You did all that, for all of us, and you never breathed a word,' she said. 'You're a good man, Horace Wallick. It's why I love you.'

His arms tightened about her. They stayed like that, swaying together for a long moment, turned away from the world, shutting out the filthy pavement of Garden Street and the stinking Hay Market ahead.

'There was a whole crate of stuff when we moved in,' he said, his voice hollow. 'And now it's all gone. The box is empty. Everyone's left.'

'We should go too,' Inna said, stepping back. Struck, suddenly, by the obviousness of it. 'Whatever old rat Madame Leman sews on your collar, you still look like a foreign gentleman. It's only a question of time before—'

But he shook his head. 'No,' he said. 'We're not going anywhere.'

There was food on the table when they got back: tea, steaming in glasses, and sugar in rough lumps in a bowl, a mound of rusks, and a big tin of sprats in tomato sauce. The four

361

Lemans and Marcus's Olympia were at the table, waiting.

'Hurry!' Agrippina said cheerfully. 'Sit down before the tea gets cold. And tuck in – imagine, sprats! We're celebrating.'

'We've got a new parcel!' Marcus chimed in.

Several months previously, Madame Leman had consulted her husband's old acquaintance, Yuri Pavlovich, an artist now more famous as the city's best ration-hunter, as to what her own family's plan of action should be to avoid starvation. Yuri Pavlovich got one parcel a month – scholar's rations – from the Academy of Art; another – a militiaman's rations – from the Cultural and Education Studio for Militiamen that he'd set up; and a third – the Baltic Fleet's special rations – for lecturing sailors on Italian painting. God helps those who help themselves, he told her. So you must thank God for the dissemination of culture to the proletariat, which the authorities are so keen on now, and start disseminating some yourselves.

Now Madame Leman talked once a week to militiamen on German literature. 'Poor bored things, how they yawn and scratch,' she told Inna.

A week ago, Maxim had finally sent word, via Madame Leman, that if Inna was willing, and if her performance was at concert level, he'd found an opening for her to go and play Tchaikovsky at working men's clubs.

'Will I be good enough?' she'd begun, but caught herself. Her old irrational dread was just a self-indulgent luxury when there was the possibility of a parcel.

'Of course you are,' Barbarian had said scornfully, in his deep man's voice. She'd laughed in embarrassment as he'd gone on. 'You could play any old marching song to them, with every note a wrong one, and what would it matter? They're not going to know the difference.'

'Where is this parcel from?' Inna asked now, sitting down. Seated beside her, Horace was beaming round at the family as if nothing was wrong.

'The Rosa Luxemburg Drops of Milk Maternity Centre!' they chorused.

'Marcus has been lecturing midwives on the history of violin-making!' Madame Leman added, grinning.

'He's going to get breast-feeding mothers' rations for it, too!' Agrippina said. Her eyes were round. 'Next time there'll be cheese! Butter!'

When they went upstairs Inna said to Horace, reassured, 'You see? They've found their feet. They don't need your stipend any more. They're going to be all right.'

After a moment, she added, 'And we should go. Because we're not.'

But he averted his eyes. 'No,' he said, too loudly, going out to wash and banging the door behind him.

Horace understood that Inna was afraid. She was always coming back from some queue with new stories from the crowd about the Cheka; about arrests, disappearances, torture. She repeated them, looking to him to share her fear. But he didn't, because he didn't really believe them. Of course people whispered. The new leaders only had themselves to blame for that, with their new censorship, which was even more stifling than the old. But things couldn't be as bad as people made out, surely? To Horace's mind, the stories about the new secret police had the nightmarish, exaggerated tone of fairy tales full of villains.

The Moscow clown who people were saying was now dead, for instance – Bim Bom – surely he hadn't really been killed just for poking fun at the politicians in his act? How could you actually believe that armed men had burst onstage and chased him around his props, shooting with pistols, making the circus crowd laugh and cheer while the grease-painted figure in checked trousers ran? Or that they'd all gone on thinking it was just another part of the show until he was shot dead, in front of a suddenly screaming audience? And what about the stories about the officer in Kharkov who was supposed to snort cocaine before interrogations, then dip his White, or maybe-White, suspects' hands in boiling water, so he could peel off their skin in perfect glove shape? (White gloves, of course?)

The horror stories had their own grotesque Gothic logic, to be sure, but Horace was persuaded they were the usual Russian exaggeration. And Inna was just reliving her understandable fear of the old police, he thought, splashing water from the jug on his face. And he wasn't going to be frightened away by ghosts from the past, when he was so interested by the present.

There was so much happening here and now, in the realm of ideas this stiff old city had suddenly become. After the dull grind of his Fabergé years, he felt jolted into electric life by Marcus's young friends from the Union of Youth, with their thrilling, shockingly modern statements.

'The past is too tight. The Academy and Pushkin are less intelligible than hieroglyphics. Throw Pushkin, Dostoyevsky, Tolstoy, etc., etc., overboard from the Ship of Modernity.'

And Alyosha Kruchenykh, bard of Beyond-Sense poetry,

the most avant-garde of all the avant-garde, had asked him only last night, with that puckish grin of his, if he'd help their friend Kasimir paint the sets for a new staging of the Futurists' opera. Of course Horace had no intention of giving up his chance to bring to life all those extravagantly radical stage characters, Nero and Caligula in the Same Person, Traveller through All the Ages, Telephone Talker and the rest. Even if nothing came of that, he had no intention, either, of leaving behind those late-night conversations, which were headier than any champagne and full of truth for today. What was it the other poet had said last night? 'The poetry of Futurism is the poetry of the city, of the contemporary city. Feverishness is what characterizes the tempo of the contemporary world. In the city there are no flowing, measured lines of curvature: angles, fractures and zigzags are what make up the profile of the city.'

Yes, Horace thought, I heard that there, in the yellow room, and then I went out today and saw it in the square, with my own eyes. Where else could that have happened?

Inna was asleep, curled over on the far side of the bed, when Horace crept back into the bedroom.

He switched off the lamp.

In the darkness, he told himself: It's right to stay, for what would I be without all the life I've found here?

In the darkness, his own private fear came on him: the fear of abandoning everything he'd made for himself, and discovered for himself, here in this city, with all its manic energy; the fear of abandoning even the debonair, knowledgeable self he'd crafted here, who sauntered inquisitively around, transforming himself into first this kind of artist, then that, as fast as his environment shifted shape; the fear of leaving behind the place his soul had made its home.

No, it was simpler than that: Horace was experiencing the dread of Home.

It wasn't that Yalta and the Whites would be so bad, in themselves. There'd be food, and respite from the snows. There'd be some of the exotic company he'd enjoyed here. But to think of going to Yalta would be to open his mind to the possibility that, further down the line, if things went wrong, there might also have to be a return to England.

England: that grey vision of half-hearted rain, bobbing bowler hats, dark umbrellas, stockbrokers on suburban trains, and bloodless, apologetic voices saying 'can't complain' and 'mustn't grumble'. The dullness. The quiet.

Shrinking even further over to his side of the bed, Horace asked himself: What would I be, what would I do, in South Norwood?

For the next few days, Inna was quiet around Horace. She wasn't angry, exactly, but maybe puzzled; keeping a tactful distance. He was pleased, at least, that if she wasn't talking much to him, she wouldn't be resuming *that* conversation. He didn't want to be nagged.

But then she burst in on him in the yellow room with a letter in her hand, looking suddenly radiant and crying, excitedly, 'Look, we *can* go – this is how!'

Horace, his heart heavy, glanced up from his newspaper. 'What is it?' he asked.

'Look!' she exclaimed gaily, waving the letter. 'God knows how it got through the censors, or even through the mail – maybe someone brought it; who knows? – but Youssoupoff has got a letter to us! It was in Aunt Cockatoo's letterbox! I've just found it!'

Horace raised an eyebrow. 'And . . .?'

'He's outside Yalta! He wants us to take his violin to him!'

Horace felt old suddenly; old and weary.

She must want Yalta a lot to have so completely forgotten her old animosity towards Youssoupoff, he thought. Well, Yalta was a legend that everyone knew and loved: the glitter of sun on sea, the dark-green mountains behind, the romantic aristocrats' castles that you saw on postcards, the yachts and military ships, the men in uniform, the summer that lasted till November and began again in March, the softness of the balmy air, the tawny-skinned locals, the palm trees . . .

He stood up. 'It's out of the question,' he said. He heard it come out like a whiplash.

Determinedly, Inna ignored him. 'He's offering very generous terms. Look, a payment in gold or valuables; because what good would roubles be? He'll put us up for the rest of the war on his estate, and, if the war goes the wrong way for the Whites, and, God forbid, they all have to evacuate, he'll help us leave too. He says we can travel with him!'

'Forget it,' Horace said harshly. 'It's insane. He's insane. You of all people should know that.'

Looking as shocked as though he'd slapped her, she paused for breath, just long enough for Horace to regret his brutal tone, and to register the desperation in her excitement.

But then she stepped closer, and said challengingly, 'He's not that insane. And he's offered to help us. Who else is willing to do that for us?'

He folded his arms across his chest. Closed his eyes. I'm

not going back to England, he was telling himself, in the dancing red cloud of light-spots behind his eyeballs.

'You're not safe here,' she persisted. 'We're not safe here. We have to leave.'

He opened his eyes. 'We can't – because of the journey.'

Doubt appeared on her face, because who would know more about this than him, after all his muttered conversations with about-to-be-émigrés whose papers he'd procured?

'We'd have to go right through where the civil war is.'

Now he could see angry tears in her eyes. 'But we'd just be *passing through*!' she said, almost childishly.

'But the time would come when someone, from one side or the other, would stop the train. Requisition it. We'd have to get out and walk. And what then?' he replied gently. 'We'd be right back there, down in the south, where it's never been good to be a Jew, among the very people you wanted to get away from before. Peasants down there who've never even seen a foreigner might be at a loss as to what to make of *me* but they won't be fooled for a moment by *you*. They'll know exactly who they're looking at. And everyone will be more feral than before with cold and hunger.'

He put his hands on her shoulders, and tried to draw her into an embrace. But she resisted.

'*You* wouldn't be safe, on the way down there,' he said. '*That's* why we're not going. *You're* better off here.'

Blinking hard, Inna nodded, shrugged off his hands and left.

I should follow her, Horace thought. But he didn't. Instead he picked up his newspaper, and sat down in the sudden silence of an empty room.

CHAPTER TWENTY-SIX

'Inna dear, I can tell you don't really want to play to the working men, because you still aren't practising, so you'd better come to see Maxim with me yourself,' Madame Leman said briskly. 'We need more parcels, and obviously Horace can't go out and get one, the way things are. Besides, he's done quite enough for us. And Maxim is full of ideas. He may be able to think of something else for you.'

It was after New Year, in February 1919. All kinds of people had started coming to Maxim with all kinds of petitions now, because he was still said to have the ear of the powerful. (Not that that made Maxim immune, as Inna knew. People had done just the same with Rasputin, once.) Still, for now at least he was a port of call for the desperate.

The scene that met their eyes in the great book-lined study-cum-dining-room at the apartment on Kronversky Avenue was like a hallucination. It was hot inside – hot! In fact, it was so hot that none of the two dozen or so people at the crowded trestle table was wearing a coat.

They were an ill-assorted bunch. There were rough

Petrograd sailors, writers, and – Inna scanned the room curiously – all kinds of other oddities bumping elbows. Inna could swear that was Tatlin the young architect, Marcus's and Olympia's friend, over there, handsome and floppy-haired, and wasn't that Chaliapin, less sleek than usual, asking for seconds in his famous bass voice? And over in the corner, looking haughty, not speaking, just intently eating, an old, old couple with a mangy dog at their feet, whom, she realized, she'd heard about: they were the grand duke and his wife, who lived upstairs surrounded by statues of the Buddha, whom Maxim was said to have rescued from the crowded jails of the Cheka soon after the Red Terror set in. Whoever they were, they were all doing the same thing she and Madame Leman were about to do: shovelling kasha (hot kasha!) into their mouths as fast as they were able.

Only Maxim himself looked chilly. He was wearing a thick grey sweater, and his sturdy but skinny body was racked by coughs. Inna could see the way his bony face, with its jutting cheekbones and big thin-lipped mouth, was constantly working to mask his tuberculosis.

Maxim's eyes lit up at the sight of Madame Leman. 'Dear Lidiya,' he said warmly, advancing to embrace her, 'come in, come in! Make yourself and your friend at home!' Turning to the plump woman dishing up gruel from a vat into whatever receptacles came to hand – a cut-glass bowl here, a tin mug there – he added, 'Moura, dear heart! Two more, over here!'

Before Inna knew where she was, they were all perched on impromptu stools made from piles of encyclopedias which Maxim had scooped off the lower shelves; they had their coats off, and warm bowls in their hands, and were eating.

'All your wonderful languages,' Maxim said enthusiastically to Madame Leman. 'Why, I've had you in mind
for some time for a project I'm discussing with the comrades
now . . .' And he was off, describing, amid the gusts of
steam and talk that seemed to come from another life, a
miraculous-sounding plan to set up an enormous house of
world literature and translate all (all!) foreign classics into
Russian, for the benefit of the proletariat.

'It sounds splendid, Maxim dear; I'd be delighted,'
Madame Leman said quickly, and, winking at Inna, put an
appealing hand on his arm. 'And it makes me wonder, right
away, whether you might also be able to find something for
Inna here?' She indicated Inna, with a beguiling smile. 'She's
a linguist, too – fluent English! And she's a good girl, too: a
hard worker, conscientious, well read; in short, one of us.'

Inna held her breath. Why, Madame Leman knew she
could only speak a few words of English. Perhaps Maxim
did too, because he didn't really even look at her. But, after a
brief pause, he patted Madame Leman on the shoulder, and
nodded, and began smiling and talking again.

Breathing out, Inna ate, and let the happy phrases she was
hearing, so forgiving of Madame Leman's wild exaggeration,
swirl through her mind: 'Plenty of clerking and copying,
so I'm sure we'll be able find some jobs,' and, to Madame
Leman, '*You*, dear lady. You are just what we need.'

It was only as she scraped the last of the food out of her
bowl that she noticed, sitting at the very end of the long
table, a fine-featured, thin-haired, wiry man, with intelligent
eyes set in a face that had lost just enough of its youthful
firmness to make you aware of the skull beneath the skin. He
wasn't saying much, and was mostly just looking around, like

371

Inna, as if enjoying the warmth in his belly, or memorizing the other guests. She'd never seen the man before; but she had seen the person hunched beside him, talking in a low, hurried voice. Even though this man had his back turned to them, and there was an unfamiliar furtiveness in his demeanour, she'd have recognized that silhouette anywhere. It was Yasha.

After a while, Inna touched Madame Leman's arm, and indicated Yasha with a nod. Maxim followed his old friend's glance across the room.

'Ah, I'd forgotten. You all knew each other, didn't you?' Maxim murmured. 'Before . . .' He gave a regretful shake of the head. 'But he's swimming in dangerous waters, that young man. And, if I may be so bold as to offer an opinion: if he hasn't acknowledged either of you, I wouldn't go up to him right now.' He leaned closer, so that Inna could hear the rasping in his throat. He croaked, fishing for a hanky from his pocket, 'He won't want that Cheka comrade he's talking with to notice you, I expect.'

Inna was startled. She'd never seen anyone from the Cheka.

Maxim began coughing terribly into his hanky. When eventually he stopped, he touched Inna's arm. 'My apologies. Damn cough,' he said weakly, almost whispering. 'He'll be avoiding you especially, because of your husband.' He looked straight at her, with watery eyes, and suddenly she was grateful for the cough, and the whisper.

Madame Leman hadn't actually mentioned Horace's name when introducing Inna, and Inna had thought Maxim didn't know who she was. But now, abruptly she realized he knew all about her, and was worried for Horace.

Maxim's smile only got sadder. 'You don't want Chekists even clapping eyes on you,' he mouthed, 'if there's the least chance they might take it into their heads that you're . . . officer class. Anyone can be a counter-revolutionary or a saboteur. Anyone can be a White. Or so people might say.'

Inna nodded. The silence that followed was full of uncertainty.

Maxim looked from one woman to the other. 'I don't think your Yasha does anything really bad,' he said at last. 'He's a good boy, at heart. He isn't one of them, not really. He just . . . just *talks* to our Comrade Bokii there, sometimes, I've noticed. Who knows? Perhaps he has no choice. We all do what we have to, to survive.'

Inna looked towards the frail old grand duke, painfully putting his bowl on the floor for the little dog to lick, then back at Maxim. 'Why do you have the Cheka man *here*, with *him*?' she wanted to ask, but Maxim was shrugging. I do what I can, he was indicating. But I can't guarantee anyone's safety. Then, smiling, clapping Madame Leman on the back, he shifted away from the difficult subject as if it had never been raised.

'There's so much it's futile for us to worry about that all we can usefully do is hope,' he proclaimed.

Madame Leman cast one last wistful glance down the table, before, with what Inna saw as the determination of a true survivor, rising to Maxim's challenge. Visibly putting Yasha out of her mind, she turned, beaming, back to her friend. 'But what we *can* do is plan for our shining future! We must make a comprehensive reading list for the proletariat!'

Inna sat very still, as if listening to the literary conversation that ensued: 'Whom should we include? Zola? Dickens?'

from Maxim; Madame Leman laughing back at him, 'But don't the poor proletarians get enough miserable realism as it is? Shouldn't we give them love, mystery, enchantment – the things they're missing?' But all Inna was thinking was, Why is Yasha talking to that man?

She couldn't help noticing as the skull-faced man got up, shook Yasha's hand, and quietly left the room. Yasha then picked up both their bowls and took them into the kitchen. That last, highly unusual act – the submissive curve of Yasha's back – alarmed her more than ever.

But when he came out of the kitchen, his face was composed. He walked towards the way out without looking round or greeting anyone.

'Why, it's a *wonderful*, elemental love story!' Madame Leman was exclaiming.

He hadn't seen her, then, Inna thought. He was going to leave without a word.

The disappointment she felt was crushing. She'd never know why he'd stooped so low as to be telling that man other people's secrets, as Maxim had seemed to be suggesting. (If that's what he *had* been doing. Informing . . . But, no, she couldn't believe that of Yasha.)

But then he stopped in the doorway, and turned his head just enough to give Inna a quick, impassive, unsurprised glance.

He did know I was here. He saw me after all, Inna thought, and was surprised by the surge of joy that came with the thought. Then, almost imperceptibly, he nodded towards the door.

Outside, that nod said. Now.

Madame Leman, lost in another world, was continuing

enthusiastically. "'I've no more business to marry Edgar Linton than I have to be in heaven; and if the wicked man in there had not brought Heathcliff so low I shouldn't have thought of it,'" Inna heard as she got up. The voice followed her as she started slipping behind chairs and benches towards the door. "'It would degrade me to marry Heathcliff now; so he shall never know how I love him; and that, not because he's handsome, Nelly, but because he's more myself than I am . . .'"

In the doorway, Inna paused. No, neither Madame Leman nor Maxim was looking her way. She slipped out.

Outside Yasha was striding down the wide street, wind flapping at his coat skirts. Shivering, with her coat still unbuttoned, Inna ran up behind him and caught his arm.

'Why were you talking to the man from the Cheka?' she panted.

He shook his head. 'Not here,' he mouthed. He turned to shield her from the roar of freezing wind and then nodded towards an archway into a derelict back courtyard. It was overflowing with stinking rubbish. Perhaps there were no dogs left to scavenge through the heaps.

'I live just through there,' he said. 'Come and talk.'

'It's not what you think,' Yasha said – muttered – as soon as they'd got to the top of the stairs.

He opened the door. Everyone was thinner than they used to be, of course. But he looked . . . diminished, Inna thought: worried, slinking, stray. Now he'd got her here, even the masterful body language had gone. He couldn't quite meet her eyes.

The dark apartment wasn't small, and it was full of things:

clothes lying in piles on the corridor floor, books heaped up, a scatter of leaflets, and unwashed plates in a bowl outside the kitchen up at the far end. But it felt very empty. Its high ceilings were fuzzed with cobwebs. There was a drip, and a bucket to catch it in.

The next thing Inna noticed in the dim light of the oil lamp he lit was a patched woman's jacket lying on one heap – an ugly one, in some sort of dark stuff. All clothes were old and ugly now, of course, but this was one that had never been anything but brutally utilitarian. She was strangely pleased.

'Your revolutionary friends are away, then,' she said, recognizing the jacket as one that only a political woman would wear and remembering, suddenly, that it had been brother-and-sister comrades he'd been talking about moving in with back then, though somewhere else. Feeling a stranger, she wondered if he and those people she didn't know had moved on here together.

'They've gone.'

Holding the lamp, he moved her towards the nearest door. She kept her eyes on the jacket. There were several stockings, too, she saw: thick ones, darned many times, most worn through at the heel. Ugly though they also were, she was less pleased to see such intimate female articles so close to Yasha's room.

'That's why I'm in this mess.'

Inside his room there was a small rough table, a chest and several more heaps of clothes. Drawn curtains kept out the grey daylight. There was no chair; she perched modestly at the foot of the rumpled bed. Yasha put the lamp on the floor and slumped down on the pillows at the other end, sinking his head despairingly into his hands.

Without being prompted, he began to tell Inna his story.

A year or so ago, back when the Cheka started, he'd been recruited to help fight counter-revolutionary sabotage by a tall Polish man with a pointy beard at a political meeting. He'd been excited, but the work had turned out to be nothing special, just writing the kind of leaflets he'd once written for the Bund. It was a harmless little job, involving nothing more than going into an office, from time to time, with the copy he wrote in this room. Back then he hadn't known anything more, except what they told him to put in the leaflets.

He'd been living with his friends, still, then: Fanny and her brother. They were trouble, because until Lenin came and they fell under his spell they hadn't been Bolsheviks, but Socialist Revolutionaries, and when all the opposition parties started being shut down, and their former members arrested, Fanny and her brother hadn't seen it was all for the good of the Revolution. They'd taken it badly. Yasha wrinkled his brow. 'Bitching and kvetching, they were. But why should I have wept over that? The Bund was dissolved too.'

Then Fanny went off on a trip to Moscow, and never came back. Just disappeared, no word, nothing. And at the end of the summer, her brother vanished too.

Silence fell.

'You see, they say,' he said, wild-eyed and twitchy, 'that she was the one who shot at Lenin. That she was Russia's Charlotte Corday – the reason they started the Red Terror.'

Inna's eyes widened. She remembered the headlines and the police mug-shot. Fanny Kaplan: executed within the week.

'Though she can't have done it, you know,' Yasha added,

hastily. 'Not really. Because when she was in prison before, she was beaten half to death. She was inside for eleven years, you know, and only got out when I did. She was arrested when she was sixteen for some bomb plot against the Emperor, stripped naked, and caned with birch rods – she was just a kid, for God's sake – and after she got out she could hardly move, half the time, for the headaches. She was more than half-blind. She might have wanted to, but she couldn't have seen to shoot.'

But of course when he next turned up with some copy for one of the Cheka leaflets, they took a new interest in him. Not the bearded man any more, a different one, but he had the same kindly, intelligent eyes. They look like good fathers, all of them, Yasha said miserably; they all talk so gently, as if they know the wickedness of the world and how to protect you from it.

The new man knew everything. Putting Yasha's copy down on his table with a polite nod of thanks, he started straight in. 'Ah, yes, Kagan; I've been hearing about you. So you've been living with counter-revolutionaries, have you? And in the Bund, once, too. Well, well, you've got yourself into a pretty pickle, I see.' He stroked his beard, and Yasha trembled inside. 'There will be arrests in the Bund soon,' the man said, affectionately, 'a lot of arrests. But I can see you're a good man. We don't want *you* arrested, do we?'

And now Yasha was supposed to meet this Bokii, once a month, at Maxim's, just to talk over a meal; just to tell Bokii things about the people he'd talked to, and the people he met around town – especially, though this was never emphasized, if they were his former friends in the Bund.

'I always thought I was brave,' Yasha said humbly. 'But

now I see I'm a coward, because I do it. I've met him a few times now. Sometimes I tell the other people I talk to that I've been asked to inform but refused, just as a way of warning them not to tell me their secrets, because who does refuse the Cheka? Who'd dare? So you see, I try not to make it bad. But it is.'

They sat quietly, Inna listening to Yasha's breath; to hers; to the slow drip of water into the bucket outside the door.

After a while she saw his lips twist into a mirthless grin. 'It was all going to be so different when we were in charge,' he added wryly. 'Wasn't it? When it was *our* police, and there was justice for everyone and the bright tomorrow. But what's actually changed, now we're there? Just the names of the crimes, that's all. They're still set over us. And we're all still just slaves.'

There was no more to say.

After a while, she stretched out a hand and touched his knee.

'Poor Yasha,' she said softly. 'What a terrible life that must be.'

Her heart was so full of pity for him, and a kind of astonishment too. He'd been so full of ideals. She'd never seen him without that unseen rival, the Revolution, in one guise or another. But here they were now, just the two of them, alone, without any of the pretensions that had divided them, just trust, just vulnerability, as if he were spiritually naked before her for the first time.

He shook his head. 'Sometimes I think I should just run off, somewhere. My parents made it to America in the end, you know,' he said. 'Like Beilis. But I can't. They'd find me. They find everyone.'

After another long silence, he put his hand on top of hers.

'You're as lovely as ever. I think of you, often. I always have.'

She yielded when he pulled her closer, but drew her face back when he moved to kiss her.

'Don't touch me; not if you don't want to,' he whispered. 'Don't do anything you'll regret.'

She laughed, miserably. Whatever her mind was telling her, her hands were still roaming over his back. 'I can't not,' she whispered back. 'I never could.'

She was sleeping. There was a faint flush on her cheek. She looked so peaceful. Yasha raised himself on his elbow and softly brushed the hair back from her face.

She stirred, and reached for the hand touching her face; she stroked it and took a deep inward breath. For a moment, Yasha dreaded what would be in her face when she woke fully and turned to look at him. Would he see a slow-dawning horror at what had happened? Panic, even?

But when her eyes did open, it was only as part of a sinuous stretch that brought the entire warm length of her body against his, under the heavy pile of blankets that no longer felt damp or cold. She was smiling right at him, *knowing*, he saw, with unspeakable relief, as his arms twined across her smooth back, his legs around hers.

And when her lips parted, it was only to say one word, in a dreamy, happy murmur: 'You . . .'

'And you, what about you?' he whispered.

He could see the cloud passing over her face as she came to, properly, and remembered everything else. 'Me . . . I don't like it here any more either. I want to leave. But Horace won't.' She sighed. 'Let's not talk about it now.'

How beautiful her voice was. 'No, tell me,' he said, not wanting the moment to end.

And so she did, in a hurried, worried whisper: how Horace had been keeping the family afloat by hiding valuables for his Fabergé colleagues; how that was over now that the Fabergé people had all gone, and it was up to her to start keeping him; how, even though Madame Leman was so good at sourcing parcels, there was never enough to go around; and, also, about the other fear she lived with, that her Horace's undisguisable foreignness would, sooner or later, bring the lynch mob to their door.

When she fell silent, eventually, Yasha kissed her parted lips, very gently. She pulled him down on top of her.

Through the red haze that came on him then, as their bodies started to move again, he heard her whisper, 'If only things had been different. If only we hadn't let ourselves get so trapped by life, you and I . . .'

She drew in her breath, sharply, as his hands touched her breasts. 'I love him, of course I do. But not like this. Not like I've always loved you.'

She woke again, at dusk. She looked sadder this time. She sat up, oblivious of the cold and her nakedness, and whispered, 'I have to go.' Her breath was white.

Only when she was dressed, right to her coat and hat and boots, did she come back to the bed, and sit on the edge of it, and kiss his lips. There were no words. Nothing either of them could promise. Just sadness.

'Will you come again?' Yasha asked.

She shook her head. And then she was gone.

CHAPTER TWENTY-SEVEN

They'd abandoned the second attic room as it was too hard to heat, but she found Horace, in his overcoat and hat and gloves, in the bedroom, feeding pages from a book into the little stove he'd improvised for them when the building's central heating started getting unreliable. He'd made it from a square biscuit tin from England – you could still see the name Huntley & Palmers under the soot – as well as from various metal conserves jars, bound together and shaped into a long wonky tube that went out through a hole in the window pane. Everyone was making these stoves now. They were known, with the class sneer that had become habitual, as *burzhuiki*: bourgeoise women.

She stopped in the doorway. He turned, and said, with a relieved smile, 'Ah, *there* you are. You've been gone for hours. I was worried.'

Horace had chopped up his bedside table for firewood, so there were small, kindling-sized bits of wood piled neatly by the bed. There was no need for one any more, he'd said. You couldn't read in bed any more, not with only a couple of hours' electricity a day. He'd moved his book and reading glasses to the window, next to the *burzhuika* – the light was strongest there, of course; and it was warm, too, if you kept a hand on the tin containing the little fire. His book, which he must have abandoned at dusk, was still there, face down on the floor. Something English, she saw; and felt obscurely comforted by the reminder that he was *from* somewhere, even if it wasn't a place he ever talked about with much affection, if at all.

'I went for a walk after the lunch,' she said dully. (Lying was so easy, to those who wanted to trust you.) She walked in, coat, hat, wet boots and all, not wanting to take anything off; not wanting the smell of Yasha's body to give her away; not wanting to wash it away, either, which was when she'd really have to accept her reality. She sat down on the bed.

Horace said, 'Are you hungry? Because Agrippina was lucky in the market.' He reached down for his offering, with an expectant, innocent look that felt like a knife in Inna's heart. On the little plate he was holding out were two slices of bread and a hard-boiled egg.

'Horace, we have to leave,' she said, looking straight at him, suddenly knowing that, if they didn't go away, she wouldn't be able to resist going back to Yasha.

'We really have to leave,' she repeated when he didn't respond. He was still holding out that plate, but he'd dropped his eyes.

'I know you say I'd be in danger if we went south to Yalta. But I've been thinking, and really it isn't likely that the train would take us straight to a battle, or a lynch mob. The likeliest thing is that we'd just pass quietly through. It would take a few weeks, but after that we'd be safe. Just imagine:

parasols, and sea breezes, and gypsy singers in cafés – not to mention food in the cafés – and all your old Fabergé clients – and safety.

'And maybe, when it's all over, we'd come back here again . . .' she added, but by now her voice was faltering.

'Marching in triumphantly behind the victorious White army, do you mean?' Horace answered, rather mockingly. 'As some distant royal cousin renames the city St Petersburg again, and proclaims himself the new Emperor?'

She sighed. No, she couldn't really imagine that happening either.

That old life seemed unimaginably remote now, as if decades, not just two years, had passed since anyone called himself Emperor. The brief euphoria of the revolutionary spring seemed no less a dream, though she knew Horace still found comfort in the enthusiasm of his young artists. Yasha's disillusioned voice echoed in her mind: *What's actually changed? They're still set over us. We're still just slaves.*

'And you realize, don't you, that we certainly wouldn't be marching back triumphantly behind the victorious Red army, if they came in and found us in Yalta with the Whites – and then won?' His voice was getting harder. 'Because we'd almost certainly be dead. Going to Yalta doesn't just mean going for a holiday by the sea any more, till things somehow "calm down". All those people waiting around down there, making fools of themselves with their seaside strolls and their parties, are only fooling themselves; you must see that. What going to Yalta almost certainly means, now, is accepting you'll soon have to leave Russia altogether – forever.'

He pushed the plate towards her. 'Do eat,' he said. 'You must be hungry.'

But she didn't want to be coddled like a child any more. 'All right,' she said. 'Then let's leave Russia altogether. Look it straight in the eye, and do it. We have to. We're not safe here, either of us.' She hurried on, before she could be seduced by the memory of what was putting her in most danger in this city. 'And if you're so worried about going south on a train, which as far as I can see is the soft option, then let's get out the other way, north, and walk over the lake ice, before the thaw, and get ourselves over the border to Finland. I don't mind how we go. Who cares if everyone says it's a long, hard walk over Lake Ladoga: cold and rough. If Anya Vryubova, that fat old thing, could get out over the ice, as they say she has, then surely we can too. Would you rather try that?' She could feel her eyes flashing.

Horace bit his lip. 'You really want to go,' he said, slowly. 'I can hear that.'

'You have family in England, after all; we could go to them,' she went on. But as soon as the words were out, he looked away again, and his face grew stubborn.

'No.'

'Horace,' she said, more gently. 'Is it England you don't want to go to? Is that the problem? Because we could go anywhere. You could find work wherever you wanted, after all. You're a wonderful craftsman, and you've been with Fabergé for years. You speak French and Russian as well as English. And I could work, too: I could learn to play in public, or teach the violin, or make violins; I could do something. It doesn't have to be England.'

He was gazing at her now, with something she could swear looked like relief in his eyes. 'Of course it would be easiest to go where other people from here are going,' she added, 'especially for me, because of the language – though I could learn a new language soon enough if I had to, couldn't I? And they're all likely to want to go somewhere French-speaking, since so many of them speak such good French. Paris, maybe – which would be easy for you, because you lived there once and you know your way around. But we don't have to decide yet where it might be. We could follow Fabergé, or Birbaum – didn't you say he's going to try to get home to Switzerland, eventually, from Yalta? And Monsieur Fabergé had shops in London and Paris and Tokyo – he might still have them. There might be a place for you in any of them. If we could only get ourselves to Yalta, we could just see where other people were thinking of heading, and follow. We could make our plans once we got there.'

She sat down on the bed, beginning, amidst all her other concerns, to be aware of her hunger, and the bread, and the egg.

But she kept her eyes fixed on him.

'Paris,' he was saying, almost to himself, as she began to roll and crack the hard-boiled egg. 'Montmartre.'

There was something she had to do before she touched the food. She put the plate down and went out to the landing to wash and change her linen. Horace was still standing there when she finally addressed herself to the meal, as if he hadn't even noticed she'd gone out.

'Paris,' Inna was still telling herself the next evening, looking for a way to restart that conversation. Horace was thinking of it, too, she was sure, because although he hadn't mentioned it today she could see he'd kept back some torn-out pages from the old art periodicals he was slowly burning in the *burzhuika*. They were pages about the young Russian Jewish artist Chaim Soutine, and his French life supported by dealers called Guillaume and Zborowski, and his friend Modigliani, another sculptor, who'd once been in love with Anya Akhmatova and who'd escaped from the German bombing of Paris to the south of France last year, but now that the war was over was planning to move back to the French capital.

She was just framing something encouraging to say about the article when she heard footsteps on the stairs.

'Get behind the door,' Horace said suddenly. Hastily she moved, though not behind the door; she picked up the only weapon she could see – Horace's book. Horace picked up another, a big Dahl's dictionary that he never consulted but always kept by the bed. They stood near the door, together, breath rising white from their mouths.

The knocking was hard and aggressive.

Two men stormed in. They wore ragged military coats, like deserters or thieves, but they carried cards with official stamps which they waved threateningly every time they barked 'REQUISITION!' Inna and Horace could do nothing but stand helplessly while the men pulled out drawers and banged doors at will.

Within a few minutes the room was turned upside down.

The men were bulky, and had big slab faces, with broken noses and cauliflower ears, like criminals, Inna thought.

They paused for a minute over Horace's books, looking briefly hopeful at the gold-tooled set before sweeping them off the shelf to the floor to join the woollen stockings and bedclothes.

'Foreign,' one grumbled. 'What use are they?'

Bolsheviks they might be, but Inna supposed they still had this in common with the ordinary thieves they so resembled – that, even if they wanted to humiliate the person they were robbing, and rub their nose in their shameful class origin, they'd also want to confiscate stuff they could sell in the market later.

It didn't take them long to see there was nothing much worth taking in this bleak little pair of garret rooms. No typewriters, no smart lamps, no jewels. Even the violins were all locked up in the storeroom downstairs.

Inna's head was full of a not so distant memory: of Horace, holding her, swaying in the street, of the grey of the afternoon sky, and the misery in his voice when he'd said, 'It's all gone. The box is empty . . .'

Even if they take the floorboards up, Inna told herself now, they won't find anything. But she couldn't be sure. Horace looked so pale.

Hardly daring to breathe, she watched the men give up.

'There's nothing here,' said one. 'They gave us a bad address, didn't they, the bastards.' He kicked the *burzhuika* and Horace's improvised pipe came away from the window with a metallic shriek.

Horace stifled his reproach, but a tiny sound came from his throat.

The one who'd kicked the stove turned towards him, looking at him properly for the first time. However shabbily you dressed Horace, Inna knew his bearing, the refinement of his features, gave him away. There was a brief silence as the man's mouth curled upwards and he started to nod. He could now see he was looking at a class enemy, all right; he just hadn't yet seen any way of profiting from having found him.

'Waistcoat,' he said, triumphantly, and pulled open Horace's coat. 'He's wearing a bleeding waistcoat, look, Van.'

The other man stepped eagerly forward, too, as they both saw the watch in Horace's waistcoat pocket.

Horace didn't give his watch up without a struggle. The dictionary he'd been clutching fell to the floor. But the scuffle lasted only a moment – not even long enough for Inna to shout, let alone start banging them about the head with the book in her hands, as she so wanted to. Then, pocketing their swag, they were strong-arming Horace down the stairs towards the street, and she was running down after them, with her heart pounding in her ears.

Outside, in the dance of firelight, the first man into the courtyard grabbed the doorman. The doorman in his raggedy cap cringed away from the stranger's touch as his own drunken friends abandoned him, shuffling back from the little fire they'd been sitting around, making themselves small against the dark courtyard walls. But they all edged forward again when the man said, 'Shovel, mate, get us a snow shovel,' and the doorman rushed eagerly, cravenly, to fetch it.

Meanwhile, the man who'd punched Horace as he'd taken the watch put the shovel in his hands.

'Clear the snow,' he jeered, 'your bleeding excellency.'

For a moment, Inna's eyes met Horace's.

The doorman, with a bit of a crowd now muttering behind him in the archway, shouted, with savage pleasure: 'Yeah, sweep up, go on, all of it. Don't forget the corners.'

Horace, his face drooping between bowed shoulders, scraped.

They might all just have gone on like that for five or ten

minutes more, until the onlookers got bored and went back to their bonfire, if the doorman hadn't taken it into his head to point at Inna and call out, 'And what about *her*, brothers? The wife, here, the Queen of bloody Sheba?'

At that first hint of a Jew sneer, Inna felt the crowd beginning to look at her. 'Isn't *she* going to get a bit of what for, too?' the doorman mocked.

Then everything changed.

She was scared now, black and sick with it. She shut her eyes. But that didn't stop the cackles and catcalls and whistles from all around her. 'Run,' she heard urgently, but whose voice it was she couldn't tell. 'Run,' the voice whispered. 'Innochka, run . . .'

And then she was back in the huge doorway, looking for Mama. She was in her white nightgown, twisting her blanket in one hand and her hair in the other, looking up into the smoke at the men towering above, with their backs to her, in a ring. She was wondering what they were all doing here, in the dark. Wondering why Mama had let them in, and where Papa was. Trying to make sense of the movements and the scuffling sounds and the flickering light and the smoke and the men laughing and saying things.

And then, from somewhere in the middle of it, down on the ground in the dark, actually below hers – where nothing grown-up should be – she saw Mama's eyes. Fixed on her. Nodding. Jolting. And the whisper, over and over, 'Run . . . run,' which she could hardly hear, because the big dark men were saying things now, so loudly, so rhythmically, so fast. Horrible things. 'Run.'

But she didn't, because she knew she had to stop the men. They were alarming Mama, weren't they, hurting her, and they had bright policemen's piping on their shoulders, and it wasn't right. Mama needed help.

But then she looked around, and saw the other thing in the room, almost at her feet, on the floor where Papa's violin lay, or what was left of it, because someone seemed to have walked on it, and its neck was snapped. The thing was as big and unmoving as a felled tree trunk, but a tree trunk covered in the dark wool of Papa's suit, so that it looked like a still version of his chest.

There was something else, something red and smiling at the far end of the thing, in the dark – a giant clown-grin she couldn't understand, stretching right across the top of its vague shape.

It was a horrible shape, red and glistening as paint.

It was only after she'd finally made out the pale still lips of Papa's real mouth, further away still, that she finally understood that what she was looking at was his throat. The smile was in his throat. The red was his blood, a great long line of it. Running from ear to ear.

Shocked, sickened, she turned away.

'Run,' she heard, the whisper in her ears again. And now she could imagine the men turning to her, on her; the feel of their arms on hers; the smell of their breath.

So, feeling as though she were floating, she began to tiptoe very slowly and quietly away, down the stairs, counting the banisters drifting past her eyes, humming to herself and twisting her hair in one hand and her blanket in the other. It wasn't that she was running away and leaving Mama, she told herself; not really. Aunty Lyuba downstairs would know what to do. Aunty Lyuba would stop them . . .

Somewhere very close, she heard a huge roar of rage, then

the thud of something hard landing on bones, and a scream. And suddenly she wasn't in the fear of that other place any more, but here again, screaming.

Desperately she took a breath, opened her eyes, and saw Horace, his face contorted with fury, swinging the shovel. Horace's boot had been split open, and Inna realized that someone must have gone down savagely on it with that shovel a moment ago. But one of the men was on the ground, just near her, clutching his head and starting to groan, and several of the crowd were edging back out of harm's way, muttering to each other, 'Call out the guard!' and 'Man's gone crazy!'

The other man had already begun dancing backwards towards the safety of the archway that led back to the street.

Then he stopped altogether, because another man came in through the archway, took in the scene, grabbed him by the scruff of the neck and strong-armed him back into the courtyard, to face the suddenly hushed little crowd.

Yasha, Inna saw. It was Yasha.

Inna watched as Horace grinned – a look of triumph – clanked down the shovel on the cobbles, so hard it nearly sparked, and shouted, 'Don't ever think of laying a finger on my wife again, you filthy haemorrhoid!'

The fickle cluster of bystanders changed sides at once. With contemptuous nods towards the thugs, they began to leave, one of them kicking the man on the ground as he slipped away.

Horace limped the two steps to Inna, and pulled her close.

It was Yasha she watched, astonished at the extraordinary coincidence that had brought him through the archway at that moment. Not just she; all eyes were on Yasha.

But it was Horace she clung to, treasuring the feel of the rough dark wool of his coat.

'What are you up to here then, comrades,' Yasha said sternly to the men now cringing abjectly in front of him. '*Scaring girls?*'

They backed away as the doorman shooed his family back inside, and the last of the spectators left the scene.

'Do you know what I call that, comrade?' Yasha went on, his face a mask of disgusted anger.

Miserably, they shook their heads.

'I call it betraying the Revolution.'

There was a low growl of agreement from the doorman.

'So hop it,' Yasha added brutally, 'before I turn the pair of you over for some People's Justice yourselves.'

Inna knew she should feel more, much more, than she was feeling. She should be thanking Yasha for appearing. She should be thanking Horace for his heroic attempt to save her. But all she actually did was to turn around and stumble back inside the staircase door, heading not for the attics but for the unviolated rooms of the Lemans, just one floor up.

CHAPTER TWENTY-EIGHT

'But I didn't hear a thing!' Madame Leman kept saying once she'd got Inna and Horace safely in her kitchen. 'It makes my blood run cold to think of it! You could both have been murdered, just like that!'

Yasha hadn't come in. He'd just nodded, curtly, as Inna stumbled towards the stairwell. 'Get her in, and get that foot bandaged,' he'd told Horace before he turned on his heel.

'Well, it was all very quick,' Horace kept replying now. He was keen to keep things calm. Marcus was out for the evening with Olympia and the poets. He was aware of Barbarian's and Agrippina's round eyes, fixed first on his beaten-up face and then on Inna's pallor. He didn't want to mention his throbbing foot. He didn't want them more scared than they need be.

Horace caught Madame Leman's doubtful glance at Agrippina in her green dress. She wouldn't say anything, because of course she didn't want to make him feel unwelcome, but she was clearly imagining what might happen next time thugs came hunting in this building for foreigners. He could see she was beginning to be afraid for her daughter.

'You mustn't worry,' he said reassuringly. 'It won't happen again.'

It was only as he said this that he realized, with dawning sadness, why.

'Inna and I have been talking,' he went on. 'Not because of tonight – we were discussing it anyway, before this happened – but this makes it easier. We've decided it's time for us to leave.'

In the pandemonium that followed, with the three Lemans each talking at the same time, shouting, 'What do you mean, leave?' and 'How could you possibly?' and 'Where would you go?' and 'Are you crazy?' (but not, Horace noticed, 'Why?'), he saw Inna, very slowly, raise her head and smile at him.

'You see, Youssoupoff wrote,' she told the Lemans with a strange calm. 'From his estate at Koreiz, in the Crimea. He wants his violin.'

'So we're going to go to Yalta first,' Horace said. 'And then I think we're going to make for Paris.'

There was nothing else for it. He could see that. And he could so clearly envisage the first part of the journey on the train: the seat, the bunk, the pistons, the chuffing, the mournful hoots and the landscape streaming backwards. To this picture, he could easily add soldiers, massed in those cornfields through the murky glass of the windows, glimpsed through the round peep-holes they'd rub, some in Red uniforms, some in White (stick-men figures, shooting at each other with looks of surprise and muffled pops). Yet whatever he'd said to Inna about the dangers, crossing the war zone still seemed too unreal to prompt any emotion. It was the

395

unknown lying beyond that was saddening him, he knew: what came once they'd crossed the unmarked line from Red to White Russia. Because there was no way back from the Crimea.

So he only nodded as they all started exclaiming again, 'Paris!' and 'Yalta!' The lump in his throat might have given him away if he'd tried to reply. He could see something of the same mixture of emotions on Madame Leman's face, as she took in the news that he and Inna would be unlikely ever again to sit in this kitchen with its gurgling pipes, eating whatever she'd managed to bring in from the market and joining in the usual arguments about art, or who should queue for what in the morning, or Barbarian's table manners.

But, even though she brushed an impatient hand across glistening eyes before she spoke again, what she said was, 'Well, the last thing I want is to say goodbye to either of you, you know that, but I do see why you feel you must.'

Mixed up with the sadness of parting, he saw, was quiet relief. She wanted her children safe. Perhaps he'd been a fool to resist for so long, and put the people he cared for most in danger.

'I'll go and see Maxim in the morning,' Horace said, getting carefully up on his uninjured foot and going to stand behind Inna. 'We can be off as soon as he can get us travel papers.'

'Be safe,' Maxim said, embracing Horace and kissing him on both cheeks before wiping water from his eyes.

The envelope had already disappeared inside Horace's greatcoat.

With a tenderly mocking salute, Horace stepped back. He would miss this. 'You, too,' he said.

Outside, it was a perfect winter's morning. There was no wind, no ice in the air, just a celebratory light blue sky with tiny white clouds. Great white pillows of unspoiled snow lay everywhere, and the little golden boat at the top of the Admiralty spire glittered in the pale sun.

Horace knew he was saying goodbye.

He knew, too, that it wasn't as important to him as he'd once thought, being here. He'd been a fool. It was far simpler than he'd realized. The main thing was for Inna to be safe. A man can live anywhere. Home is where the heart is.

Still, he'd have liked to tramp right round the city one more time, making private farewells to all the places he'd been happy in here: to the canal sides, and the river banks, to the concert halls and garrets and palaces and basements.

But his injured foot was throbbing too much. He limped on home.

And as he walked, he found his thoughts returning to what Maxim had said before his Moura had come in with the tray bearing the little painted flask of vodka and the two glasses and the obligatory bit of bread to sniff after their farewell shots.

'Have you seen anything of young Kagan recently?'

Some instinct had stopped Horace from answering straightforwardly. 'I don't suppose we will now,' he'd said lightly. 'It's been a long time since he worked at the Lemans'.'

Maxim's eyes were always compassionate, but for a moment Horace had thought something steelier was glinting in them.

'He comes here sometimes, and talks to Bokii the Chekist,

you know,' Maxim had said, shaking his head. 'He's in over his head, I'm afraid. He never did know when to stop.' And then Moura had arrived. 'How much time one spends worrying about people,' Maxim had added, reflectively, taking the tray from her. 'But at least there's no need to worry about *you* any more.' He'd poured out the shots with a lavish hand. 'You're well out of all this.'

That evening, when they gathered in the kitchen to eat, Madame Leman brought out every luxury she could manage.

There was tea. And not just tea, but jam with the tea.

There was fresh bread, and she made a point of telling Inna that she'd parcelled up the rusks she was always making out of the stale bread and that the parcel, with a bottle of tea, was for them to take on the train.

Horace had meant to go and stand in a queue to get something for this farewell meal, but his foot was hurting again. And at least he could share the presents Maxim's Moura had given him: a carefully wrapped box of darling doves, with at least a memory of meat mixed up with the buckwheat inside the cabbage parcels, and also, miracle of miracles, a long piece of sausage.

He couldn't go up all those stairs to their rooms very easily, and anyway the *burzhuika* he'd made was broken, so he and Inna had been sleeping these past couple of nights down in the yellow room, on the divan. Inna was still in that dazed, mute state she'd been in ever since the attack – a perfectly understandable frame of mind, considering the shock she'd suffered; he could only hope she'd recover her usual quickness of wit on the road. In the meantime, while he trudged around town getting documents, he'd charged her, Agrippina and Madame Leman with clearing out their space in the attics, scrubbing both rooms clean and bringing down all the belongings they wouldn't be taking with them. Everything except a couple of changes of clothes, and of course the violin, was to be shared out among the family.

Since Horace was rather enjoying the mood of decisiveness that had come on him since he'd realized they had to leave, he'd hoped the sheer practicality of that task might energize her, but she'd only nodded, looking quietly acquiescent. Horace had the distinct impression it was Madame Leman who'd actually taken charge of the work. In any event, it was all ready now, and their possessions – two small bags, one battered violin box, and Inna's reticule – were out in the hall.

He'd got Inna, rather than anyone else, to bring down the big dictionary, the one he hadn't managed to hit the Bolsheviks with, and put it on the kitchen dresser.

Once Madame Leman had poured them each a thimbleful of Aunt Cockatoo's dark-gold cognac, he got up and heaved it over to the table. It was as big as an English family Bible and you needed both hands to lift it.

'I have a farewell present for you all, too,' he began.

He sensed the slight disappointment in the air. He could imagine what they were thinking: what good was a dictionary? Yet they kept their polite smiles firmly on their faces, as if, however inadequate his unwanted gift was, they knew they must accept it with good grace, because they loved him.

'Can I have a knife, please, Barbarian?' Horace asked. 'A sharp one?'

They all laughed at that.

'We can't eat the dictionary!' Barbarian cried. 'Not after this meal!'

'Not without boiling it first!' Agrippina added, tears brimming in her eyes.

Horace took the knife Barbarian gave him and inserted it between the solid black leather of the binding and the first of the pages.

'Are the pages glued together?' asked Inna, looking curious for the first time in days.

Horace said nothing; just grimaced, and yanked.

He was a bit breathless by the time the leather front finally dropped away, with a tearing noise, to reveal hundreds of pages, all stuck together with violin-making glue, to make the sides of a box – a box with a deep square cut in the middle of every page. It was an idea he'd had when he'd first done his deal with Fabergé to hide things from oafish requisitioning Bolsheviks: the perfect hiding place. Little boxes and glittering jewellery tumbled out on to the table.

The Lemans squealed, leaned forward, and put their hands out to touch. They opened the boxes, and more shining objects were revealed. They oohed and aahed as they lifted from the shimmering mound an egg pendant on a fine gold chain whose bottom half of faceted violet amethyst was separated by a gold band from a top half of smoothly creamy enamel; a curvy photograph frame of translucent grey guilloche enamel, decorated with a tracery of silver-gilt lilies of the valley; a delicate bracelet, shaped like another bouquet of foliage and flowers and ribbons, made of sparkling gold, diamonds and enamel; a perfectly lifelike onyx bulldog, with emerald eyes and a miniature golden collar, whose bell actually rang; an art deco brooch in silver-topped gold, with a large aquamarine and a smaller diamond at its wider end; a pair of peasant figurines, in semi-precious stones and enamel, full of the patience and gentleness of old Russia; a pair of gold and enamel cufflinks, with a swirl of tiny lilies across the blue background; and a blue-and-gold enamel cigarette case, with a snake coiled elegantly around it, its tail in its mouth.

'My own savings, these,' Horace said, but no one was listening.

'Take what you want,' he said, a little louder. 'I can't travel with all this. We'll share them out.' He was aware of Madame Leman's sudden sharp-eyed glance – of the disbelief in it, for she must be doing the sums and seeing that, if sold, these playthings of the old rich would keep them in bread and jam and sausage for as long as she could imagine – but he only smiled wider (how they'd always laughed at his quick English smile) and gestured with his hand: take, take. Gradually, they all started to smile, too – soft, radiant smiles. Their hands slowed, reflectively sifting through the beautiful little objects. The charmed look of yesterday was in every pair of eyes.

'But you, Horace,' Madame Leman said gently when, even after Aunt Cockatoo furtively stuffed the picture frame into her jacket before he could change his mind, he didn't move to touch the pile they were fingering, 'you must take something for yourself, too.'

Horace hadn't found these little trinkets so remarkable when he'd been putting them by, over the years. They were beautifully made, of course, but too mannered, too refined and dainty to be truly art, as he understood the term, with the sweep and love of experiment and roughness he loved most.

401

But now, seeing them gleaming on the table among the greasy plates, he was swept with a nostalgia so intense it felt like pain for the lost world they belonged to.

'Yes,' he said, simply, reaching forward too, and picking out the ice pendant. Now that *was* truly lovely, so apparently simple it took your breath away: a long, irregular, octagonal form in rock crystal, frosted and faceted, subtly etched, here and there, with the thin jagged lines that frost draws on glass – icicles, Carl Fabergé had called them – which were applied with rose- and brilliant-cut diamonds so they sparkled when the pendant moved, with only the border of tiny, regular, brilliant-cut diamonds giving away the artificiality of the piece's creation.

He turned to Inna. 'This is for you. To remind you of the snows.'

She hadn't been touching anything, any more than he had, and now looked lost as he fastened the pendant round her long narrow neck. The others all cheered and stamped their feet.

They were right to applaud, Horace thought, appreciatively. Inna was wearing a black dress, and the crystal took on its darkness, but the tiny gemstones winked and sparkled with her breath. With her black hair piled up carelessly on her head, and that magical curve to her cheekbones, that added flash of glamour lent her the air of a grand duchess. If only her eyes weren't so clouded, Horace thought . . .

Perhaps Madame Leman guessed at Horace's anxiety, because she leaned over and, kissing Inna's forehead, said, tenderly, 'You don't have any idea how beautiful you look, I can see. You never have had. But, oh, the havoc you could cause, in that . . .'

Inna put a hesitant hand to her neck, and touched the chain. Looking bewildered, she nodded her thanks.

'And for the journey,' Madame Leman prompted, 'Horace, do have some sense and take at least one or two things with you. You never know when you'll need something pretty to please someone on the road.'

Horace nodded, grateful for the tartness in her down-to-earth voice. He picked up the amethyst pendant, and the slim, showy cigarette case, which would be easy to carry. Felix Youssoupoff had had one like it, he recalled. He slipped both items into his pocket.

'And what's this?' Barbarian was digging at the square hole in the dictionary. There was one more box still wedged in there, quite a big one, which Horace hadn't managed to tip out.

'Ah, yes,' Horace said. Using the knife, he levered out the package.

There'd been a time, long ago, when he'd thought of simply posting this to England, to his sister, for her to keep for him, so it was wrapped in brown paper, string and sealing-wax, and addressed to Mrs. William Ingham Brooke, The Rectory, Barford, Warwickshire. He cut through the string.

Inside the paper was a silk Hollywood box, lined inside with velvet, and with the lid satin stamped, heartbreakingly, with words written in the old way of yesterday's Cyrillic: 'Fabergé, St Petersburg, Moscow, London'.

'Open it,' Agrippina said, wide-eyed.

Horace did, taking out a fist-sized egg vertically striped in green-and-cream enamel, on a delicate golden stand, with an emerald set at the top.

'Press it,' he told Inna, setting it before her.

When Inna touched the emerald, a tiny catch moved. At once, the little egg sprang open, into slices that concertinaed smoothly outwards: each oval slice hinged to the next, each one turning out to be a glassed picture frame bordered by tiny, perfectly matched seed pearls, each frame containing a miniature vista of a different St Petersburg street, in pastel colours, the throat-catchingly lovely way those streets had all used to be . . .

They all stared; remembering, suddenly; eyes filled with tears.

'*That*,' he told Inna, 'I always thought, would show our children and grandchildren where we'd first met. That's my gift to them.'

As Inna looked at the egg, something in her face finally relaxed. Then, at last, she turned to face Horace, and put her hands in his.

CHAPTER TWENTY-NINE

Sitting on the bags in the hall beside Horace, Inna joined the Leman family in the ritual minute of silence before departure. Then she left the apartment and walked through Hay Market in a daze.

It was only at the station, on the platform, with the clank and swoosh of trains all around, and bitter little eddies of snow in the air beyond the station building, and the ragged men with guns checking the papers of every person who passed them, and the young Lemans inside the train energetically cramming the bags into the overhead rack of the packed carriage, sandwiching the violin between the two softer ones, and laughing quite hysterically at unfunny things, that Inna looked around at the family and realized she was really leaving.

Her eyes filled with stinging tears.

Her heart lurched at the thought that struck her next. She hadn't said goodbye to Yasha. Yasha, who, only days ago, she'd felt so close to, spiritually as much as physically, and who must have felt the same; Yasha, who'd helped to rescue her, and who was as trapped as she was, now, in a life not of his choosing; Yasha, more herself than she was, who knew everything about her and always would; Yasha, whom she loved and would never see again.

Suddenly every complexity, every nuance of emotion she'd ever felt was burned away in the awful simplicity of this truth. She yearned to see him, to feel, taste and smell him so desperately that she felt faint with it. Three days, she reminded herself, in an agony of self-reproach – *three whole days* – and I never tried to see him, not even to say goodbye . . .

And now it was too late.

She looked up the platform, searching for his face.

But there were only strangers, hundreds and hundreds of strangers.

Instead she fell into Madame Leman's arms, hugging her harder than she'd intended, knocking hairpins flying from that white-grey hair, reassured, for a moment, by the familiar home smell of bread and lily of the valley, murmuring broken snatches of words, 'I'll never be able to thank you enough, never, dear, sweet, good Lidiya Alexeyevna. I've been . . . you'll be . . . we'll . . .'

Madame Leman hugged her back. 'There, darling, there,' she said soothingly. 'Don't you fret, it'll all be fine, and soon we'll—' But then her voice broke too.

'Look after Horace,' Inna heard next, but only vaguely, for she was looking along the platform again. Could it be? But no, it was only Marcus, emerging from the crowded gloom, limping towards them with newspapers tucked under his arm.

'They're fresh ones,' he said, trying to look cheerful. He

gave the smudgy folded sheets to Horace. 'Come back and see us,' he added. 'And send your children to me, when they're old enough to be apprentices; I'll make luthiers of them all.'

Balancing on his crutch, he gave Horace a one-armed hug. Then he hugged Inna, too, looking hungrily into her eyes as if he were memorizing her for the future. 'And *you*, dear heart. Look after yourself, look after your husband, look after your children when they come, be happy, wealthy and wise forever, and always as lovely as you are today.'

She clung to him. 'Dearest Marcus,' she whispered, trying to laugh, remembering the puppy of a boy he'd once been, and his father rumpling his hair. How proud old Leman would have been to see him now, looking after the family. 'Marry Olympia, have babies, write poetry, and open up the workshop again soon, do you hear?'

For a moment, behind Marcus, she thought she saw a tall silhouette in the distance: black hair cut short. Her heart stopped. But, as the man came closer and his outline resolved into detail, she saw he was just another nobody; one of the multitudes of strangers the world was filled with; not the shape she was looking for.

The whistle went piercingly in her ear. 'Get on, quick,' Madame Leman was saying, wiping her eyes. Horace tugged at her arm.

Panic rose, catching Inna's throat. She couldn't go yet.

And then there were arms around her from behind.

She wheeled around, suddenly breathless with expectation—

But it was only Barbarian and Agrippina, both together, breathless themselves from climbing out of the carriage at high speed, both flinging themselves on her, nearly howling at the prospect of parting, 'Innochka! Write! As soon as you can! Don't forget! We'll be waiting! We'll check the mailbox every day!'

Bitterly ashamed of the disappointment that must briefly have shown on her face, she kissed them both back just as frenziedly. 'I will! I promise! And you be good for your mother, both of you, and for Marcus, and work hard, and . . .'

Behind them, the train hooted mournfully, then screeched into slow motion. She couldn't. She hadn't. She must. She looked desperately up the platform, through the thickening snow, one more time.

'Get on, Innochka!' the children were screaming. 'Hurry!'

Grabbing the handle on the carriage doorway, Inna leaped on to the latticework outer step behind her husband.

Even when the train speeded up, Barbarian and Agrippina went on running along the long platform beside them, faster and faster, waving and breathlessly shouting, with tears streaking their cheeks and snow pushing unheeded into their faces, until the adults behind them were just a grey huddle against the lit-up silhouette of the station; until, eventually, they fell back, laughing, crying and collapsing breathlessly against each other.

And they, too, dwindled away into points in the darkness, until they were swallowed up in it altogether, and there was just the rhythmic clank of the train, and the conductor closing the door, and the sudden stillness of the sweaty air inside, and the sway of the yellow lamp, and Horace beside her, tall but slightly bowed, blowing his nose and dabbing at his eyes. He was opening the last little package Madame Leman had pressed into his hands, which, Inna could see, even through the mist over her own eyes, contained a dozen hard-boiled eggs and Maxim's wife's piece of sausage. 'Well, that's that. And now let's find our places,' he said shakily, taking her arm, and guiding her into the carriage.

Long ago, when Inna had come north, alone, by train, the journey had been frightening. But the empire had still existed, and everything about the actual travel arrangements had been as sleek as the gendarmes' shiny-buttoned uniforms. Her entire trip, with its one easy change of train in Moscow, had taken, what, three or four days?

Going south, now, in the People's Russia, was an altogether different matter, even up here in the north, where there was no war to worry about. The crowded, broken-down trains limped, agonizingly slowly, from one siding to the next, one tumbledown village or town or city to the next. People got on or off. And everyone argued.

It took four days just to get to Moscow. And Inna wept all the way.

'So many tears,' Horace said, gently, with his arm about her. 'A lifetime's supply.' And it was true that the endless flow of salt liquid down her face surprised even her.

They were sharing a top bunk. They lay down on it by night, with the violin under the two bags at their feet, and the dwindling parcels of food on top of everything, and the eggshells slowly filling up the tube Horace had made of one of Marcus's newspapers. By day they sat on the bunk, side by side, arm in arm, with their legs swinging down in the faces of the people below; or, if the compartment was crowded, as it usually was, they went on uncomfortably lounging on the rumpled bedding and – in Inna's case – quietly sobbing.

She was aware, even as she cried, that they shouldn't be drawing attention to themselves. So she tried to stop. There's so much you don't need to think of, she kept telling herself. You just have to hold on to what you need: that we're going to get through the war, that we're going to find Youssoupoff, that we're going to be all right. But, however surprised she felt at her collapse, however angry with herself, the tears would well up again, regardless, dripping on to the newspaper, swelling over the eggshells, soaking her front.

Yet, as it turned out, it didn't much matter what she did, in this rhythmic, trance-like movement from past to future. Many of the passengers didn't even seem to be aware she was there. Mostly, they were too busy with their business: particularly the fattish, smooth-jowled men, with their mysterious bundles and their suspiciously good clothes and their supplies of chicken drumsticks and brandy and cards and cigarettes.

They liked to sit up half the night chomping, and gaming, and smoking, and warbling sentimental folk songs out of tune in their rough voices, and even when the singing of one merry band ('Spreading o'er the rii-veer, Golden willow tree-eee; Tell me true: my lover, Whe-e-ere is she?') reduced Inna to audible sobs in the middle of the first night, long after Horace, with his head by her feet, had fallen into a heavy, exhausted sleep, the men just laughed, not unkindly. One got up, and, in a fiery burst of brandy breath, grinned at her. Frightened, she pulled away from him, but all he did was hold out a square of chocolate, unwrapped and half melted in the heat of the compartment. He said, 'Here, girl, don't take on so, it's all going to be all right,' and watched, as if she were a child with medicine, while she swallowed

410

his little black-market luxury down. She kept her breathing quiet after that, although even then the water squeezed out under her eyelids, as she lay willing herself to sleep.

Sometimes, kindly matrons, of whom there were fewer, also looked sympathetically up to their high bunk. One reached up before she got out, patted Inna's knee, and said, 'Heading south, are you? No need to be so scared; you're in God's hands,' before making the sign of the cross over her. Another passed Inna a hanky, saying hoarsely, 'Keep it, dearie; I know a broken heart when I hear one.'

Inna told Horace the first evening that it was the shock of having remembered her parents that was making her cry, that she felt as though she was only now beginning to mourn them. Horace nodded as she spoke, as if everything about her were coming together in his head and making sense at last.

'That's why you've always been so frightened, isn't it?' he kept saying, unbearably kindly. Once, kissing her hair, he even added wistfully, 'And maybe now you'll lose that fear. Who knows, perhaps you'll even become a violinist at last, and take Europe and America by storm?'

'You don't think, do you, that *she*, my mother, felt . . . abandoned . . . when I went away?' Inna whispered.

'Oh dear heart, no. It was exactly what she wanted – for you to get away and be safe. It was what she was telling you to do. You don't ever need to feel guilty for having obeyed her. You were absolutely right,' he replied, holding her close.

He also said that it was a blessing to have remembered her family, even with all the pain that the memory had brought. Because she'd felt alone in life, hadn't she, until now? But now she knew that, however badly things might have ended

411

for her parents, at least they'd known the greatest joy in life: having her. And she could take real comfort, at last, in having brought her parents that happiness; having been at the centre of their world; and in knowing that she hadn't been alone at the start. 'You had their love,' Horace whispered. 'And you have me now. You'll never be alone again.'

But I am alone, Inna thought then, in spite of all his kindness, and, out of despair at her own ungrateful contrariness, cried again.

Moscow, city of bells and onion domes and lopsided little yellow houses with their stucco falling off in great patches behind the red banners, came creeping up around them one overcast dawn.

'Look,' Horace said, waking Inna with a bristly kiss. She stared through the dull glass in dull surprise, and then began scrambling to do her hair, and assemble her coat and boots.

When the train finally stopped in the north of the city, they picked up their bags and walked across town to the next train. They needed to save the money sewn into their coats, and, more importantly, were anxious to avoid attracting attention in an unfamiliar place where political sympathies were uncertain.

'You're still limping,' Inna said. Marcus had tried to repair Horace's boot, but the big string stitches through the uppers only just held the leather together. It would let damp in: maybe this was the problem?

'Oh,' said Horace, 'it's nothing.' He smiled, and the care seemed to lift from his face. 'You sound happier.'

Moscow was just the first change of many on the itinerary

Horace had tentatively drawn up to try and skirt anywhere the war further south was likely to be.

The war, Inna imagined, was only ever a place; quite a small place, perhaps, with people leading something quite like their normal lives only a road or a field away. But the war was also like a storm that might move on at any moment. The important thing was to keep up to date with the war news, and listen to rumours on the trains, so you could have the most recent information about where the fighting might be, and how to avoid it.

But even Moscow, still in the north, was alien territory to her and Horace. They walked, slowly, for an hour, towards the station for Kiev, through the black, icy snow of a city full of bonfires outside, and the exhaust pipes of *burzhuiki*, inside, sticking out of windows. The violin was slung across Inna's back and she was carrying the two bags in her hands.

'Let me,' she'd said with sudden pity when she'd seen Horace grimace as he picked them up. 'They're not heavy.'

She couldn't cry here, as she had to ask strangers the way. They had decided it was unwise to let Horace, with his accent, open his mouth. On this journey, she felt in no particular danger – yet. But Horace, with his foreign voice, was a potential victim in this hungry crowd. She was going to protect him.

It turned out that Kiev, the most obvious next stop on their journey, was not a good place to head. She wasn't sorry when Horace ruled it out – in a whisper.

Kiev was almost certainly too dangerous now, he said. With the German wartime forces gone, their puppet government of Ukrainian nationalists had vanished too, leaving behind Whites, Reds and a mysterious Ukrainian peasant army slugging it out in the streets or in the fields. Wildly contradictory press reports spoke of first one lot and then the other trouncing the rest and forming governments with strange, wild-sounding names.

Nor could they head straight for Sevastopol, the main port of the Crimean peninsula, south of Kiev. It was their logical destination, since from Sevastopol it was only a short drive along the coast to the Youssoupoff estate, and Yalta. But, like Kiev, Sevastopol was too important not to be dangerous. Ever since the sailors of the imperial fleet moored there had mutinied – hacking their officers to pieces, burning them alive in the ships' furnaces, or throwing them into the Black Sea with iron bars tied to their legs – it had been off-limits.

Horace and Inna picked a quieter route, one they thought would most likely allow them to avoid trouble, though you never knew. This quiet worry, this fretting and eavesdropping and anxious reading of newspapers as you crawled around the edge of the hostilities was as much part of what war was, she now saw, as the battles she and Horace were trying to avoid. And there was always the possibility everything would have changed once you got there.

And so they zigzagged across country.

From Moscow, they took a train to Kursk.

'At least the bags are getting lighter,' Horace murmured, subsiding with relief on to another top bunk. Inna nodded, though not so happily. The bags were lighter because the food was gone.

Below them seethed another sea of the dispossessed: crying children; women with haunted eyes, trying to watch too many bags and babies at once; profiteers; soldiers.

Horace, with his back to her, spent a long time easing his boots off.

'Let me take a look at that,' Inna said.

He only laughed. 'Thank you, but no. Leave it. There'll be water on this train for another day or two, don't you think? So I'm going down, right now, to change the dressing – and have a shave, too. Or next time you see me someone will be asking me for a blessing, because they've mistaken me for an Orthodox priest.'

He leaned over and touched her hand before he started easing himself down, with his wash-bag. 'I'm glad you're feeling better,' he added.

She nodded distractedly. She wasn't going to cry any more. The time for tears had passed. She was worrying now about his foot, admiring the gallant way he made so little of his misfortunes, wishing she'd thought as much about him, before now, as he always had about her. She was thinking: I need to see why he's limping.

Pine forests, villages, birch forests, dogs barking, little towns, the occasional man on a cart, whipping on his horse down a country lane: the mournful immensity of Russia. This time their journey took a week.

She acted for both of them: bargaining for food and newspapers on station platforms; showing their documents to all the checkers while Horace shut his eyes, as if asleep. He was a biddable charge; falling obediently quiet whenever she shushed him, wedging himself awkwardly into the little space of their bunk, head on the fiddle box, reading and eavesdropping. But he didn't sleep much. Even when his thoughts seemed far away, he was wakeful, sitting up late into the night, gazing out of the window. His eyes were almost always open before dawn, too, however early she woke. Was he in pain? she wondered sometimes. But he didn't say, and she couldn't tell.

By now they were living on stale bread bought from station salesmen, or, sometimes, if they were lucky, on pies filled with unidentifiable meat. Rat patties! Horace laughed, rather uncertainly. Cat rissoles!

Once, starting to smile, he whispered, 'I don't think we've ever spent so much time, so close together, have we?'

And she smiled back, and squeezed his hand.

It wasn't Horace's fault that she still felt that wrenching private pain in every joint and muscle. She wasn't unhappy with Horace.

One night – the night before they reached Kursk – she woke, to the jolt of the train, with her body agonized by the memory of Yasha. There was moonlight in the stuffy carriage. She opened her eyes to see her husband's gaze on her.

Startled, she pretended to yawn and rub her face, wondering guiltily whether he'd guessed her painful thoughts, and then, with a different kind of jolt, whether he was awake because he was suffering from that foot.

But he just nodded at her, with that amused look of his, preventing her from asking. 'It's hard to sleep, sometimes, with all the shunting, isn't it?' He tightened his arm round her, settling her on his chest.

'I often wonder what Kagan was doing in our courtyard that night, you know,' he said reflectively. 'Don't you?'

Inna took a cautious breath. This was new terrain.

'Maxim said he thought he'd turned police informer.'

Horace's tone was neutral. 'He was concerned that all that political enthusiasm was taking him a step too far.'

Inna shook her head. It didn't seem to matter what the actual facts were. She just wanted to protect Yasha, since he couldn't speak up for himself.

'And he turned up just at the right moment, didn't he, to weigh in for you with those thugs, the Bolshevik police or whoever they were.'

Her surprise was genuine, this time. 'Yes,' she said. 'He did.'

'Though not for me, ten minutes earlier.'

'I was just lucky, I suppose,' she parried, with a strange moonlit feeling inside, as if her innards were about to be cut open and rearranged.

'It did occur to me that he might have sent them, for me, you know.'

'Oh, no, Horace,' Inna whispered, as the doubt began to sink in. That couldn't be right: Yasha wasn't like that. He wasn't deceitful, or hadn't been. But, well, it was always possible that he just *might*. You could never tell with Yasha. He always *might* go too far. And the mere possibility that he might have wanted to harm Horace, who harmed no one, felt unbearable. 'Don't even think that. It can't be right. Please,' she begged.

'Well,' he said philosophically, and rather too loud for a man who was only supposed to whisper. 'I'm just glad we're away.'

Kursk was quiet.

So was Inna. But she couldn't stop thinking: might Yasha really have done that?

417

She was thinking it as she went down the platform in search of food. A boy in ragged britches was standing among the pie vendors, offering a fresh-cooked trout, with burn marks striped down its crispy side. Despite all that was on her mind, she registered that the trout smelled more delicious than any food she'd ever imagined: of wood-smoke and summer.

The boy wrinkled his nose at the handful of coins she held out. 'That's no good here,' he said. But his bright eyes lit up at the sight of her gold bracelet.

Might Yasha have . . .?

The bracelet was far too valuable an exchange for a fish. But she gave it to the boy, hardly aware of the joy with which he scampered off, calling to his mates.

'Shall we try Kharkov next?' Horace said, sitting on a bench on the platform, biting into his last chunk of fish. He was in good humour, and it wasn't just from the food. He'd found a stream. He'd washed his foot and rinsed out the dirty bandages, which, disgracefully ragged, were flapping on the string he'd tied up behind them. His foot was stretched out on the bench. 'It's getting better,' he said, but he still wouldn't let Inna examine whatever was under the clean bandages.

There were no papers on sale, and Inna hadn't been able to find out much from the locals either about what they might find up ahead if, as seemed likely, Kharkov was no longer the capital of the Bolshevik Soviets of the imaginary republic of Ukraine, which had been conjured into existence a year earlier.

The stationmaster had only shrugged when she'd asked. 'Plenty of people still go to Kharkov, lady,' was all he'd said.

Kursk was certainly full of people asking about tonight's

train. And there was spring in today's cold sunshine: a lift of hope. The snow on the banks beyond the tracks was glistening, turning transparent, ready to melt. Kharkov was further south, and it would be warmer still there.

Inna was surprised at how much, suddenly, she longed for sunlight and journey's end for them both.

'Yes,' she said. 'Let's go to Kharkov.'

Could Yasha have done that to Horace . . .?

Could *she* have . . .? But, no, she couldn't bear to think *that*.

The flat landscape outside, which hadn't seemed to change for so long – snow, pines, birches, villages, snow, pines, birches, villages – did, at last, start to look different as they chugged towards Kharkov. The trees thinned out, and the snow did, too.

Inna sat inside, swinging her legs, alternately watching Horace sleep – he had started sleeping more and more, these last two days, even in the daytime; he answered her uneasy queries by saying the warmer air was making him tired – and staring out at the great rolling fertility of the south outside. Last year's corn stalks were still poking through the speckled snow on the black earth, and this year's startling growth was already marshalling itself underground under vast golden-blue skies.

She gazed, more curiously, at the flags that she had begun to notice whenever the train passed near a settlement. They were the first real evidence, apart from the usual crowds of refugees and food shortages, that there was a war being waged down here. Tattered and forgotten, the flags had been left to fly over abandoned village buildings. Often, in the distance, she saw the blue, white and red tricolour of old Russia, or the yellow imperial standard with its double-headed eagle; sometimes the red of the Bolsheviks, and, more and more often, the further south they went, the black, white and red tricolour of the recently departed German enemy. The war had been here, and not long ago.

On the evening of the day she first noticed the flags, they passed near a village that wasn't just empty, but had been burned. Recently burned. The roofs were still crackling and falling as the sun set, and some of the dark shadows on the ground, far away out there, didn't look like the usual piles of manure or broken carts, but more like bodies lying on the roads.

Her first sighting of the war didn't frighten her unduly. Seen from the tight warm compartment of the train, it felt too unreal. Anyway, as she thought later, they were still moving forward.

She just wanted to get beyond this landscape, with its slow melt and its uncertain loyalties. She was willing them forward. She could smell the spring.

Even now Inna still looked up whenever a door opened, half hoping to see Yasha. But she couldn't stop the restless new doubt, which had resolved itself, in her mind, into two questions. Was it because of Yasha that those heavies had come to make trouble for Horace? Or was it because of *her*?

Yasha had told her himself that he talked to the man from the Cheka, hadn't he? She could hear the despairing bitterness in his voice, even now. *Who does refuse the Cheka? Who'd dare?*

But that hadn't stopped her telling him Horace's secrets: how he'd kept things for the Fabergé people; how he'd worried that his being foreign would bring trouble to their door.

And, a day later, trouble had come.

I still can't believe it, she told herself. But the worst thing was, she could.

Watching Horace doze, curled up, with an arm resting on the violin case, and the tired lines of his face relaxed into trust, she was suddenly overwhelmed by repentant protectiveness. Whatever the truth about that night was, whatever Yasha had or hadn't done, *she'd* certainly done more dreadful, damaging things to Horace than he would ever know. But at least she could make amends now, and look after him with the love he deserved, because they'd got away unharmed, and were together. She leaned over his sleeping shoulder, moulding her body to his, and lightly kissed his clammy cheek. 'I'm sorry,' she whispered. 'I'm so, so sorry.'

Kharkov was quiet, too, what little they saw of it, a day later. But it was best not to linger too long, trying to find out; best just to slip the man by the gate that cigarette case with a bit of glitter about the serpent's head and get yourself inside the train to Crimea and away.

Now, on their last train – a local train, where there were no more bunks, just seats, packed with peasant women selling things in baskets, and chickens – Inna finally let hope take root that they'd slipped across the lines, and bypassed the war.

Simferopol, still ahead, sounded reasonably safe. And beyond Simferopol, right down to the coast, as far as they could tell, everything was White. There were British and French ships docked in the Black Sea, keeping watch. Those Romanovs who remained alive after the killing of the

Emperor and his family, all the royal cousins who'd been set free by the Germans last year, were down there too: fighting, or dancing in the restaurants at Yalta, along with what was left of the court.

Halfway from Kharkov to Simferopol, they got down from the train and drank tea and ate – what? – something savoury in pastry at a place called Sinelnikovo. Inna sniffed the air and smelled catkins and willow-buds and said, 'Spring.'

And after that the landscape began to change into monotonous scrub-pasture with, every now and then, a surprising mound, a burial site like a child's drawing of a steep hill, lightly dusted with icing-sugar snow.

The next day, at the next station buffet – Alexandrovsk – even Horace noticed the spring. Lifting his head, he breathed in the unfamiliar southern smells with wonder. 'Look,' he said. Over in the distance, by the hollow where the river must be, she saw a green cloud – a great mass of luxuriant foliage.

After that, it was swampy rivers, rushing with torrents of meltwater, and gentle-looking German Mennonite peasants in the fields, with their blond hair and beards. From Akimovka on, they saw sloe-eyed Tatars and strangely shaped rocks set in desert. Unfamiliar flags, too, were painted on buildings and half scrubbed off: Inna wondered whose fly-by-night governments they had celebrated.

Ahead of them, beyond the water of the Putrid Sea, lay the flat, ugly northern part of the Crimean peninsula, and then, at last, as they chugged endlessly on, there it was: the hazy blue zigzags on the horizon that signified the northern approaches of the hills of Yaila. Beyond, Inna knew, lay the magical coast, full of palm trees, pale castles, steep hillsides, winding roads, and estates with exotic Turkic names.

Inna put her hand over Horace's. 'You did it,' she said, excitedly, gratefully. 'We're safe.'

He startled awake. 'What?' he muttered. Then, smiling into her eyes, he said, 'No, dearest: *you* did it.'

CHAPTER THIRTY

It was only the next morning, almost at the end of the journey, when they got out at yet another station, that Inna saw Horace wasn't better, but limping worse than ever, and decided to intervene.

'Can *I* rebandage your foot, please?' she said, briskly. 'Let's get it washed.'

He lifted a hand, like a stop signal. 'It's nothing.'

And so she didn't insist, not straight away. But once they were seated in the buffet, she slipped off to the stationmaster's wife and asked for a bowl of warm water and some rags. And when the water was brought to the table, and when Horace was again insisting, in a whisper, 'Truly, it's nearly better, and anyway we can sort everything out once we arrive,' she was grateful that the stationmaster's wife was there too, in her bright red Little Russian sarafan, standing inescapably behind the carbolic-smelling basin.

'Oh no, dearie,' the woman said loudly. 'I don't like the colour of you, and – begging your honour's pardon – I don't just mean the train dirt. So let's not be silly about this, eh?

Let's get that foot out and see what's going on with it, shall we?'

Horace was mortified, Inna could see, though she knew he must also feel as reassured as she did to hear the title 'your honour' again; a small sign they were past the danger, back in the White world, where it was acceptable to appear to be a gentleman. But there was no gainsaying this woman. She was going to wash that foot, and that was final.

'Not in front of everyone with their tea, at least,' Horace said, speaking at a normal conversational volume, almost for the first time since they'd left Petrograd.

Inna was glad they'd moved back to the bench outside the stationmaster's room, away from the curious eyes, when, at last, the bandages came off.

The smell . . . Why, it reminded her of her nursing days; of those boys, lying in the Youssoupoff ballroom, rotting.

He hadn't escaped unharmed after all. He must have been in agony for all these days and weeks. Why hadn't he said?

But she knew the answer. He'd been concerned to keep *her* spirits up, to stop her weeping. She didn't like to think any more why she'd been crying on those first nights in the train. She just shook her head, beyond words.

Horace winced as the woman – Yevdokia, her name was – unlaced his boot and pulled his foot out. He winced again as, very gently, she unwound the filthy scarf underneath. His exposed foot, pink and raw round the heel and ankle, was hot and stank with infection further down. From the middle of the foot to the toes: a mass of purple, yellow, red and white, and, through cracks everywhere, leaking with pus.

'Into the water with it, there's a love,' Yevdokia said, without a hint of the guilty panic Inna felt at the sight of that infection. It wasn't dark with gangrene, at least not yet, but it was so inflamed that it looked as though it might poison his whole body. 'Let's get that nasty foot clean, now, eh?'

When his foot went in, Horace breathed very sharply and muttered, then clenched his two hands together in front of his mouth till the knuckles went white.

'You should lie quietly somewhere for a week or two and let this heal,' Yevdokia was saying. 'I don't suppose there's any chance of that, is there?'

Horace was too busy rocking back and forth to answer.

Inna shook her head.

'You'll be stopping at Simferopol, at least?' Yevdokia asked hopefully.

Again, Horace didn't answer. He seemed to Inna have lost touch with the outside world now that someone was finally tending to him and letting him concentrate on his pain. Bitterly reproaching herself for not having found a way to care for him better herself, earlier on, Inna shook her head again.

'We've got to find a way on to Yalta,' she told Yevdokia. She went over to Horace and put her hands round his shoulders. He leaned back against her and Inna kissed the top of his head. 'At least, we were heading for Yalta. If,' and she sensed from the quality of Yevdokia's silence that even this was over-ambitious, 'you think it's safe?'

'That foot's infected. He won't be able to walk on it. No point in thinking he will,' Yevdokia said briskly. 'It might turn nasty if he doesn't stop and look after it a bit.' She examined Inna with her bright little eyes. 'As for where's safe, well, even *we* can't make head or tail of what's going on any more. And we're local. All you can be sure of is that half the gentry of St Petersburg are wandering round here. And it's not safe for any of you any more, or it soon won't be, not now all the foreign soldiers are leaving. Simferopol's all right still. My brother's there, at the station – a cab driver, he is; he sends word most days. So I can send you to him, and, if you want to go on to Yalta, he's the man who'll know how to get you a ride down to the sea. He might even take you himself. But as for whether it *is* still safe, down there, on the coast . . . well, I just don't know.'

Inna bit her lip. Here, where they called Horace 'your honour' and there wasn't a red banner in sight, she'd thought they'd finally reached safety. It only now occurred to her that this might not be the case.

They only had one real plan: to get as quickly as possible to Yalta, and from there the ten or twelve versts down the coast road to Youssoupoff's estate at Koreiz to give him the violin, thereby getting whatever money or shelter or help with onward travel he could give them. Vaguely, they'd thought that if things were safe and stable – if the Whites were winning – they could then sit out the war in the south. But now it didn't sound as though they would be safe here either. No, it was becoming increasingly clear that they would have to exchange the violin for something they could live on, and find a boat out.

'What have you heard about Yalta?' she asked.

Yevdokia responded with gloomy gusto. 'Oh, Yalta. Well, with all those royals there – the Dowager Empress and half the court – of course there must be Reds buzzing round, and every other kind of anarchist and assassin, too. Bees to a honeypot. Stands to reason. That's why there are English ships waiting to take her highness away – though she won't

427

go. Not yet. She says her presence is stabilizing the country. But it's only a question of time till Yalta falls too.'

The sunlight, which a moment before had seemed so welcome, seemed to be thickening and congealing. Inna shivered. So Yalta was not the paradise of peace she'd imagined. Soldiers were circling it; men with knives in their teeth and murder in their hearts were creeping through the bushes . . . But here, at least, in the station, all was quiet. Here felt safe. There were bees buzzing nearby, and an avenue of trees with white-painted trunks stretching away down the road. Wild flowers shone in the fresh green meadows all around.

'Perhaps,' Inna said 'we should stay here for a bit, until my husband gets better?'

She was surprised to feel Horace stop his quiet, painful rocking.

'No,' he said, firmly, and she was surprised, too, at how strong his voice was. 'Let's bind up my foot. We've got a train to catch. We've got to get to Yalta.'

'All right,' Inna said, making an effort to keep her face composed, grateful she did not have to take responsibility for the decision alone. They would continue.

'If there are English ships off Yalta, then there's more reason than ever to get there fast,' Horace had been saying all the way to Simferopol. He'd been full of his new hope. 'Whether or not we find Youssoupoff, an English ship has a duty to me. The captain will take us on board, with or without the Dowager Empress, and evacuate us. Which we might well need, if things are looking so uncertain.'

He'd lain, thinking, gazing out at the innocence of the countryside.

'Maybe that would even be better,' he'd said, eventually, as night fell. His eyes were glittering as he touched her hand; feverish probably, Inna thought, fearfully. 'If we just got on the English ship, and never managed to deliver the violin at all . . . if you actually *played* that violin, and really did take Europe and America by storm . . . well then, to Hell with Felix Youssoupoff, don't you think?' He laughed, too wildly, and she stroked his hand.

She'd so seldom seen Horace vulnerable, as he was now, and a part of her feared that laughter of his, that clutching at straws. He was putting too much faith in shadows, she thought. But all mixed up with her alarm was something else: a soft, magical tenderness. It wasn't an entirely unfamiliar feeling, she realized. As it stole through her, even while she worried about the clamminess of Horace's hand under hers, she was trying to pinpoint when she might have had this same urge to protect him before, this dizzying sense of having missed the obvious, this dawning awareness that everything might, after all, be simpler than she'd seen.

And then she remembered. It had been years ago, in the Stray Dog cellar, on the night Horace had taken on the policemen who were harassing her, and she'd realized, just as his attack on them faltered, that he also meant to propose to her afterwards. When, unexpectedly, she'd been visited by this strange serenity, this understanding that the answer to the questions she'd been asking had, all this time, been right under her nose.

It was why, as they'd climbed the stairs up from the cellar that night, she'd laughed softly when he'd given her the box containing the ring he'd bought and then, not knowing quite how to put the question, paused. It was why she'd gently taken it from him and slipped the ring on her finger herself. Because everything else was confusion – the animal heat of the body, the tumult of the moment – but it was Horace she loved.

Horace had always tended so carefully to her, and encircled her so fully with his love, that she hadn't needed to think very much about her feelings for him. It had only really been on this journey, now that she'd seen his frailty as well as his kindly strength, that she could fully understand the strength of the love that she bore him. But, for all the confusion that she'd felt, in these past months, hadn't a part of her always known this, deep down?

It was Yasha she'd watched, the last time she'd seen him, as he strode into the courtyard and rescued them. But, she also now remembered, with a rush of emotion that went far beyond the affection she usually owned to feeling for her husband, it was Horace she'd turned to. And it was Horace who'd brought her away from Petrograd, towards safety. It was Horace she wanted to start a new life with.

'I don't care about taking Europe and America by storm, or impressing the world,' she said, very tenderly, wanting, more than anything else, to put Horace's feverish mind at rest. 'All I want is to have a normal life somewhere safe with you. Everything else can wait.'

But a flicker of something long forgotten went through her, all the same: a memory of that strange little Scriabin tune, with all its dancey double-stops, that she'd once played for the Lemans; and how, as her bow flew over the strings, she'd felt as light as if her feet had stopped touching the ground.

That feeling, she thought suddenly, might be happiness, and it was what Horace had always wanted her to feel.

Perhaps that private, joyous lightness was what her father had felt, too, playing the violin she could now just recall lying smashed on that floor beside him? Wasn't that ability to make your own brief happiness a more real kind of freedom than the kind the revolutionaries talked about so incessantly, as they replaced one form of bondage with another?

Perhaps it showed on her face, whatever she was feeling, this unfamiliar, painfully sweet twisting of the heart, because he smiled as if in relief. But his words answered hers. He was still repeating, 'Yes, we'll be fine if we can only get to the English ship,' when, suddenly, he fell asleep.

Despite the brilliant spring sunshine, Yalta was locked down when they arrived: shops boarded up, shutters across windows, seagulls squealing. It was all eerily quiet.

Yevdokia's brother Selifan, as fat as she was, had driven them from Simferopol. Inna had struck a deal with him, that he'd see them out of Russia within the week, with all transport, accommodation and food included, in return for the amethyst pendant, to be delivered at journey's end. Selifan had borrowed a rough farm cart for the trip – he wasn't risking his own smart little carriage on the coast road, not these days, when you never knew whom you might meet round the next corner, he said darkly. And he had brought them straight to this deserted hotel on the seafront and knocked till the scared old watchman, the only person left on duty, opened.

The two men clearly knew each other. They'd muttered together for some minutes, until finally the old man – who had trembling hands, and cloudy blue eyes, and looked as though he hadn't shaved his white prickly chin for days

– nodded, and led Inna to a room on the ground floor which, though dusty and in twilight because of the closed shutters, did have a pair of made-up single beds.

Wheezing crossly, 'Heavy, i'n't he,' Selifan half carried, half dragged Horace to the nearest of the two. 'And hot. Burning up.' He looked around the room. 'There's no food, and no light. But he'll bring you tea in a bit.'

'And hot water, please,' Inna said, 'to bathe his foot. We'll get a room for you, too, of course,' she added as she drew a quilt over her husband, and stroked his forehead, and hoped she could afford whatever the no doubt enormous price would be. She could see how important it was to make Selifan feel appreciated. He might be surly, but he knew how things were done here. She didn't want him just to take off in the night. She'd need him tomorrow, after all, to drive her and Horace along the coast road, as they looked for the Youssoupoff estate at Koreiz, or to go looking for English ships, whichever of the two seemed the better course in the morning.

But Selifan only shook his head, making the jowls flap on his greasy chin. 'I don't need a room. I'll sleep with the horses,' he said. 'I don't want any scallywags messing about with them. We'll be off early, will we?'

'To Koreiz,' she agreed, thinking of Youssoupoff.

He nodded. 'Where the English ships are,' he replied, as if in confirmation, 'that'll be taking the Dowager Empress away.'

Inna stared. 'But she won't go,' she stammered. 'Your sister said.'

Selifan blew out his fat cheeks in disgust. 'Oh, that's all changed. Things have got too dangerous for any more of her stubbornness. The old bloke at the door here was telling me just now. The Reds are on their way, for sure, and she's said she'll go if they'll also take all the aristos who want to get out – and they all do, believe me, every single toff who was here. They're desperate to get away before the Reds find them. Haven't you noticed how quiet it is? They're all camping out up the coast near where she's staying – making their own dinner, even, who knows? They've left their servants behind to take their chances here, so they've got no one to do it for them any more. The English sailors are building a special jetty there so that Her Imperial Highness doesn't have to come all the way to the port here to embark, and none of them wants to miss the big moment. The word is that the jetty will be ready by tomorrow. So I expect your Prince Youssoupoff will be there, fighting for his place on the first-class deck like everyone else. It'll be madness. But it's the place to head for.'

Speechless at the discovery that her two possible ways of escape had diminished to just one, Inna nodded and Selifan disappeared.

The old man, cringing away from her, brought hot water and tea. Then, after staring silently as she undid Horace's bandage and lowered his foot into the basin of water, he disappeared too.

For a long while, in the interior twilight, with half a dozen thin strips of bright sunlight from between the shutters making the dust motes in the air dance, Inna soaked Horace's foot in the slowly cooling water.

Sitting on a chair beside his bed, she wiped his hot forehead with a damp cloth. She whispered, to the rhythm of her own movement, 'Come back, come back, come back,' but more to comfort herself than to connect with him, for

Horace was elsewhere. He was utterly absent from this cool, dark room, with its gracious reminder of yesterday's space and care, with its flowery basins and recently pressed linen and curved mirrors and fresh paint. The fear in Yalta could only have come in the past day or so; that there were candles and matches laid out on the tray, at least, spoke of ease and plenty to anyone recently living in Petrograd. Horace groaned, every now and then; sometimes he seemed to say a word; but he was too feverish to make sense.

Outside her room, Inna could half hear the creaking of someone moving softly around. The old man, she thought; and even though she thought he was probably scared of her, she was scared of him, too, tiptoeing around out there, in the artificial dark, in yesterday's luxury, with his mysterious thoughts.

What she heard next at the door was less a knock than a scrabble: the sound a mouse might make. It alarmed her, imagining the old man out there, waiting for her. When she opened the door, just a crack, with her heart thumping, half expecting to have to push him back in some ugly tussle, she found him patiently standing, a big step back, with his head humbly lowered and something she couldn't make out in his hand.

She opened the door a little wider. She could see better now. In his hand, the man had a folded cloth of fine linen, which must have come fresh from the hotel's laundry cupboard, and a flat metal can, the kind men carry tobacco in, or maggots for fishing.

'If you'll pardon the liberty, your excellency,' he said hoarsely, not lifting his eyes to hers. 'I think I could do something for that wound.'

His white-flecked chin was trembling. She didn't think he'd be able to give any real help, but she warmed anyway to the sound of the south in his voice and to the timid concern, so she stepped aside.

He sidled over to the bedside with Inna following close behind. 'No need for you to trouble yourself, your excellency,' he said without turning. 'I'll just put a little poultice on it; it'll be all done in a minute.' When she stayed where she was, he ran a trembly hand over his chin and looked cautiously round at her. 'Now, your excellency, you take these leaves I've got here and mash them up with your tea, see,' he added, in his quavery voice. Digging into his pocket, he pulled out a twist of paper. 'We'll put a little of that down him too.'

'What is it?' Inna asked, half wanting to believe in a miracle.

'Dandelion,' the old man said proudly. 'It's full of healing, is dandelion.'

'I see,' Inna said, gently, feeling the flicker of hope go out of her, but still grateful for his kind intentions. She crushed the weed's leaves up with her fingers and a spoon till the tea smelled fresh and sharp with the green tangle floating on top. It was something to do, after all.

When they'd fished out the fibrous greenery, she passed the glass to the old man, who gently spooned a few drops of the liquid over Horace's lips. Inna couldn't really even tell if any had gone in, but the old man seemed pleased.

'There,' he said softly, touching the crucifix at his neck. 'Now, you leave him be, and, if you would be so good, your excellency, don't you touch that cloth I've wrapped round his foot with the poultice for the rest of the night. Just leave it to do its good work, and, God willing, he'll be feeling a bit better by the time he wakes up.' And, without waiting to acknowledge her whispered thanks, he crept to the door again.

Inna washed the dirty rags the man had removed – the last of the bandages, as Horace's other set had finally disintegrated – and the rest of the linen they'd been wearing, and hung them up to dry near the window.

Horace carried on sweating and muttering. From time to time, she murmured something encouraging; '*That*'s better,' or '*Now* we're on the mend.' But she gradually fell silent. From time to time, she wiped his face.

She drank the cold tea and put the glass outside.

And then there was nothing left but to listen to the sound of the sea, and the gulls, and the creeping outside, as she watched Horace. After what seemed hours, he subsided into what looked more like a restless, dream-filled sleep.

'I'll look after you,' she whispered to him, willing this to be the turning point; willing him to wake up refreshed and himself again. 'You'll be well again soon. Everything is going to be all right.' But she couldn't sound sure. She'd staked everything on her hunch that, down here, they'd have a better chance of safety. It had never crossed her mind that journey's end would look so empty, or that, just as she was realizing all that he meant to her, he might die.

The shadows in that dusty room thickened and the dust-flights dimmed, like hope fading. To stop herself panicking at having ended up like this, alone with her thoughts, in a hotel room in a town about to be overrun by the enemy, to stop herself wondering just how safe she might be without him, she made herself think instead of the Lemans, of how much she missed them all. She called to mind the yellow room, and Marcus proudly watching his Olympia toss back her hair and declaim her poems, and Barbarians and Agrippina's boisterous squabbling, and Madame Leman, chatting peacefully to her dead husband's portrait, as she sometimes did while she sat there sewing. For a moment, she even thought of Yasha, whom she'd run away from, and whose very memory she'd started to fear . . .

But conjuring up *his* face made her shrivel inside. She couldn't help but be aware that it was her attempt to escape the dangerous overcrowding of her married life – which she alone had sought out, and for which her husband was in no way to blame – that had landed Horace and her in their predicament here.

Looking penitently down at the noble profile, the proud nose, the cleft in his chin, the line of neck and shoulder – all so familiar, yet strange too, now that Horace's form wasn't lit up with his usual kindly amusement but lying so still – she asked why she had been so slow to appreciate her husband, to understand.

She could never have left him. She hadn't just chosen him for the security he'd provided until now. She loved him: the look of him, the laughter, the gentle life that no longer animated his face. She knew that now. She couldn't imagine – couldn't bear to think of – a world without him.

'It's you,' she said aloud, touching his clammy hand. 'It always was, really. I don't know why I didn't realize.'

Yet the sound of her own voice, so small and uncertain in the eerie silence, only unnerved her further. Getting up from the chair, longing for the touch of him and the reassurance of his warmth, she lay down gingerly beside him, careful not to touch his foot. She curled herself along his back and laid

437

an arm over his shoulder, excruciatingly aware, now that it might be too late, of how naturally her body fitted to his. 'Don't go. Don't go, my darling,' she said, though perhaps the voice was only in her head, because he didn't stir.

There was a great deal of grey in his wiry hair, she saw, trying to keep her fear at bay, but feeling it seep in anyway. There were deep lines on his cheek. 'It will all be all right, don't worry,' she repeated, feeling desperate. 'I'll make it be.' But what would she do when even the brilliant bars of sunlight had faded, and there was nothing between her and the silence?

Who sleeps in an empty house after dark, in a war, when anything is possible?

Back on her chair, Inna listened to sounds. Little whispery sounds, coming closer: creaks underfoot and the clangs and bangs of possible steps, or the wind, at the window. Then it got so quiet, she wondered whether the old man was still here at all, or whether he'd run away, or was whispering with men in the street. She wondered what she would hit them with if they burst in.

To keep her spirits up, she found herself humming under her breath as she padded around, checking things, fretting at the candle's wick with her fingernail – how was it burning so slowly, when it had been dark for so long? – and wondering why the bandages wouldn't dry.

The frisky tune on her mind was from long ago. She stopped when she realized it was the Scriabin piece. The memories it brought flooding back, of the yellow room, were too poignant now.

She could open the window and get a breeze through.

That might help with the bandages and linen, she thought. But she shivered at the thought of letting the night in, and whatever was out there wandering around in it.

Inna tried to put her dulled mind to thinking what to do if the bandages weren't fit to use by morning. There was nothing else dry.

If the rags weren't ready, she might be reduced to finding the untouched little pile of cloths she'd put into her bag for her own use, for her monthly bleeding.

No, of course not, she thought, a moment later, almost relieved to have had that absurd, taboo idea for which she could laugh at herself. They weren't that desperate. She was, for tonight at least, back in the land of gracious living. She'd just take one of the hotel's pillowcases, or a towel, and rip it into strips.

And then, less certainly, she began to wonder: why were the rags untouched? She hadn't thought, hadn't counted; but shouldn't she have needed those rags a good fortnight ago? Why, after all these weeks – what, three, four weeks – away?

Her breath caught.

The thought that struck her now was so utterly unexpected that she couldn't give it a name. Oblivious, all at once, to the wind and gulls, to all the possible creeping of feet outside, and even to what sounded like banging at the front door, she bit her lip and hunched forward. She'd intended not to think of Petrograd, or what had happened in those frenzied final days, for a long while, perhaps forever. She could still avoid thinking, maybe. But she needed to count.

CHAPTER THIRTY-ONE

When Yasha walked into the room, that's how she was: frantic-eyed, with her fingers up in a circle of candlelight, muttering numbers under her breath.

She looked up at him in the doorway – flickering and uplit from the candle he was carrying, and stubble-bearded from the train – as if he were a ghost.

He was carrying a bag, and had a violin strapped to his back.

For a long moment, she just stared. 'Is it really you?' she whispered, wondering if she were dreaming. 'Yasha?'

There was nothing ghostly about his grin.

She sighed away all her fears, put a finger to her lips, got up, picked her candle up, and drew Yasha out into the corridor, away from Horace's sickbed, with a trembling hand. Yes, she breathed to herself, he was really there. She was suffused with a golden feeling that she would once simply have called happiness, though now, with all she'd been learning on this long journey, she also thought it might just be the relief of not being alone with her imaginings any more.

There'd been moments – all right, she would admit to them – when she'd believed that never touching Yasha again would be a kind of death. She'd felt, in all the moments when her mind, skirting the edge of sleep, had escaped its inner policemen and had run away into unpatrolled, unthinkable byways, that if she ever saw him again, they'd kiss; fling themselves at each other; pull each other's clothes away. She'd put her lips to his skin, and fill her nostrils with his smell. At other times she'd thought she would accuse him of things she couldn't, for the moment, even remember; argue about things that no longer seemed important. And, just an instant ago, she'd been yearning to have him there to help her with her frantic counting. But now the sheer wonder of his reappearance outweighed everything else. She realized she didn't want to do anything more sensual than feel the reality of his back under her hand, and his hand on her hip, and smile at him.

In the hotel corridor's curly art-nouveau mirrors, hung between dusty potted palms, their two intersecting circles of gold were reflected from glass to foggy, speckled glass. His reflections were staring at her, none of them exactly like the Yasha she remembered, and all of them were smiling too.

She watched her many reflections lean towards his. But then she stopped watching them, and just looked into Yasha's long eyes.

'I thought I'd never see you again,' she whispered. 'But you've come.' She could smell him; see the creases round his eyes as he grinned. He was really here, as handsome as he'd ever been, and so warm under her hands. Yet something was missing. She was still aware of every movement, of the way his eyelashes brushed his cheeks when he closed his eyelids, but it only was the near-miraculous familiarity of that sight that moved her now. There was none of the disconcerting heat and giddiness she remembered from before.

'I've been so lonely,' she stammered, wondering at its absence. 'So afraid, and worried, because Horace is ill, you see, terribly ill, and I think he might . . .' She couldn't finish that thought. It was too complicated, too painful, and it might let in all the contradictions her mind didn't have room for right now. Yasha didn't respond, anyway. She hadn't expected him to. He only liked big, bold ideas and had always treated Horace as an unnecessary encumbrance.

She sat down, rather suddenly, on one of the ornate sofas. He sat down too, and she laughed when he winced and wriggled as the violin dug into the sofa back, rejoicing at the comfort of his being here, now, by her side. She went on uncertainly, 'But how did you get all this way? Why are you here?'

'You went away,' he said. She couldn't help the sudden lurch of her heart, the twinge of uneasy pleasure, as he added, 'You didn't say goodbye. I needed to see you again.' He'd never said he loved her, never put her above all the other things he valued; but surely this action spoke louder than any words?

But when, a moment later, he continued, 'Because you've got the wrong violin,' the illusion that whatever he was about to say might, after all, sweep her away on a tide of uncontrollable feeling gave way to the scratchy, dawning disappointment of reality. He added, with satisfaction, 'I've brought you down the Strad.'

She didn't believe him, at first; she made him get his violin out of its box.

She tiptoed into the bedroom, and got out the one she'd been carrying.

It was only when she'd picked up the two golden-brown bodies, and turned them round, and compared them, that she saw he was telling the truth.

'You see?' he said. He looked pleased.

At first, all Inna could do was shake her head in astonishment. How could they have been carrying that box around with them for all these weeks, guarding it so carefully, when it hadn't even had the right violin in it? How could she have just taken Barbarian's word for it that he'd got the Strad up from the store? Had she really been so dazed, before they left, that she hadn't checked for herself? The thought of Felix Youssoupoff accusing her of stealing his violin was making her go hot and cold with shame.

'Thank you,' she kept murmuring. 'I don't know how to thank you.'

She so wanted to be grateful; she so wanted Yasha to have made this heroic dash south purely to save her. But had he really, prompted a niggling voice inside her, or was this just his way of escaping the dangerous mess he'd got himself into back there? Yet it was graceless even to think that, she told herself, her head spinning, for how incredible it also seemed, how single-minded, how devoted, to have tracked her down here, right at the other end of Russia . . .

'But how did you find me?' she finally remembered to ask.

He only grinned wider. 'Maxim said you'd gone,' he said simply. 'And Marcus told me where. And this is the only hotel still working in Yalta.'

So it took a while before she plucked up courage to ask the

other, harder question that had been slowly forming in her mind. 'But why did you have the Strad anyway?'

He laughed. 'Oh, it was a mistake,' he said carelessly. 'I've never been one for detail. I put the copy and the real one in the wrong boxes, ages ago. I'd been meaning to come back and sort it out for months. I just didn't realize you'd take off like that.'

He swung her to him, and she let him. Again she was quietly surprised that she didn't melt into him, as she once would have been unable to prevent herself from doing. Her body seemed have unlearned how to fit his. She could feel the cautious stiffness in her limbs.

'None of that matters, anyway,' Yasha finished. 'The details. What matters is that I've found you, and here we both are.'

He sounded so happy, as if he hadn't noticed how strangely detached she was feeling. For his sake, she wanted, or almost wanted, to be able to share his pleasure; to lose herself in this moment, to forget Horace and tomorrow. She certainly didn't want the prickle of unease she now felt, the knowledge that something Yasha had said was wrong – something separate, that is, from the bigger wrongness that she felt of being in his arms at all.

'Yasha,' she whispered, stepping back, trying to work out where this suspicion might have come from. 'There's something I have to ask, something I've been wondering. Did you send those men to beat up Horace?'

He gave her a blank stare. 'Me?' he asked, looking bewildered. 'Why would I do that?'

Almost against her will, she believed him. Relieved, she squeezed his hand, mutely asking forgiveness for her question.

It took a moment more for her to realize that whether or not Yasha had tried to harm Horace no longer made any difference to what happened now. What mattered was that she'd realized the damage *she'd* done him. What mattered was the new, trembling, overwhelming desire she'd become aware of in these past few days to get to safety with Horace; the hazy vision beginning to emerge in her mind of how they would be happy afterwards. That was what had stopped her humming the Scriabin tune, earlier on, she suddenly saw: not just the memory of playing it to the Lemans, long ago, but the hope of playing it again in some other yellow room, in some other time, with Horace listening. That was what she wanted.

She held tenderly on to Yasha, wishing she could somehow convey all this to him without hurting him, wanting him to know how much he still meant to her, even so . . .

And then it came to her.

'I remember when you last touched those violins,' she said, suddenly. Yes, she'd put her finger on it. All the doubts she'd ever had came crowding in. 'It was months ago, a year or more. You came round to hand in the fiddle you'd been varnishing to the workshop – your copy. You went off to the storeroom to compare it with the real Strad. And then you left. It couldn't have been just a mistake that you left with the Strad. You weren't supposed to leave with anything.'

'Well,' he said, looking cornered now. 'Well . . .'

He hung his head, and then looked at her reluctantly.

'All right,' he said eventually. 'It wasn't a mistake. I did mean to take it.'

She nodded, bleakly disappointed to have caught him in a theft, or at best a lie; thinking how sad the Lemans would have been if they'd heard; remembering the darker side of Yasha that she'd tried to forget on the train. He'd have some explanation, of course. He always did. That was how he'd always been, wasn't it? Seeing everything too simply; sweeping aside what he called 'details' and she thought of as 'other people'. She'd wanted to believe it was just the revolutionary in him, and that falling out of love with the Revolution had changed him. But this was who he was.

'It's not what you think,' he added, and, for a moment, she was moved by the unfamiliar note of uncertainty in his voice, the pleading. Surely that hadn't been there before? Then, looking ashamed, and scuffing at his feet, he added: 'I didn't steal it. Well, I did think, for a while, that I might requisition it, and give it to the Commissariat of Enlightenment, as a Former Aristocratic Person's belongings. But that was just . . . an excuse I was making to myself. Really I just took it to look at for a while. Because I didn't think I'd see you again. And it reminded me of you, sitting in the workshop, with your hair falling down over it, concentrating . . .'

Inna was surprised at the tears in her eyes.

'You must believe me,' he whispered. 'You do, don't you? I was just a fool. I didn't know how to put things right. And I put off even thinking about it, because I was nervous of going back to the Lemans' . . .'

He took her back in his arms. The clear lines she'd felt she was drawing began to sway and dissolve.

For a while, neither of them said anything. They just clung together, teetering between past and future.

'Did you know', Yasha said, eventually, 'that there are English ships moored in the next bay over?'

'Yes,' she said.

'Well,' he said, nuzzling at her neck, 'I've been thinking.'

'Mmm?'

'If I go with you tomorrow, to those ships, and help you get your Englishman on board. If we make sure he's safe among his own kind . . .'

She stiffened. Waited.

'. . . will you stay with me?'

He made it sound so easy. He raised his head, and looked at her, as if all she had to do was to say yes.

'And do what?' she asked.

'I don't know,' he admitted candidly. 'Go down the coast to Constantinople, I suppose, if we can get there, get jobs, find a ship to take . . .

'We'd be all right together,' he said after a moment, and she almost believed it. 'We'd get somewhere we could make a proper living sooner or later. Mending violins, even, maybe. We'd get by.'

She put her hands together over her belly, thinking. Wishing she didn't remember all the details Yasha had forgotten: that, quite apart from her own feelings, she had a husband who loved her, and how devastated he'd be to wake up on board an English ship and find her gone.

'We have the violins, after all,' Yasha was saying. 'Two of them, and one's a Strad. It would fetch a good bit of money, if we could only get somewhere we could sell it.'

But, a shocked voice in her mind said, *I wouldn't want to sell it.*

'We might even make it to Chicago. My parents are there. They write, you know. They want me to join them. They say there's a trade union movement there that could use a person of my experience: because who better than me to teach the workers how to campaign for better conditions?'

She smiled, sadly. So that was his new dream, the one that had replaced the Revolution. He always had big ideas.

'I can't, Yash,' she said softly, 'I think I'm going to have a baby.'

CHAPTER THIRTY-TWO

It was the old man who woke Inna. Slumped on the chair beside Horace, she looked around in a daze. The creeping terror of the night had gone. Instead there was the cool expectancy of a hot day in the air, and dust motes dancing in the shaft of sunlight coming in through the windows. The old man had another basin of hot water and another two immaculate hotel towels.

Inna hastily rose to her feet, rubbing her eyes. All her limbs were stiff and achy. She muttered something grateful, but the stubbly old man only darted a cautious glance at her and sat down in the seat she'd vacated before uncovering Horace's leg and, very carefully, unwrapping the poultice over his foot.

'Don't you look now, girl,' the old man said, not unkindly. His elaborate hotel formality seemed to have gone with the night. Now, with Horace's foot in his lap, and his back hunched over it, blocking the sight from Inna, he sounded more as if she was just another girl in a country inn, needing to be comforted. 'You fetch in the tea I left outside for you.'

And, because she could see at a glance that Horace's

breathing was steady, and there was a little colour in his cheeks, Inna dully obeyed.

It was only when she stepped outside the room for the tray in the corridor that she saw the long shape lying curled up on a hard gilt-backed divan several sizes too small for proper sleep, under a coat, with a kitbag on the floor, and two violin boxes. It all came rushing back: the decision she had to make.

Yasha was here, asleep. For a moment she almost laughed when she recalled how he'd looked when she'd told him about the baby, the way his mouth and eyes had seemed slowly to turn into a series of big, astonished Os, and he'd forgotten all about taking ship to Chicago and leading the trade union movement there.

She'd half thought he might immediately ask who the father was, as if he doubted. She'd half expected him to look mortified – or trapped – at the answer. But she hadn't had time to imagine in advance how he might take it, so all she'd really had to go on was that she didn't remember him ever talking about children, and, if she was honest, that she often thought of him as still just a boy himself.

In the event, all that had happened was that his face had slowly softened into an expression of something close to wonder. 'That afternoon in my room,' he'd whispered. 'It was then, wasn't it?'

And she'd nodded, overwhelmed by the simple fact of having put this secret thought into words.

It was Yasha who'd broken into the quiet that had fallen on them both, speaking so gently that it almost broke her heart, and looking so serious that he seemed somehow older. 'What do you want to do now, Innochka?'

When she'd opened her mouth to reply, no words had come. She'd just shaken her head dumbly and felt tears forming in her eyes. She couldn't think beyond this quiet conversation on this sofa; she couldn't. She'd lived for so long with the belief that she faced an impossible choice between the man she loved and the one she'd married. And now that the moment for choosing was here, the choice had become bafflingly different: between the man she now knew she loved and the father of her child. But it was no easier. The altered, gentler Yasha had gathered her in his arms again, and repeated, very kindly, in the heartbreaking certainty that he understood the reasons for her turmoil, 'It's all right; it's all right. Don't say anything now. There's time. I'll still be here in the morning, and we'll all walk together as far as the English ship. This will wait. I will wait, I promise,' until she'd composed herself.

'Go back and sit with him.' Yasha had nudged her. 'I'll sleep out here.'

And here he still was, saying something she couldn't hear in his fitful sleep, waiting for her to choose.

Quietly, Inna bent and picked up the tray, and went back inside.

The walk was beautiful: a coastal road through cypresses and pines and, sometimes, walnut and hazelnut and apricot trees.

Inna had never seen water so glittering as the sea at their side. The air smelled of thyme and rosemary, salt and heat. She listened to footsteps, birdsong, wheels crunching over grit and the patient clop of hooves.

As midday approached on the road, it was properly hot. In crumpled linen stretched tight over his belly, Selifan was sitting on the rough bench at the front of the cart, holding the reins loosely in one hand as the horse plodded on. Inna, who had taken off her coat and was walking beside him in her own faded skirt and blouse, thought that she might easily be taken by anyone who didn't know them for another local peasant like him.

Horace was lying in the back of the cart, facing back towards Yalta, on the boards where the driver had lain him. He had his foot up on the blindingly white hotel pillow Inna had taken from the room, his head on Inna's bag, which now contained the Strad, and Inna's coat wrapped round him like a blanket. Inna had reached down for his hand as they left town. She was still holding it now as she walked, and she could feel that he knew, because there was answering pressure from his fingers. He was holding on to her.

Horace's eyes were shut. If he'd recognized Yasha, heaving him into the cart with Selifan before they left the hotel, he hadn't acknowledged him. But his temperature was down, and when the old man had finally allowed Inna to the bedside to look at his foot and bandage it for the road, she'd seen to her astonishment that it had been much cleaner, with the hot hard anger gone out of the flesh and the edges of the wound a hopeful, uninfected pink. It was almost miraculous. 'How did you do that?' Inna had asked.

The old man had only lifted his shoulders awkwardly. 'I've tended a lot of soldiers in my time, miss,' was all he'd say. 'I know how easy it is to lose a good man once you let the badness in.' And then he'd got quietly up and taken away the basin, covered with cloths so Inna couldn't see the water inside. But he'd drawn Yasha aside before they'd all set off and given him a paper-wrapped parcel, and whispered to him. Yasha's eyes had widened for a moment as the old man talked, and he'd glanced down at the package and then at Inna, but after he'd heard the old man out he'd just nodded and put the parcel in his bag.

'What was that about?' Inna had asked as the cart had set off.

'Towels for bandages,' Yasha had said briefly. 'And some poultice.' And then, turning away, he'd walked back, away from the lumbering cart, and slipped the old man some money. Inna, suddenly remembering how he'd done the same kind thing, long ago, in the poorhouse, hadn't been able to bring herself to speak for some time afterwards.

Now Yasha was loping along in front, by himself. His bag was swinging jauntily off one shoulder, and the violin he'd made was in the box under his arm. She could see herself in that long body, the dark intentness of it.

Sometimes he turned round and looked at her, expressionlessly. She could see herself in his eyes and his cheekbones.

She couldn't help staring at him. He was right in her line of vision.

There was so much holding them together, even now. Especially now.

She touched her free hand to her belly. She couldn't help thinking, If I get on that ship I'll never see him again.

She couldn't help the tightening of panic at the thought.

The road twisted into a new bay and, down in the distance, the embarkation near the horizon came into view. There were two English ships flying flags with red, white and blue crosses: a smallish dark-grey destroyer and a much bigger carrier vessel. Near a toy-like jetty, stretching out into the blue, were hundreds of tiny forms, rushing to and fro among steamer trunks. 'They're not leaving empty-handed, the aristos, then,' Yasha remarked drily.

Their footsteps rose and fell. The sun got hotter. The ships got bigger.

Inna held Horace's hand, and watched Yasha.

The ships seemed much bigger by the time Yasha dropped back and started walking next to her.

His face was studiedly neutral. But she could feel the hope in him, just as she was aware of Horace lying trustingly in the cart on her other side, with his hand holding on to hers.

The road went on, all the way up the coast. But, any minute now, they'd reach the place where their cart would need to turn off to get to the water's edge. She could get on the ship with Horace, or she could carry on up the coast with Yasha. She'd have to decide soon. Now it was coming so close, it felt to Inna as though her whole life had been leading her here, to this moment, to this crossroads, to the choice she'd have to make once they got to the mêlée ahead. And she still didn't know what to do.

She saw Yasha glance down at her hand in Horace's.

The pressure of both men's expectations felt as crushing as a physical burden. When her ears caught a new sound mixing with the breeze and the rustle of leaves: the faint hubbub of the crowd ahead, she felt sick.

Letting go of Horace, she grasped the side of the cart with both hands and clung on, dizzy and grateful for the rough wooden support.

'Is there any water?' she asked Selifan faintly. They'd drained his flask during the morning, but he jerked a thumb at the wooded hillside just behind them. 'There's a spring up there,' he said, 'under that big rock, see?' He handed the bottle to Yasha who put down the violin box he was carrying on the open back of the cart, by Horace's feet, and scrambled away through the bushes to refill it.

The horse ambled on. Inna tried to concentrate on nothing more than the sunlight on her back and the sound of hoof and wheel. After a few minutes her nausea began to pass. She straightened up and felt for Horace's hand again.

It wasn't much of a noise, what came next, barely enough to make the horse put its ears back. But Selifan looked up when a scatter of pebbles fell on the road ahead. Following the direction of his eyes, so did Inna. For, unless he'd gone a very circuitous route through the trees above, the pebbles were coming from the wrong place for Yasha to be returning.

Inna saw three men emerging from behind the rocky outcrop ahead. They came shambling out together from a patch of shade. One had a rifle.

Inna was aware of Selifan swearing under his breath; her own breathing seemed to stop. The cart kept moving forward through the honeyed air towards the men. There was nowhere else for it to go.

Inna could see the red armband on the one with the apology for a coat – the officer, she supposed, if these Reddish irregulars had officers in the normal sense of the word. They looked more like bandits. They were also close enough, by now, for her to see the twitch in the cheek of the one standing next to him, with the gun, and the dragging leg of the fat one at the side.

The cart's wheels crunched in the scree. Selifan kept walking, though more slowly, as if he were hoping to go past them without a word. But his forehead was wet.

'*Stoi*,' the man in the armband told him, not loudly. 'Stop.' And the man with the twitch in his cheek raised the gun.

Selifan reined the horse in, and it dropped its head and put its nose peacefully to the nearest grass. Inna saw that Selifan's clammy cheeks were pale and his eyes cast down in an attitude of utter dejection.

'Are you lot headed for that lot?' the man with the armband asked Selifan. He nodded his head towards the crowd of gentry in the distance.

'Just driving along the coast,' Selifan answered cagily. 'That's all I know.'

'You.' The man turned to Inna. He beckoned.

How unreal it felt to be summoned forward, in the dappled light, with the sea sparkling at her side. She was dully aware of the irony of being stopped at the very last minute, when they'd got so close. But all she could really focus on, as she let go of Horace's hand and stepped towards the man, was the fact that all the buttons were missing off his torn coat, which was far too heavy anyway for this hot day.

'Going for a boat ride?' the man asked her in turn. The mockery in his voice got the other two men snickering. 'Your excellency?'

Inna lifted her head higher, hearing in her head a voice from long ago, Aunty Lyuba's, saying, 'Walk tall . . . stare them down, like a princess.'

She came eyeball to eyeball with the man. She was on the point of telling him, with dignity, that her husband was sick and they were out searching for a doctor when suddenly her mind started working again and she realized that it would do her no good at all to be seen by these desperadoes as a woman with no male protector.

'No,' she said, emphatically, and the act of speaking this one word out loud, and knowing it to be a lie, because she did, overwhelmingly, want to get on that ship with Horace, brought her back to life.

She could see the man didn't believe her.

'Requisition!' he bawled, right in her ear, making her jump, and his two grinning mates immediately leaped forward and rushed round the side of the cart to start scrabbling for stuff from the open back.

There was too much at stake for Inna just to let them do whatever they wanted. Instead she rushed after them, feeling that if she once let fear root her to the ground and her eyes drop, as Selifan had, she'd never get back the will to resist. 'Stop, stop. There's a sick man in there—'

And then there was another scattering of pebbles, and Yasha was jumping down from the bushes above the road, between the men and the cart. Her heart leaped. The men all stopped dead.

'What's going on?' Yasha yelled. Then, without stopping, he grabbed Inna and pushed her down to sit on the back of the cart, so hard that she only just managed to avoid Horace's bandaged foot. She saw Yasha's mouth move quickly, and a bright, encouraging flash of eyes, though it was a moment or two before she disentangled the words his lips had formed and realized that he'd said, 'I love you.' It was too late to respond. By the time she'd understood, he'd already picked up the violin case that was lying next to where she was now sitting, at the back of the cart, and turned towards the men.

'Look here,' he was saying, striding straight past the sidekicks towards the man with the armband: the boss. 'Look at this. Never mind what those poor bastards have got in their luggage, brothers, because it won't be anything much, any idiot can see that; they're in rags. But just you take a look at what I've got here. They won't have anything like *this*, I can tell you. And you won't, either.'

The three men could see by now that Yasha was unarmed. They could easily have rushed him. But his decisiveness, speed and flow of talk seemed to have disoriented them, and they were just staring at him in uneasy fascination, and following him as he stepped away from the cart. Perhaps they'd been too confused to even notice that he'd only picked up the violin box when he'd pushed her down? Perhaps they hadn't realized that the box had been in their cart all along?

Inna couldn't tell. All she could be sure of, as she hunched fearfully down in the cart, not knowing what to expect, was that Yasha sounded so confident that the bandits had let themselves be taken right off the road, into a patch of shade under a tree several paces behind the cart.

Out of the corner of her eye, she became aware of Selifan, also hunched up, sitting very quietly on his driver's bench up in front. He hadn't quite given up hope after all, she could see; he had pulled up the horse's head, and had the reins taut in his left hand and his whip ready in his right.

'Now, let me just get these clasps open, and then you'll see,' Yasha was saying, retreating under the tree, step by step, until the bandits, craning forward like children eager for a fairy story before bed, found they had to stoop to avoid the low branches and look down to avoid the knotty roots. When the gun started bashing awkwardly against the tree, the man who'd been carrying it leaned it against a branch and took another step forward. 'This is a priceless thing I've got here, brothers, I'm telling you, something that's going to set me and my lot up for life.' Yasha was sweet-talking the men on. 'When you've had a good long look at it, I'll tell you how I came by it. Because that's a tale in itself.'

Then, grinning around at them, he went on, 'Ah, to Hell with these stiff locks, I'll take my knife to them; here, hold this for a moment,' and, unexpectedly, Inna saw him shove the violin box towards the man who'd had the gun.

Quite what happened next Inna was never certain. But suddenly the shadowy space under the tree was all grunts and blows and movement and the splintering of wood, and Selifan was looking around and swishing the whip in his right hand, ready to use it as soon as the moment was right. Then someone rushed out from the fight under the tree with the rifle in his hands, yelling, and it was only when he got into the sunlight that Inna saw that it was Yasha, and that he was shouting something at her, or Selifan, and it was only much, much later that she made out the words he was shouting: 'Go! Go! Get the Hell out! Get her away!'

And by then – and certainly by the time she screamed – the cart was creaking into life and rolling down the road away from him, with Selifan standing up at the front of the cart, yelling like a madman too and whipping on his panicking horse until it bolted in earnest.

Only Inna saw the shadow emerge out of the branches behind Yasha. As Yasha, heeding her warning, began to turn round, the fat man at his back tripped over a root, falling heavily against Yasha and knocking him to his knees. Only Inna saw a thinner, harder shadow, with a flash of red at the arm, run out too, and grab the gun. Only Inna saw this man whack the rifle butt down on Yasha's shoulder and knock him flat, then, twirling the heavy weapon round with the speed of adrenalin and rage, point it down towards the prone body below.

But everyone heard the shot.

As the man with the gun raised its barrel away from the bloodied ground, and began swaying round towards the road, as Inna began screaming in earnest, Selifan, still shouting too, and fighting the foaming, rearing horse, forced it on, out of the sunlight, round the bend.

They fell quiet as soon as they'd got into the shade, though with the cart still rolling and jerking dangerously underneath them. They fell quiet enough to start hearing Horace's stifled groans as his injured foot was banged from side to side. But they went just as fast: a blur of breath and snapping leather and terrifying jolts, with the cart feeling as though it would topple any moment or come apart altogether. For what felt a long time, Inna could hear running behind them. And then, finally, the footsteps stopped.

'Nasty, that,' muttered Selifan, slowing to a walk again round the next kink in the road, wiping the sweat from his brow and fixing his eyes on the green and gold dance of the waves at their side. His voice was trembling.

The once formless crowd ahead was close enough by now to have separated into people, Inna saw: arms, legs, heads, parasols, valises, fob-watches, voices, arguments. A whole new life was beckoning her forward, a future that felt remote and dream-like now but which she knew she should, and would, come to value in time, because Yasha had given up his life so she could live it.

'Close range. Now, better check on your man. That ride won't have done his foot any good either.'

CHAPTER THIRTY-THREE

The sun was still hanging over the jewelled sea. Horace, in his chair on deck, tucked under a blanket but with his head up and colour in his cheeks again, was watching it sink into the sea. His foot was mending nicely, the English ship's doctor had said. That might be because of the poultice the old man in Yalta had put on it – maggots, the doctor said – or it might just be because Horace had the constitution of an ox and was destined to live. At any rate, he'd managed to get up and limp to his chair this evening, leaning on a stick, with Inna at his side.

She'd wanted them both to see the sun set on Russia. There's God in the glitter on that water, she remembered Father Grigory saying in St Petersburg long ago, back when he still had his innocence. And now Inna could understand why. It was only now, looking at the great oblivious majesty of it, the tranquilly deepening gold of the horizon ahead, that she could calm the anxious whirring of detail in her mind; that she could understand that Yasha was truly gone, but that, because of his last magnificent act of self-sacrifice, the

461

two of them were safe and heading towards the future, and give thanks. Yasha had despised his own cowardice before getting away from town, but that was just the trap his idealism had caught him in as that world back there went wrong. She wouldn't remember him like that, but as he'd been at the last – and long ago, too, before politics had changed him. She'd remember his idealism. His selfless kindness.

The first crisp naval officer she'd found and pulled towards Horace, back at the jetty at Koreiz, had barely wasted a moment listening to his weak whispering before having space cleared on the gangway for him to be stretchered on board. There'd been strong young ensigns assigned to walk alongside, too, carrying their bags and keeping off the fretful, panicky press of other people; and the sailors had waited on deck with their burdens for Inna to pull the amethyst pendant out of her waistband and, with hasty thanks and handshakes, slip it into Selifan's hand, before stumbling back along the jetty to rejoin them. Yet despite all this, leaving Russia hadn't been quick or easy.

While the passengers were still milling frenziedly around on board, their two ships had stopped, almost immediately, offshore from Koreiz, to meet a third British craft at sea. This sloop had braved Yalta to pick up four hundred officers of the Imperial Guard who were to be set down again at Sevastopol. And then they'd all stopped again, this morning, at Sevastopol, and, after the Imperial Guardsmen had been put ashore, taken on more White refugees. There was no room on the smaller ship ahead, the *Marlborough*, where Prince Youssoupoff and his family, and many others of his kind, were accompanying the Dowager Empress, but this ship, the *Princess Ena*, had somehow found space for the stragglers.

There'd been clouds and choppy seas at Sevastopol: thin clouds rising from the fires in town, and billowing grey in the sky, too. Fidgety and claustrophobic, morbidly curious to see what had become of Sevastopol, Inna had left Horace sleeping in the officer's little cabin, which he'd given up for them, and come up on deck to stretch her legs and get a breath of air.

As the sloop carrying the Imperial Guardsmen had set off to take them back to land to fight the advancing Reds, Inna had seen the Dowager Empress and Grand Duke Nicholas and a crowd of others gather on the quarter-deck of the *Marlborough*.

For a moment, Inna had thought she might also see Youssoupoff, whose violin they still had – because of course there hadn't been a moment, in the chaos of departure, to think of running around trying to find *him*; and Horace's first word, when he'd opened his eyes in the cabin and seen the fiddle box propped up against their cabin wall, had been a hoarse but deeply satisfied 'good'. And so she'd briefly wondered whether, if she did spot Youssoupoff on that other deck, she should wave and make herself known to him, or just turn her face away.

But then she'd forgotten all about Youssoupoff, because, at the sight of their former Empress, the Guardsmen had started to sing. As the solemn words of the old anthem Inna had never expected to hear again began ringing out – 'God Save the Tsar' – the hair had risen on the nape of her neck. The noisy conversations on the crowded deck of the *Princess Ena* – the where-next question that everyone on board had been trying to answer since they'd found out these ships would only take them as far as Malta, the my-cousin-in-Paris, my-aunt-in-Rome, opportunities-in-Switzerland, chances-in-London cacophony of hopes – had died away in an instant, too. All those who'd been sitting were on their feet, suddenly, and the men were standing to attention. Some had saluted, like the Imperial Guard. There'd been handkerchiefs, too, and closed eyes, and sobs, and Inna had seen the undisguised glitter of tears. For this was goodbye.

Inna thought she'd never forget the melancholy sight of that little elderly woman on the other ship, standing apart from all the others under a white flag marked with a bold red cross and with the complicated crossed blues and reds and whites of Britain in the top left-hand corner, stiffly upright as she prepared herself for exile, listening to the deep voices drifting across the water.

Inna would never forget, either, the long, long silence that followed.

She'd gone back to the cabin, feeling hollowed out but strangely healed, wanting to share with Horace the feeling of completion that the singing had brought her, and hoping he might feel able to come on deck for their last Russian sunset, and make his peace with the past, too.

Now Inna leaned against the deck rail, finding herself once again able to rejoice simply at the fact of existence, at the wind in her hair. The gold was slowly fading from the sky, as the first faint stars came out in the dusk. Horace was as lost in his thoughts as she was in hers.

Here, at vanishing point, the past seemed as unreal as the future. Inna let her mind wander back all those hundreds of versts north to St Petersburg, where there would still be snow on the ground, yet the Lemans might be looking out into the deepening heavens at the same stars as her. She closed her eyes, and suddenly it came flooding back, and she could almost smell the brutal, scouringly salt air of the city she'd left behind, and imagine Marcus and Olympia laughing over a parcel, or Madame Leman looking exasperated as her two youngest quarrelled over the size of their portions of kasha. For a moment, too, she was lost in the painful poignancy of another memory, a kiss in the deserted street, late at night, with litter blowing at her ankles, and her heart full of the certainty of youth, and snowflakes melting on his eyelashes . . .

She opened her eyes. The landline of Russia was already far behind, over the horizon. Ahead lay nothing more definite than a shimmer of transformation: the hope of a new life and an uncharted happiness. But that was enough.

Out of habit, she curled her fingers into her palms to touch the old scars – angry wounds once, faded now to a gentle silvery trace. Then she let her hands straighten again. If surviving this journey had proved anything, it was that she was strong enough to face whatever the future held for her unaided. She didn't need the help of those lines any more.

She shifted against the rail, wondering if that was the beginning of a swell in her belly that she could feel through the stuff of her coat, and then whether the baby would be a boy or a girl, and then, with the sorrow for him that she knew she would soon feel still strangely suspended, what it would be like to hold this child – Yasha's share of infinity – in her arms, and see a new being grow up whose cast of eyes, or turn of calf or cheekbone, would always remind her of him.

Then she became aware of movement at her side.

Horace had turned and was smiling up at her from his chair, with the beginning of his old carefree grin. She wasn't sure yet what he remembered from the time when he'd been so ill, or whether he even knew that Yasha had been there for those few precious hours, but she was certain he was vaguely aware that something important had happened to her. He hadn't asked, though, any more than he'd started to wonder, aloud, what was uppermost on the minds of everyone else on this ship: what to do after Malta? She had the sense he was just grateful that they were together, and that the worst of their journey was behind them. But she'd tell him everything when he was stronger, she resolved, or at least as much as she could without hurting him, and there would be no more secrets in the life they were about to begin.

Inna looked tenderly down at him.

'When the sun comes up tomorrow,' he said, 'I wonder where we'll be, you and I?'

AFTERWORD

This book is a very personal story for me, and not just because I drew so heavily for it on the seven years after the end of Communism which I spent living in Moscow and St Petersburg, or because I made the Leman family with whom my heroine lives in early twentieth-century St Petersburg so very like the wonderful Karpov family with whom I lived with in modern St Petersburg (they share an address), or because my own parents are musicians, or even because, in the course of describing violin-makers in Russia, I learned to make a violin myself.

There's one even more important thing. One of the book's three central characters is an Englishman called Horace Wallick who worked for Fabergé the jeweller's in pre-revolutionary St Petersburg. He's drawn from real life. He was my great-great-uncle.

The real Horace Wallick was, just as I have him in the book, a jobbing artist who painted miniatures – the kind that went inside lockets, or in miniature portraits, or on top of jewelled boxes. From 1910 to 1919, right through the last days of Tsarism and both the Revolutions of 1917, he lived a few streets away from the Fabergé shop and worked for the Swiss firm. Then he escaped from the starving city during the civil war between Red and White forces that followed 1917. Like many White hangers-on, he ended up among Whites in the southern resort of Yalta. Eventually he was spirited away by a British ship in 1919, along with a good chunk of the defeated Russian aristocracy, just as the Reds won the day. He never returned to Russia.

I can't claim that I learned Russian as a schoolgirl, or travelled to the Soviet Union as a student, or loved the art of the early twentieth century, or went to work in new Russia as a journalist as any kind of homage to Horace Wallick.

In fact, I only discovered he existed when I'd already spent years living in a Russia that was returning to the overblown, turbo-charged, thrillingly transgressive form of capitalism he must also have experienced nearly a century earlier. In my Russian 1990s, hardly a day went by without a coup, or a war, or a banking battle, or a smear campaign, or a corruption scandal, or a shoot-out, or a millionaire being caught in a post-KGB honey trap. You gasped and stretched your eyes at all the exaggeration, but you were never bored. I couldn't leave – I was always worried that, anywhere else, I *would* feel bored. And yet I'd been there so long that it was beginning to seem I might end up staying forever.

And then I found Horace. I went back for a quiet weekend in London at my family home, still the house where my great-grandmother, Horace's sister, had died, and still full of many of her books – I'd found my first Chekhov and my first Tolstoy, in old Everyman editions, on those bookshelves. And I saw an old catalogue of a London exhibition of Fabergé eggs from the 1950s. That's very Russian, I thought, and it might come in handy if I have to write about Fabergé starting up again, which was always being talked about at the time. So I took the book back to Moscow with me.

To my astonishment, when I flicked through it, I saw it was full of notes. What drew my attention first was simply nostalgic pleasure that they were written in my much-missed grandmother's handwriting. They told the story of my 'new' relative and his hasty departure from Russia on the British *Princess Ena* from Yalta to Malta and on to England and, as she sweetly wrote, 'peace and plenty'.

I was thrilled to find this unexpected family member who had lived in Russia even longer than I had. Between us, we neatly book-ended the Communist years. And I was also thrilled to find this connection to the city where the Russian family I loved lived. It was a joy to be linked to the place where I'd spent so much of my recent life. I knew very little about my father's relatives. Feeling rather rootless was part of the reason it was easy to live abroad for years on end – but, at the same time, it had left me wondering quite where 'home' was. St Petersburg seemed like a pretty good answer.

I spent a year trying to find out more about Horace Wallick's time in Russia. I had only the patchiest of success. I went to libraries and archives and Russian Aristocracy Associations, where the very Soviet-looking doctors and lawyers behind the office doors barked into very Soviet-looking orange plastic phones on giant desks but answered to the recently revived title of 'your excellency'. But no one could tell me anything. The past, as one of my interviewees said, really is a foreign country in Russia. You might never find out.

Back in London, eventually, I raised the subject of our shared relative with my father, and discovered that he had not only heard of Horace Wallick, but knew him, and remembered him as 'Uncle Horace'. All I learned, though, was that Horace had stayed too long enjoying the glitz and over-the-top drama of Russia. He'd let his own life drift. He was spoiled for England. He never quite settled back into quiet English phlegmatism, into 'can't complain' and 'mustn't grumble'. He drifted around, doing bits of art jobs for friends and relatives and making ends meet. He used to show my teenage father pictures of what my father called the Tsar's treasures. He always wore slightly grubby white gloves, my father remembered, and he liked a luxury or two, though he couldn't afford them. From time to time, he used to bust out of the old people's home in Richmond where he lived and come over to cadge a fiver off my father's parents, to keep him in gold-tipped black Balkan Sobranie cigarettes. 'I got the impression Russia hadn't been kind to him,' my father said.

Still, I've always been very grateful to Horace Wallick, grateful enough to want to write him a happier ending in this book. Finding out just when I did that he'd spent his years in Russia, with all their parallels to my own, but that no trace of him remained from that time, helped me decide to stop hanging around there myself, and come home to make a grown-up future before it was too late. I can't help thinking that it's all thanks to Horace that I did.